Disney

Unbirthday

A Twisted Tale

LIZ BRASWELL

AUTUMN
PUBLISHING

Published in 2020
First published in the UK by Autumn Publishing
An imprint of Igloo Books Ltd
Cottage Farm, NN6 0BJ, UK
Owned by Bonnier Books
Sveavägen 56, Stockholm, Sweden
www.igloobooks.com

0121 003
4 6 8 10 9 7 5 3
ISBN 978-1-83903-117-5

Printed and manufactured in Italy

For my sister, Sabrina.

We are not Mathilda and Alice but have moments of each.

I forgive you for that time you tricked me into eating
a fancy chocolate with a hairball inside.

Sort of.

— L.B.

A gentle note, Dear Reader:

As you are probably already aware, this book is a work of Nonsense.

That being said, it behooves us to remind you that the Mad Hatter is a fictional character and doesn't conform to the strict rules of our own world.

To wit: mercury is deadly poisonous.

Hatters really were said to have gone mad in the nineteenth century because of exposure to mercury in their hat-making processes: in effect, they suffered long-term mercury poisoning.

You cannot eat the fish from many rivers and lakes of America even today because of the deadly mercury that lies on their muddy bottoms eternally, the result of toxic industrial pollution.

In this book the Hatter drinks mercury.
You, dear reader, cannot.
It will kill you.

— L. Braswell

Alice as You Remember Her

Chapter One

Morning sunlight waved a cheery hello on the papered walls of an equally cheery bedroom. It had rained overnight, a proper rain – hard with big droplets – and the day came freshly scrubbed and eager. The air that drifted through the open window was chill and sharp and had a bit of a kick to it. A flock of little sparrows who had been nest mates barely a week earlier chirruped excitedly back and forth in a way that would eventually result in either a sudden flight en masse, or feathery fisticuffs.

Even the hammer strikes of Mrs Anderbee's solid heels against the floor downstairs sounded springier and more energetic than usual.

The girl lying so peacefully in her brass-frame bed,

thick golden hair spread around her head and neck like the resplendent halo of an angel, was coaxed from sleep to wake at once by the abundance of all these cheerful noises. Her eyes snapped open, the long lashes on her lids waving like wheat with the suddenness of the motion.

"Today," Alice declared, "is a perfect day for adventure!"

She grinned and basked in the glory of her decision for a moment, then shot out of bed. Dinah, a cat both grumpy and unwilling to see the day for what it was, stretched once in place (where formerly her mistress's warm feet had been), then closed one elderly eye to the day and was asleep again seconds later.

"Sorry, old girl!" Alice said, giving her a kiss. "But *tempus fugit*, you know; time waits for no one!"

Of course, this being the time and place that it was, adventurers couldn't just run out the door in their chemises. It would be scandalous. And so Alice began the tedious process of donning all the layers necessary to going out into the world as a respectable young English lady. She had:

Drawers that went down to her knees.

A *crinoline* that looked like a cross between a bee skep and a cage. It was basically a series of steel hoops in diminishing circumference that circled her lower body from her calves to her waist. This held the skirts worn on top of it out from around her like a giant bell with her legs the clapper.

Corset.

She didn't tight-lace, despite the fashion and the pressure from friends. On this one thing Alice and her sister agreed: it was pure foolishness. Her waist was fine as it was, thank you very much, and she left the corset to its main job: keeping her back aligned and her womanly attributes smooth and in place.

Petticoat.

Petticoat.

Actual dress. A nice summer-weight gingham in blue and white.

Jacket and *hat.*

And finally, *camera* bag.

Alice hurried through all of this as fast as she could and then nearly skipped like a girl much younger than eighteen as she ran down the stairs… only remembering to try to keep her footsteps silent at the very last – and far too late – minute.

"*Alice!*" a strident female voice cried out. Mathilda, her sister. Of course.

Well, since she had been heard, she might as well have some breakfast.

"Good *morning*, Mother, Father, Sister," she said grandly, sweeping into the dining room. Her family was gathered at one end of the long table like refined squirrels, cracking soft-boiled eggs, spreading jam on toast, sipping tea and coffee, and generally looking completely at ease in the formal and bric-a-brac-filled room. Her mother turned a plump, still-pink cheek for a kiss and Alice obliged. Her father's face was mostly hidden behind the newspaper, but she managed to get in a quick peck, not quite on his mutton chop.

She patted her sister on the shoulder dismissively, as if brushing off some dandruff.

"Married yet?" her father asked from behind the paper.

"No, Papa."

"In the stocks yet?"

"No, Papa."

"Hmm. Good." He shook his paper to facilitate the turning and folding of a page and then continued reading about things happenings in foreign places, his favourite type of story.

"Are you *sure* it's good, Papa?" Mathilda asked. She was severe, beautiful in a slightly off-putting way, dark eyes and lashes and hair where her younger sister's were light. Her sombre dress was as drab as Alice's blue-and-white one was gay and summery. But if they had ever really made an effort to go out together – and if Mathilda ever made an effort with her appearance beyond brushing her hair – they could have owned all of the town of Kexford.

Not that Alice wanted to own Kexford. But it would have been an absolute gas for one party at least.

"She's eighteen, you know," Mathilda prodded, spreading jam on her toast most seriously.

"And I believe you're twenty-six," her mother observed.

"*I* have prospects!"

"Yes, yes you do," her mother said quickly and soothingly.

"I'll keep my baby girl Alice for as long as I possibly can," her father said from behind his paper. "Don't go interfering with that."

"My dear friend Mr Headstrewth has a friend – Richard Coney," Mathilda said, turning to Alice and ignoring her parents. "I believe I have told you about him a number of times. I think you may even have met him once? Very bright young man. Handsome. With a great future before him – he's already working on Gilbert Ramsbottom's election campaign. I have invited him—"

"Oh, he sounds *lovely*, yes, thoroughly interesting, fantastic, do keep me informed of his doings, absolutely! Good morning and goodbye!"

Alice winked at her mother, who tried very hard not to smile.

Then she grinned and spun away, and it wasn't until Mathilda turned back to her breakfast with a huff that she noticed her carefully buttered and jammed toast was missing.

Walking down the sunny road, Alice thoroughly enjoyed her purloined breakfast, so expertly buttered and jammed. After wiping her lips and cheeks with the back of her hand like a cat she raised her face to the sun, enjoying its warmth as it hit her skin. For only a moment, of course, before it did any real damage. She adjusted her hat and—

"Oh dear."

She had forgotten her gloves.

"Oh, my fur and whiskers," she sighed. "Not respectable at *all* today."

A momentary feeling overcame her. It wasn't *sadness* exactly. But it wasn't just nostalgia, either. There was a golden drop of happiness in the feeling, whatever it was, as warming and delightful as sunlight. A memory of old dreams that had worn thin like the comfiest pillowcase one couldn't bear to throw out.

Wonderland.

The details had dimmed long ago but the feelings remained: adventure, magic, fascinating creatures. True, not all her imagined adventures in Wonderland had been fun or safe. And not all the people had been particularly nice or polite. Some of the flowers in Wonderland were downright violent.

And the Queen of Hearts! She had wanted Alice *dead*! "Off with her head!" The phrase still sent shivers down Alice's spine.

But…

She hadn't had another dream like that one since.

"Stuff and nonsense," Alice declared, shaking her head. "It's a gorgeous day! Let's go find the magic right here!"

Right here was, of course, Kexford, a shining little town of university professors, ancient halls, glorious green parks and glittering canals. There were gleaming white pavements, ancient stone buildings and gardens so tiny and bright they practically sparkled like jewels. Everything was ordered and perfect and old in these hallowed grounds – even down to the properly wrecked, robed students hurrying to class after late-night partying or discussing Petrarch.

(Alice's house was just north of the university area, a fine large place with gardens and a lawn; not too long a walk to where the action was in town, but not close enough to hear 'Gaudeamus Igitur' being belted out at three o'clock in the morning.)

After waking from that magical dream ages ago, little Alice had devoted all her free time to searching the town for anything that reminded her of Wonderland. No place was safe from her explorations: every bell tower she could sneak into, every alleyway she could slip down when her parents' backs were turned. Top to bottom, high and low, nary a stone unturned.

(Mostly low: rabbit holes and mushrooms, tiny caterpillars and large spider webs, dumbwaiters and surprisingly small doors in other people's houses she really ought not to have explored and opened.)

Her wooden treasure box had contained rather more than the usual number of strange trinkets children tend to collect: tiny brass keys, tiny glass bottles, leftover halves of unusual biscuits, a left white glove, a right off-white glove, scraps of paper with the words EAT ME and DRINK ME laboriously written over and over again as she tried to match her flourishes to memory.

Alice hadn't been a morose girl – far from it – but she wondered sometimes if the reasons she never again dreamed of Wonderland were just a little bit her fault.

"Of all the silly nonsense—
this is the stupidest tea party
I've ever been to in all my life!"

"Well, I've had enough nonsense.
I'm going home – straight home."

"Oh no, please. No more nonsense."

No more nonsense. There, she had said it herself. And her subconscious had obliged and kept her nightly excursions to a world with little nonsense in it at all.

So Alice had tried her hand at drawing the few things she remembered clearly from her dream (the Cheshire Cat, the White Rabbit, a pretty little golden key) or the curious things she saw while she was out exploring (a student with surprisingly pointed ears, an interesting clump of moss, part of a stone wall with vines that looked like they could be pushed aside to reveal a hidden entrance to somewhere fantastic).

"Hmm," her father had said, looking over her sketches.

"We don't have much artistic ability in my side of the family, either," her mother had commented.

"She *does* notice many… obscure things. Even if she can't… reproduce them."

"Yes, she spends quite a bit of her spare time *noticing* things. Perhaps she needs some sort of focus for that—er, besides drawing, I mean?"

And that was where Aunt Vivian had come in.

She couldn't draw, either, but she could sculpt a fair piece, hosted literary salons, was occasionally involved in rather scandalous doings, and wore trousers like a coal-hauling pit lass. Her house was running over with fringed lamps, art made by her friends, incense burners and velvet. She was not married. In fact, she was just about everything a family could hope for in a black sheep.

And she helped her brother and his wife (and their

daughter) by fulfilling that role perfectly: she bought her niece a camera.

One of the latest models, a Phoebus box camera. It was a beautiful little thing and extremely portable, requiring neither a tripod nor bellows. It fit very nicely into a medium-sized case and could be brought out to quickly capture whatever took Alice's fancy – provided the light was bright enough.

(Aunt Vivian already had a darkroom sufficient for developing its glass plates; she was famous for the costumed tableaus she took at her salons with a much more traditional and giant-sized portrait camera.)

Alice was delighted. There was something inherently Wonderlandy about the whole process: light and shadow and mirrors and glass and lenses and images appearing magically.

A side effect of the new hobby was spending a lot more time with her aunt, which relieved her parents (who were concerned about her wandering the streets of Kexford by herself) and worried her sister (who believed Aunt Vivian was a terrible influence; not so much *modern* as *profligate*). Mathilda need not have been over-concerned, however; Alice loved her aunt, but she was now eighteen and had her own agenda – which had nothing to do with artists or vermouth or poppies or trousers.

Alice of course used the camera to document anything the remotest bit mysterious. She spent her days on what she called 'photo walks': looking for objects and people that hinted at a hidden, fey or wild side, which she would try to coax out with her camera. Once she found a potential subject she worked long and hard composing the shot, sometimes with additional mirrors or a lantern if it was in a dimly lit alley. She developed these images in her aunt's darkroom and then laid them out around her own room, studying them and trying to conjure a world out of what she saw there. Sparkling dew on spider webs, gloomy attics, a pile of bright refuse that might have hidden a monster or poem. The elfin qualities of a child, her eyes innocent and old at the same time.

She never told her parents (or her sister) about her visits to the less storybook parts of Kexford. But it was where things weren't kept quite as neat or perfect or orderly that she felt magic and nonsense had a chance to bloom.

And that was where she was heading on this glorious day.

Down the road and south… and then east, away from the pretty campuses and annoying students. She chose her route to pass Mrs Yao's tea shop. Really it was too beautiful a day for a cup of oolong and gossip, and she was still full from her stolen bread and jam for a sweet bun. But she turned down the tiny twisty street anyway and contented herself with a smile and wave to the woman behind the window. Mrs Yao smiled and waved back. She served her customers out of brightly mismatched cups and plates from England, China and even Russia – which was magical, and felt a bit like Wonderland.

Just past the tea shop, under a rain pipe, was a tiny, delicate fern that had not been there the week before. Alice's questing eyes immediately spotted its out-of-place bright greenness, its patterned and gracefully uncurling frond. *Definitely* magical. She gauged the light then pursed her lips sadly. The narrow street was dismally dark, she had no lantern or mirror, and only a few more film plates left. None to waste on potentially terrible shots.

"Apologies, young master fern," she said, giving it a little curtsy. "Maybe next time, when you've grown a bit."

Or *opened up like a telescope*, really.

Following the twisty street round, farther into a tangle of old buildings, she stooped through a low archway and finally emerged at her real destination. At one time the little open area had been officially called Wellington Square but was now known as simply *the Square*. As in *the Square* where many of the local children met up and played, often the sons and daughters (or orphans) of immigrants who weren't necessarily welcome in the nicer parks. Alice took their portraits and listened to stories of their homelands and travels to England—some of which, especially with the younger sitters, were mixed up with fairy tales from their mother countries.

Today several of the children had a ball and were playing with it in a corner, scuffing up the dirt. In another corner three girls were playing a counting game, effortlessly switching back and forth between English and Russian and Yiddish. Alice took out her camera and began composing possible images in her head.

"Oh, look, it's the famous English girl come to take photographs of the poor but pretty foreign children."

Alice spun round, affronted by both the words and tone. A young man not much older than herself leaned lazily on a worn statue of a cannon and gave her an indecipherable smile. His clothes were very different from the rest of the crowd here: they were adult, for one thing, pressed and clean and grey and professional. His jacket was spotless, his waistcoat well fitting. He didn't have a watch, but his purple cravat looked expensive and silken. His hat was carefully brushed. Under it was red hair so dark it was nearly black, trimmed very neatly around his ears and neck. His eyes were a light hazel that was nearly orange. His cheeks glowed a healthy shade of rose.

"Tell me," he continued, reaching down to pet a stray cat that quickly disappeared round the corner, "do your patrons enjoy weeping crocodile tears over portraits of the other half and how they live?"

"I beg your pardon," Alice replied coldly, straightening her spine – until it cracked. "These photographs are for my personal use, and the occasional private viewing with my aunt to a select and discreet crowd. I am not some sort of terrible charity vampire preying on the sorrowful state of others."

"Oh? And how much do you know about their *sorrowful state*? How much do you know about them at all?" he pressed.

Alice regarded him coolly for a moment.

"That girl over there, in the jacket with the large bone button. Her name is Adina. She is from a shtetl too far from St. Petersburg to be safe from the pogroms. Her mother is dead; her father and her aunt Silvy are her only family in the world." She gestured at another child. "That's Sasha. He is probably five years old and prefers cheese to sweets. His mother sews piecework and his father collects rags for the paper companies and his sister is dying of tuberculosis, although he doesn't really understand that yet.

"I never speak to them patronisingly and I never bribe them to pose with coins or sweets. If I bring anything it is enough for all of them and it is just because it pleases me to give. I treat even the littlest one with the same kindness and respect I expect out of *every*one." She said the last bit pointedly, glaring at the stranger.

"All right, all right." The young man laughed easily. "I apologise. I accused you without knowing whereof I spoke. I was a cad and a scoundrel."

He gave a bow, and it wasn't ironic at all.

"You are forgiven," Alice said, polite but still distant. "May I know whom I have the – *pleasure* – of addressing?"

"Katz," he said, taking his hat off. "Abraham Joseph Katz, Esquire. Barrister at Alexandros and Ivy. But you can call me Katz. At your service."

"I'm—" she began to introduce herself.

"Oh, everyone knows Alice and her camera around here," the man said, waving his hand. "The one and only Alice. But seriously, you have to understand, these children – even those of us who have grown up here – have not had the greatest experience with your fellow countrymen. Either it's spit and sneers, or cold charity and exploitation. There's rarely a middle ground."

"Us? You sound—you look—" Alice faltered, wondering if she was being rude. "British."

"I was born here. My parents were not," he said with a shrug. "They worked hard and I studied hard. Now I help out when I can with a little pro bono work. Sometimes someone with legal power needs to step in and save a child from the poorhouse or a parent from jail. Or worse. Sometimes a *patron* – say, with a camera – takes a child they fancy away entirely. For display, or ostensibly for charity, or for… things best not spoken of."

"That's dreadful," Alice said with feeling. "I am deeply, deeply sorry for all of it. All the same you can't blame me for the actions of a few of my terrible countrymen. That would be just like me treating you all poorly because of one bad apple that came in from Russia."

"A perfectly fair point," he agreed immediately. "In that case, I offer my stunning visage in case you ever decide you want to come back and take a portrait of *me*. I am an adult and a child of immigrants – and can legally agree to fair usage of my likeness, should it come to that."

There was nothing untoward in his tone. He did not wink at her or enunciate any word suggestively. He smiled and it was innocent; he did not even tilt his head dramatically as if posing. Alice felt neither flirted with nor threatened.

It was a little strange.

"Your English is better than that of many of my 'country-men'," she said slowly while she tried to work out what that meant. "My neighbours, at least."

What on earth was she talking about? Was that rude?

He had grown up here – he'd just said that! Of course he could speak English perfectly well!

"Ah, well: barrister, remember? I know Latin as well as Russian and English. *Quo usque tandem* and all that. I should probably learn French, however, so I can at least pronounce the wines."

Alice felt the world spin a bit like she was tumbling down a rabbit hole. What a strange man to meet in such a strange way! Normally she either avoided the young men pushed on her by her sister, or quickly forgot the ones she somehow met herself. Most were dull and unlikely to be found in this forgotten square. They all made unamusing and lewd jokes and references to Roman scholars they thought she wouldn't get.

She never had a desire to take a picture of any of them.

Unlike Mr Katz.

"I didn't bring enough film today," she lied. But she *did* have lots of film already exposed at Aunt Vivian's waiting to process. Really, that's what she should have been doing instead of spending the day adventuring. "I was just realising that when you approached me."

"Oh, I was joking about the picture. It's just that I have nothing besides my handsome good looks to offer you, to make up for my insults. I should keep a packet of sweets on me at all times. Remember that – always keep sweets around for emergencies. Someday it may save your life.

"Or, if you have any rats around your house, I could get them for you. I have a friend who is an expert at it."

"That won't be necessary," Alice said quickly. "I'm fairly certain our gardens are rat-free."

"I don't know. Rats are pretty sneaky. Sometimes they even make it into elected positions. Sometimes if you let them get out of control they even become mayor."

Alice couldn't repress a smile at that, and it almost became a snigger. He was very obviously referring to Ramsbottom, the candidate her sister and the boring Mr Headstrewth so fervently supported. There was only one other person running, and for the life of her Alice couldn't remember his name (he was quite forgettable since he had no party affiliation and didn't write letters to the *Kexford Weekly* about building workhouses for the poor, kicking out foreigners and giving the police bigger clubs).

"Well, I should be off, then," Alice said, putting her camera firmly back in her satchel and closing it up.

"Come back soon," Katz pleaded. "You're the most interesting person I've talked to in ages."

Not *you're a bright light in a dark corner of the world*, not a *fair face in a gloomy neighbourhood*, not a *muse* or a *nymph* or an *angel with a rosy smile to bestow on her willing supplicants*. None of that nonsense verbiage men usually offered her. He asked her to return, very simply, because he wanted to talk to her.

Alice curtsied, because it was always good to curtsy while you were thinking of a reply, then hurried off, unable to think of one.

Chapter Two

She found herself walking quickly away from Wellington Square – more quickly than before, and far more quickly than was strictly necessary. She forced herself to slow to a more lady-like stroll and concentrated on adjusting her breathing (not that hard with a corset already restricting her deepest breaths). Her cheeks felt warm and were probably a beautiful rosy shade.

It wasn't *entirely* a lie. She really *was* heading straight to Aunt Vivian's now to develop her pictures.

She remembered herself enough to cross to the other side of the street so she could peep into the window of Willard's Finest Haberdashery. His sign had gold letters and silver flourishes and the hats in his window were stacked artfully on top of each other like a carnival act, complete with fancy plumes and ribbons and spangles. It was delightful – and also felt somehow familiar. In fact, Alice had made friends with Mr Willard because he reminded her a bit of someone she once knew in a dream, someone she couldn't quite remember.

When *he* shared a cup of tea with Alice, the cups matched, they sat quietly and he discussed the advantages of an economic system in which the common people controlled the means of production – or at least regulated it – and medical care and legal help were free to all. Also advanced schooling and university would be provided gratis.

While this was a trifle boring, it was also quite mad, and his hair was white and wild. He and her aunt had hit it off splendidly – not romantically, but they were bosom companions at once and he became a fixture at her salons.

Today he wasn't at his worktable but standing outside his shop, eyes closed and face turned up to the sun like a flower, enjoying its rays.

"How do you do, Mr Willard?" she asked, curtsying. He opened his eyes and smiled at her, his cheeks crinkling into a thousand happy lines.

"Oh, my dear, I am just enjoying this day. The sun is still free for everyone – never forget that. We can *all* enjoy its life-giving warmth as much as we want."

"Absolutely true, Mr Willard. As is the clear blue sky."

"Quite right, my girl! Say! Did you develop that portrait you took of me? Not that I'm vain or anything – all right, perhaps I am. A silly old man indeed! But I would dearly like to see it and show it to my friend Mrs Alexandros. She is fascinated by photography but not perhaps as brave as you to take it up as a hobby."

"Why, I'm just on my way to Aunt Vivian's right now, Mr Willard. I shall have it developed directly."

"Oh, excellent. And say hello to your aunt, would you? Tell her I have a hat I think she will absolutely love. Also a pamphlet concerning scientific principles that may prove once and for all that alloparenting – the act of a non-parent helping to raise a child, a niece or a nephew, say – is not just normal, but in fact *integral* to our evolution as a higher species! Not everyone need have a litter of kittens to be part of the great human cycle, I mean."

"Alloparenting. Kittens. Yes. I shall, Mr Willard. Good day!" Alice said, curtsying again.

"Good day, Alice!"

She strolled happily down the road filled to a surfeit with the bonhomie of the moment, the sun and a day full of the possibility of everything. Of course there was also that young man she had just met… *He* certainly added a certain sense of wonder and potential to the air.

She forgot herself, pondering this, and cut through the market: sometimes a place for wonderfully interesting photographs and sometimes a bore, full of gossips who had very strong feelings about Alice and her prospects. She started to duck and hunch over before she caught herself.

"Alice," she told herself in a patient but chastising tone, "you are eighteen years now, fully grown and an adult, and you can no longer be ordered around or bullied by other adults. Please behave as such."

She took a deep breath, thanked herself for the reminder, and straightened up, proceeding past the stalls of cabbages with her head high in the air.

"ALICE!"

She slumped.

"Hello, Mrs Pogysdunhow," she said as politely as she could. "Good morning, Mrs Pogysdunhow."

The short and red-faced woman (*Piggysdunhow*, as Alice used to call her to Dinah) pushed her way over to talk. She looked exactly the same as when Alice had been of the age to run away from her at first sight: flat grey hair pulled back under an old-fashioned bonnet, dark old-fashioned dress with nary a crinoline or fancy stocking. Despite being the mistress of the rather respectable house up the street from Alice's family, she dressed and spent like a skinflint from a previous century – and screamed like a tavern matron from a previous millennium. Despite this, or possibly because of it, Alice's parents had occasionally employed her to look after Alice and her sister when they were younger. Her food was terrible and her breath worse. Somehow she was also always with babies, either children or grandchildren or other young, innocent, and heretofore harmless members of her extended family.

"ALICE, HOW IS YOUR MOTHER?"

She had a baby under her left arm right then, rather like a ball, tucked and restrained despite its desperate squirms in the name of freedom.

"She is fine, Mrs Pogysdunhow. Thank you."

"DID SHE GET OVER THAT BIT OF GOUT SHE WAS EXPERIENCING?"

"Er, yes, Mrs Pogysdunhow. She's quite well now, thank you."

"COMES FROM TOO MUCH MEAT, YOU KNOW," the older woman offered confidentially, which meant lowering her voice to mere half-scream volume. *"IT'S ALWAYS WISE TO TEMPER A ROAST WITH A FEW DAYS OF PORRIDGE OR HASH AFTERWARDS. A GOOD TURNIP HASH WILL CLEAR IT STRAIGHT UP!"*

Alice tried very hard not to shudder.

"That seems reasonable, Mrs Pogysdunhow. Excellent

advice. But if you'll excuse me, I'm on my way to see my aunt now, and to develop the portraits I took last week. Including the one of you."

The other woman shook her head. *"OH, YOUR AUNT. WELL THERE'S A BLACK SHEEP IN EVERY FLOCK AND THERE'S A PLACE FOR BLACK WOOL IN EVERY SHAWL, I SUPPOSE. GIVE YOUR MOTHER MY REGARDS – AND YOUR FATHER MY SYMPATHY."*

"Yes, Mrs Pogysdunhow. I shall."

Relieved almost to the point of fainting at such an easy escape, Alice tried not to rush away. While their relationship had improved somewhat since Alice had the dowager sit – with several babies – for a portrait, she was still mostly an unpleasant, cabbagey woman whose habits had involved making young Alice and Mathilda read long, archaic passages about the importance of… well, things Alice couldn't even remember. She shuddered at the memory of endless hours of endless sentences in books that made no sense.

And which probably cost the good woman no cents, Alice added thoughtfully, knowing well her tightness.

Down the hill now, she entered the more bohemian section of town, a poor area with pockets of strangely upbeat residents. Some were truly penniless philosophers who would rather read than eat; some were artists who spent every last coin on supplies and refused all patronage. Some were of semi-aristocratic descent, enjoying the decadent atmosphere around their artistic friends (and sometimes even actively contributing). Aunt Vivian was one of the latter.

She had a whole building to herself instead of just a flat, perhaps in slightly better shape than those around it. Alice rang the bell and let herself in; the door was never locked. She immediately began to cough. Besides all the usual apparatus of an artistic lifestyle (half-silvered mirrors, enough silk fringe draped everywhere to curtain a small theatre, great and terrible paintings hung on every square inch of wall, etc.) her aunt was a big believer in *incense*. There were braziers everywhere, and blue smoke hung heavily in every room like a scratchy wool canopy. Alice gulped several mouthfuls of air through her fingers, trying to get used to it before her aunt appeared.

"Alice."

Her aunt strode in from the hallway with her usual drama and even clapped her hands. She wore soft trousers that came down to her calves, exposing a pair of shiny, chic boots. A thick tunic of velvet made for a shirt, and this was protected with a small apron. She also wore a small pair of gold-rimmed glasses and had her light brown hair back in a bun, which meant she was sculpting.

The two women embraced, and her aunt gave her a very Continental kiss on each cheek.

"You have a bit of a backlog in the darkroom," the older woman said a little accusingly as Alice carefully took off her hat and removed her satchel. "We shall have to work together, overtime, to get everything developed. It's a good thing I ordered all those compounds from the chemist – I knew we would be doing heaps..."

Alice wasn't really listening. She was looking at the various portraits around the room she had seen a thousand times: farmers, actors, politicians, labourers, midwives, a princess, boys, girls, babies, all in rich and luscious tones. Photography captured someone exactly as he or she really was, but left out the colour in the cheeks. If she were to take a portrait of Katz, it wouldn't capture him completely unless she used some pink pastel on his face afterwards. And some gold for his eyes.

"Hello? Alice? Where are you?" Vivian demanded, narrowing her own pale grey eyes. She shook a finger at her niece. "You are not here. You are entirely elsewhere. What are you thinking about?"

"Oh, the difference between the arts of photography and painting..."

Her aunt regarded her silently.

"I just met someone, that's all," Alice finally admitted, waiting for her face to flush, but it didn't.

"A boy?"

"A young man. A barrister. He was with the children at the Square. He helps out the families there sometimes. His parents were immigrants, too."

"Oh. A Jewish boy. Your parents are going to *love* that," Vivian said with a wicked grin. She grabbed Alice's hand and pulled her farther into the house, into the basement where the darkroom was.

"No, it's not like that..."

"No talk. No lies. Just work. Work and art!"

Vivian took a burning joss stick from a brass holder as she went by and waved it before her as if clearing the air.

After putting on (bigger) pinnies, the two women were nearly silent for the next hour. The darkroom was tiny and smelled of fresh chemicals and magic. Well-practised in what needed to be done, each worked as if she knew the other's movements beforehand: Pour this solution into that pan. Dip the dry plate in it. Dip the plate in the stop bath. Carefully set out to dry. Repeat.

Most of the ones they were working on were Alice's (although a few of the photographs were her aunt's, one a particularly detailed large-format re-creation of *The Death of Socrates*). She couldn't wait to take a look at them under real light; in the dim glow of the lantern with the red filter, she could barely see anything even when she tilted them back and forth and squinted.

Eventually they finished, tidied up the spilt chemicals, and left the plates to dry on a half dozen pressed and clean tea towels.

"I'm going to have a bit of vermouth and see if I can't get Monique to make us a light lunch," Vivian said with a heavy sigh, as if they had spent the last hour lifting weights. She crankily stuffed a piece of hair back into her bun and disappeared into the smoky rooms beyond.

They were supposed to wait an hour or so before handling the plates, but, always impulsive, Alice couldn't help herself. She sneaked one into her palm, knowing that if she was caught her aunt would lecture her about how Patience and Time were the lost twin sisters of the other muses, the extra ones no one ever talks about (as compared to the more showy ones like Terpsichore and Urania). Alice quickly made her way to the little solarium off the study, where the brightest light in the house would be.

The portrait she had grabbed was of Mrs Pogysdunhow; she caught a glimpse in the photo of the settee from the staging area where she had taken it. Alice couldn't remember if the sitter had been scowling or grinning with her two weirdly wide rows of tiny white teeth. Maybe it would be a masterpiece of artistic realism, or maybe just a horrible mockery that she would never be able to show the poor woman. The babies had been squirming. The exposure time had been approximately half a second – too slow to freeze the little tots; they would be blurry around the edges. But then weren't babies a little blurry around the edges all the time anyway, with their drool and blankets and fuzzy hair?

Alice slipped into the bright sun of the solarium and anxiously tilted her hand round, trying to get a good look without glare.

Her eyes widened when she saw what she really held.

It wasn't a portrait of Mrs Pogysdunhow at all.

It was the Queen of Hearts.

Chapter Three

Alice stared at the piece of glass in her hand, slick and thin and flat like a mirror, and tried to convince herself that she was wrong.

" 'Tis a trick of the light," she murmured aloud to make it true. Too scared to believe.

It was a smudge, a drip, a chemical defect. A distortion that was her fault somehow for not making sure the solutions were properly mixed and properly spread. There was a bubble in the fixative.

But when she held the negative up to the blue sky beyond the panes of window glass – also rectangular, like her photo plate – there was no mistaking it. The horrid, imp-like thing gawping in the middle of the picture had too massive a head, too vicious a grin even for Mrs Pogysdunhow. And there were no babies.

Also she was wearing a crown.

A tiny, strange angular distortion of a crown – the sort of crown you'd give a playing card to wear if it had come alive. The Queen waved a fan (in the shape of a heart) at the viewer as if to say, *Yes, it's really me, don't look away, you horrid girl*. Her hands and feet were tiny. Too tiny for her barrel-like body.

Alice realised she hadn't breathed in several seconds.

Wonderland!

Exactly from her dream.

But—

It was… real?

Alice wondered if this was what other girls felt like when they claimed they felt faint. The air in the tiny solarium *was* a little close. But instead of suffocating her, the warmth from the sun felt alive and rich on her hands, her skin soaking up its power with relish.

Yet even that, and everything else – the sky and brightness and the whole beautiful day – had become drab and unreal next to the strange grey-and-black image on the plate.

Alice peeped at it again almost from the corners of her eyes, afraid it would be gone, afraid it was a momentary hysterical delusion now replaced forever with a picture of a sadly all-too-non-fictive person. The Pogysdunhows of the world were too real to deny.

But no, the Queen was still there.

Alice laughed aloud and almost danced in the tiny confines of the solarium. Her smile and tossed golden hair put the glorious day outside to shame. She had Wonderland in her hand!

"Fancy that!" she breathed.

And yet...

Alice examined the picture more closely. There was *hate* in the negative-bright eyes of the Queen. Her smile was triumphant and cruel and looked like it could eat cities. True, the Queen of Hearts was malevolent and, in modern parlance, *unbalanced* in her constant sociopathic desire to take off everyone's heads, but she had said and done everything with the callous antipathy of any unpleasant child playing with dolls. Not with any real feeling about the situation.

"Alice!"

She jumped at the shout. Her aunt was looking for her, swishing in and out of rooms with languid yet efficient movements, trouser leg wiffling against trouser leg.

"Yes, Aunt Vivian?"

She let herself back through the solarium door, the tiny brass doorknob reminding her of other things: tiny keys, tiny glass tables, tiny doors...

"Oh, getting a little sunlight, hmm?" her aunt asked appraisingly, looking at her over the tops of her glasses. "Probably quite healthy after the darkroom. Opens your pores. Here, these just came for you in the morning post."

Alice took both the cards with surprise. Who had possibly known where she was, who was so formal and needed her? Which *two* people?

Breathlessly she cracked the first one open. In her excited state she wondered dizzily: Would it say EAT ME? Or DRINK ME? Or be some sort of invitation to a playing-card ball? Anything was possible!

But the handwriting was immediately – and sadly – recognisable as her sister's.

My dearest Alice,

You did not let me finish speaking at breakfast in your haste to go running off to Our Aunt's.

You will be delighted to hear, I am certain, that Mr Headstrewth will be visiting with us during receiving hours. More than that, however, he will be bringing his good friend Mr Richard A. Coney, whom I was also telling you about at breakfast.

Let me refresh your memory on the fine attributes of Mr Coney in case you have forgotten: He is a very educated, intelligent young fellow destined for great things in our Party and the world in general. His hair is a brilliant platinum to your golden and I am certain you two will get along famously.

We will be receiving them at noon; a light tea will be served.

Ever yours,
Mathilda.

"No," Alice said, her disappointment so severe it felt like gastric distress. Or perhaps that was merely the mention of Coney. "Absolutely not."

"I don't blame you," her aunt said, having read the note over her shoulder. "Sounds ghastly and bourgeois."

With something like feverish desperation Alice cracked open the other card. In the best of all possible worlds, there would be a tiny etching of a rabbit on it.

There was not.

Alice dear,

Please do not bother yourself in making up an excuse that we would never believe anyway.

Come or we shall never hear the end of it from your sister.

— Your Loving Mother.

Vivian let out a terribly unsophisticated bark of laughter. "She's got you there."

"Bats and cats," Alice swore, crumpling her hands into fists. "Bloody—"

"Aha, language," her aunt said, tsking. "You had better go. Otherwise I doubt you will ever be allowed over here again."

"But the other film plates!" Alice cried desperately. "I want to see them! They're almost dry. Let's do just have a peek first..."

"They shall be waiting for you when you're done. Or no—I can send them over in the late post. Or by errand boy. Along with your camera. Come along, you'll have to hurry if you want to make it home in time. And you must never let them see you run, of *course*."

But Alice did run. She ran as fast as her leather shoes, corset and crinoline let her. She felt strangely naked without her camera satchel but at the same time light and free – the only thing she carried was the glass plate of the Queen of Hearts (it didn't *quite* cut her hand as she gripped the sharp edges). Her hair tugged in its hastily reassembled chignon. Her arms spread out behind her like wings for a moment, memories of the freedom of chasing a white rabbit and thinking of nothing else but catching him.

As she rounded the corner to her house she slowed and adjusted her breath, slowing it as well. She swept her hands back over her hair to neaten it. Not that she *really* cared, but she didn't want to hear her sister making nasty little remarks about it.

Sedately and calmly she strolled up the cobbles and let herself in.

Everyone was already in the sitting room and looked up at her expectantly as she approached. The men stood. First and foremost was Corwin Headstrewth, Mathilda's 'young man'; older than her by seven years, a smidgen overburdened with health and wealth. He was overall light brown in his jacket, trousers, waistcoat, hair, skin and eyebrows. Like a happy rodent. Obstinate lips rested uneasily when they weren't moving (which was almost always).

Next to Headstrewth was a younger man, almost his direct opposite. He was so pale as to be milky, with light blue eyes that would have been gorgeous had they not been framed by red lids and nearly invisible eyelashes. His hair, an extremely acceptable shade of gold, had so much pomade in it that it looked crunchy.

"We were just expecting you," Mathilda said pleasantly. She was wearing the medium blue dress with rosettes at the neckline that she thought was especially fetching on her – and was that a hint of powder on her face? On *Mathilda*?

Alice looked to her mother, the only person in the room worth looking at. She had on a bright smile and confused eyes, perhaps a shadow of the old woman she would someday become. For now it was less dementia and more like *Well, I'm here, but wouldn't I be better off somewhere else – with my sewing or in the garden, perhaps?* Alice's father was nowhere to be found. He didn't like young men coming after his girls and had decided the future could be avoided by avoiding young men in general.

"Yes, of course," Alice said. "How do you do." She extended her hand politely to Headstrewth's friend.

"Richard Coney," the man said, bending over and kissing her hand instead of shaking it. Alice gave her mother another look; her mother covered her mouth with her fingers, hiding a mischievous smile that hinted at the girl she once was. Alice groaned inwardly: she would get no help there. "Your sister has told me so much about you."

"Really," Alice said neutrally. "How positively of her."

No one noticed the lack of adjective: quite rightly, she assumed each would fill in whatever he or she thought sounded most appropriate.

"Oh, let us have some tea," her mother said, ringing the little bell next to her. "And I know it's a bit early for a heavy bite, but Mrs Anderbee just made a tray of macaroons."

"That sounds delightful, Mother," Mathilda said.

Alice didn't say anything: she was trying to sneak another look at the glass plate in her hand. Here she was stuck having tea with two of the most boring men she had ever met – she assumed – when all of Wonderland was out there waiting for her!

"What do you have there?" her sister asked. "Might you not share it with us?"

"Oh, it's just a picture I developed at Aunt Vivian's. It didn't come out the way I had expected," Alice said, holding up the glass and trying to tilt it back and forth specifically so no one could focus on the image.

"It's Mrs Pogysdunhow," Mathilda said, her sharp eyes seeing it immediately. "And her two grandnieces. What an odd subject. I salute you for your charity."

Alice frowned and looked back at the plate. No: for her it was still just the singular Queen of Hearts. Fascinating!

"You're one of those 'photo fiends', eh?" Coney said, not even bothering to take a look. "Snapping pictures of everyone everywhere?"

"I beg your pardon. I always ask permission. I would never invade anyone's privacy."

"*Richard* has a hobby, too," Headstrewth said broadly and awkwardly, perhaps competing in some unknown competition for *worst segue ever.* "He helps print up and distribute pamphlets for Ramsbottom's campaign – he is the campaign manager, along with Quagley Ramsbottom. He's even organising the big rally next Tuesday!"

"Do tell," Alice said, not even trying *not* to sound bored. She turned her attention to Mrs Anderbee, who had come in with the tea tray. Her mother didn't offer to pour, looking distractedly out the window, probably thinking of birds.

"Ramsbottom is the man to go with. England is changing," Coney said, taking up the new topic excitedly. "We're in a time of great upheaval. Factories everywhere, new technologies, unparalleled growth – why, the very definition of *labour* is changing. It's a tremendously exciting time to be alive. But with all this change it is vital to make sure we keep England – you know, *England*. English values, English ideas, English *citizens*."

Alice wondered if the sudden pain in the top of her nose was the beginning of the same sort of headaches her mother developed when her father grabbed his toolbox and claimed he could fix something himself.

"This tea, I believe, is from India," she said aloud, taking a delicate rose-covered cup from Mrs Anderbee with a nod. "This cup, China. The fabric of Mathilda's dress is from Paris. My locket was made in Italy. There are no doubt more countries represented in this room than there are actual English *citizens*."

As well as one from Wonderland, she added to herself.

"That's all very well and fine," Coney said, eagerly rising to the argument. Mathilda and Headstrewth gave each other nauseatingly familiar and knowing smiles. "As long as the locket makers stay in Italy and the tea farmers in India. If you know what I mean."

"I am sure I *don't* know what you mean," Alice said with a deceptively innocent face.

"Oh, but look at some of the lovely photos Alice has taken of the children in the Jewish quarter," her mother said unhelpfully, pointing out to Coney a pair of pretty silver-framed portraits. Alice was particularly fond of those; she was close to the two young sisters. When the family had moved to York, they continued to stay in contact by post.

"Wouldn't you rather be handing around lovely pictures of your grandchildren?" Headstrewth asked her mother with a knowing smile.

"Are you and Mathilda setting a date, then?" the older woman replied innocently, taking a prim sip of tea. Mathilda gave her a nasty look. Alice almost snorted her own tea out her nose.

"Yes, yes, these are very picturesque," Coney said. "And I'm sure – in their own way – these orphans are very appealing."

"They're not orphans, they're—"

"Yes, yes, I'm sure. You have it in your head to save them; that's very charitable of you. But look here, why not come to the lecture we're doing as a fundraiser for the rally? It will be quite intimate and fun, just for Ramsbottom's closest supporters. He'll give a little talk – short, I promise – and then take questions. See it from our side – it might open your eyes a bit. You could be my guest."

"Oh, that would be fun," Mathilda said excitedly. "We could make it an outing. A foursome!"

"Oh, that does sound lovely," Alice said. "An evening taken up by an informative disquisition on xenophobia with, no doubt, an aside or two about the benefits of being a Luddite. But I am sorry to say I have a previous engagement that day."

"We haven't said what day yet," Mathilda said, narrowing her eyes.

"Yes," Alice agreed sunnily.

The bell rang; Mrs Anderbee went to answer it.

"So many visitors," Alice's mother said. "Perhaps I should be around to receive them more often.

"Or… perhaps move further away from town," she added reflectively.

But Mrs Anderbee came back without any additional

guests; instead she carried Alice's satchel and a small packet tied with ribbons.

"My photographs!" Alice cried, leaping up joyfully and taking them.

"Children today," Headstrewth sighed. "Always checking the post, too anxious to hear from friends who aren't actually present, or what the news is – so busy with such intangible communication..."

"I beg your pardon," Alice said, dipping a curtsy like the child she was accused of being. "I have been waiting for these. A pleasure meeting you, Mr Coney."

"Alice, you're not leaving?" Mathilda said incredulously.

"I am afraid so. This absolutely cannot wait. Good luck with—whatever." Alice nodded at the men and rushed up to her room. Would there be Hades to pay later? From her sister, and, reluctantly, her mother?

Who cares? Alice thought resolutely.

She sprawled on her bed and ripped apart the neatly tied velvet knot.

There were three photographs: one supposedly of Mr Willard, another of a little boy named Ilya, and a third of a pretty wind-shaped pine from the park, by the river.

Mr Willard, standing behind his desk, a pile of hats

on either side, was most assuredly not himself. Instead he was…

"The Mad Hatter!" Alice practically screamed in delight as the memory came rushing back. The tea party, the songs! The riddles! And there he was, just as she remembered him: short, with a nose that took over his entire face and a head that was the size of his tiny body. He wore a giant top hat with an equally giant tag that said IN THIS STYLE 10/6. He must have been standing on a chair, because he loomed over a desk, his hands firmly placed on it as he leaned forward.

But… he was turned, as if something off camera had caught his eye. He didn't look so much Mad as suddenly worried about whatever it was he saw, as if he was just about to entreat the viewer, beg her for something, when he was interrupted.

And while that was strange – even for a strange land – Alice quickly flipped to the next plate, eager to see what else there was. Ilya had become a spectacle-faced bird in his photo, one of those that had taken pity on Alice when she felt her most lost and alone in Wonderland. The boy had a sensitive face in real life; the bird in the picture looked equally empathetic despite the lenses for eyes and very sharp shaft for a beak. He was running, his feathers blurred.

"This is truly astounding!" Alice said in awe. "The

camera somehow sees through the real world and channels *Wonderland* through its lens instead!"

There were of course crackpots who used new photographic technology to claim they could capture ghosts or fairies or the auras of people, 'scientifically': with chemicals and light and mirrors. This was obviously not that. Alice had complete control over her equipment, the process and the plates. And there was nothing hazy, indistinct or unbelievable about these images.

The tree in the last photo turned out to be a flower.

A swaying flower the size of a house (or perhaps the camera and artist were shrunk small) with lips at the end of her petals. Alice wasn't even sure what kind of flower it was; certainly nothing as easily identifiable as a rose or a jonquil. Even a rose or jonquil with eyes.

"Oh, I bet she can sing!" Alice cried. "This is fantastic! My dreams were all *real*! Here they are right before my eyes!"

But why had they chosen to make themselves known now? Why couldn't anyone else see them? And if it was all real, where had Wonderland been for the past eleven years? Alice hadn't found a single hint or peep of it – and she had been looking ever so hard! She had *dozens* of photos of cherubic children and many interesting personalities from around town, several years' worth at least.

Also walls and flowers and designs in the cobbles and a few even at the beach – and up until today all the pictures resembled their subjects.

"Best not to question the magic," Alice decided. Whenever she had questioned anything in Wonderland from her last… *visit*… she had never received a straight answer; sometimes people became even ruder to her as a result of her asking.

So: the Queen of Hearts, the Mad Hatter, a spectaclebird and a singing flower. Every single one of her plates was a glimpse into Wonderland.

"Is it a world that mirrors ours? Hidden somehow? I wonder if everyone – if every*thing* has a double, like a reflection," Alice said thoughtfully. "Curiouser and curiouser!"

Well, there was really only one way to find out.

She repacked her camera bag and checked her film – there were four dry plates left. Only four! Time to order or make more.

Dinah, who had quite profitably spent the morning on the end of Alice's bed and hadn't moved an inch since, watched her mistress with one lazy half-open eye.

"Dinah! Of course you! I'll bet you're the Cheshire!" Alice cried, nuzzling her nose into that of the grande dame. Then she carefully set up the camera to take a long, slow shot of the cat because the room was dusky. She needn't have worried, however; the old kitty fell asleep, or pretended to, and didn't move a muscle until she was done.

Or after, either.

Alice then carefully changed film and ran downstairs and was on her way out the door again – before she remembered her hat.

"Oh, my ears and whiskers," she swore cheerfully, going into the parlour where she had left it. Once there she saw that Headstrewth and Coney were taking their goodbyes formally at the front door. Mathilda had her own hat on, and a shawl; perhaps she was going to escort Mr Headstrewth into town.

"Saved by a hat," Alice said with a deep breath of gratitude, touching it to her head reverently. Such a thing seemed like perfect Wonderland nonsense, too. She tiptoed back the way she came and left out the kitchen door instead.

With only three plates remaining, Alice had to choose her subjects very carefully. She tried to find Mr Katz – just for laughs, just to take his portrait, mind you – but none of the boys and girls at the Square had seen him since that morning. So she took one of Adina instead. Then she made Aunt Vivian pose, despite her aunt's weak protests of lethargy – and that she had done one already. Vivian seemed, however, to find the energy to fetch a turban with a long feather and a cape of gold and donned both. She draped herself across a cushy couch, and held an incense burner in each hand like some sort of unknown tarot card.

And then… Who for the last plate?

Alice knew even before she picked up the camera. In the back of her mind she had known all along.

She carefully set it on a table, aiming it at the opposite wall. Then she took one of her aunt's ivory-handled walking sticks, stood very still in front of the wall, and set the camera off by stretching her arm and lightly tapping the shutter button with the tip of the cane.

Her first – her only – self-portrait.

Developing the film was agony.

Her hands shook. She wanted to get it done quickly but had to be extra careful. It took too long. She wanted it to be perfect. She wanted…

She made herself leave the darkroom and take a walk while the plates dried. She would not look at them when they were imperfect and wet, encouraging wild speculations and guesses. She nibbled on a couple of cucumber sandwiches and a slice of cold Welsh rarebit (the cheese had solidified and was a little chewy, just the way she liked it).

She wondered what a picture of *it* would result in: a plate of iced biscuits with the power to cause sudden growth? Or did some real-world things remain just that – things in the real world?

Finally, unable to delay any longer and driven mad by her own thoughts, Alice ran back and looked at the plates against the sitting room window.

Dinah was… Dinah. Just a cat.

Alice bit her lip in disappointment. She'd felt *certain* Dinah would turn out to be her beloved Cheshire, the strange smiling beast who sometimes helped, sometimes hindered her travels in Wonderland. The kitty before her looked just as normal and sleepy and grumpy as she always did; no hint of a smile at all.

Well, that answered that question: some objects or people (or cats) were *this* world things alone, without doubles in Wonderland.

Unless…

What if the magical moment was over? What if Alice was back to taking pictures of real, normal things now – things that remained real, normal things?

She flipped quickly to the next plate.

All her worries were immediately dispelled when she saw what was there: Adina was a bird with a delicate neck and a mirror for a face. Without eyes it was hard to tell what she was thinking or feeling, but there was no trace of happiness around the beak. Her head was tilted, regarding the viewer a trifle too intently considering that there was nothing where its face should have been but a ghostly reflection of the camera itself.

Alice hurriedly put that one aside.

She looked at the next and couldn't at first remember who or what it was originally; all elements of the real world were pushed to the edges or erased entirely. The creature who starred in the portrait was large and segmented – and not a little terrifying – until she suddenly remembered who it was.

The Caterpillar reclined languidly on his giant mushroom top, clouds of vapour twirling around his uppermost appendages in thick, almost recognisable shapes. Alice was torn between delight and annoyance. He had the same unhelpful, obnoxious smile on his face as when she had first met him. Very disagreeable.

On the other hand, he was really there, resplendent in detail down to his nose and little golden slippers.

"Oh my goodness! He's Aunt Vivian!" she suddenly realised. His short arms were spread the way Vivian's long ones had been, to either side, and the mushroom top was almost like a couch. Alice giggled, putting a hand to her mouth despite being the only one there. "I had no idea you were so polypedal in your soul, Auntie Viv."

Then, knowing who was left, she slowly pulled out the last plate.

And immediately grew cold.

She had no preconceptions, no idea what to expect; visions of bright-coloured creatures and toddling oysters of course flickered through her mind as possibilities, but all she really thought she would see was… Alice. She was the only Alice in all of Wonderland, as far as she could tell. Alice in the real world and Alice over there.

But… this…

This other Alice, this Wonderland Alice, on the other side of the glass, was someone very different.

She had dark hair, for one; stringy, long, unkempt. The rest of her features were hard to distinguish because a thick, ratty white blindfold was tied around her head. Streaked and streaming down her cheeks from beneath it was thick black blood. Her lips were cracked and also bleeding, her bare neck and shoulders smudged with dirt.

Alice swallowed. She had never seen anything like it. Even at the theatre the blood was bright red and flowed easily and didn't cake up so. This was not a tableau; this was not fake blood. It was all too real – like something out of a scene of war, of a horror story, of a nightmare worse than any Alice ever had.

And then the picture moved.

Suddenly the other Alice was either screaming or grinning – impossible to tell which with her teeth outlined in more blood, her lips pulled away from them. She was holding up a banner that was delicately penned despite the poverty of her apparent surroundings.

MERRY UNBIRTHDAY

Chapter Four

Alice almost dropped the plate.

The image didn't move again.

She was frozen, that other girl, screaming or grinning eternally with her hideous missive.

Alice's heart thudded loudly within its double cage of ribs and corset. The house around her was silent and the light didn't change, but somehow she felt that everything had shifted when she wasn't looking. Opposite versions of the same emotion pulled in her belly: fear that the house had transformed into an expected nightmarish or Wonderlandy version of itself – and fear that it hadn't. She looked around.

It hadn't.

On the walls the pictures were all the same, on the floor the rugs were the same, the furniture… everything the same, same, same.

"Merry Unbirthday," Alice breathed.

In spite of the hideousness of the image as a whole, it was obvious the reason for it – perhaps the reason for all of the Wonderland images – was this written message. A message for her, real-world Alice, from this wretched counterpart. Who was she, exactly? Alice closed her eyes and tried to remember. Who looked like her, even a little, from the other world?

She recalled something about the White Rabbit, the one who had started everything. He *never* let her catch him. And he didn't even seem to see Alice as a distinct human being: he always confused her with someone named Mary Ann. *That* girl seemed to be his servant, and responsible for the white gloves he was constantly missing.

Was this she? Was this Mary Ann?

Alice ran a finger along the bottom of the picture, the edge of the banner, thinking about Unbirthdays. The Mad Hatter had said that she had only one birthday a year, so that left three hundred and sixty-four other days to celebrate Unbirthdays.

But what has that to do with anything? Alice wondered. It wasn't the Mad Hatter greeting her, nor anyone else from the tea party. This was someone she didn't know, and no tea was involved, and it certainly didn't look merry. It was a mystery.

"Or a puzzle, rather," she said thoughtfully.

Weren't there puzzles in Wonderland? Getting yourself the right size to fit through a door, eating or drinking the right thing for the intended effect?

Alice knelt on the ground in front of the sofa and took out all the photographs, laying them carefully next to each other on the soft velvet surface like a very slow game of solitaire.

All the Wonderland residents looked upset. Nervous. Scared. The birds looked particularly spooked. It was a little hard to tell with the Hatter, because he wasn't even looking at the camera – but *why* wasn't he? The flower seemed as if it was ducking its head, trying not to be seen. And the Caterpillar didn't look as smug as Alice initially thought; she had been rewriting the image with her own memories. His eyes weren't haughty; they were sad and old. And wait…

She squinted at the clouds around his head and hands. The *almost* recognisable shapes. There was something very odd about them. If she had a decent projector or enlarger she could have had a better look, but that was one piece of equipment her aunt hadn't acquired yet (and Alice, always a good girl, didn't like to push). She jumped up and ran to her aunt's secretary and dug around its drawers and compartments frantically. Somewhere Vivian had a beautiful magnifying glass with a rosewood handle and cabochons of jet set around the outside – but it wasn't there. The closest thing Alice could find was an old monocle left by one of her aunt's more dapper friends.

So she dutifully put it on as best she could.

It was actually quite astonishing how well it worked!

Hazy shapes resolved themselves into letters, as they had when the Caterpillar had been teasing her so mercilessly. She could almost hear his voice again.

HELP
US

The clouds seemed to swirl; Alice couldn't tell if it was the magic of the Wonderland pictures or just her eyes tearing up from the use of the monocle.

"Unbirthday..." she murmured. "Help us..."

She rubbed her head and scratched her eyebrow above the monocle. Help them *what*?

Sitting back on the floor, she looked out the window at the sky and the day as if to find an answer there. The afternoon was developing into a luxuriously warm and sleepy early-summer hug. While she was in a darkened, smoky room worried about creatures she had thought were just from a dream, there was probably a girl out there in the park happily weaving a daisy chain into a crown. Just like Alice had when she…

"Oh!" she suddenly cried. "It was a day very much like this when I fell asleep and dreamed of Wonderland!"

She went to her satchel and fumbled around until she found the journal in which she kept her film and exposure observations. It was a slim leather-bound notebook printed with all sorts of useful information in the front, including a nearly perpetual twenty-year calendar (as well as recipes for homemade salves and lotions). The tiny numbers on the mostly decorative calendar were nearly impossible to decipher. Once again the monocle proved its use.

"I do believe it was May when I went to the park with Mathilda for my lessons, years ago. Early May. It was a Thursday. I remember that clearly because I wanted to tell Mother and Father all of what I dreamed, the adventures that had happened to me, but they had gone to dine with the Ruthersfords as they did every Thursday. So I had tea in the nursery and had to tell Mrs Anderbee about it instead, the poor dear. And Dinah, too." She squinted and finally found the date. "Oh, my stars! It *was* today! Exactly today! Eleven years ago!"

She wrinkled her nose – a habit both her sister and her

mother tried to break her of, but Alice swore it helped her think, like callisthenics for her brain.

"Eleven… that's a prime number, and a strange anniversary. Why didn't they come to me at ten or five? That would have been far more traditional. But of course… this *is* Wonderland we're talking about."

She regarded all her old acquaintances laid out like cards. They looked back at her, scared and miserable. And the Queen of Hearts looked insane and triumphant.

Alice shuddered, remembering how terrifying the tiny little woman had been. Despite her size and ridiculous behaviour – really, quite unacceptable and inappropriate behaviour in any adult, much less a member of royalty – she was terrifying. Because whatever she said actually *happened* if her kinder, gentler husband king wasn't around to stop it. Her servants and card soldiers did whatever she asked. Everyone trembled in fear when she approached.

"Something is happening in Wonderland, something bad. *That* is why they are seeking me now. And it's to do with the Queen of Hearts," Alice said slowly. "And it is so very bad that they need my help. The – other – me seems to be quite… indisposed. They're coming all the way to the real world to fetch me."

To fetch Alice, the little Alice who had been chased and mocked in Wonderland, the girl who had tried and cried, who sang with the locals but was never really accepted as one of them. Who thought about them for years after she woke, and then slowly forgot them.

They remembered *her*, apparently, and thought she could do something.

I must save them, she decided. She squared her jaw. *I must somehow* go *to Wonderland. I will… find the rabbit hole again, or the rabbit, or someone else strange and furry to chase.*

She would return to the park. That was the first thing to do. She would find the tree she had climbed while her sister droned on and on from that terribly boring book without any pictures.

Of course she was an adult now, and without a chaperone, so things might need to be done a little differently. She grabbed her aunt's golden cape from a chair and stuffed it into her satchel for spreading on the ground, as if she were just there for a solo picnic. And maybe she would pack a few snacks, both to make it more believable and also to fortify herself for the quest.

"Well! That's different!"

Her aunt was suddenly standing in the doorway of the drawing room, an accusing finger levelled squarely at her niece.

Alice jumped, knocked out of her thoughts and strangely

scared that she and Wonderland had been discovered. Did her aunt suspect something odd was afoot? Did she notice anything was amiss with Alice?

Was she upset about Alice borrowing the cape?

"The monocle," her aunt said, shaking her finger at it. "I *love* it. A monocle on a girl. Absolutely subverting the whole masculine dandy gestalt. Oh my, you may start a trend. I wonder if I have another one…"

And with that she spun on her heel, and the forgotten monocle dropped ironically out of Alice's eye, dangling on its long black velvet riband.

Alice betook herself to the park posthaste.

But the memory of the sunny day, that golden afternoon on which she first glided to Wonderland, was not as precise, detailed or complete as she hoped. There had been the smell of moisture and sweetness of sun-loving flowers, the floating of insects and dust in the heavy yellow light, the drowsy feeling of all the earth taking her children into warm, comforting arms. There had been the drifting river, the bending reeds, the trees and the grass, her sister, the boring book, the rabbit.

But which was the right tree? *Where* had she first seen the rabbit?

As she stood on one hillock after another, peering at

the landscape between the prams, painters and picnickers, everything seemed different.

"Well, of course everything seems different, because I've opened up like a telescope since then," she said, sighing. "I'm over a foot taller. Everything *would* look different." Unlike the speed with which she changed size in Wonderland, the creeping of time and aging in this world had come upon her slowly – and yet she was still strangely unprepared.

She tried getting down on her knees for a more child-like view. Awkward and unseemly. Also it didn't seem to help.

Maybe I should start with the sort of place a rabbit would like. *An open meadow, with tasty flowers and buds, next to a thicket, a safe place for running into.*

With this idea in mind she straightened her hat, adjusted her bag, and strode off like an intrepid adventuress down a game path in deepest Africa.

Two hours later there was still no rabbit, no rabbit holes (or at least no occupied ones), no Wonderland. Only a red and breathless Alice with painful feet and aching shoulders.

"You're *here*, I know you are," she shouted, uncaring who heard her. "I've seen the pictures! You're real! So come out already! Where *are* you?"

"I beg your pardon? Did you take secret photographs of me after all?"

Alice spun round.

Regarding her curiously from farther back on the path was Mr Katz. He had a faint smile on his lips, but his eyes showed a real concern for her odd behaviour. His jacket was thrown carelessly over his shoulder and he had taken his hat off in the warm weather. He hadn't loosened his bright purple cravat, however, and it blazed like the breast of a young, strange robin.

"No, I wasn't talking to you, I was… Oh, bother." Alice shook her head. "It's complicated and a little mad."

"Well, now you have me curious. May I accompany you on your perambulations for a bit?"

"I'm rather done in, actually. I've been *perambulating* for almost three hours now looking for a rabbit. Or a rabbit hole. Or a place where I saw a rabbit once. With my sister. I also sat in a tree – was it this tree? Fie on it, I just can't remember!"

She sat down wearily at the base of the questionable tree, a lovely oak with long spreading branches like outstretched arms, amusing and useful for little girls to sit on (unlike the tight upright oaks along Pelgrew Street that made such tight and narrow acorns). This very well *could* have been her tree.

In her sweat and exhaustion and under Katz's gently amused look, she realised she had completely forgotten about her clever ruse with the blanket and fake picnic.

Now she remembered the little sandwiches and fairy cakes she had packed. She reached in and pulled out a cake, only thinking to break it in two and offer a piece to her companion at the last moment.

"Thank you." He took it very properly and popped it in his mouth, but it seemed more out of politeness than real desire. He squatted on his heels, his back up against the tree – apparently unlike the otherwise proper girl next to him, he was unwilling to sit in the dirt.

"But what are *you* doing here, Mr Katz?" Alice asked curiously.

"A friend of mine asked for help for a friend, in the friendliest way… That sounds like a riddle, doesn't it? But I cut through the park – a *long* cut, mind you, not a short one, because it's such a beautiful day. Eventually I shall have to follow through on my promise. For now, however, tell me: what is so special about this rabbit, or hole?"

Alice chewed the cake thoughtfully. What had the little treats in Wonderland tasted like? Sweeter, she thought. Would they be too sweet now? Besides growing *up* and *out*, there were other changes in her. Given a choice between a fondant-covered petit four and a bit of fat from a juicy roast, she would choose the latter.

"You wouldn't believe me if I told you. But I simply must find him. Soon. It's imperative. After a brief rest."

"Well, all right, then. You grab a kip and I'll ward off thieves and suspicious magpies," he offered chivalrously.

"What about your promise to your friend? And I'm not going to sleep," Alice insisted. "I absolutely shouldn't sleep. I feel I wouldn't wake up for hours and hours."

"Oh, I keep all my promises," Katz said with a reassuring smile. "Never fear."

"Keep me awake, then, if you don't mind delaying your errand for a bit. Tell me something interesting, Mr Katz. Tell me a story about your life. Tell me about your parents' lives. About coming here, and then having you, and you becoming a barrister. That's quite a lot."

"Ah, well, I suppose it's interesting enough to some people, but I doubt stories about studying law would keep you awake. How about instead I tell you stories I'll wager you've never heard, about a fantastic city called Chelm, full of fools and madmen?"

"That sounds *perfect*. I must in fact find a bunch of madmen," Alice said eagerly before she remembered how silly she sounded.

"Well, as the English are so fond of saying, *Once upon a time*" – and here he sat down on the ground, finally.

It was a little improper, perhaps, having the young man so close to her, but they weren't touching and there wasn't anything stupidly fantastic and romantic happening like her slowly falling asleep, overcome by the day, and leaning up against him. He didn't offer his coat to keep her warm. It was all fine.

"In the great city of Chelm in Poland there were many wise men who spent their days debating everything from the number of angels who could dance on the head of a pin to how best to save the moon from drowning in the lake at night.

"One day, the town baker came to the rabbi with a perplexing question..."

Alice listened as best she could: he spoke clearly with an educated, academic accent and sounded like one long accustomed to telling stories.

But the day was working its slow magic on her and she found it hard to concentrate. Instead of keeping her awake and engaged, the story was lulling her dangerously towards a dreamy loss of consciousness. She watched the ducks playing on the edge of the water in the reeds with a diminishing sense of interest in the goings-on of the baker of Chelm and all his in-laws.

What pretty rushes the ducks are playing in, she thought as Katz continued his story. *I gathered some very sweetly scented ones once, while we were rowing. Who was in the party? Mathilda? I cannot remember. But what are the ducks eating? Frogs? Roots?*

Look how the river reflects the sky. The water close in reflects the ducks. The sky and the clouds do not change for being reversed, but the ducks are upside down. Look at that one funny upside-down duck glaring at me like it knows something. Like it knows anything *at all. Silly duck. Well, of course, a duck on the other side of the reflection might know something. Ducks on the other side would be different. All the world is made wise and strange in the surface of the river—oh!*

She sat up suddenly. The mirror duck was staring right at her. Through the water.

"Help us," it said, rather less *beseechingly* than *peevishly.*

"I heard that!" Alice cried. "That's it – the river! It reflects the opposite of everything – contrariwise!"

She leapt to her feet and, with energy she hadn't had a moment ago, went racing down the hill towards the ducks. A small part of her was concerned that Katz would stop her; obviously these weren't the actions of a sane girl. It probably looked like she was suddenly bent on drowning herself, an English Ophelia.

But if he was chasing her, he was too slow and too silent.

"I see you! You duck there! Don't pretend!" she cried – and threw herself into the water.

Chapter Five

She fell, fell, fell, dragged down deep by her petticoats and crinolines and stockings and shoes, arms and legs tangling amongst the reeds and rushes and pointy, sticky things that tried to grab and drown her.

Self-preservation finally kicked in, and so did Alice's legs. A thought occurred to her as she thrashed and spun to push herself upright with her head pointing at the sky and her toes down below towards the depths: the water by the edge of the river hadn't *seemed* that deep. The bit off the bank she had been watching ducks swim around was little more than a few inches, just enough for frogs to slip away in quickly when you came too close. There was no way she could float suspended in the water and kick and still not touch the bottom with her feet.

And yet she felt the empty weight of limitless liquid, an ocean of it, in every direction. She hung for one unbreathing moment in this place before propelling herself reluctantly to the surface.

Alice gasped as her head exploded out of the water, her hair an unbunning mane that shed droplets and rivers. She was sitting, of course. Wide-legged and awkward. In a shallow pool.

It was a decorative, rectangular pool as might be seen in a book about ancient Roman villae. There were some decorative plants – reeds – tucked in the corners in a naturalistic manner. They were red.

Everything was red, actually.

Alice pulled her arms out of the water with a cry, thinking she was covered in blood.

As diamond-bright drops flew, she realised that only the pool itself was red: its tiles and the walls and floor around it. The water within was normal and clear, but refracted very, very red.

"Curious," Alice said, but a little sickly. She stood up and the water peeled off her; had she been paying attention she might have noticed that she dried quite a bit faster than was strictly natural.

"I did it! I'm not dreaming at all! I'm awake and alive and in… Wonderland?"

She was *in* what looked very much like the rest of a Roman villa, but all exploded and flat, or perhaps drawn by an uninspired and talentless student of the classics. The mosaics below her feet were set into what must have been different pictures and patterns, but they were all red. A single wall with a single doorway appeared before her, also red. Through the door in the distance she could see the beginnings of a lush forest – strangely drippy at the edges, and very red.

(Though if Alice squinted she could just make out organic shades here and there: a little bit of green or brown peeking through.)

The wall before her was redolent and moist.

She squished towards it, feet still heavy from the copious amounts of water sloshing around in her leather shoes. Putting out a single finger, she delicately touched the wall. Red came away on the tip. She brought it to her nose.

"Milk paint," she murmured, not entirely surprised.

Beyond the open door to nowhere was a pretty little orchard of orange trees, each and every fruit a perfect round red. Like picture-book apples. She felt very unsettled and anxious, as if something terrible had happened or was about to happen, like descriptions she had read of the battlefields in the American Civil War when brother found brother in battle, wearing the opposite side's colours. Things were familiar but horrible. Everything was red and terrifying. If photographs came in colour she was sure her picture of the Queen of Hearts would have been in all these shades of red as well.

Suddenly there came a terrible noise, horrible and loud and utterly uncategorisable. Alice flinched, covering her ears and hugging her head to try to drown it out (and probably getting red paint in her hair). The sound was a bit like a pile of something crashing – but a *giant* pile, a gargantuan stack of pots and pans. It was also a bit like a gong, like the tiny one in Mrs Yao's tea shop, but multiplied by a thousand and played by a thousand miniature mad monkeys.

She closed her eyes and fell to her knees, praying for silence.

Eventually the noise stopped and the echoes faded.

Alice unplugged her ears and saw that the sound had some effect on the otherwise empty landscape: beyond the grove of orange trees, figures were now hurrying, hunched over, along the base of a high red wall that had just appeared and was a slightly different shade of red from everything else – a little whiter and dustier, as if it was older. A portcullis slid open just wide enough for the creatures to slip through before it slammed down, locking them in.

Then everything was still and silent again.

"This doesn't seem very Wonderlandy at all," Alice

observed. The landscape was empty of movement now; not a single creature gyred or gimbled out in the open or the shadows; not a mome rath, or mouse, or bandersnatch or any of the hundreds of other creatures that normally crowded the paths and byways of Wonderland. There weren't even any woken flowers.

("Mome rath! Bandersnatch! I remember all of them now, and all the funny names, too!" Alice realised with joy.)

She walked to the portcullis – for this was Wonderland, despite its strange new mood, and what else was there to do? You went to the obvious thing, the thing that provoked your interest, following whatever intrigued you like a child. That's how *things* progressed.

Her body remembered trotting across the grounds of Wonderland with little-girl excitement; her adult legs were a little less prone to such movements. Still she strode quickly and threw in an occasional half gallop when she could resist the urge no longer. Whether it was her perspective or her imagination or Wonderland itself, the wall grew taller much more quickly than it should have as she approached, suddenly looming over her like a cat about to pounce upon a helpless ball of yarn. Its façade was smooth, of course, except for lines and bumps where stone blocks met, and the occasional heart-shaped decorative keystone. There was no portcullis anywhere.

"Of course," Alice muttered.

The door had disappeared, as doors always seemed to in dreams when someplace didn't want to be found.

But a man had appeared in its place, as if he had always been there, and at this too Alice was unsurprised.

He was all in black, the tired worn black of a high-end suit bought at a second-hand market by a farmworker who harbours some misplaced notion about impressing his peers with an outfit ill-suited to outdoor toiling. Fashionably wide trousers were tucked into high, hard leather riding boots. His waistcoat was criss-crossed with nautical-seeming belts that held muskets and bullets. The short jacket he wore seemed very proper, except that the golden fob clipped to a pocket led to a dagger, not a pocket watch. The man's hat was a dusty old bowler but had a giant black plume sticking out of it like that of a child playing dress-up.

His face was so real Alice did a double take; there was nothing dreamy or hazy about his narrow, sharp nose, the pronounced ridges above his lip, the tired crow's-feet around his eyes, or the sharpness of his dark red pupils. If she had any doubt at all that she was awake, this cleared it up immediately.

He held a scroll and a pen and was going over what was written there very closely – and seemed utterly unsurprised that Alice now stood in front of him.

"All the VIP seats for today's tea-time executions have been filled," he said, looking up only at the last minute, and then myopically, as if he were gazing at her over a pair of glasses. "Come back tomorrow. There are sure to be more then."

"Executions?" Alice asked in shock. Although from the terrible sounds and the hunched movements and the general redness of the place, this development wasn't entirely unexpected. Plus – the Queen of Hearts and all.

"Beheadings, you know. 'Off with his/her/its', et cetera," the man said, casually swiping his finger across his neck. "If you haven't shown your patriotism yet this quarter, I suggest you appear posthaste for the standing-room-only section. There's a waiting list that opens up at thirteen-thirty."

"I beg your pardon. I feel I am a bit confused. May we begin again? I am Alice." She performed the tiniest curtsy, feeling like a child again. "And who might you be?"

"I'm the Knave of Accounts," the man responded with dry surprise.

"The Knave of..." Alice blinked. "But why..."

"I know, why am I out here acting like an over-glorified usher?" he agreed with a shake of his head. "Dashed useless waste of my skills – but on the other hand, I *am* also in charge of the schedule, so maybe it all makes sense.

Speaking of which, you look like a VIP. Can I pencil you in for tomor—oh, no, no executions tomorrow. It's Cricket Day. The Thrumsday after next?"

Alice hated to disappoint; he seemed so eager. She was the only living thing within sight and very possibly the only one who ever actually took a moment to talk to him. Did he stand here all day, waiting?

"I'm sorry, but who's to be executed today, if you don't mind me asking?"

"Oh let's see, that would be…" He rolled and unrolled the scroll, lines of illuminated red hearts sliding in and out of the margins like a zoetrope. "Ah yes, the Hatter, the Dodo and the Dormouse. Quite an A-list line up, if you ask me."

"The Hatter! The Dormouse! The *Dodo*?" Alice cried. "To be *killed*? No! That's terrible!"

"That's very funny," the Knave said, squinting at her again. "Most people, after I read off the names, say, 'What did they do?' It's treason, probably, if you want to know. That's usually the reason given."

"But the King – or something – always intervenes!" Alice protested. "No one is ever actually killed!"

"Yes, tell that to all the corpses swinging in the rose garden. As for the King – well – I don't suppose you're from around here, then, are you?"

Far from it. She would definitely follow up on the King business later. As for now, she had friends in trouble.

"I should say not. But please – when are they to be executed?"

The Knave pointed his right boot; at the tip of it was a watch Alice hadn't noticed before. On the left boot was a brandy glass.

"In about a quarter hour," he answered.

"Oh, do let me in! I must stop this travesty at once!" she said, desperately putting her hands out to find where the portcullis had hidden itself.

"There's no use," the Knave said sadly. "The VIP section is full."

"But what about standing room?"

"Oh, that's the first to go so people can make their quota. Also full, obviously."

"Mezzanine?"

"Filled with ladies of the court, I'm afraid."

"I am trying to rescue my friends about to be killed. I'm about to commit what you would probably also call treason. And you still insist I need a proper ticket?"

"There's rules about these things," he said apologetically.

"I'm afraid I left my gloves under my seat, from yesterday," Alice said through gritted teeth. "In the excitement and blood I simply forgot. I'll just nip in and fetch them."

"Well-behaved girls don't lie," the Knave said accusingly.

"Please do not attempt to inform me what well-behaved girls do or don't do, or assume I am well behaved or wish to be well behaved, or even if I am a girl. I am eighteen now, you know," Alice said frostily, drawing herself up to her full height, which was still a good deal shorter than the Knave of Accounting. "If being naughty saves the Hatter, I will be the naughtiest, most rascally woman you ever laid your unfortunate eyes on. Now *open that door*."

The Knave blinked at her silently for a moment.

Then he buried his face back in the scroll.

"Perhaps there is a rule allowing patrons in to check for Lost Property."

"Oh, for goodness' sake. Let me have a look," Alice said, humphing. And on a whim, perhaps because the Knave seemed to have issues with seeing himself, or because it gave her hands something to do, or maybe it was just an Alice fancy – she would never be able to say for certain later – she pulled out the monocle and popped it in.

"*Oh!* I didn't realise you were in Accounting, too!" the Knave cried, looking at her in surprise. He held up a monocle as well – one he didn't use, apparently. Not as fine-looking as Alice's, it was trimmed in rusty grey metal and hung on a largish chain. "Or Legal. My apologies. Please allow me. Professional courtesy."

He swept a bow and at the same time the portcullis appeared, creating itself downwards and then drawing itself back up.

"*Thank* you," Alice said with as quick a polite curtsy as she could manage. With her head held high – and while trying not to drop the monocle – she went through.

Chapter Six

Alice went pale when her mind finally managed to make sense of what it saw.

Half the scene was dreamy Wonderland nonsense. There were stands and seats in tiered rows made from all sorts of inappropriate things: a sofa on legs that was in imminent danger of growing bored and walking off with its sitters still on; wicker thrones with silk parasols attached; chairs sat on the wrong way, upside down.

The standing-only area was fenced off with giant wooden forks and should have been as raucous as similar sections in Angleland at cricket matches or political speeches – especially considering the miniature elephants, large-mouthed ants and strangely-shaped humans all pushing each other for a view.

But no matter which tier they were in or what manner of creature they were, the spectators were all – quite rightly – subdued. Unlike Alice's previous visit, when the Queen had just shouted *Off with her head* wherever she went – croquet court, alee in the gardens, parade grounds – this was a place that had been custom made for her gruesome orders.

The focus of attention was a large, strange pile that haunted the centre of the arena. It was made from rubbish and junk and all the detritus of a fantasy world: teapots and tiny castles, golden eggs and rubbish bins, locked trunks and suits of armour that didn't seem like they were quite emptied out of their owners yet.

Balanced precariously on top of this was a stage stained a different shade of red than the red with which everything else had been painted. Darker. More permanent.

The castle in the background was the same as Alice remembered from her dream, such a dark red as to almost be black, but now it was the tallest thing in any direction of a flattened, red-rubbled land. Ominous black smoke poured out of its loops and murder holes. Everything smelled faintly of burnt tarts.

On a strange little pavilion to the left of the pile was a gigantic puffy red heart. Standing (carefully behind a railing) on the ramparts atop this were a pair of old familiar faces: Tweedledee and Tweedledum. They grinned, their mouths practically splitting their ridiculous faces, and waved to the crowd as if they were the main attraction at the event. Tweedledum wore a giant pin that said BEST BOY. Tweedledee wore a giant pin that said BOY, BEST. Below each of these was a second pin, large and glittery and tacky: a ruby red heart.

"Well," Alice said to herself, "it's safe to bet whose side *they* threw their lots in with. But where is the Queen herself? Shouldn't she be overseeing this business?"

A horn sounded: a long, beautiful golden horn with red banners trailing from it that would have been achingly lovely had not what it summoned been so horrible.

(Also, it sounded itself; there was no horn player present.)

Prisoners were marched out, bound up and miserably shuffled along by something Alice decided was a kind of ogre, as well as a grumpy-looking elephant who stood on her two hind legs. Alice caught her breath. Hatter, the tiny Dormouse and the Dodo looked so sad. Not terrified, as she would have expected. Exhausted and dirty and dried-out and somehow ancient, too old for their time. The Hatter gazed at the crowd with a face that didn't beseech, only wondered *why*.

Behind them came what had to have been the method of the execution and the executioner all in one: a giant creature with a black hood over its eyes and ears and top of head, its snub-nosed, razor-toothed muzzle wide and ready to snap heads off.

Alongside this gruesome parade came the soldiers. Hundreds of cards marched stock-straight at attention, eyes unreadable and sharpened swords all identically at the ready. Were Alice to charge them, it would be death by a thousand paper cuts.

"Most decks only have fifty cards – fifty-two at the most, surely," Alice breathed.

"Oh, she's been building her ranks again, haven't you heard?" an old gossipy sheep said, shifting her knitting aside to look over her glasses at Alice. She lowered her voice to a raspy whisper. "Playing rummy and a new one called Spite and M'alice to maximise her offence."

"But where is she? Where is the Queen?"

"Oh, she don't come to executions any more. Too many of them," the sheep sniffed. "I suppose we watch them *for* her."

"Is that what it is about, the quota? Does everyone have to be here for a reason?"

"You must be from the Outer Board – or as dumb as a hat on a tove. *'Course* we have to be here, at least once a quarter, or it's treason. Beg pardon now. I don't want to lose my seat." The old sheep passed Alice into the middle tier, where she held up a heart-shaped ticket to an anteater usher and was then escorted to a church pew.

"And they all just come and watch the executions?" Alice asked wonderingly.

How on earth would she save her old friends? If the soldiers were countless and the crowd unlikely to rebel, terrified for their own lives, what could *she* do?

There had to be something. There was always an answer in Wonderland, if you just knew where – or how – to look.

And then she spied it.

In the VIP section was a prettily set table with refreshments for the upper crust. There was tea, punch, tall crystal glasses of what could only have been champagne, delicate sandwiches shaped like hearts, and trays and trays of tarts and biscuits.

(Ironically, the other sections also had food – pie and cider and the like – but these were *sold* by vendors. The refreshments for the rich were free. *More Wonderland nonsense*, Alice thought.)

But she was drawn to one particular stand made of delicate gold wire and glass. It held trays of fondant-covered petits fours delicately iced to say EAT ME.

"That must do something!" Alice cried. "It will either allow me to grow tall and step over all the soldiers, or tiny so I can slip between their legs!"

So she pushed her way forward to the gated VIP entrance, where a fox in a dashing cap stopped her.

"VIPs *only*," he purred politely.

"But I'm a knave," Alice said quickly, popping in the monocle again. "In Accounting," she added, rather more hesitantly.

"Oh, quite right, then," the fox said, stepping aside and opening the gate for her. He whispered: "And about bloody time, too, if you ask me! Women have a lot more to contribute than just as queens and ladies-in-waiting. I've a kit would love to be a Foxen Spy if she were only given the chance."

Alice nodded politely, afraid that saying anything else would give her away.

She was dimly aware how bad it looked, her diving right into the refreshments instead of exchanging pleasantries with the pig-nosed marquesses under their parasols, the nearly extinct dukes, the viscounts and vultcounts. Everyone here was also subdued and stern, and they spoke to each other sotto voce, and the dresses were large and lovely. But time was ticking.

Alice plucked a lovely vanilla-looking square with lavender bits on the top and was about to pop the whole thing in her mouth but remembered at the last moment to nibble.

"Last time I ate too quickly, my neck lengthened until I looked like a serpent – and scared the wits out of that poor bird!"

She swallowed. And waited.

Did her toes feel tingly?

Were her fingertips itching?

Was the ground suddenly farther away – or a great deal closer?

No. None of it.

Nothing happened.

Another horn blew. Alice watched in dismay as the prisoners and their executioner were led up a rickety ladder onto the platform. An officious-looking creature that seemed to be half pangolin took out a megaphone (really, a toucan held by its feet, beak propped open) and began shouting out a list of what were presumably their crimes, but between the noise of the crowd and the laziness of the toucan it was impossible to hear what precisely they were.

Alice anxiously – but cautiously – nibbled a bit more of her petit four.

The Pangolin on the platform bowed and stepped away, finished with whatever trumped-up charges he had announced. The elephant and the ogre prodded the prisoners forward to the front of the platform and then down to their knees. The Executioner scampered behind them improbably on its four large paws.

Alice still didn't grow.

Or shrink.

She stuffed the rest of the cake down her throat and grabbed a teacup in each hand, throwing back the pleasant lemony liquid like a drunken sailor.

NOTHING!

Nothing at all happened.

"What am I to *do*?" she wailed.

"Cut back on your between-meal snacks a bit, I'd say, lassie," said the servant bear who quickly replaced the treats she had scarfed down.

The Executioner opened its wide mouth. A surprisingly cute pink tongue, acres in size, lolled to the side. There was nothing cute about its teeth, however; ivory-coloured, sharp as death, and springing out of pitch-black gums. It bent over the prisoners…

"STOP!" Alice cried out, unable to think of anything else to do.

And everyone *did* stop.

Everyone.

They all turned to look at her.

"Stop this nonsense at once!" Alice ordered, trying to sound regal. But her voice was shaking.

The prisoners spotted her and the Hatter made a face that broke her heart: his exhaustion melted into a relieved *smile.* Nothing Mad about it at all. As though – as though Alice was here now and everything would be all right.

"What in blazes is this?" the Pangolin demanded from below, his voice perfectly audible without the toucan (the poor bird now hung forgotten at his side). The crowd looked at him with delight. "This is highly unusual. Out of the ordinary."

"Release the prisoners at once!" Alice demanded back, pointing. It was very rude, but these were dire circumstances.

The crowd craned their necks to look back at her – rather like they were watching a tennis match.

"Release the *prisoners*?" the Pangolin cried. "They are enemies of the state. They are treasonous, foul miscreants. Didn't you hear their crimes? *Gathering with the purpose of undermining the Queen's authority, spreading spurious lies about the Queen, stealing tarts, redistributing property properly seized by the state and eminent domain...* It's all there, and you want me to release them? Don't be mad."

"We're all mad here!" Alice shouted. "Has there even been a *trial*? With a judge and jury and barristers and tea?"

The crowd began to murmur and talk to each other, nodding like this was a good point.

"The Queen doesn't require a judge," the Pangolin said haughtily. "She's the Supreme Authority."

"Well!" Alice said, uncertain where to go from there. "I hardly think so. Now release them before I come down there and do it myself."

"Are you a knave or… a queen?" the fox guard whispered in awe. "You're certainly not a pawn."

The Pangolin, meanwhile, was snorting himself into a fit. The crowd quieted in wonder while he guffawed, choked and made other terrible noises with his nose. He bent over with his arms crossed in front of his stomach.

"You?" he finally managed, the apparent laughing fit over. "Against Her Majesty's army?"

"They are just cards," Alice said, stepping forward – but slowly. "Shan't be a problem at all."

The prisoners weren't wasting a moment while everyone was distracted; they were conversing quietly amongst themselves and untying their bonds.

"Get on my back," the Dodo ordered the Hatter.

The Hatter scooped up the Dormouse with one hand; with the other he grabbed the Dodo's neck and swung himself aboard.

"Be off with you!" Alice shouted at the soldier cards, making sweeping motions with her hands. "Shoo! Or I shall scatter you directly and let the maid sweep you up. You'll all be replaced with a nice fresh pack of clean, well-behaved cards."

She moved forward menacingly. Worried spectators moved out of her way.

As was always the case with perspective in Wonderland, it switched quickly; in no time Alice was down at the level of the field and realised she was no taller than the cards. Though she remained a good deal thicker round the middle, one of them could easily curl itself around her like a rug and finish her off by squeezing – without even having to touch his sword.

"I'm going! I'm going!" the Dodo shouted.

And indeed he was.

Alice, the spectators, the card soldiers, the Pangolin and the fox usher all watched in awe as the ungainly bird flapped madly and took off into the sky. The Hatter grinned triumphantly and waved like royalty to the crowd.

(He waved with the hand holding the Dormouse, which seemed a little unfortunate for the poor queasy thing.)

"I rather thought dodos couldn't fly," Alice said in wonder.

"Might as well, since he's extinct," the knitting sheep said with a sage shrug.

As soon as the fugitives disappeared into the sky, all attention was turned back to Alice.

"You're responsible for the prisoners escaping!" the Pangolin spat in a frothy fit of rage. The soldiers all flexed, almost as one, with eagerness and anger.

"Seems more like it's those two?" Alice suggested, pointing at the ogre and the elephant. The guards looked at each other in surprise. The Executioner was bored and had taken to chasing its own tail round and round for a bit.

"Idiots!" the Pangolin raged.

"If you'll just excuse me," Alice said politely to the people in front of her, stepping around them.

"Don't let her escape, too!" the Pangolin cried.

And then Alice ran.

Chapter Seven

Alice could hear the *fwip fwip fwip* of the cards running after her. How she longed to be huge, to turn round and gather them up and shove them in her pocket like the naughty little things they were.

If she died in Wonderland, did she die in real life?

She pushed people and creatures (and creature-people) out of her way and dived through the portcullis out to the other side. She had a vague vision of the Knave of Accounts looking surprised somewhere on her right but barely registered it. Wonderland had rearranged itself a little during her time in the arena, as was its wont, although this didn't impact Alice's escape plan for the very good reason that she didn't really have one. She just heaved hard to the right and kept close to the wall on the slim hope that the soldiers would assume she had actually dashed straight ahead and into the plains beyond the castle, back through the orange grove.

The wall surrounding the arena split off and became two walls, and then three, and then joined into a number of smaller and thicker walls at strange angles. These were in turn soon replaced with boxwood and topiary. With a flash it came to Alice: she was now in the horrid maze that had nearly entrapped her forever last time in Wonderland!

It was even more ominous now, all painted red. Drippily, thickly, large gobbets of paint clumped on top of curling and dying leaves.

Alice risked a glance behind her.

The soldiers had not been fooled. They *fwipped* closer, legs matching gait perfectly and arms held up identically, short spears at the ready. Where were the silly cards of before? The bumbling buffoons mis-painting roses and acting as croquet hoops? It wasn't their alien build or the general wrongness of inanimate objects consciously attacking her that was the most terrifying; it was the perfect synchronicity with which they did it.

But they were without a non-card commander or lackey. The Queen was still absent – which relieved Alice a bit, to her surprise. Everything seemed more *survivable* and less confusing without her constantly shouting death threats.

"You win," Alice growled at the maze. It might lead to problems later, but right now it was her only hope for losing pursuers.

She chose her route at random, left right right left and up a little ramp. The paint had pooled underneath the bushes into thick, goopy lines on the ground, an ugly mess of red sludge over dust. Her hair was entirely undone now, and when she cut a corner too close it whipped against the wall and came away heavy and sticky.

Sound echoed strangely amongst the high bulwarks of red bushes and trees, and just like last time, it was unclear if the sky above her was the same as it was outside the maze or just a very high ceiling. But the noise of the cards grew quieter behind her, and Alice began to feel a little safe: as safe as a mouse in a maze escaping a cat. Out of the frying pan and into the laboratory.

She slowed her pace, and her own footsteps grew loud. Loneliness increased exponentially as a function of time away from the entrance of the labyrinth.

She swallowed an incipient sob and nearly choked on the dust and her own dry throat. Her ears rang with the beats of her heart. Her breath came in short gasps.

"When I return to Angleland, I really must engage in a routine of physical exercises and callisthenics," Alice told herself, focusing on being out of shape rather than lonely and scared. "One never knows when one will be forced to run away from an army of playing cards. Or angry dogs."

She turned down a path at random, because what did it matter? She crossed an intersection. At the end of one of the paths was a figure: a strange fellow, mostly human, wearing a bell-shaped garment of bright red that went to the ground and a sort of matching upside-down bell-shaped hat. The stitches were large and obviously hasty. Alice was pretty sure she saw a bent nail or two put to use in holding it together in place of pins.

"Bless you, my child," the strange man said, making a gesture with his hand.

"I beg your pardon?" Alice asked politely.

"We are all pawns hoping to make it to the end of the Game."

"Pawn? You look more like a bishop," Alice said, pointedly looking at his hat.

"We are all pawns," the man repeated, also pointedly. "We arrive at the end equal and unafraid. Actually very, very afraid. All hail the Queen of Hearts!"

"What game?" Alice said, advancing on him. "*Not* cards? Is it chess? Or have we wandered off into entirely different realms now, like pachisi or quoits? Does this have something to do with the executions?"

"May She be the last standing!" He looked around nervously. *"Say it,"* he urged her in a desperate whisper.

"Why?" Alice also whispered.

"Everywhere they are listening, *you* know that! *SAY IT!*"

"I don't want her to be the last one standing. I don't want her anywhere at all, much less standing in it. She seems to have grown completely out of control since the last time I was here. Wonderland looks like it was razed to the ground by a terrible cyclone or other act of God. Now I repeat: what game, what ending, and why has her murderous behaviour suddenly become so – rigorous and systematic? And why is everyone just kowtowing to her whims? She's ridiculous. Together you needn't be afraid of her."

The man saw something past her, over her shoulder, and went pale in despair. "Look! They heard me! Here they come!"

Alice spun round. There was no one.

When she turned back the man was gone.

"People come and go in the most curious ways here," she said.

"You never answered. *Are* you for the Queen of Hearts?" came a whispering voice from inside the wall next to her head.

She peered in between the thorny, desiccating and blood-coloured branches. Therein crawled a tiny serpent, pale green with large black eyes. It looked adorable and utterly harmless, but Alice had read several cautionary tales about snakes from Africa whose poison was so strong it could kill a man in ten steps after he was bitten.

Also, the Bible and all.

"I can't be for anyone or anything unless I know the full situation," Alice said politely. "But I would say probably not. Are you the reason that poor man disappeared? Are you the one listening for the Queen of Hearts?"

"Why does a silly girl need to know the *full situation*? And anyway, I work for the White Rabbit, not the Queen. It's a simple question: are you for her or against her?" He pulled a twig aside to get a better view of Alice: she was fairly certain he didn't even have his pale, almost translucent front appendages before.

"Oh, put a sock in it," she said crossly. "A serpent in a walled garden indeed. Very subtle. I doubt the devil was so rude."

"I shall record your recalcitrance and reluctance to respond posthaste!" the little thing screeched.

"Do. Please. I insist," she said, letting the branch snap back. The cry of the flung lizard grew immediately softer as he fell into the shadowy depths of the bush.

Alice sighed and set off again. "Now, how to best get out of here and find my friends?"

As she wandered down a long narrow path, she thought about how strange that was; the term *friends*. None of the three creatures she'd helped save was precisely her *friend*, much less even polite to her. Yet she thought of them as such – dear old friends she missed and hadn't seen in years and was very anxious to become reacquainted with. Which was strange, because until the photographs, she had forgotten most of them. It was obvious that whatever note their relationship had ended on before – Alice stomping angrily out of a mad tea party to which she hadn't even been invited – the Hatter, at least, thought of her the same way: with hope and nostalgia. She had seen it in his eyes.

Thank goodness they *had* managed to get away, despite Alice's failure to mount a dramatic rescue. It was unsettling the way the tiny cakes and Wonderland tea had no effect on her whatsoever. The last time she was here she couldn't eat or drink a single thing without something happening. Mushrooms, elixirs, cakes… even smelling perfumed gloves had altered her physical self dramatically.

Was the Queen of Hearts responsible for this change as well, somehow? She seemed to have literally taken over most of Wonderland – did she now have sway over its rules and effects?

"What terrible things have happened while I was gone," Alice thought sadly.

Of course the denizens of Wonderland had been afraid of the Queen of Hearts before, but not in the crazed sort of way the Red Bell Man was, or the beaten-down crowds who came tiredly on demand to watch the execution of their fellow fantasy citizens. And what was all that about being the last one standing?

She explored the maze a little diffidently, no goal in mind beyond avoiding the soldiers and trying to find the Hatter and get to the bottom of things.

"But you were never supposed to be *gone."*

Alice whirled round: there was nothing there.

She waited impatiently.

She crossed her arms and tapped her foot.

Eventually a mouth full of teeth appeared, but its smile wasn't the moon-sliver grin of old; it was wry. A pair of eyes eventually appeared above it, more resigned than mad.

"Cheshire! About time. What do you mean, 'I was never supposed to be gone'?"

"You were saying—oh, you were *thinking*—" The rest of the cat appeared in the air and twisted languidly there like he was rolling on a particularly soft and tufted couch. "I have it out of order. It's a problem with hypercativity. In your head a while ago, not aloud just now. But it's just as true as it ever was. You were never supposed to be gone, the both of you."

Alice had to resist reaching up to scratch his neck the way Dinah would have liked. One probably didn't touch sentient creatures without their express permission – at least not on first meeting. She wondered if there was a children's book in Wonderland somewhere full of useful rules of etiquette and proper Wonderland behaviour for good girls and boys.

"But whatever do you mean, I was never supposed to be gone?" she asked. "I didn't ask to leave, although I was terrified for my life – the Queen wanted to kill me. I just, as you know, sort of woke up."

"Yes, but you woke up too early. You didn't see it to the end, because Mary Ann didn't end it then."

"Mary Ann? The White Rabbit's Mary Ann? But she was the one with the message about the Unbirthday! She called me here!"

"Like calls to like," the cat said, now bored. "One or the other. You save, she saves, he she it saves, we all save. In Latin it's *pipsquo*."

"It isn't, either. But..." Her last memories of being in Wonderland were of chaos: a large-headed queen screaming bloody murder and *off with her head* and soldiers and everyone running which-aways and Alice wanting to shout and cry. "Mary Ann was supposed to save you? But – why wait for *me*, then?"

"Why not you? You're not from here, but you were there. You're Alice from another Land – Angleland. Not as good as Mary Ann, but you tried. You rose to the occasion. Literally."

"But I cannot rise at all now," Alice protested. "Not like bread or anything. I had the Eat Me cakes and the drinks and nothing at all happened to me."

"Well, of course." The cat twisted again, but only his striped purple-and-orange body: it rolled all the way round while his head stayed fixed and his eyes on hers. "You're finished shrinking and growing now. You're at your tip-toppiest. You can't be taller than your tallest, my Alice."

"That's an assonance," Alice pointed out smugly. "Of course I'll help you – and Mary Ann – if I can. But what precisely is happening here? What game is the Queen of Hearts playing at?"

The words, the tit for tat, came rolling off Alice's tongue as if they had been waiting all her life for someone else's dialogue to play with. It felt like a game, a grown-up one, and she hadn't played for years. It felt *good*.

The cat regarded her with an eyebrow raised.

"'Hands she has but does not hold; teeth she has but does not bite; feet she has but they are cold; eyes she has but without sight'," he recited.

He fell to the ground – feet first, of course – and looked up at her inscrutably. Like a normal cat.

"Oh, you're no help," Alice said crossly. "All recrimination and riddles."

"You're not much help yourself. You're certainly no Mary Ann. She's the real hero. If you want my advice… you'll figure out my riddle and find her. The *her*o."

It looked like it physically pained the Cheshire Cat to speak so plainly. He went green and chuffed and coughed up a fur ball – which opened bright pink eyes and then went running off into the bushes.

"Fair enough." Despite a strange incipient jealousy of this superior girl, Alice had to focus on the fact that whatever kind of hero she was, she was in trouble. She needed help. All of Wonderland did. "But how do I do that?"

"Ask around…" the cat said, drifting up into the air again. He yawned and put his head on his paws. "Keep your ear to the Grunderound, if you please."

"Grunderound?" Alice asked. "What? Where? How? Oh – he's gone."

The smile remained, inanimate, in the air.

"Of course," Alice sighed.

"The answer is *doll*, by the way," she added, sticking her tongue out at the smile. "Oldest one in the book. Are you saying the Queen of Hearts is a doll? That Mary Ann is?"

Then a distant squawk caught her attention.

In the glary sky above her an undiminishing speck resolved itself into a large awkward bird and its larger-hatted rider. They bobbed and burbled as they went. Someone from the castle must have finally found a suitable anti-aircraft weapon and was firing giant crossbow bolts at them. Alice flinched, but the heavy things, made out of dark orange cheese, all fell far short of their mark.

"Hatter! Dormouse! Dodo! I'm coming!" she cried, and took off after them.

Chapter Eight

Alice tried to keep an eye on the trio flying above her but soon lost them behind the high walls of the maze. She paid little attention to the twists and turns now, ducking in and then out of the cul-de-sacs haphazardly and not bothering to memorise the changes of direction she made as a result of this. Things crept behind her and pattered away in front of her, and she paid them no mind. All she really *did* mind was the length and breadth of her skirts, which impeded her speed and occasionally caught on curlicued signs that pointed to nowhere.

At some point the maze happily disappeared.

The sides of the labyrinth were replaced with thick and wild shrubs that poorly mimicked the boxwood. A spectacle-bird, perched with its giant toes wrapped round a low branch, eased from one foot back to another as if guarding – or perhaps merely watching – the imaginary entrance to the labyrinth.

"Pardon me, but have you seen the Mad Hatter?" Alice asked it politely.

The bird thing looked at her inscrutably, not an iota of kindness, interest or curiosity in its strange eyes. And this was the most alien thing of all. The last time she had been here Alice was gently accosted by all sorts of odd, harmless creatures – curious fauna who wanted to play with her, or run away from her, or perhaps loom menacingly over her to keep her away from their territory. But never had they displayed this frigid disinterest.

"I wonder if I am entering the Tulgey Wood again," Alice said with forced casualness, turning away from the bird and feeling strangely embarrassed, as if she were the cause of some Wonderland faux pas.

(*Tulgey Wood!* She remembered it so clearly, the name and the place. But if asked what street she lived on back home, she would have said, "Baxterflashenhall!" And then, "No, that's not right at all…")

It might indeed have been the forest from her previous visit: the trees were thick-trunked with storybook branches, and darkness grew under their leaves like a living, breathing entity. Ghostly green moss glowed and flowed around roots. Little flowers – eyeless, mouthless – poked star-shaped blossoms up from the forest floor. Strange pastel lights flickered off and on at unpredictable distances. It all felt very familiar.

And yet.

Once there were signs everywhere espousing nonsense: THIS WAY or THAT WAY or OVER HERE, nailed several to a tree, roughly carved into pointing shapes. The signs were still there, but in place of the friendly and useless words were bloody hearts painted slapdash upon them. Thick, ugly drips of red ran down their fronts like tears.

"'All ways are the Queen's way'," Alice repeated to herself with a shudder.

She walked into the woods.

The first thing she noticed was how silent it was; the beeps, warbles, burbling streams and qworking duck-bulbs were silent. There were of course no paths and she had only a vague idea of which way her friends had gone. It was like chasing the White Rabbit all over again.

"And where *is* the White Rabbit, anyway?" Alice mused. "He wasn't at the executions. Usually he's right up front with the Queen and other important people. But of course the Queen wasn't there… so perhaps he is out with her, wherever she may be. What did that lizard thing say?

That he *worked* for the White Rabbit? What does that even mean?"

Suddenly Alice spotted something at the base of one of the gloomy trees: a little flash of unnatural colour. She bent down and saw a single mome rath, a bright pink one, desperately trying to pretend it was a flower.

"Excuse me," Alice said gently. "I understand that you may not be able to tell the difference between regular people, especially girls, but I am not at all associated with the Queen of Hearts. And I could really use your help. If you please."

The little tufted head lifted up just a smidgen so that the tops of two large and innocent eyes could gauge her trustworthiness.

"Really," Alice said as patiently and calmly as she could. "You can see there isn't a spot of red on me. I just freed my friends from the Executioner, and now I'm looking for them. It's the Hatter, the Dodo and the Dormouse. Although if you knew anyone else who was left – the March Hare, for instance – I would love to see him again, too."

The mome rath raised itself up out of the ground on a pair of purply-pink and cautious legs. Keeping both of its large eyes on hers, it tottered, unconvinced, around her feet. Alice stayed perfectly still, resisting the urge to scrunch and unscrunch her toes away from it.

Finally the tiny thing made up its mind and went whirling into the woods. Alice wasn't entirely sure if it had decided to help her or was off on a mission of its own, but she followed nonetheless.

"I thought you fellows always travelled in crowds," she said to make conversation. "When I was here last, I only saw you in packs. Or flocks, rather, or – what *do* you call dozens of mome raths? A herd? A murder? A blessing?"

The creature stopped long enough to look back at her with sad, baleful eyes. Then it stretched its legs out and fell to the ground, eyes closed.

"Oh. I see. They were stepped on," Alice said softly. "I'm so sorry."

The mome rath gave her another look that was impossible to interpret without a mouth or other point of reference. Then it leapt up and toddled on. Alice followed, continuing her conversation – but with herself this time. That way there was no more chance of her accidentally saying something hurtful to the other party.

"Eleven years later and I'm still mucking things up," she chastised. "I used to laugh at little Alice for telling the Dormouse all about Dinah. What an improper thing to do, bragging to a mouse about a cat! And now here I am in a war-torn land asking about the Queen of Hearts' latest victims as if they were no more than a background image, a picture or illustration with no real feelings. Naughty Alice. Be more careful! Think before you speak! Remember what happened last time and learn from it!"

She opened her mouth to say something nice and soothing to the little creature, but the mome rath was gone. It had just faded out of consciousness as if it had never been there at all. Alice found herself beside a small brook that broke apart and foamed over rocks into a lovely little pool below – but it was all absolutely silent. *Impossibly* silent.

"No, none of that. Nothing is impossible in Wonderland," Alice said with a sigh, dipping her hand into the water and whipping it round with her fingers. Even that made no noise.

Then she heard the faintest bit of *something.* A song that was started and then stopped suddenly… a chorus? In the middle of the woods?

"Oh, that's rather mad," she said, cocking her head and listening.

"Oh!" she said again, realising what the music reminded her of. "It *is* Mad! Mad as a Hatter!"

Cautiously Alice picked her way to the sounds. It was far harder than it should have been: the Wonderlandians' now very recognisable voices grew louder for no good reason and then suddenly shut off like a door had closed. She had to stop, wait, then turn round and try different directions. She suspected that it was the trees. They scattered sounds they didn't like or didn't want to hear, or perhaps translated it into something closer to *tree*.

She rounded a particularly large oak and the source finally revealed itself. It nearly broke poor Alice's heart.

The escaped prisoners had found the perfect camouflaged hiding spot: a small clearing between trees so large that their branches knotted around each other overhead.

(Alice found herself suspecting that some of the tangled branches didn't actually come from the trees at all and had just grown ex nihilo in place.)

On the ground were several large, flat boulders suitable for sitting. Between them, tuffets of tall grass had been quickly and inexpertly plaited together to make a kind of a flat surface. This swaying, delicate top was set with a number of unlikely objects: a couple of broken teacups; a shell; a flat, concave stone; a snuff box. All were filled with water and rested on broad leaves.

Two of the old friends slumped tiredly on the big rocks. But the Mad Hatter kept his back straight, shoulders back, elbows close, and pinkie out as he picked up the snuff box with one hand and used the other to hold a leaf beneath to catch any spills.

Besides his familiar green top hat with the label sticking out, the Hatter now sported a much tinier one over his left eye. Alice gasped when she realised that the doll-sized velvet hat was there to cover up what was probably an empty socket; there were terrible scratches around his lid and cheek. The bags under his right eye had bags. He was gritting his teeth.

He also seemed to be taller than last time, almost normal height, and his head of a more conventional size. *Normal* and *conventional* being the operative, and therefore terrifying, words.

"No, properly now, let's, and..." he was saying with a forced smile.

The Dodo, missing his wig and a number of feathers, picked up his own 'teacup', the concave rock, with a resigned look on his face.

"This is where he would start to sing," the Hatter prompted sotto voce. "The March Hare. He would sing: *Ohhhh, a very merry...*"

"'Fraid I don't know the words – but I could learn 'em if you want. Or can we run a race instead?" the Dodo suggested. "That might cheer us up! A good old-fashioned caucus race!"

The Dormouse lifted his head up out of the snuff box the Hatter was just about to sip from. He, too, looked exhausted, but his eyes were wide and unblinking and he shivered a little.

"TWINKLE TWINKLE LITTLE BAT," he screamed. "IF I WERE A BAT I COULD FLY LIKE THAT ALL AWAY FROM EVERYTHING!"

"Sssht!" the Hatter said, snapping the snuff box shut desperately. As water squirted out its sides, he suddenly realised the danger to his friend and snapped it open again. The Dormouse popped back up like a jack-in-the box – wet, but with the same wild look in his eye.

"Oh dear oh dear oh dear!" Alice cried, stepping forward, unable to watch any longer.

She probably should have restrained herself a little. The Hatter leapt up, pulling the snuff box close to his chest and holding his other hand out to – what? Fend off an attack? With nothing? It was a crushingly valiant gesture. The Dodo stumblingly turned round and tried to hiss like a lizard or something far more dangerous. And while he wasn't at all a dangerous creature, he *did* have the mad look of someone, no matter how awkward he seemed, who had definitely had enough.

"Alice!" the Hatter cried. And again that change of expression on his face: the softening, the relief, the desperation, shot right into Alice's heart. It was the least Mad she had ever seen him.

"Alice? What's an Alice?" the Dodo asked, patting himself down for a pair of glasses or something he obviously no longer had. "Oh, I know you – did you ever wind up getting yourself dry, my dear?"

"Yes, thank you, I have," she answered. "I'm so glad you managed to escape!"

"Yes, *we* did," the Hatter said, his face falling again. "Yes, we did," he repeated softly.

"Please, tell me what is happening," she begged. "I received your message, your cry for help. I am here now. What can I do?"

"It's monstrous. *She's* monstrous," the Dormouse sighed in his quavering voice, swaying in the snuff box like a cobra entranced by a flute.

"A pox on the Queen of Hearts and her caucus bans!" the Dodo said, trying to pound his fist – wing – onto the tabletop, which resulted in nothing but the grass bending and being crushed under his force. The shell of water slid precipitously towards the ground. "I'll drink to her removal!" He grabbed up his own concave rock, toasted everyone, and took a sip. "Fine vintage," he observed.

"But what exactly is the Queen hoping to accomplish? What is the scope of her operations? What is it her intention to *do*?"

"*Do?* Intention?" the Mad Hatter said, suddenly fixing Alice with bright aqua eyes that were clear for just a moment. "What a question! Does it matter? She is sweeping her armies across the entire land and burning everything as she goes. She is throwing everyone into prison. She is seizing everyone's property. She is executing anyone who dares ask why or stands up to her. *Executes* them!

"*Why?* I have no idea why. Ask the eye I no longer have. Ask the friends who are no longer here. She… just… wants it. All. All the cake. Whatever."

"Ooh, a nice bit of cake would go well with this port," the Dodo observed.

"It's tea," the Dormouse corrected gently, as if the Dodo were mad and to be handled with care. "But do try the chestnut pudding. It's delightful."

And with that he hurled a prickly cocklebur at the bird's head: it wasn't even a horse chestnut, much less pudding. The Dodo caught it in his rock cup and gulped it down, which of course resulted in a fit of choking and coughing as the little hooks grabbed the inside of his throat.

Alice closed her eyes and counted to ten. They were all Mad here. She had to remember that.

"But mightn't it help if we knew what her eventual goal was? Croquet and cards – it's always all about *winning a game.* What is she looking to win? The rule of all Wonderland? Alone?"

"Rule?" the Hatter scoffed. "Rule is for rulers. And protractors. And perhaps slides."

"Well, one *might* just as well ask what the use of War is," the Dodo said philosophically. "There is no purpose. You just pull out your cards over and over again, and whoever has the most at the end wins."

"There is no purpose," the Hatter repeated darkly. "You just put your soldiers out over and over again, and whoever has the most bodies at the end wins."

Of course it did make a strange sort of Wonderland sense: in the end the Queen of Hearts was nothing more than a card grown too big for her britches. Alice used to play War – or Battle – all the time when she was little. Mostly against Dinah or her dolls, since grown-ups and Mathilda found the game random, tiresome, pointless and silly. It made Alice blush to remember how sometimes she used to secretly stack her half of the deck with all the royal suits to give herself a leg up against the opponent kitten.

Still, it seemed a little strange that the Queen was so energetic and directed in her undefined violence. Something didn't quite fit.

"So for all we know, she is just rampaging until she destroys all of Wonderland?"

"Or until the Great Clock ticks its last," the Hatter said with a weary sigh. He scratched distractedly at the tiny velvet top hat over his left eye.

"Yes, what you have seen in Heartland is just the

beginning," the Dodo said with a sigh. "A view of what's to come."

"All right, we have a mad Napoleon on our hands," Alice said briskly. "I'm not sure what I can do to help – she has an *awful* lot of soldiers on her side, and as you saw, I can no longer shrink and grow as I used to."

"You cannot grow because you have decided you have stopped growing," the Hatter said diffidently. "You haven't grown in ages and you've lost the knack."

"Well, I beg your pardon! In *my* world you don't get to decide whether or not to stop growing. My mother is rather short, my father is not overly tall, and I believe I am about average for an English lady."

"You 'believe'," the Hatter mused. "'Twas a time you used to believe six impossible things before breakfast, if I'm not mistaken."

Alice started to retort but then sat back on her heels and considered: she was the odd man out here, so to speak. These locals knew the realities and rules of their own land. Perhaps she *had* decided to stop growing. It seemed possible, since she had such a ready and pat answer about her parents.

"You haven't done much growing up at all actually," the Dodo said, a trifle rudely. "*Except* for your height, I mean. You've stayed the same, in the same house, trying to do the same things you've always done."

"Excuse me!" Alice said, frowning. "I have a passion for photography now and am finished with my schooling. If you had contacted me earlier, perhaps I could have come sooner and prevented some of this mess."

"Mess?" the Hatter said wryly. "I wonder if that's what the March Hare would call this, rest his poor long-eared soul."

"Oh..." Alice crumpled.

Everyone was silent. The Dormouse swayed sadly.

"I am so very, very sorry," she said softly. "I did not mean any disrespect to the poor thing." She took a deep breath. "*But* if we are to prevent such horrid occurrences from happening to anyone else, we must strategise. Work together. Plan. Isn't that why you wanted me here? To help you stop this?"

"*Mary Ann* wanted you here," the Hatter said moodily. "She was trying to stop it all. She had the odd notion you could help."

Mary Ann thought *she* could help? Alice tried not to let this thought distract her. But how could this other girl know anything about her?

"Mary Ann!" the Dodo squawked. But not like one would imagine a dodo squawking, or any bird at all; he squawked like an over-dramatic man. "Now *she's* the tardigrade's petard!"

"The—I'm sorry, I haven't any idea what that means," Alice said, not trusting herself to repeat the confusing phrase correctly.

"Tardigrade's petard. The echidna's phalarope. You know."

"I'm afraid I don't know. I suppose it's a good thing?"

"A *good* thing? A rare thing indeed!" the Hatter snorted. "Have you ever seen so tiny a petard that would suit a tardigrade? The Dodo's a bit dim at times, but he has it on the knuckles there: Mary Ann could fix everything up."

"All right," Alice said uncertainly. It was strange and a trifle naughty, but she couldn't help feeling a *bit* put out at the constant lauding of Mary Ann, this other version of her. The first time she had been in Wonderland, with all the growing and shrinking, she had wondered if she was still Alice at all afterwards. She even considered the possibility that she had become another girl entirely. Including specific girls she knew who had terribly boring lives full of lessons and empty of toys. How dreadful that would have been!

But here Mary Ann was the saviour of the fantasy land, Alice the Anglish girl who had led a comparatively boring, normal life until called for help. Well, that was a turnaround! And a bit painful for the ego.

"Really, dear girl," she reproved herself. "Even if this

Mary Ann turns out to be more vexing in person than she is in stories, she is the one who seems the most able to save everyone. Set your childish thoughts aside and do what is right!"

Aloud, she said:

"How did she do it? Contact me, I mean?"

The Hatter shrugged. "She had to wait for your Unbirthday. The proper one, I mean: the eleventh anniversary of your first visit. I suppose there was nothing else to do in prison but wait and hope and wish."

"That explains why she appeared the way she did in the photograph," Alice said, remembering the blindfold and the wounds and shuddering a little. "She certainly looked like she was in prison."

"She travelled to you by photograph?" the Dodo asked curiously.

"She *appeared* in a photograph. Of me. Actually, quite a few of you appeared in place of the pictures of people I knew. I suppose each of you is reflected in a real-world – excuse me, Anglish-world – version of yourself."

"Really? Whatever do you mean?"

"Well, Hatter, in my world you are – well, a hatter."

"Really?" he asked, looking delighted for the first time since she had arrived. "I'm a *hatter* in this other land? How exciting! And what kind of hats do I make?"

"All sorts. Especially large fancy ones for ladies."

"Think of it! Ladies' hats!" He took a dreamy sip from the snuff box, forgetting about the Dormouse. The mouse seemed more curious than upset.

"But Mary Ann is no longer *in* prison, now," the Dodo said. "She's free! I rather thought because of what you said that maybe she escaped by photograph."

"Really! How wonderful!" Alice said, clapping her hands. "I think the best thing to do, then, is for us to find and join her."

The Dormouse swayed dreamily. "It's said she is hiding out in the Back of Beyond..."

"*I* heard she went all the way to Helenbach," the Hatter added casually, sipping his water as if they were discussing where a friend was spending the summer.

"I heard she was drumming up a resistance, gathering revolutionaries and mendicants," the Dodo said confidentially.

"I heard it was flutes," the Hatter mused.

"FLUTY WOOTY DRUMMY DUMMY DONE-Y," the Dormouse whistle-sang before slumping to sleep in the water, splashing a little out.

"*Regardless* of whether it's drums or flutes," Alice said quickly, before they went off on another Wonderland tangent, "could she be someplace called the Grunderound?"

Everyone looked at her in shock.

"How do you come by this intel?" the Hatter asked suspiciously. "Nobody knows exactly where she is!"

"The Cheshire Cat told me," Alice said, not seeing any point in hiding the truth.

"Ah. Well, he *is* nobody," the Dodo conceded, nodding. "Most of the time. And nowhere at all the rest of the time."

"What *is* the Grunderound, if I may?" Alice asked timidly.

The Hatter tapped his teacup impatiently. "You know – when you're looking for secrets, or where you've hidden that last lump of sugar, or where the thieves go to sell their stolen tarts. You *grunder around* looking for the right wrong thing."

"Of course," Alice said, putting a hand to her head. "Grunderound. That makes loads of sense. Anyway, how do we get there?"

"Generally by walking," the Hatter said with a shrug.

"I prefer rocking chair myself," the Dodo mused.

"Haven't been flocks of those around since the Red Doom," the Hatter said, shaking his head. "I wonder if she's killed them all – or thrown them into her mews."

"Faster by bottle anyway, since the Sea of Tears," the Dodo said with a significant, accusing look at Alice.

"All right, can we shrink somehow? To fit into a

bottle?" Alice asked hastily. She had created the Sea of Tears herself years ago, when as a giant girl she had cried about her situation. It had flooded the place – and made a lot of Wonderland inhabitants grumpy and wet.

"No, but it's always up to me, isn't it?" the Hatter said grumpily. "Not allowed to be Mad even a quarter of the day now." He leapt up and began patting down his jacket, searching his pockets.

"It's true," the Dodo whispered to Alice. "The poor chap had the Nonsense knocked right out of him along with his eye. Hasn't been the same since."

"Oh my," Alice whispered back, concerned. That would explain his normal height and head; he was becoming sane.

"He keeps *trying*. To be Mad, I mean," the Dodo went on sadly. "It just doesn't come naturally any more."

But the Hatter succeeded this one time, at least: he pulled an enormous umbrella out of his waistcoat. With a flourish he snapped the black and arabesque-y thing open. A shower of raindrops fell out from underneath until he shook it dry.

"I don't—" Alice began.

"You never do," sighed the Hatter.

And so saying, he tossed it, handle up, into the stream that Alice had dipped her hand in before (and that must have provided the 'tea' for their party). But she was fairly certain it hadn't been *right next to them* until just now. Yellow cowslips smiled up from the banks – literally, of course. Their heads nodded and waved cheerfully, as Alice always imagined the wild happy flowers would. With a courteous bow – and another flourish of his hands – the Hatter indicated for Alice to get into the umbrella.

"Thank you, dear sir," she said with a little bit of a curtsy and, trying not to show any reluctance, stepped in. Whether she finally shrank or the umbrella grew mattered in the end not at all; the *getting into* it was not carefree and graceful as one might imagine in a fairy tale. It tipped just like it would in the real world, and Alice had a very hard time, swaying and balancing, not upsetting the whole thing. The Dodo half fluttered in next to her, more like a delicate canary than a large (mostly) flightless bird. The Hatter leapt in between them.

And the umbrella began to drift downstream.

Chapter Nine

If their quest had not been so urgent, Alice would have truly enjoyed travel by umbrella. It was restful, and all three escapees from the Queen looked grey and exhausted and absolutely filthy where there weren't streaks of blood. They could have slept for a week, it looked like.

The Hatter scratched thoughtlessly under the tiny top hat covering his eye socket.

"If you don't mind my asking, Hatter," Alice asked, knowing she shouldn't. But she was always a curious girl. "Whatever happened to your eye?"

He looked over at her, and she was startled by the moment of lucidity in his good eye.

"Jubjub birds," he said bleakly. "She threw me to a nest

of them she kept hungry just for such a purpose. Wanted to know where Mary Ann was. I never told. I wasn't the one who betrayed her."

"Oh, how very brave of you," Alice breathed. "I'm so sorry."

"Bravery is for kings and wingless pigs. I'm just a Mad Hatter. Well, I was, once upon a time."

Everyone lapsed into silence again. The umbrella twirled and the landscape rolled by, a little too slowly for Alice's liking.

"I haven't heard any poetry yet," Alice eventually ventured. "There is always ever so much poetry in Wonderland. Has the Queen of Hearts done away with that, too?"

"Poetry! I say! Poetry!" the Dodo said, pounding one wing into the other. "Just what we need a spot of. Dormouse, wake up. Dormouse! Some nice refreshing poetry! Come, come!"

Dismissing without wages the usual sleepy stages between unconsciousness and consciousness, the Dormouse immediately stood up, straight-backed, in full recital mode.

A dog and a cat and a droll wombat
Ran off to the Similung Sea
The sun shone fair in the immutable blue

'Twas as daylicious as a day could be.
"I spy a fish!" said the critical cat (who liked
trout fried in salt pudding).
"We haven't a pole!" the little dog barked
as the 'bat was sticking a foot in.

A flunder leapt up and glared at the three
"Our kind is not for your pleasure!
Go back to the sands of old Angler-land
On the beach you'll find great
... numbers of shells and something really sparkly and nice to take home and put in a cabinet, maybe."

And with that the Dormouse fell straight forward onto the handle of the umbrella and began snoring.

"Oh," Alice said, trying to work out what she had just heard. "That didn't end properly."

"I beg to differ. It ended *most* properly," the Dodo said, flicking a bit of lint off his cuff. "They left the fish alone and found some lovely thing like a pearl or an oscilloscope to bring back to Mother."

"But, but—oughtn't it have ended, 'On the beach you'll find great heaps of *treasure*'? That makes sense, and moreover rhymes with *pleasure*, the way the other stanzas have the second and fourth lines rhyming."

"You asked for poetry," the Dodo pointed out. "*I* certainly didn't ask for a poetical lesson. Next time recite something yourself. Actually, this *is* the next time, because you're next. Up, girl, recite."

"Oh, I shouldn't," Alice said quickly. "Everything I ever try to say here comes out all wrong."

"Try something really easy," the Hatter said casually – but there might have been a twinkle in his eye. "Your national anthem, for instance."

"Oh! Of course! I know 'God Save the Queen' back and forth," Alice said. "My sister and her silly man friend sing it all the time, even before they go to one of their ridiculous rallies."

"Only forth, please," the Dodo said hurriedly. "I don't think we have time for back as well."

"I can't stand in the umbrella without tipping it," she said, shuffling her feet. "I hope no one is offended." Then she cleared her throat and sang the familiar tune:

"My country, 'tis of thee
Sweet land of liberty
Of thee I sing...

"No, wait, that's not right," she said, frowning. "It doesn't even mention the Queen."

"I rather like it," the Hatter said. "That's what we need right now, anyway. *Liberty.* And no more queens. *Ever.*"

Somehow the trees had fallen away without her noticing; the cosy forest had been replaced by what seemed like endless silver water that rippled and waved randomly. Alice dipped a finger in and tasted a drop; it was indeed salty, perhaps even saltier than the North Sea. And much, much warmer. *Body* temperature, one might even say. They had come to the Sea of Tears.

"Does this leave us off in the hallway with the keyhole?" she asked.

"Only in March. Everyone out!" the Hatter ordered.

The Dodo scooped up the Dormouse and stepped forward; the umbrella, now somehow washing up onto a tiled floor, was much more stable, and he disembarked with great aplomb. Alice followed and the Hatter came last, pushing his umbrella back out into the water.

"Aren't you taking it?" Alice asked.

"No, it has filled out its term of service. Time for it to be free." He took off his (large) hat and waved goodbye. The umbrella handle uncurled and waved eerily back. Then it sort of pointed itself and dived underwater like a sea serpent, its cloth and spine splitting into two rear fins.

The black-and-white tiled floor they now trod on continued on an uphill slant away from the water, occasionally making sharp slanted turns into still wave shapes – it took Alice a moment to realise they were *dunes*. The squares changed size as required to fill in properly, but never curved or altered their straight lines and angles; the resulting mosaic was dizzying and impossible to focus on. Beyond this they came to a well-grazed monochrome sward, and beyond that a lovely little English village.

At first glance, any rate, it *appeared* to be a lovely little English village: there were houses, a main street, a horse fountain, people hurrying about at market. All the colours were right; all the movements seemed normal.

But the houses were built one on top of another. Literally. A large family house painted bright yellow with an airy porch and slate shingles was balanced on the roof of a lovely flag- and river-stone one-room cabin, and squarely on top of that was a narrow three-floor brick town house. A green witch's delight with round towers and intricately decorated eaves supported a solid farmhouse, perfectly symmetrical with three windows on the upper floor and a door between two windows on the bottom. The chimneys had to stick out sideways, of course, because this abode had what appeared to be a seaside shack – complete with a bathing machine – atop.

The fountain or horse trough in the market square didn't seem to be working and was moreover too high for horses.

A stone pillar held up a wide concave disc filled with water. When someone wanted a drink, he or she perched on the rim and bent over, taking delicate sips.

And therein lay the biggest surprise (or perhaps not so much, considering it was Wonderland). The people of this village had somewhat avian tendencies. Most sported beaks. Many had feathers, though the women often kept theirs under caps or oiled up into fancy designs and curlicues that looked like hats at first. Wings were used like hands and unshod feet had claws.

"What the blazes is going on here?" the Hatter asked, blinking at the sight.

Alice looked at him in surprise: surely *he* couldn't have found anything particularly unusual in the scene? This was his native land, and strange was normal, the odd the everyday to Wonderlandians.

So she looked at everything again, trying to imagine she was a local.

Then she saw it.

The inhabitants moved as if haunted. They slunk in the way birds shouldn't, hunkering down so their wing bones made it look as though they were hunchbacked. Their heads turned quickly this way and that, birds' eyes taking in the view in quick and feral glances.

Everywhere signs had been hastily amended with

splatters of paint: the symbol of a rabbit added to a sweets shop, a butcher, a tailor. Sometimes it was a red heart, but mostly a rabbit. Sometimes the rabbit was red, but mostly he was white.

In the market around the birdbath was a large, ugly and hastily-made statue that looked like it had been hammered together from spare bits of wood. Like a giant shrine, its base was covered in offerings of all sorts of food. But Alice couldn't figure out *what* the statue was at first; boards stuck out of it willy-nilly.

Then, as she was cocking her head and stepping back, it suddenly came to her all at once:

It was a rabbit.

"Hatter," she said, nervous but unsure why.

"No I don't like it no no no," the Hatter said, sort of agreeing, but it was clear he was finally a little Mad and of absolutely no help at all. He even seemed to have shrunk a little. The Dodo was busy washing his wounds in the bath, and of course the Dormouse was asleep. So Alice screwed up her courage and approached one of the lories hurrying by with a market basket on her arm. It was not, as Alice would have guessed, filled with seed. Instead there was a mound of luscious-smelling soft hay and three beautifully washed carrots.

"Pardon me—oh *my*."

It wasn't the giant hooked orange beak or gorgeous yellow-and-blue chignon the matronly woman had that shocked Alice; it was her hastily tied headscarf. The two long ends were starched and twisted up a bit *to look like rabbit ears.*

"What is going on here? Why all the rabbits?"

"There is only the one rabbit!" the woman angrily hissed and whistled. "If he comes by we're ready. We like rabbits here. All bless the Rabbit and keep him and his mistress safe. *And out of our business.*"

"We're a good town, we are," a budgie in a morning coat and bowler insisted as he walked by. There was a bit of white fluff sewn on his rear for a little tail. "Absolutely loyal. We gave up immediately, we did."

"To whom? The Queen of Hearts?"

"Never! To the Rabbit's men. *He's* to be trusted, of course. If he says that's what the Queen wants, that's what we'll do," the lory said with a determined air and a sniff. "You tell 'im that if you sees 'im. Whatever he says goes with us here. Mayhap he'll put in a good word to the Queen. Maybe she'll skip us on her next raid."

"But of course, whomever the Rabbit follows, we're right with him," the budgie added quickly.

Alice knew there was a song about this sort of thing but couldn't quite remember it just then.

(In fact, she was thinking of 'The Vicar of Bray', but when she tried to remember the lyrics about the man who changed sides for whoever was in power, all she could come up with was *"Whatsoever," sings the train, "Still I'll be quicker in May, Sir!"*)

"Alice, I don't like it here," the Hatter said forlornly. "Let us move on."

"Look right there," the lory said, pointing proudly at a rapidly growing pile of produce, offerings, at the feet of the rabbit statue. "A *pile* o' lettuce. That's from me. Much as it pleases him."

"And peases for him?" the Dodo asked interestedly.

"It appeases him," the budgie agreed sagely.

"Wait, that's not right," Alice said, but she wasn't really paying attention any longer.

For as strange as it was to see a town of birds be suddenly taken over by a fawning loyalty to rabbits, something stranger still managed to catch her eye. A shawled figure was adding her – his? – own offering to the pile of rabbit treats; he or she was entirely covered with robes and capes and cloaks and hunched over even more than the others. He gripped the edge of the cloth tightly with claws that weren't wingy at all.

Alice rushed over and grabbed the shawl and yanked it away.

"Aha!" she cried.

(Wondering – vaguely, in the back of her head – when she had decided it was all right to act like a seven-year-old ruffian again.)

Spinning out of the linsey-woolsey fabric wasn't a bird, although he did indeed have some bird-like attributes: a beak and wings certainly allowed him to hide out amongst the townsbirds, but his ears and tail and lion hindquarters had to stay firmly under cloth to pass. He let out a fearsome yelp, exposing teeth within his beak – again, certainly not bird-like at all. Then he curled his arms together quickly as if protecting something.

"Oh," the Hatter said, as if nothing untoward had happened. "Hello, Gryphon."

"A gryphon!" Alice cried out. "I've always thought you were imaginary and fantastic beasts!"

"Well, there's a fine how'd'ye'do," the Gryphon said a little wryly, looking left and right and trying to protect whatever it was on his arms. "I don't suppose there's any use in telling you that as of this moment you are the only little girl in Wonderland, and just as imaginary and fantastic?"

"She's not little any more," the Dodo pointed out, still preening.

"But what about Mary Ann?" Alice asked.

"Hush! Hush!" the Gryphon said desperately, putting

one clawed paw awkwardly over her mouth while keeping the other one curled around something protectively. "Do you want to get us all killed?"

"What's that you've got there?" Alice asked (somewhat muffled), unable to contain her curiosity and reaching for his paw. She pulled back with a cry when something horrific and tentacle-y extended and retracted itself. Whatever it was snaked quickly up the Gryphon's arm and under the voluminous cuff of his coat, reappearing as a lump at the nape of his neck.

After a moment the capped head of a timid green thing with golden eyes peeped out.

"Oh!" Alice cried in relief. It wasn't, as she had feared, the horrid thing from the maze at all. "Bill! Poor old Bill the gardener!"

But rather than being equally excited by this reunion, the little lizard fainted dead away, mumbling something about her being "even bigger this time".

"I don't understand this at all," Alice said, frowning. "I'm the same size as these townsbirds, who ought to be small, like real birds, oughtn't they? But I'm normal-girl-sized compared to Bill. Are we all small, or are the townsbirds large, or has something happened to Bill?"

"Leave it to an Alice to be talking about the general size of things when we're all about to be killed," the Gryphon said mournfully. "Silly, fantastic creatures, these little girls."

"Actually, we're on our way to join with *M-A* right now," the Hatter said with meaning.

"Come join us," the Dodo whispered. "We'll travel to the Grunderound together."

"*She'll* never fit in there. She's far too big!" the Gryphon squawked in a whisper.

"Now which fantastic imaginary beast is wasting time talking about my size?" Alice demanded, hands on hips. "Oooh – look at that."

A shop had opened and folded out one of its horizontally shuttered windows, locking it so it formed a shelf. On top of this, a baker set out pies to cool – caramel black thistle and ginger worm – along with tiny square seed cakes that smelled amazing. Not that Alice had ever *smelled* a seed cake before or known beforehand what a good-smelling one smelled like; perhaps time in the bird town was changing her. EAT ME was spelled out in pine nuts upon the top of each cake.

"Let me just try one of these. Perhaps I shall shut up like a telescope," she said, taking one and nibbling at it. The baker's wingy hand slapped ineffectually at her, but there were no other ramifications. The cake was nutty and buttery with a distinct hint of grasshopper.

All five of them waited to see what would happen: the Dodo, the Hatter, the Dormouse, and even the Gryphon and Bill, holding their collective breaths.

Nothing.

Alice gulped down the rest of the cake, barely chewing – which seemed a waste, it was so delicious.

Still nothing.

"Perhaps you really have forgotten how," the Dodo said.

"I can't imagine that's so," Alice said. "I remember exactly what it felt like…"

"Remembering isn't the same as knowing," the Gryphon said accusingly. "You've been schooled terribly if you think that's so."

"That's it!" the Hatter cried. "You've filled your head with all the wrong things since you left. You pushed all the good things out. You need to unlearn them. *Unremember* them."

"You with your uns," Alice said fondly. "Like Unbirthdays. But everything I have learned is necessary, in my world… And anyway, I couldn't *un*learn it all if I tried."

"But you haven't even tried. What's nine times ten? Forget it!" the Hatter shouted.

"What is the capital of Cumbria? Forget it!" the Dodo shouted.

"What is the airspeed velocity of an unladen sparrow?

FORGET IT," shouted the Gryphon, apparently also forgetting that he was hiding from anyone or anything.

"I beg your pardon," said a passing sparrow, unladen except for a small briefcase.

The four travellers (Bill was still passed out) began to sing:

"Forget the cheese and forget the fife
Forget the flies a-buzzing
Forget the one about the pair o'
brick-red Bristol cousins

Forget your name and forget your meat
Forget the Earl of Plumbing
Forget the time and forget the words
And all commence with humming!"

And of course they hummed the last stanza, whatever it was.

"We shall take her to the Forest of Forgetting!" the Hatter cried. "Then she'll forget all the silliness of the other world and start again with shrinking and growing and become a powerful weapon – and then we can get to the Grunderound and we'll find Mary Ann and we'll all have tea!"

"I'm not sure I like the idea of forgetting everything," Alice said uneasily. "Or being some sort of powerful weapon. But if it's for the good of Wonderland, I suppose it's worth a try." She had been suspicious of the shrinking and growing the first time round as well but rapidly – well, grown used to it. Maybe this would be the same.

And the Hatter was, at least, beginning to act like his old self. A little more logical than he ever was, but shouting nonsense and songs and poetry. His head did seem a trifle bit larger, too.

"Let us go, then you and I—" he began, taking her gallantly by the hand.

"No! No dramatic, subtextual, free verse poetry now – stop, we're done with that. Rhymes only," the Dodo said, dragging him away by his ear.

As they walked out of the village and through the bright sunlight, Alice observed how strange it was for her companions to be *staying* with her. Generally in Wonderland she spent only a little while with each creature or person – or both – before everything changed and she moved on to the next thing. But they were a little marching band now, the Hatter even pumping his arms like a drum major. The Gryphon mostly walked upright beside him but sometimes dropped onto all fours and trotted like an absolutely enormous dog with wings. The Dodo chuckled to himself, and Bill had consented to ride on his beak, keeping one wary and distrustful eye on Alice. The Dormouse slept in someone's pocket.

The landscape did that thing it always did: seamlessly and silently roil into something entirely different. The vague seaside air with its accompanying grasses and black-and-white-checkered floor became more of a golden meadow, which, as often happened in late afternoon, wound up in deep, lush shadow from some hill or knoll no one could see. A lovely forest sprang up rather suddenly, like a fog had disappeared and revealed what it hid: soft pine and cushy oak and dappled spots of sunlight like a painting by Corot. A ridiculously straight-running brook – almost a canal – bordered it, but was apparently natural, insomuch as anything in Wonderland was natural.

"I'm remembering it all now," Alice mused to herself. "Everything here changes unexpectedly… but somehow you always wind up right where the next thing, the next bit of action is. When I was little I just *went* and *did* and followed my impulses and wound up at the next place. I should keep that in mind. Wonderland knows where it's taking you. I should trust that."

There were only two off notes to the otherwise perfectly

Arcadian scene. One was a whiff of smoke that came from somewhere beyond the forest. It wasn't from a wood fire and smelled foul.

The other was a sign hammered up on an otherwise innocent oak, whitewashed and red painted:

FREE OF TRAITORS
INSPECTED BY W. RABBIT
WEDNESDAY

A crude symbol of a rabbit was hastily daubed on at the bottom.

"Which Wednesday, I wonder," the Gryphon mused, scratching his chin. "One from the last batch, I assume?"

"I think the next ones are all full," the Dodo said, pulling out a pocket watch.

"Is it still always teatime with you, Hatter?" Alice asked curiously.

"Oh, Time and I made up a long time ago," the Hatter said moodily. "He wanted to make amends before he went. And with the Queen of Hearts in charge, there is never tea any more. For anyone."

"Isn't it funny," Alice said, reaching out a hand to tentatively touch the sign. "Last time I was here, all I wanted to do was find and chase the White Rabbit. And this time, no matter how hard I try to avoid him, his presence is everywhere."

"All right, here we go, then!" the Dodo said, puffing out his chest and reaching with one large and awkward foot to step over the stream.

"Not you, foolish bird!" the Hatter cried, pulling him back. "We need to fish out clean Alice on the other side, when she's back to the way she was. An empty girl. We can't do that if we've forgotten who *we* are and what we're about as well."

"Empty girl?" Alice said. "I don't think—"

"Off you go!" the Gryphon cried gamely and pushed her over the stream.

Chapter Ten

She stumbled and fell against the trunk of a comfortable tree but nearly lost her shoes in the stream.

"Dear me, what just happened? I tripped over—wait, is this the forest I'm supposed to be in?" she wondered, taking her shoes off and tipping the water out of them. "I've forgotten… where… I was going…"

She put her shoes back on and looked around. The stream seemed wet so she went the opposite way. The grasses she trod on were sweet and the pine woods she entered also smelled lovely. A bread-and-butterfly flapped languorously by, proboscis out, looking for weak tea.

"Do *you* know where I was going or who I am?" she asked, half addressing the insect. She was not the least bit worried, only a little perplexed. "I'm fairly certain I'm a girl – from my dress, I mean. And, well, I just *feel* like a girl. Oh, but wait! What if I am a lizard or a satyr going to a fancy-dress party? How frightening that would be to discover – only because I can't remember my life at all..." She spread one hand before her and felt her head and face with the other. "No, smooth and lovely. No scales. No horns. Wouldn't that be a horror, to have forgotten who I was and then found out I was someone else entirely."

She ducked under the bread-and-butterfly and skipped a little. "Well, I suppose that now I can be anyone I want, since I am no one at all. I can *do* anything I want as well. And no one shall be able to chastise me later: How *dare* you do this or that; don't you know who you are? And I shall say: But I *don't* know who I am. So it's hardly fair.

"I wonder what I always wanted to do that I couldn't do before, before I forgot everything. Fly? Could I fly now, I wonder? Or grow a moustache?

"If I *am* no one now, that means I could *be* anyone. Perhaps I get to choose. Let's see: I could be queen, I suppose. But I think despite all the parties and parades, it would mostly be boring and stodgy and I would have no time for myself.

"I could be married with a sweet little husband and some enormous strapping children in a cottage with a garden and painted eaves. That would be lovely, if a bit dull. Perhaps someday.

"I suppose what I would *truly* like to be most of all is myself, whoever that is, and have all sorts of adventures in wonderful fairylands when I wanted. But not *all* the time. I would need days to think about them and tell my stories to friends and strengthen up for the next adventure—oh!"

She had been really enjoying herself and this flight of fancy when she nearly stumbled over another inhabitant of the otherwise empty forest. He was a lazy-looking, thin fellow stretched out at the base of the tree. But he must have been someone a bit fancy, for he wore a lovely sharp hat with long feathers and a beautiful blood-red velvet tunic over black breeches. There were crumbs on his lips and what looked like a hint of raspberry jam – or blood – on his cheek.

"I beg your pardon. How do you do?" she said politely.

"Haven't the slightest," the man said with a smile. She was struck by the light in his eye and the ironic yet plaintive expression on his face. "I can't seem to remember either *how* I do or *what* I do at the moment."

"I can't, either. Did you have a pie?" Alice asked interestedly, pointing at his face.

"A tart, actually. Raspberry," the man said with relish. He still wasn't getting up, which was a trifle rude. "I found several of them with me when I ran in here. I would offer you one, but I ate them all."

"Oh, how gluttonous!"

"I suppose," he said with a casual shrug. "There was no one else here at the time. If *you* had been here, I would have shared, of course. They were quite tasty."

He leapt up rather suddenly springily – on account of his pasteboard thinness, Alice supposed. Crumbs fell out of the rich fabric on his lap and he brushed off the remainder with artistically graceful and narrow fingers. His fine feather bobbed and swayed with a life of its own, matching the arch of his insouciant eyebrows.

She found herself quite taken for a moment.

He wasn't at all like—

—like—

"Mr Nobody of Nowhere," he said grandly with an intricate bow wherein he touched his middle with one hand and threw out the other behind him and then immediately somehow took *her* hand and brought it *almost* to his lips, but not quite. "At your service."

"Miss Nothing of Neverbeen," Alice answered with a smile and a curtsy. "Shall we walk on together?"

"*Nothing* would give me greater pleasure," he said without a wink, and she found herself laughing.

She took his proffered arm and they strolled down

a little path, tan and dusty between the pine needles. Everything was delightful. She wasn't even concerned about her inability to remember anything. It was like… a holiday for her brain. She did wonder vaguely what was happening in her life that meant her brain required a holiday. She looked down at her clothes and skirts again to see if they would reveal her occupation, but couldn't come to any conclusions. They were cleanish and well sewn and mostly comfortable, though a little restricting.

"Just being by your side is utterly pleasant," the man next to her said eventually. "I'm sorry to not be making conversation, but I seem to know and remember Nothing – and Nothing is more pleasant than you in my sight. So there isn't much to say, is there?"

"Lovely weather," she remarked wryly. She gave his arm a squeeze. It was fine and hard. "This is quite all right. Let us do just… *be*."

Too soon, or after many hours, or somewhere in between, the trees came to a sudden halt as if ordered by a mean sergeant. A narrow stream ran by at the trees' edge that was inhabited by chunky golden fish who stayed solidly on the bottom, waddling only a little hither and thither on their fins with great effort. On the other bank, sitting with their backs towards the strolling couple, was an odd collection of creatures warming themselves in the sun. They made black silhouettes free of fine detail – which only accentuated their strange shapes: tall heads, long beaks, too many legs.

"Wait—" she said vaguely as the gentleman made to cross the stream.

"Whatever is the matter?" he asked, concerned.

Alice frowned, trying to think. "I feel as though once we pass over, everything will change."

"Change isn't always a bad thing," he said, patting her arm for comfort. "There's no adventure without change. And no buying sweets, either. Have you ever tried to buy a lolly with a thousand-pound note? Disastrous."

"I suppose—" Alice said tentatively. His point made sense, although it didn't seem to apply specifically to *this* situation. Clutching his arm, she made a wide step over the water…

"I'm Alice!" she cried. "Always and forever Alice!"

For some reason the thought cheered her immensely. She was a young woman from Angleland with nice hair from a nice household who had a lovely camera and aunt and boring sister and everything was generally good. "And I *do* have a lovely home to return home to, and Wonderland adventures! Isn't that just perfect!" she cried.

Her gentleman friend had a similarly joyous reaction: he leapt over the stream with as much grace and skill as

Jack o'er the candlestick and landed with triumph on the other side.

"Well, what do you know!" he cried, laughing. "I'm a knave! How fortuitous!"

The shadowy figures on the berm beyond had heard the shouts and leapt up. Alice ran forward to meet them.

"No! No more this way, no further," the Hatter implored. "One or two brooks is fine, but then you cross another or another, and then after the eighth one you're no longer our little Alice, you're a queen..."

"I think I'd make a rather good queen," Alice said, her desire to gather her friends in a great reunion hug tempered by his words.

As her memories came back, they took a faster route than normal, as when one is trying to push through a crossword puzzle and can't remember the right word. Empty Alice became full Alice in less than a minute; she saw, through new eyes, her nearly adult height and all the changes and growth she had gone through in the last eleven years. All the subtle things that made her who she was today – which her Wonderland friends couldn't see. Subtle wasn't a function of Wonderland.

"But not yet," the Hatter begged.

"Alice! Step away from that man!" the Gryphon cried, hissing at the pretty fellow who ate tarts, and grabbing her with his talons. He could have done with a good trimming, Alice thought peevishly as they pinched her skin through her dress.

"Oh, alarm clocks and bearbells!" the Dodo said, shaking his head. "Alice, do you not know who you're standing with?"

"Knave of Hearts, at your service," her companion said with a bow, this time doffing his beautiful hat and winking at her.

"He's a shill for the Queen!" the Hatter whispered far too loudly to do any good. "He'll report us all!"

"Oh, I don't think so, not any more," the Knave said with a sigh, dramatically brushing more crumbs off his waistcoat. "I'm on her wanted list now. I stole all her tarts, the ones she was saving for tea."

The Hatter raised an eyebrow sceptically. "*You* stole the *Queen's* tarts? But why? You were her favourite, her second-in-command."

The Knave shrugged. "They were delicious."

"And she made them herself, didn't she?" Alice said, remembering the rhyme:

The Queen of Hearts, she made some tarts
All on a summer's day
The Knave of Hearts, he stole the tarts
And took them right away.

"Fancy her having time to make tarts with all her wars and killing and executions," the Dodo said, tsking. "But no wonder you ran away. She would have your head on a pike, she would."

"No, the King would beat him," Alice said. "That is all, and he would return them. According to the rhyme, anyhow."

"Alice, the King has been dead or imprisoned or otherwise out of commission for over a fortnight… Have you not been paying attention?" the Hatter asked, exasperated.

"Well, I can't very well return the tarts anyway, now can I?" the Knave said with a sigh. "The Dodo's right – the Queen would have my head and then decorate her ramparts with it. Silly of me to run into the Forest of Forgetting. I forgot and ate them."

"You could have at least saved one," Alice said, vexed. "I could use a tart to see if I could grow again."

"Oh! And how do you feel, little Alice?" the Hatter asked, dancing. "Fresh and new? Ready to start all over again? Are you unremembered now? Can you shrink and grow as the moment requires?"

"Please don't call me little. At least not until I shrink. You and I are about the same size," Alice pointed out. "And I am full-gr—ah, an adult now. Just like you. I am not your little *anything*."

"Bah, sounds like she still knows her maths and all," the Dodo said. "Failure!"

"Well, we shan't know until we find a treat of some sort. And anyway, one might just as well assume that life experiences and knowledge gained over the last eleven years have taught me to grow or shrink even better than I did before."

"And yet grow and shrink you don't," the Hatter pointed out. "Q.E.D."

"This is all a waste. We may as well go on to M—" the Gryphon started to say, but the Hatter took off his hat and hit him.

"Where are you off to?" the Knave asked, catching on immediately that there was a secret.

"None of your business, Queensman," the Dodo said haughtily.

"I told you, I'm no good to her now," the Knave said, hands out and open in supplication. "I'm a dead card walking if I show up anywhere near the castle. So you might as well take me with you. Perhaps I can even help, if you're – you know, planning something."

"Are you good with a sword?" the Hatter asked.

"Or a bootlace?" the Dodo added.

"Both, and both would be dedicated to – the cause," the Knave said with a bow. "Or at least to your lady here."

"All right, but you'll have to carry Bill, then," the Dodo said, putting his wing out so the little capped lizard could scramble over and up the fancy card's sleeve. The Knave's painted face seemed to blur for a moment into a look of disgust but soon smoothed out. Alice couldn't fault him that. She wasn't sure she would particularly want a strange lizard suddenly so close, crawling on her skin.

"Maybe after we had been properly introduced and chatted a bit it would be all right," she said to herself.

The group set off in a direction that was argued about several times before everyone managed to agree on it. The air seemed sunsetty – the sun, however, was feeling tardy and hung in the sky high away from bedtime. The moon sulked on the eastern horizon and turned away from its sibling, who always seemed to hog the attention.

In that light, the grassy plain quickly became a cosy landscape of tangled scrub bushes, old apple trees and an abandoned hazel copse whose woody residents preferred to grow their new shoots in spirals like a little girl's hair gone wild and unruly – very hard to pick around. The mirrorbirds loved them for roosting, however, and Alice couldn't help stopping now and then to see how she looked just for the novelty of the types of frames they sported. Some of the reflections even changed her hair and lip and skin colour! Her friends hurried on ahead, chatting amongst themselves and listening a little too raptly to stories of the royal court in its current deadly phase, as told by the Knave.

Alice lingered at one particular mirrorbird whose reflective face gave her image freckles. The fashion in Angleland was of course to try to minimise tanning and other effects of the sun, at least for young women of breeding, by use of either powder or sun hats. But she rather liked the healthy, friendly look they gave to her otherwise clear face.

"I see Alice has *spotted* herself," said a musing voice from behind her. Since Alice knew who it was, she didn't turn around immediately, preferring to give herself one last nose wrinkle to see how witchy she looked with the freckles.

The Cheshire Cat was of course lolling on a spiral branch behind her, like a series of circles himself: upon the circular branch, his head and his body wrapped round and round, and his eyes seemed to bounce a little in his face as if to emphasise the conceit.

"How very original of you," Alice said dryly. "But I still like cats, however jejune they appear – fortunately for *you*. Kittens as well as mangy old striped things." She scratched him under the chin to soften the words.

"Mmm..." The cat rolled his body and thumped his feet, obviously enjoying it. But his head stayed in the exact same position, of course: impossible.

"Why don't you come with us, instead of just popping up now and then?" Alice suggested. "I really would like your company, and I think you might help the Hatter regain a bit of his Nonsense. You could sit on my shoulders, if you like, or I could carry you."

"Oooh, and be petted the whole time by the Great and Powerful Alice," the Cheshire said saucily. He twisted so she could get to his belly better, but his head popped off for a moment to give her a wink. "At least until we get to Mary Ann."

Alice stopped petting him and glared.

"All right, all right, I'll bow quietly out when she takes over you lot. I'm not a leader, or trained in the ways of rebellions or civil disobedience. I don't have much to add to your side. But I will still take comfort in seeing the Queen of Hearts dethroned and punished for her actions so everyone can return to their normal – ah, absurd – and safe Wonderland lives. So come with us, rather than making jokes, and help!"

The Cheshire Cat gave her an inscrutable look. Then he feigned fatigue.

"I *am* helping… You don't know how hard it is to keep a straight thought in a place like this." His body suddenly became a series of sharp angles and squares, from rectangular ears down to his long looping tail that was now a spiral of not-quite-ninety-degree turns. He stood out in orange-and-purple starkness against the coiling organic growth of the trees behind him.

"Time is running out on you. He didn't even pay his portion of the bill."

Now he stood and made a triangle with his paws above his head; his head then began to drain into his body like sand in an hourglass. "Beware what churches and suits and jails all have in common."

"Is that another riddle?" Alice demanded. "Is it—oh, he's gone."

Of course the cat faded out of view, eyes last, which rolled up into the now invisible head. Then they bounced and rolled through the spiral branches like tiny croquet balls.

"Bother! How people *still* come and go in this place!" She allowed herself exactly one *humph* and stamped her foot exactly one time like the seven-year-old she once had been, and then ran after her friends. They were chattering nonsense at each other, not having even noticed she was gone. The cat's puzzle reminded her of another one from Wonderland, long ago.

"Hatter! Hatter! Do you remember your old riddle? The one you told me the last time I was here?"

"I don't own any riddles," he responded, pulling out his pockets to show how empty they were. Needles and pins fell out. They scurried to the side of the path to not be trod on. "I borrowed one once, but I doubt the March Hare will ever be able to collect on it now."

Alice took a deep breath.

"Why is a raven like a writing desk?" she prompted.

"I don't know, why?" he asked gamely.

"No – you asked *me* that, last time. I never figured out the answer myself. But I asked everyone when I woke up—er, came back to Angleland, and even read a great many books on puzzles and riddles to try and solve it. So now I have several answers. So tell me which one is right!"

She began counting on her fingers.

"One: because they both have quills dipped in ink."

Her audience just looked at her gravely.

Alice hurried on to the next.

"Two: the American author, Mr Edgar Allan Poe, wrote on both."

The Dodo and the Gryphon looked at each other and shrugged helplessly.

"And three – my friend Charles came up with this – because each can produce a few notes, tho' they are very flat!"

She sat back on her heels, much pleased with herself, and waited for a reaction.

The Hatter took her gently by the hand. "Ah – it doesn't *have* an answer, my dear girl. That is the point of a riddle."

"That is *not* the point of a riddle!" Alice almost shrieked.

"I think the heat has got to her," the Dodo whispered badly to the Gryphon.

"But I just gave you *three* answers!"

"Well, you had better take them back, they would best be used elsewhere. Here, there they are," the Hatter said graciously.

Alice regarded them all silently for a long moment. "I'm remembering this from last time," she finally said. "*Nothing* gives satisfaction in Wonderland. You always think you say the right thing, do the right thing, figure the deuced thing out – and you're always wrong. *Always!* The key is too far away. You're too short. The rules of etiquette are all skewed. The rules of *croquet* are insane. It's like the most beautiful and yet worst sort of dream where everything is upside down consistently and *could* be beautiful and perfect but instead just drives one to fits!"

"Definitely the heat," the Gryphon whispered back.

"Well, what is it like in *your* world?" the Dodo asked politely.

"In Angleland, if you learn the rules, and follow them correctly, you generally get where you want to go or receive what you want to have."

"Seems boring," said the Dodo.

"Seems easy," piped up Bill.

"No matter who you are? No matter what your height is?" the Hatter asked curiously.

"It doesn't at all matter what you look like, or..." Alice

paused, thinking about the children of the Square. "Well, perhaps it is a little easier if you're Anglish. Born in Angleland."

"And what if you don't have the luck of that?" the Hatter asked. "Can you change it?"

"Where you were born? Of course not!"

"Seems a bit arbitrary to me," the Hatter said. "Sounds *harder* than here, where you merely have to run twice as fast to get anywhere. At least you can choose how you run."

Alice rubbed her temples. He wasn't wrong. For a brief moment she had a vicious wish that all her Wonderland friends could spend a week in London, figuring out the trains and how to get a cup of tea they had to pay for, talking to alley cats and dormice who didn't speak back.

"Well, anyway, forget *my* riddle. Perhaps you can help me out with a new one."

("I thought she said it was the Hatter's riddle," the Dormouse whispered to Bill. The two tiny things nodded knowingly at each other.)

"We're already out, and there's no place to go *in*," the Gryphon said testily. "Speak plainly, girl."

"Call me *girl* again and I'll have you on a lead before you can say *bandersnatch*," Alice snapped. The Gryphon's eyes widened and he shrank back behind the Dodo. That was the other thing she remembered about Wonderland; the random, abject cruelty that was constantly threatened. Well, when in

Rome… "What do churches and suits and jails all have in common?"

"Oh, that's a good one! I don't know! What *do* churches and suits and jails all have in common?" the Dodo asked eagerly.

"I. Don't. Know," Alice said through gritted teeth. "I was told this riddle but not its solution, and it might be important to our mission."

"That's a trifle rude," the Knave spoke up. "Demanding the answer to a riddle you have no answer for."

"Try out one of the other answers that you kept," the Hatter suggested eagerly. "Poe wrote on both, perhaps?"

"It doesn't…" Alice began. "Besides, there are three things there, not 'both'."

"Does a church produce notes?" the Gryphon asked the Dodo.

"If its bell tolls, or it's Lutheran," the Dodo said sagely.

"All of 'em have quills dipped in ink?" Bill joined in enthusiastically.

"Oh, forget it!" Alice cried. "I'll work it out myself. You're no help at all with your nonsense. Let's just keep going to Mary Ann."

The Knave's eyes widened when she said that, but he said nothing.

Chapter Eleven

The denouement to their search was dreary and disappointing. Even in ancient Greek plays, the deus ex machina was a fellow let down in a basket draped in flowers and cloth of gold or whatever so that everyone could tell a god had come to save the hero at the last minute. It was ridiculous but glamorous and made good theatre.

But our travelling heroes had merely made their way to an even less Wonderlandy place than usual: a scrubby edge of nothing. There were dead leaves and duff, unraked, in ugly drifts. The sharp-edged green grass that thrived here was interspersed with many dead yellow companions. The bushes and hazel had small leaves, smaller than they should have, and looked generally unkempt. The whole place resembled an abandoned park in a bad part of town.

That's what it was, Alice realised; the place looked *real-world* unkempt. Not "mysterious etching of a romantic moor" wild or "carefully contrived, abandoned and folly-filled gardens of the wealthy" wild. *Bad* wild. Ungoverned, and possibly with bears.

"There it is!" the Hatter cried. Then he looked around, alarmed. "There it is," he whispered.

Alice finally saw it, too: a worn and weathered sign whose bright colours had faded to the dim shades of the vegetation around it, saying: GRUNDEROUND THIS WAY. It pointed to a plain hole in the dirt whose edges had grown smooth and hard with roots over time. It was not unlike the rabbit hole Alice had first fallen down, except that it was even smaller.

"Oh, what are we to do?" the Dodo moaned.

"We could dig it out," the Gryphon suggested, holding up his claws.

"You know the defences are prepared for that," the Hatter said accusingly.

"What defences?" the Knave asked casually.

The other three gave him silent, frosty looks.

"Let the little ones go first. Bill and the Dormouse," Alice suggested. "Perhaps they can tell those below to let us in – somehow. Or at least see the lay of the land."

The Hatter shrugged and lifted off his hat. The

Dormouse, who had been sleeping on its brim, tumbled down the Hatter's arm and neatly rolled like a billiard ball into the hole without so much as a peep. Alice wondered if the fall had even woken the poor thing up. Then the Knave plucked Bill off his chest like an oversized military medal and dropped him, rather quickly and perfunctorily, into the hole after the Dormouse. He too tumbled, feet over feet, but at the last second whipped his tail and landed, clinging to the side of the entrance. Despite his sleepy and anthropomorphic expression (and cap), he scuttled off *most* lizard-like into the darkness.

"Well, here's a fine mess. And you not even able to shrink," the Hatter said, then crossed his arms and sat down in a huff.

"And what about *you*?" Alice demanded, pursing her lips. "How were you, the Dodo and the Gryphon supposed to be able to get down?"

"Oh, we're not important, you know that," the Hatter said grumpily, waving a hand at her like a ninety-year-old granny.

"So this is the hideout of the infamous Mary Ann," the Knave said with a sniff of distaste, kicking some sand into the hole. He took out a tiny flacon, unscrewed its tiny gold cap, and prepared to take a swig. "No wonder the rebels are losing. To the Queen!—Er, Queen's defeat, that is," and he made to drink it down.

"No! Give it to me!" Alice cried, forgetting herself and all her good manners ("Ironic, that," she observed; she had been out of the Forest of Forgetting for a while now). She grabbed the bottle from the Knave's hand and without a word of apology or excuse tossed the entire contents back. It burned in a cardamomy, cinnamony, peony sort of way.

"Surely this will do something," she thought. "It *feels* strong!"

"I say," the Knave said, a little dismayed that his quaff had been quorffed.

Only the Dodo and the Gryphon looked hopeful. The Hatter just turned away and rolled his eyes, grumbling.

Alice stood, arms out, legs spread, body parts removed from other body parts, fingers and toes splayed and nothing touching itself, waiting for the magic to come.

Nothing happened.

"You see?" the Hatter said sourly. "You're too grown. You..."

"Oh, shut *up* already," Alice snapped. "Do you know, I'm really *growing* weary of your constant comments about me and my physical relation to Wonderland. Why should *I* grow and shrink, anyway? Why should *I* remember or forget according to what you think will work? 'Get small to fit in the tiny door, Alice.' 'Get big to get the key, Alice.' Get too big and scare the birds. Shrink, and the birds and mice walk all over you. I'm tired of being something else for everyone else.

"It's long past time Wonderland started changing for *me*."

And, not quite sure she knew what she was doing but full of red and rage, Alice marched over to the hole and pulled it open.

It was a bit tricky and didn't budge at first, like a cold piece of leather, but after a tug or two and an unladylike groan she managed to stretch the hole several feet across – quite large enough for herself, the Knave, the large-headed Hatter, the hexaped Gryphon and the portly Dodo.

Everyone blinked in surprise.

Alice recovered herself quickly and tried not to look surprised, too.

She did it. How had she known she would do it? *Had* she known? It was and yet wasn't like a dream where you realise you have to do something and somehow it works. In dreams everything was fuzzy with no clear beginnings or embarrassing ends; here she could have failed spectacularly and just wound up clutching dry dirt.

She had just trusted in herself, and Wonderland, and... it worked.

"Remember that," she marvelled to herself. "Trust in yourself and Wonderland."

The Hatter whooped in delight, taking off his hat and whacking the Dodo with it. "She did it! Alice did it!"

"Alice always does," the Dodo said proudly, like she was his daughter.

"But never in the way you expect," the Gryphon added, also like she was his daughter.

Alice rolled her eyes at them. "All right, I'm first. Here we go—"

And she leapt into the darkness and unknown, for that was what Alice always did.

But she did not land in an abandoned hallway with a charming door leading to an even more charming garden. Nor was it a forest, nor a castle, nor an oversized banquet, nor a bucket on a sea of tears.

It was like nothing Alice had ever experienced before.

It was *loud*. Dozens, perhaps a hundred or two hundred different voices muttering and cursing and wailing and soothing and talking and sighing with the occasional strident laugh. Creatures of all stature and make sat, stood, padded, milled or lay on benches in – well, in some sort of building. Something large and cavernous with a vaulted roof. From the smell – hoppy – and the size of the place – infinite-seeming with shadowed corners – Alice thought it might be a tavern, or perhaps a Viking longhouse, or something she had no name for in which people of all ages gathered but that wasn't a church and stank a bit.

"Wounded in the bedrooms, please," a long-necked duck told her tiredly. His hat was beaten about the brim and his bright yellow neckerchief was spotted with blood. He held a clipboard and what Alice couldn't help noticing was a quill pen – but black. Dipped in ink. Someone else's feather.

"A raven's, perhaps," she mused.

But before she could focus her thoughts on what was actually going on, the Hatter hit her squarely in the head in his tumble from the skylight (which was dark, of course, and opened onto absolutely nothing at all). She fell aside and managed to just avoid being landed on again, by the Dodo this time. The Gryphon spread his elegant wings and coasted to the top of what looked very much like a bar.

"Dear me, this place has changed a bit," the Hatter said, swallowing.

"Don't tell me you frequented this notorious joint," the Dodo said with a wink and an elbow in the ribs.

"When I was younger, and a little less Mad," the Hatter said with dignity, pulling out his cuffs and straightening himself. "But there were more refreshments then. And fewer... wounded..."

The duck had decided that the newcomers were fine and wandered off, checking in on other recent arrivals.

"But who are all these people?" Alice asked as what looked like an overgrown hedgehog and three baby brushes woefully waddled past her. The mother – Alice assumed – clutched a pathetically small bag of possessions and had a bandage around one broken arm, which didn't really work because of her spines tearing up the wool.

"People with nowhere else to go," the Hatter answered with a shake of his head. "I thought the Grunderound had just become a place for conspirators to meet, for the resistance to convene, but it looks like word has got out. These are all refugees from the Queen of Hearts' War."

"My *doll*! They took my *doll*!" one of the baby brushes cried.

Alice frowned.

Hands she has but does not hold...

Nothing in Wonderland was a coincidence. Especially not with the Cheshire Cat helping her.

"*Who* took your doll?" she asked as gently as she could, kneeling down to look her in the bristles.

"The soldiers, of course," the mother snapped,

pulling her child back protectively. "They took Earnest's cup and ball, too! Ruffians! Thugs!"

"But you still have your bag… and a necklace…" Alice said, confused. "Why would they bother with toys and let you keep your valuables?"

"Who knows? But their father is missing and we have no home. Doll's the least of our problems now," the mother said, trying very hard not to cry by frowning and marching away.

"Odd," the Hatter said, which for him was also odd.

"Let's find Mary Ann," Alice said, swallowing as she saw a—well, hard to say what it was. Something long and furry and bound entirely from head to hoof in one long bandage. Its blue mouth let out a groan as a pair of pigs tried to carry it gently over to a bench. "Perhaps she can clear up this mystery for us."

"They would be in the back room, in the hidden casino," the Hatter said, pointing. "Behind the false cabinet."

How he knew that was more than Alice wanted to consider at the moment. She pushed her way through the crowd and round to the back of the bar, someplace she never in a thousand years imagined she would ever find herself – either in the real world or Wonderland. There was a point in her childhood when she assumed that the men and women who stood behind bars in pubs had no legs at all but were merely puppets who moved back and forth behind their wooden stage as they magically produced glasses and froth.

She squeezed herself along the large set of wooden shelves that at one time must have been full of bottles of whatever passed for imbibables in Wonderland. There were a few tiny brown jars of bitters and cordials that remained, dusty, on a lower shelf; these Alice hastily grabbed and stuffed into her sleeve. DRINK ME said one, VIOLETS said the second, HOURS said the third.

She tried pulling the cabinet away from the wall as if she were opening a normal, if oddly shaped, door. It didn't budge.

"Not another Wonderland puzzle," Alice moaned.

"*Slide* it, you silly girl!" the Hatter said impatiently. "Have you never been in a secret room before?"

Alice pushed, and the whole thing simply slid away from her with very little effort. She allowed herself exactly one Wondersecond of chagrin. A cold, dank wind blew from the slim rectangular opening as if it were trying to escape whatever was within. Reluctantly she stepped in, taking the Dodo's wing and Hatter's hand and pulling them behind her.

(The Gryphon stayed behind. When she last looked, he had been allowing a sick person to be loaded onto his soft, furry back to be better examined by a doctor magpie.)

The room they entered looked just like Alice would have

imagined the hidden base of a secret rebel cause: cold and dark but for one candle on a crate being used as a table. Filling the darkness was the smell of stale sweat and exhaustion, sour at one end of the scent spectrum and earthy and mouldy at the other. Four bone-weary creatures huddled on sacks of supplies: a large muskrat, a man all dressed in newspaper, a ruby-eyed white bird and a—

"Caterpillar!" Alice cried.

He was not as the Caterpillar should have been. The arrogant, plump morsel only too perfect for a bird to snap up was now skinny in the wrong places and flabby in the others, as if a caterpillar without the right things to eat or think shrank into itself like a sponge. There were deep bags under his eyes.

Alice wondered for one wild moment whether, if she gave him a big juicy leaf or glass of lemonade, he would puff back up again into his former glory.

At least his bearing was the same: he turned a desultory head towards her and regarded the girl with exhausted, world-weary eyes.

"Of course it's you," he drawled. "*Who* are you?"

"I'll tell you who she's *not*," the muskrat snapped, voice rasping and almost cutting out entirely. "She's *not*..." But the Caterpillar surprisingly and deftly clapped a stubby foot over his mouth.

The white bird began to flutter and coo. It shook its wings and head, and feathers flew out from under its arms.

"Where is Mary Ann?" the Hatter asked, looking around as if he expected her to leap out and shout *Surprise!* from behind a barrel or shadow. "We've come to join her and you. I believe Alice – that is her name, you know. *Most* girl children have them. Names, I mean, not Alices. She was summoned here by Mary Ann specifically to help us against the tyrant."

"None of us knows what you're talking about," the muskrat muttered, looking away.

"Oh, for heaven's sake!" Alice cried. "You're in a *hidden* room in a *hidden* place called the Grunderound. You're tending to the wounded and frightened out there, and in here you're plotting your next move against the Queen of Hearts. Mary Ann came to me – she *called* me here to help. And so did you, Caterpillar! So please, produce her at once!"

"Produce her," the bird cackled hysterically. "Turn her into produce. Yes, yes. A pumpkin or an egg. That would be much, much improved. Compost."

"Well, that's very rude!" Alice said. "To say that about your leader."

"No, you don't understand. We're just no good without

her. We're lost," the man in paper said sadly, watching the bird. "Her words were worth a thousand pounds a letter."

"Yes, I can see that," Alice said, taking a deep breath and trying to remain patient. "Where. Is. She?"

The bird cackled again. "Where is one when not in Wonderland? When the other's won and you're Undone?"

"I don't..." Alice began, but she began to suspect.

The man in paper looked at her with gentle, doleful eyes.

"Mary Ann is dead."

Chapter Twelve

"*What?*" Alice gasped. "No! In the picture, when I saw her..."

Well, if truth be told, and Alice tended to tell the truth, at least to herself, the girl did not look well in the photograph. She seemed to be incarcerated. There was blood and a blindfold. But she had been alive.

"Where was that?" the muskrat demanded.

"Don't you mean *when*?" Alice asked shakily. "How long ago it was?"

"Time is meaningless, unless he's offering to pay, you know that," the Hatter said, but the words were thin and scratchy, and his heart wasn't in it.

"She was being held against her will somewhere. But I thought she had escaped!"

Alice wrung her hands and twisted her lips to avoid tears. Why was she so distraught? She had never met Mary Ann. Not even during her first time in Wonderland. Mary Ann had always seemed like a figment, a ghost just out of reach, a white rabbit. Now she was beyond Alice's grasp forever.

She hadn't felt anything when the other girl had died, had she? Some sort of tremor or echo of feeling? If each resident here had a counterpart in Angleland, surely there was some connection she would have severed when she passed away? A phantom pain in Alice's own neck?

For surely—

Off with her head—

"The Queen of Hearts," Alice murmured. "She did it, didn't she? She found and executed Mary Ann."

"Less execute and more *murder.* Less capitalism and more capital *punishment*," the Caterpillar said sourly.

The Dodo sat down suddenly next to Alice, collapsed, like a human boy rather than a bird, feet splayed out and a dumbfounded look on his face.

"She didn't come back here – she didn't want to draw the Queen's attention here, to have her find out about us and the refugees. We had hoped she made it to the Unlikely, but she didn't," the muskrat said woefully.

"Mary Ann *always* gets away," the white bird trilled. "She always gets away with it somehow."

"I guess her luck ran out with the postman," the man in paper said sadly.

Everyone was silent. This had been Alice's one lead, her one goal, and it was gone.

She voiced the thing everyone was thinking.

"What are we to do now?"

"Why, you're to take over the resistance and lead us to victory in her place, of course," the Hatter cried. Then he scrunched up his face in pain and pulled his giant hat down over it. "Oooh, it hurts to make sense!"

"I haven't an ounce of tactical or military knowledge!" Alice cried. "You would be foolish to put your and everyone else's fate in my hands! Apparently I can open holes – that's my singular talent here now. I can't—"

"Hush!" the muskrat hissed.

"I shall not!" Alice cried. "*Listen* for once! You need a leader with experience. Wonderland always puts one in the most ridiculous positions – judging caucus races, choosing between identical brothers… But this time it is deadly serious! I have just learned that a poor innocent girl has died, and now you have me taking up arms like a centurion! I was to take you to Mary Ann, not *take her place*."

"But Mary Ann thought you could do it," the Dodo said softly. "She brought you here."

"No, *hush*; do you hear that?" the muskrat repeated, cocking his head.

Everyone immediately grew quiet, but to Alice's ears there was nothing but the rise and fall of the chaos outside.

"Hatter, Dodo, let us find the Gryphon and Bill and the Dormouse at once," she said after a moment, trying to bring some semblance of order to her thoughts. "And the Knave. Sadly, you are the closest thing I have to an advisory council. Somehow I must make sense of all this."

She made herself stand up and went back through the secret door, desperate to get out of the dank and suffocating room full of sad people.

For, despite her protests, Alice was already moving past the sad revelation of Mary Ann's death. Her arguing with the Hatter was merely an instinctive reaction. She had promised to take them to Mary Ann, and she had done her best. Now there was another job to do. She had no idea *what* to do or *how* to do it, only that she must. It was inevitable and solid as a boring granite statue of some bewigged leader of yesteryear at a park. In the same way that as a child she had just *done*, she would just *do* now. Maybe it would work out. The deceased Mary Ann had apparently put all her hope in Alice. What other choice was there?

The question was: what *could* she do? She wasn't a native of Wonderland, well versed in its rules and laws and shifting geography. She had no great military knowledge, having ignored all her sister's boring lessons when she was a child (fancy that actually coming back to haunt her!). She had never actually been engaged in any sort of job or organised anyone else to do anything.

Then again, the poor Wonderland creatures couldn't get themselves together even when actively trying to help one another. Back in the secret room, the leaders of the rebellion were just sitting around grieving and waiting for another Mary Ann to come along and save them. And outside, in the temporary hospital ward…

Alice watched as a mole ran round with a nice sterile bit of moleskin in his paw, shouting, "I've got it I've got it!" and, like the answering call of a mated duck (a midwife duck, in fact), came a quack back, "I need it I need it! Where is the moleskin?"

Who else, in the end, *could* save them?

Only Alice.

"There's the Gryphon," she said, spotting the creature, who was kindly giving a few lost tots a ride on his back to cheer them up. "I don't know how we'll ever find the others, they're so tiny. *BILL! DORMOUSE!*" she shouted, hands cupped round her mouth.

"Have you seen a lizard, about yea high?" the Hatter asked an owlet. He still had his hat down over his face but was somehow making the correctly sized motions with his hands.

"A small Dormouse, probably asleep in something," the Dodo explained to a goose-necked lamp-goose.

"And the Knave, let us grab him, too." Alice looked around, surprised when she couldn't see him. Surely he would have stood out in his immaculate red velvet doublet and hat. Actually, he would be the only person in here at all with a fancy matching suit.

Matching suit.

"A knave in a matching suit," she said to herself. "Why does that ring a bell?"

But it was hard to focus on the beginnings of what seemed to be a fairly important thought: a low vibration began to thrum across the Grunderound, irritating and disruptive.

Ba-Boom. Boom. Boom.

It wouldn't stop, working its way into Alice's bones in a very upsetting way, along with the thought she couldn't quite complete.

"Hatter," she said slowly.

Boom. The vibrations grew louder, like a giant was striking the earth with a mighty hammer.

Boom.

Boom.

"There he is," the Hatter said, jumping up and down and gesticulating at a chandelier onto which the Dormouse clung. The tiny creature was strangely awake and pointing desperately.

Alice turned to look. At the far end of the great hall was a vaulted ceiling and multi-paned rose window, which taken together made it all look like the apse of a church. The thin glass shuddered with the strange vibrations, bowing in and out with the force of the thumps.

"Funny," she said to herself, "if that really is the apse, then the tavern bar is the chancel! And the place I fell into is like the nave...

"Oh," she said as it all came together in her head at once.

Boom.

Boom.

Boom.

Everything rattled; creatures were screaming.

Matching suit.

"Hatter!" She took his hand, which surprised him into stillness: he looked at it as if the whole idea were outrageous. "What do a church, a jail and a suit all have in common?"

"Alice, this is hardly the time for riddles—"

"*Knaves*, Hatter! Knaves!"

The Hatter blinked.

"Churches have naves, jails hold knaves, every suit of cards has a knave! He's gone! I don't know if he even came down with us!"

"*He went back to the Queen,*" the Hatter said, swallowing.

"Oh, the Cheshire *knew*! He tried to tell me..." Alice lamented. "We must leave this place immediately – I don't know what is going on, but it can't be a coincidence that he's gone and now this is happening..."

"Quickly, out the back door," the Dodo said, nodding.

"We're in the *Grunderound*!" the Hatter cried. "There is no 'back door'."

"Of course there is. This is Wonderland," Alice said fervently. "There's always a tree with a door or a hole in the floor or a door in a door. Come on. We'll find it and then—"

And then the booming stopped. So did everything else in the Grunderound: for one magical moment all the chaos was still, every eye and antenna frozen, every beak, muzzle, pair of lips and snout open but quiet, everyone immobile, waiting.

And then the walls caved in.

"Just like a house of cards," Alice observed a little crazily. "Or a really cheap pasteboard house, or one of the paper balloons your uncle likes to fold out of a discarded magazine."

There were no real bricks behind the brick walls, no stone or log to hold them up – not even dirt, as one might expect underground.

The edges of the building folded down, thin and flimsy, and soldiers marched over the crumpled remains.

Not that the soldiers were much heartier than the Grunderound itself, but there were so many of them: tens, nines, eights and aces, all in blood-red armour. They wielded short, ugly swords and viciously sharpened axes. Row upon row came over the ruins of the old tavern, crushing it into dust under their feet and flowing over the rubble in a relentless flood.

"Run!" Alice cried. "Everyone, run! *Run!*"

This time she stood her ground.

She had no idea how big she was compared to the cards; the sight of them was so terrifying she didn't even stop to see if she could put them in her pocket. Like mad ants, like nothing she had ever imagined, they filled every bit of free space and attacked every Wonderland creature in their path.

"No!" she shouted.

She flung her hands out in front of her, unable to think of anything else to do.

"*No!* It doesn't end this way! *NO—*"

Chapter Thirteen

And then, of course, she woke up.

Alice as She Is

Chapter Fourteen

"Easy, steady on!" a voice was saying.

A voice that had a smile in it – but no matter how friendly it sounded, a voice that irked Alice entirely. Wrong tone, wrong time…

She continued to struggle and strike out with her hands, but her waking mind already knew the indisputable truth of where and when she was.

"No! You mustn't! I must go back!"

"Back where?" the young man asked with faint amusement.

Alice stopped her pugilistic feints and sat up. She was under a tree – the big spreading oak she had fallen asleep against so many years before, as apparently she had done now. The ground was hard and a little chilly, even through the golden cape she had put down. Katz had carefully laid his coat over her. It smelled faintly of an aftershave with warm and pleasing lower notes of moss. There was, an idle part of her mind noticed, a single piece of purple thread or hair stuck on the back.

In her hands were dead leaves, left over from last year perhaps, crunching like flimsy cards.

Katz was smiling down at her, a little confused but not concerned.

"You know, *back*," she snapped. "I have to go back to – to..."

But there she paused, feeling as lost as her body was. Already her latest adventures in Wonderland were dissipating, spun on a breeze back to wherever they came from, too fragile to remain long in this world. The urgency she felt had the urgency of any nightmare upon waking. Real – but not.

"I have to find a way back there," she said helplessly. "They need me. I've left them again."

"If you were anyone else I would ask if maybe you were overindulging in laudanum," Katz said, offering his hand to help her up.

"Not at all, I'm afraid." She sighed, taking his hand, and creakily rose. She wished she could tell him everything, even if it would be just like telling a dream. It might keep the memories in her head a little longer, and it would be nice to finally share the stories with someone.

"That would be a most convenient excuse," she said instead. "The laudanum, I mean. If a terrible revelation. Here is your coat back – I'm afraid I've rather crumbled some leaves on it."

"Oh no, leaves, heaven forfend," he said mildly, and the space under his arched and solid brown eyebrows made two little sunrises of skin; he was a man who could smile with every part of his face and not have to move his lips at all. He took the coat and threw it over his shoulder carelessly.

Alice busied herself with patting her dress down and carefully shaking out the cape and folding it back up while she flushed, trying not to look at him.

She had to figure out how to get back to her friends and save them – because they *were* in trouble, weren't they? It was all soft and blurring now. The Queen of Hearts was involved somehow... She had to be defeated... Right?

But Alice *also* had to get home before anyone had a fit because she had been gone so long. There was the sun finally yearning for the horizon, its rays stretching out to the west as if it couldn't wait to be there.

The two walked in silence for a while, for which she was supremely grateful. Katz seemed to sense she needed a little quiet time. He wasn't asking her questions and demanding the due diligence of a sexist etiquette that usually came with these sorts of situations: *There, I watched you and loaned you my coat, now you owe me conversation at least.* In some ways, being with him had the ease of being with a Wonderland resident. As a two-time and now experienced visitor, Alice realised that for all their frustrating mannerisms, at least one didn't need to feel indebted or obliged to follow the commandments of social customs there. It was like tea with a toddler: messy but without guilt or rules.

(Although, *un*like Wonderland folk, Katz was fully human and had lips the same colour as his cheeks, only several shades darker.)

"What the—*what in blazes is going on here?*"

Alice looked around the park, expecting some sort of crime or other shenanigan being perpetrated. But there was nothing. Before them on the path was a governess and her two young charges who ran back and forth happily. Beyond them a hunched-over and ancient couple wandered up a hill hand in hand. The scene was as serene as it could be.

Behind them, however, was Mr Coney – really, of all the bad luck! – striding quickly to catch up. Now he wore a moderately trendy milk chocolate suit with wide trousers, long jacket and a crisp straw hat. This sat almost perfectly down on his voluminous, macassar-oiled hair; Alice wondered if he had to put it on while still styling his locks.

If she didn't imagine how it smelled or felt, it came across as very stylish.

She heard the wisp of a sigh from Katz, but that was all: his smiling brown eyes crystallised into stoic blandness.

"Who are you? Is this man bothering you? Stop harassing this lady at once!" Coney ordered. "Leave her in peace."

The children playing up ahead giggled at his behaviour. It was more than obvious that Katz and Alice were friendly and no one was bothering anyone.

Alice felt bad for everyone involved in or watching the situation, even Coney – but mostly she wished he would disappear. Down into a rabbit hole, perhaps.

"In peace?" she asked dryly. "From what?"

"I hadn't realised my appearance was so frightening. Unless you already knew I was a barrister," Katz said easily with a mocking little bow.

"Now that I see you up close, I realise I *do* know you. You're the one who is always engaging with all the street rats and rabble from Wellington Square," Coney said accusingly. "You visit with pretensions and airs of doing good – but really with *schemes* and *questionable motives*."

A shade of rose deeper than normal came and went over Katz's face like a single ripple across an otherwise still pond. It left nothing in its wake, disappearing entirely.

"No pretensions, good sir; I leave that to those who have time for leisure and stylish hats. The children of the Square and their families are often at the mercy of a system weighted against their favour – I should know. I just help even the odds a bit."

"Mr Coney," Alice said as politely as she could. "How pleasant to see you again. Where are you off to?"

She hoped he understood the not so subtle hint. *Off to.* As in, away.

"I am in fact hurrying to a meeting specifically about saving our country from these – those – pestilential parasites," he replied with an impressive amount of hauteur. "Before they wind up staying here permanently, agitating to destroy England as they are trying in Russia. They have no patriotism, you know, even the so-called citizens who were born here. They have no loyalty to anything save each other and their – their – *golden coins.*"

"Shekels, I think you mean to say," Katz offered politely.

"They are trying to unseat the tsar!"

"Are you *kidding* me?" the other man said, finally losing his composure. His face showed a mix of genuine disbelief and a terrible tiredness; for a moment the edges of his eyes made him look far older than his years. Somehow this distinct *lack* of rage and the intelligence behind it, sparkled in his eyes like a treasure, ancient and precious.

Alice felt her chest tighten. It hurt and felt wonderful at the same time.

"That story is just that – a *story*. It's anti-Semitic filth. My people have been suffering at the hands of the tsar and our fellow countrymen – not the other way round."

"Of course you would say that," Coney said, moving forward into Katz's space, glaring down at the slightly shorter man.

Katz gazed back at him impassively.

Alice wondered, perhaps for the first time – although certainly not the last – if all human conflicts were started by men who thought they were doing it for a woman.

"I'm not *entirely* certain why you're concerned with the fate of Russia's tsar," she said, interrupting what appeared to be a heavy-breathing match, "but I do think you're being rather unforgivably rude. Mr Katz and I are friends, and we just happened to bump into each other in the park. Rather like you're just bumping into us, now. He was offering to walk me home."

Katz blinked at this unexpected statement and smiled stupidly before recovering himself.

"Indeed?" Coney said on a long inhale. "Well, I shall relieve him of that duty. I was heading that way myself to meet with Corwin and then pick up your sister. We are all attending an organisational meeting for the Ramsbottom

fundraiser tomorrow night. I am in charge of the souvenir pins."

"Oh, of course you're supporting Gilbert Ramsbottom. That xenophobic troglodyte," Katz said, rolling his eyes. "I wonder whom you will get to scrub your floors and fetch your coal and wet-nurse your babies once he has kicked out everyone *not* named Harold or Arthur or William. I shall bid you good afternoon, then; have fun shaking your fasces at the rabble. Alice."

He gave her a quick bow and sauntered off into the late afternoon, whistling. She watched him go with wonder: somehow he had exited the scene without appearing to have lost the conversation.

"Alice?" Coney demanded. "He has the gall to call you by your Christian name?"

"Oh, do shut up," Alice said, at the last minute trying to put a droll spin on her words. If she had been a true Wonderlandian, of course, she wouldn't have bothered. "If you're going to walk me home, let us hurry, at least."

And she set off grimly to the park's exit.

She had hoped to shake the terrible young man loose before actually approaching the door of her house; if he was seen by one of her parents, or God forbid, her sister, he would no doubt be invited in, and then she would have to bear even more of his now-loathsome presence. She put what appeared to be a delicate hand on the brass doorknob and gripped it with a strength that rivalled a carnival strongman's.

"Thank you, Mr Coney, good evening," she said, opening the door as narrowly as possible.

"Alice? Are you home? Who is that?" her mother called from the foyer.

"Is that your mother?" Coney asked.

"Not at all," Alice promptly lied. "Good evening, Mr Coney."

She sidled her way round the edge of the door to the inside in the most unladylike, serpentine manner and slammed it behind her, leaning against it as if to keep all the Visigoths out.

"Unwanted suitor?" her mother asked kindly.

"Would you please tell my sister to keep out of my affairs? Forever?" Alice demanded. She made to go upstairs – there were other, far more important matters on her mind to sit in private and consider than this nonsense with boys.

Her plans were derailed by a single mild, infinitely vexing statement from her mother.

"She means well, you know that."

"But who does she mean well *for*?" Alice cried, whirling round. "She has set ideas in her head that will not be changed for anything despite the fact that the entire rest of the world doesn't live in that same head, with that same head's rules. What if *I* tried to introduce her to someone *I* thought would be a lovely boy? A painter, perhaps? Or a boatman?"

"You would never do with a painter yourself, Alice," her mother said with a mischievous smile. "You have more imagination and buoyancy than a hundred young artists. Now a boatman, who could take you on trips down countless sleepy rivers – and earn coin while he did – I could fair see that. Your father would be disappointed, of course, and worry about your financial future, but perhaps not if he could fish a bit from the prow."

"As long as I had a good, solid, loving husband, it wouldn't matter?" Alice prodded, pretending she didn't fully understand why this question was suddenly so important. "It wouldn't matter at all who he was, or what he did? Or who his family was?"

"Not at all. As long as you are happy, unlike your—" And here her mother's eyes whisked away and back.

"Unlike my aunt," Alice finished softly. "She *is* happy, you know. And financially her future is fine."

"But what would you know about that? The finances, I mean, not the happy part," her mother said quickly, not wanting to dwell on whatever unconventional things made her eternally single sister-in-law happy.

"Oh, never mind. I'm exhausted from my present 'buoyancy'. Would you mind having Mrs Anderbee bring me up some warm milk? I think I shall go to bed early tonight and miss supper."

"And also miss your sister at the table?" her mother asked archly.

Alice pretended not to hear her.

Twice she had actually gone to Wonderland and not just dreamed about it. But twice she had come *out* of Wonderland by waking. Perhaps sleep was merely the door, the way back in.

She ripped off her many layers of clothes as fast as she could and donned her warmest, snuggliest chemise. She grabbed Dinah where the poor thing was just having a quiet lie on the window sill in the sun and brought her into bed with her, tangled in with her own blonde hair. Dinah didn't resist and even curled around her head, purring into her ear.

Mrs Anderbee came up with the milk and a suspicious frown.

"It's no' the right time for your *flowers*," she said in her thick Northern accent. "Tha'd better not be getting ill."

"Thank you for keeping so close a track on my health," Alice said with faint amusement, taking the milk. *Flowers* was such a lovely metaphor for it. "But I do definitely feel a bit of malaise."

"Girls today with their *humours* and *mal-ays*," Mrs Anderbee muttered. "In my day you strapped on what rags you needed to and got on with work. Farms wait for no swoonin'."

"Thank you, Mrs Anderbee," Alice said around a smile and a mouthful of milk. *At least if you were outside leading a dray horse around a field*, she thought, *you wouldn't need to worry about accidentally bleeding on a prized needlepoint cushion.* The old servant showed herself out and closed the door as quietly as possible. She did care beneath her hard exterior. You just had to ignore what she said and pay attention to what she *did*.

Warm milk down, Alice found herself sliding into sleep most delightfully, as if she hadn't spent half the afternoon napping under a tree in a park.

Chapter Fifteen

But of course she woke in Kexford.

Chapter Sixteen

While Alice didn't make it back to Wonderland that night, she had come very close; of that she was certain. There was a feeling of liminality when she awoke, like her dream-self had just touched whatever skin separated England from that other place.

It's very similar, she thought with a strange premonition, *to an old person dreaming of youth.* Not quite young again in reality, but near enough that upon waking there existed a certain confusion as to which version of age inhabited the current body.

She had a nightmarish glimpse at the strange bodies of Wonderland creatures tumbling over each other as they fled the card soldiers. Beaks and tails and crazed inhuman golden eyes and people with strange hats. There was the *smile of the Knave* – ooh, how she wanted to slap it off him.

There was blood dripping from roses. *Not* red paint.

Also a glimpse of a placid castle in a remote valley that seemed important somehow. Did she know it? Was it familiar? What did it mean?

If only she could have reached out and pressed through, somehow!

"Oh, wake up, you lazy thing!" said a voice that wasn't Alice's. "You have been asleep for ten hours, easily! This is what comes of not having a real project or even a suitor or *anything* to occupy your time."

Alice kept her eyes closed, hoping the voice would go away, trying to keep the few moments she remembered distinct. The castle was important. The wounded, fleeing creatures were important.

Everything was important except for that irritating voice calling her away from Wonderland.

"*Really!* I'm talking to you, Alice. Open your eyes at once! I can tell you're awake."

"Do shut up," Alice told her sister as she scrunched down into the covers further and put a pillow over her head. Mathilda had to disappear. If Alice could just have a few moments to herself, maybe she could remember everything and figure out what it all meant. "You're very rude to come in without knocking. I'm quite busy at the moment. Go away."

"I will *not*," her sister said with some amusement.

Alice opened one eye and saw the severely bonneted Mathilda regarding her with a raised eyebrow and *almost* a twinkle in her eye.

"Please. Leave," Alice said as seriously as she could. "I am trying to remember something very important and you're making it impossible."

"What nonsense. Trying to remember a dream? That is not being *busy*. I must speak with you."

Alice took the pillow off her head and just looked at her sister, uncomprehending. There she was, utterly composed, utterly *smug* in her position, perching on the end of the bed. As if the only proper way the universe could run was when older sisters with ideas they thought were important could barge into rooms unasked, to wake up happily sleeping people, to correct them of their (presumed faulty) personal lives and routines.

That was what really irked Alice about Mathilda, she suddenly realised. Besides the unasked-for lessons when she was younger, the unwanted introductions to terrible young men now that she was older, the constant and unrelenting sermonizing aloud of her beliefs and politics – besides these things, underneath it all was an unshakable smugness, an undefeatable certitude in all things she did. Which she did without hesitation or question. There was only one worldview possible, and it was Mathilda's. It wasn't even that she rejected other people's beliefs; she literally didn't see them.

"You have two minutes," Alice said levelly. "And if you ever so much as come into my room without asking again, you will wake up the next morning with a blancmange dripping down your face."

Mathilda's brown eyes widened in extremely satisfying shock. "This is precisely the sort of thing that I wanted to discuss with you, Alice," she said, a little more shrilly than she probably meant.

(Another unbearably irksome thing was her constantly calm, patronising tone. Her losing it was a little *tick* of winning in Alice's game-board mind.)

"You were exceedingly rude to my friend Mr Coney yesterday."

"*He* was *extremely* rude!" Alice shot back. "He acted horribly – like an uncle or an older brother or zoo keeper in charge of the Alice beast. He said some horrible, really filthy things to *my* friend Mr Katz. And he did so first, I might add."

Mathilda was shocked into momentary silence. She had obviously not been told the whole story by whichever snitch passed it on.

But she did not question what Alice said.

"Well, but Mr Katz isn't… known… to us…" she began instead, sounding apologetic. It was all too obvious what *isn't known* really meant.

"He could be a satyr or a demon and it still would behoove an Englishman to behave with a modicum of politeness if no insult to his person has been made," Alice said frostily. "And as Mr Katz is neither, but a barrister moreover, perhaps he even deserves a modicum of respect."

Mathilda sighed and then nodded, looking this way and that, almost nervous. She smoothed the front of her dress out. "You are right, of course. I just… Coney is a close friend of Corwin's, and Gilbert Ramsbottom's right-hand man."

Alice jumped a little at that: Mr Headstrewth was *Corwin* to her sister now. That was a step!

"He will have quite the political future, perhaps not as an actual elected official like Ramsbottom himself, but as a person more behind the scenes. An organiser, a doer. None of which matters, of course," she added quickly, seeing the look in Alice's eyes. "It's just that he is making things a trifle difficult for Corwin right now because of your… interactions yesterday. It has put me in a very difficult position. Perhaps I never should have introduced you the way I did, but now… He cannot seem to take a hint, or let you go – like a bulldog when its jaws are locked."

Alice wondered both at this strangely vivid metaphor from her otherwise dull and placid sister and the *almost* apology that came before it.

"Corwin understands that you don't want anything to do with Coney – I think a passing pigeon would notice that – but the man is his friend. Could you—I'm not asking you to *see* him as a favour to me, but could you perhaps… perhaps leave your relationship on less of a sour note than a literal door slammed in his face?"

Alice wanted to scream. And not just because of the imposition she was being forced to endure – which was all a result of her sister's initial nosiness. Silly Mathilda was wasting her time rambling on about boys and friendships and relationships and what was little more than gossip while an entire world was on the brink of some sort of disaster.

While the fate of her friends was on the brink.

Yet with the hours that had come and gone since she was expelled from Wonderland – even with the dream-reprieve of the past night – the urgency of the situation had lessened even further, at least emotionally. The feeling of desperation was fast becoming more like wishing to return to a book whose plot has just reached a climax when one is rudely torn away by workaday matters. The devout reader is anxious to return to those pages… but the need to do so is not felt as strongly as, say, the need to make sure there's enough milk for the baby.

When Alice focused back on her sister, she saw a fretful young woman who was worried about her relationship with her suitor – whom she obviously loved – and her friends. And she had basically just admitted it to her young, 'silly' sister. She had admitted weakness.

All of which was touching, but Alice still had to get her out of the room as quickly as possible.

"Fineallrightwhatever," she said grumpily. "I will speak to him one last – *last* – time with you and *Corwin* present. But no long-time commitments and nothing intimate like a carriage ride or dinner at the club. Also something that has a definite terminus."

"Splendid! I have just the thing!" Mathilda cried, eyes lighting up. She did not, however, say *thank you*, Alice noticed. Instead she pulled out one of her loathsome pamphlets. Alice's heart sank. "Tonight is the fundraising lecture for the rally. Mr Ramsbottom is giving a talk to his biggest supporters. There will be light refreshment. The four of us shall attend – and that way I also get you to actually come to one of my meetings."

"Great yes fantastic you win now get out," Alice said,

scooching like an inchworm back into her covers and putting all the pillows back over her head. She felt the bed shift and the pressure in the air change as her sister stood up and left the room.

"Clubs," Alice said for no good reason, and resumed trying to dream.

But she never got close to leaving England or even falling asleep. And somehow, remarkably, as the day progressed, Wonderland slipped away so much that she forgot it entirely for minutes at a time. Bathing, getting dressed, attending to what little correspondence she had, and avoiding any more contact with her sister took up most of the afternoon. When she found out that Mathilda had invited Mr Headstrewth (*Corwin*) over for a spot of tea before the lecture, Alice slunk out of the house entirely with the message that she was going to fortify herself for the evening as well – but at Mrs Yao's.

(Also there were several specialty teas in her stock that were conducive to sleep: lavender, chamomile, valerian root, etc., which Alice thought she might avail herself of.)

This day wasn't half as glorious as the previous ones. It was misty and dark – practically begging for a good lie-in. A *duvet day*, as one of Alice's closer girl friends called it. Certainly not one for attending hateful and boring lectures.

"Then again, perhaps I shall be *so* sleepy and dull at the talk tonight that I will simply doze off… just as I did when my sister was reading to me so long ago – and thereby make my way back to Wonderland!"

That thought put her into a much sunnier mood, at least until she turned the corner and saw the tea shop.

Its dainty window was smashed to bits, its sign cracked in two.

"Good heavens!" Alice cried, rushing through the door. The bells that jingled merrily upon her entrance had at least not been ruined.

Mrs Yao sat slumped at her counter with her lower lip sticking out sadly. But she broke into a smile as soon as she saw Alice and quickly busied herself measuring out the right quantity of Alice's favourite tea and pouring hot water from a constantly bubbling kettle over it.

"No, stop," Alice pleaded. "Let me do something – you look a wreck."

"Being busy keeps me from being sad," Mrs Yao said with a wry grin. "Also, I have to pay for the damage somehow. Can I sell you on two biscuits this time?"

"You may sell me a half dozen. What has happened? Was it a bird?"

"Sure. If birds sank like stones from the air," the proprietor said sourly. She lifted up the stone in question from where it had sat in an icy-looking puddle of cracked glass. It was smooth and fist-sized and unlike something you would pick up from the wayside or a cobbled road. It was a beach stone, its origins far from Kexford. A string was tied tightly around it, attached to which was a surprisingly neatly and prettily written note:

go back to whence you came

"Oh dear," Alice said. "That's terrible!"

"I know who did it, too," Mrs Yao said, going back to working on the tea service. "That wretched little Danny Flannigan. But I don't think it was his idea. He can't write. Or read."

She presented Alice with a pretty tray holding two teacups and mismatched saucers, a couple of fancy nibbles and an enamelled pot whose steam smelled divine.

"Has this sort of thing happened before?"

"Oh, you can't live here and look different from everyone else and not hear things like that from time to time. Breaking the window is new. But I have been told worse."

"I'm so sorry," Alice murmured. "I had no idea."

"Why would you? But I appreciate your sympathy, I really do. It's nice to think I have an ally – with good taste in tea."

Alice smiled and poured a cup for her friend and then for herself, breathing in the lovely-scented steam issuing from the pot.

"You should talk to Danny's parents. Even if the boy can't pay for a new window, he could help fix it or run errands for you until you're square."

"I am certain he was put up to it by someone else. He's not this clever. He's just a brat." She smiled mischievously. "We had brats back in Nanjing, too – and they *also* only targeted Chinese shop owners."

Alice sighed. "I just wish there was something I could do. Oh!" Her face suddenly brightened with an idea. "Can I take a photograph of you? Next to the window? Holding the rock? I could submit it to the newspaper. 'The scene of a hateful crime!' It might not do much, but it would shed a light on this sort of thing, and might also act as an advertisement for your business."

"Oh, that's an interesting idea! But I don't want Danny's name in the paper. I don't think he's the real villain – and anyway I'm fairly certain his father would beat him for it."

Alice spent the next hour setting up the shot. It was a tricky business because of the backlighting from the window itself, but she needed the shards outlined. Also,

Mrs Yao wanted to smile for the camera; Alice had to keep telling her to look stern or sad.

But as she worked, she couldn't help thinking:

I wonder if she *has a Wonderland double, and who it might be…*

Chapter Seventeen

After she left the tea shop, Alice spent what little afternoon there was left looking for hints of Wonderland everywhere and taking photographs of anything – or anyone – she thought might be a likely prospect for a double in the other world. Then she tried napping again, faintly hoping the world would end before she woke.

Evening came despite her best attempts to avoid it. Soon enough Mathilda – hair specially combed, more of that powder on her face! – appeared at her bedroom door. She looked a little disappointed at Alice's outfit, unchanged since the morning. It wasn't a formal dinner they were attending (and Alice didn't *want* to go, anyway) so her rather plain dress with red diamonds seemed just fine. She had shined her shoes a little to get the dust off and combed and restyled her hair, but that was all.

"Ready?" Mathilda asked, visibly restraining herself from commenting on Alice's clothing choice.

"As I shall ever be."

"That's not—you're not bringing your camera, are you?"

"Of course I am. Why, will your party members do something they don't want me to take a picture of?"

"No, no, of course not."

Mathilda shook her head swiftly, more like a dog than a person, unsubtly trying to reset the conversation. "Isn't this fun? We're going out – on the town – together!"

"*Très* droll," Alice responded, not quite rolling her eyes.

Downstairs, Corwin Headstrewth was sharing a brandy with Alice's father. Coney was meeting them at the lecture. *That* was something, at least.

"How delightful!" Headstrewth bellowed, beaming. "I shall have a sister on each arm tonight."

"You may only have the permanent use of one," Alice's father said with far less humour than that sort of joking statement should have accompanied. "And that I grant most reluctantly."

"We should take a picture to remember this happy occasion," Alice said, and only her father picked up on her tone. He hid his smile behind the snifter of brandy he held.

Mathilda made a few negative sounds but Headstrewth was tickled pink with the idea. He brushed down his front, carefully moved a stray tress on Mathilda's forehead (such an intimate touch!), and proudly held her in front of him.

Definitely a pair of bandersnatches, Alice thought. She couldn't wait to see what would develop.

But on the walk over, even she had to admit that Headstrewth could sometimes be charming – if loud. He didn't mention the lecture or Ramsbottom or Coney at all, but kept up a fairly amusing dialogue about the shops and people they passed and even the street itself.

Mathilda must have schooled him on what subjects to avoid, Alice thought with a faint snigger.

Aloud she said, "Oh, did you know? Mrs Yao's tea shop had one of its windows smashed – by a small ruffian with a stone."

"That's a pity," Mathilda said sympathetically. "She's a lovely woman."

"It was one of those little foreign thugs, I assume?" Headstrewth interrupted, more matter-of-factly than maliciously. "That gang from the Square?"

"Not at all," Alice said through gritted teeth. "It was one

of the Flannigans, but egged on and abetted by someone who writes with a pretty hand. I took a photograph of Mrs Yao and the note. Perhaps if it is printed in the newspaper someone will recognise the handwriting and we can get to the bottom of it all."

"Indeed!" Headstrewth said like this was the most brilliant, heady thing he had ever heard.

Alice fumed and focused her attention on the gutter, where all her goodwill to the man beside her had just flowed.

The venue for the lecture was a large and lovely house, much grander than Alice and Mathilda's, with a special room off the library just for gatherings like this one. In it there was a stage with a lectern and space for at least fifty seats. Red, white and blue bunting had been draped around the windows, but any potential festival air was squelched by the intense conversations of the attendees, who all had serious eyes and grim mouths. A gaunt young man with a close-shaved beard stood at a table offering buttons and ribbons that said RAMSBOTTOM FOR MAYOR. There was also a small pile of the sort of pamphlets that Mathilda was so fond of.

Not even the least bit droll. Alice sighed.

"Oh! I'm so glad you could make it!"

Mr Coney approached the trio delightedly, arms spread

to encompass at least the *idea* of Mathilda and Alice and Headstrewth. Alice marked the look in his eye: it was delight, to be sure. But it wasn't *rapturous* delight, the sort of emotion one might expect from a young man infatuated with a young woman – one who had seemed to allow him into her good graces once again.

I wonder how much he actually likes me, Alice mused to herself, *and how much it would merely be good for his career to be married to Mathilda's sister. Mathilda and Corwin, Alice and Richard, going to lectures and promoting mayors and taking the Grand Tour and making their way to London gatherings of like-minded political folks…*

Mathilda and Headstrewth were exchanging a quick, *very* familiar look, like an old couple. Worry/hope/dismay/fear-of-embarrassment.

"Wouldn't miss it for anything," Headstrewth said aloud.

"We absolutely endorse Ramsbottom, as you know," Mathilda added.

"I brought my notebook," Alice said, pulling out her journal. "So I could take notes. And my camera for after."

"Splendid!" Coney said enthusiastically. "I have saved us four seats up front. Normally I would be up there, with the pins and buttons, you know. But I wanted to spend this time down in the trenches, as it were, with you."

Alice, unable to think of anything to say that wasn't sarcastic, dry or ironic, said nothing at all. Apparently satisfied with her silence, Coney led them to their seats and traded chuckles with Headstrewth.

It turned out that Quagley Ramsbottom was the grim fellow subbing in for Coney at the table with the pins and pamphlets. Apparently the two brothers were twins. But aside from their political theories, they had little enough in common, at least physically: Gilbert, the politician, was broad, friendly-looking, prone to smiles.

"Gentlemen Tweedles Dee and Dum, I've no doubt at all," Alice murmured, taking out her camera quietly and setting up a shot.

"Thank you all for coming out tonight," Gilbert began. Alice noticed he had a RAMSBOTTOM FOR MAYOR pin on his lapel. Was that normal or egotistical?

She heard him say very little else after that and was elbowed only once by Mathilda for too obviously sketching the Hatter in her notebook, which was the real reason she had brought it. Words and phrases would occasionally make their way into one of her ears and thence to her mind: "... everybody, of course, but focus on the real backbone of England: its own children..." "... darkening our doorsteps..." "... exotic philosophies and religions and even food, anathema to our traditions..."

Alice looked up at Mathilda at the last one. *"Food, too?"* she whispered.

Her older sister looked a little chagrined but shrugged, lips tightened.

Mostly what Gilbert said *sounded* upbeat and positive—on the surface at least. He touched on how sad immigrants must be, so far from the shores of their real homes. Women and men alike in the audience murmured in sympathetic assent over this. He talked about the need to take care of them (though this sounded ominous rather than charitable) and how the planet had conveniently put giant bodies of water to separate the various races of men. The audience ate it all up.

When it was over Alice did not applaud.

"There's a question-and-answer session," Coney told her with a winning smile. "Won't you stay for it?"

"Oh," Alice said, "I think I have all the answers I need, thank you. And what I need now is a cold drink."

"Absolutely! I'll join you outside in a bit!"

I will be long gone by then, Alice promised herself but did not say aloud. She made for the exit as quickly and discreetly as she could, without waiting for her sister. Outside the lecture room there were refreshments and people milling about, speaking more animatedly than before, their spirits awoken by the hateful, upbeat nonsense of the would-be mayor. Alice wished she had brought a fan. It was hot and she wanted to leave at once – but it would be rude without her sister. She found the punch bowl and dipped herself a mug, then stood in the corner to drink it as guiltily as a child sulking with a cup of milk who wishes to remain unseen.

But then she saw something that nearly made her choke on her first sip: *Aunt Vivian.*

She, too, was by herself and sipping punch! But she did it somehow without looking lonely; she held herself like she was the queen of the room, vaguely bored, waiting for some dullard to approach her. Her dress consisted of layers of emerald velvet and silk and tassels, topped by a small but exquisite polygonal hat.

"Aunt Vivian!" Alice cried, approaching her with more gratitude than she could contain.

Her aunt's world-weary eyes widened.

"Alice, dear, whatever are you doing here?"

"I'm with my sister and Mr Headstrewth. And Coney," she added after a moment.

"Oh, that's right, your sister buys into this nonsense. I keep forgetting that; she is so level-headed in every other aspect of her life."

"But what are *you* doing here? Do you support Ramsbottom?"

"Heavens forfend! I'm here as a favour to Willard," she said with a spin of her wrist and a roll of her eyes. "They won't let him into their little gatherings any more – not after the last one. Gave Gilbert quite the what-for, and all his nasty little cronies. I am to report back on the latest developments! But sadly I do not have much to tell aside from the usual hate-mongering drivel this crowd eats up."

"Perhaps if Willard is so inclined against Ramsbottom, *he* should run for mayor," Alice said a little archly, thinking of the Hatter and his constant search for other people to lead the way. Mary Ann, herself…

"What an idea!" Vivian said, shocked. "I absolutely love it. Ooh, hush, hush, dear, *They* are approaching."

She nodded over Alice's shoulder. Gilbert himself came up to them, flanked by Coney and Quagley. The would-be mayor was nodding and grinning and his little helpers were clearing the way, Coney practically hopping up and down with excitement. Mathilda and Corwin followed.

"You're looking lovely as ever, Miss…" Ramsbottom said, nodding at Vivian. "It *is* still Miss, is it not? There's no Mister in the picture?"

She could have said "I'm afraid not," or "Not yet, sadly" but instead she looked him in the eye and said simply, "No."

"Oh, but you come from such a good, strong family

line, English to the core," Gilbert said with a smile, this one with his fleshy lips closed over his teeth, just the corners of his mouth turned up. "We need good women like you to make sure there are future generations of such."

"But there *is* another generation," Vivian said calmly, putting her hand on Alice's shoulder. "I wouldn't trade my nieces for the world."

"I have a law in mind for situations such as this, should I ever be so lucky as to make it into a higher office than mayor," Ramsbottom went on with pleasant menace. "A law about... *unwed* women. Preventing the sort of dissolute lifestyle that not having a stabilising marriage to a man generally encourages."

Alice didn't react; she was too busy watching Mathilda and Headstrewth, both of whose eyes widened in shock.

"Oh, well, it's a free country, Gilbert," Headstrewth managed. "Vivian's no burden to the system. She supports herself."

Apparently even they have a limit, Alice thought.

Coney said nothing but grinned like both his master and his friend had said the cleverest things in the world, and he was anxious for a fight betwixt them.

"Well, hopefully women will get the vote before your law is discussed seriously," Vivian said, tossing the rest of her drink back. "*All* of us women get the vote, I mean, including the ones you fear are invading our country. Alice, do come home with me – it's early yet and past time you started earning your keep in my darkroom. I have a friend who wants a portrait of her own pretty little *English* niece. But she could be Welsh, or even French, so don't quote me on that."

And with that Aunt Vivian turned with the grace of a goddess and sauntered out of the room, Alice practically giggling as she followed.

She took giant gulps of the cool night air and enjoyed the feeling of her flush departing. The close smells of the party were replaced with moisture and horses and evening greenery. It was quiet on the street. Alice felt herself unfurling like the fern.

Then a trio of men exited the club next door, talking loudly and laughing uproariously, in fine – if raucous – spirits.

"Oh, look, there's Ramsbottom's stupid event tonight," one of the older men said, pointing his silver-handled cane mostly at Alice and her aunt, though meaning the building behind them. "I say! Let's crash the party!"

"George, yes, let's do!" another otherwise distinguished white-haired gentleman agreed enthusiastically. "I hear they have quite the spread. Oh, it would be so fun to tweak the nasty little start-up – he daren't order us out! He would just have to take it, hoping for our support!"

"Perhaps not, gentlemen," the youngest member of the party said soothingly, with patience and humour. "We should really call it a night... *Alice?*"

She had a terrible premonition just before he turned, she really did, of who it would be.

(Terrible?)

(Or *hopeful*?)

It was A. Joseph Katz, Esq., of course, and those were most likely Alexandros and Ivy, also esquires, the partners in the firm where he worked.

Any excitement she might or might not have admitted upon seeing the young man was immediately tempered by the look in his eyes: they flicked over to the house she and her aunt had obviously come from, and his face fell in disappointment when he realised why they were there.

"I hadn't realised you were so political after all," he said with a forced smile.

"I'm here because of my sister," Alice said quickly, without even the courtesy of a proper greeting, too eager to correct his assumption. "I owed her a favour. That is all."

"*Vivian*, it's been too long!" George (Alice assumed) called, waving his cane. "What the deuce are you doing at Ramsbottom's?"

"Stealing the silverware, of course," Alice's aunt quipped. "How is your wife?"

"Oh, she's a fighter! She's doing just fine, the old lass! She'll be up and about soon, and we'll take that trip to Italy I promised her the moment she's better! The air there will do her a world of good, I'm sure of it!"

The other lawyer was still looking a little myopically at Alice and Katz, who were silently looking at each other.

"You know this young woman, Katz?" he asked.

"We're acquainted," Katz said shortly.

"George, walk with me? Ahead? With your partner?" Vivian suggested, tilting her head at the younger people, giving her friend a knowing look.

"Absolutely! Always willing to help out a damsel in distress!" he said, pulling Mr Ivy after him.

"But *I* should like to steal some silverware," the other barrister said longingly. "Or at least a glass of port."

The three older people strolled ahead, and Alice and Katz, somewhat embarrassed, followed. Alice put her hand on his arm. They walked in awkward silence.

"I think Ramsbottom is just terrible," Alice finally blurted out. "He is loathsome. I don't know why my sister supports him – she is many things, but not stupid. Anyway, I have paid up my debt to her and will not be returning for an encore."

"I'm glad," Katz said with a smile.

"Are you glad I do not support Mr Ramsbottom? Or glad I will not be mingling with his supporters, perhaps?" she asked, a mischievous twinkle in her eye.

Katz didn't respond, at first looking chagrined and then smiling at his own obviousness. Alice felt a funny little thrill when he gave her a sidewise, conspiratorial look: *oh, you got me there!*

"Both, if I may be honest. But did *you* ever resolve whatever park-tree-rabbit-friends issue you were having?"

Alice laughed and it was perfectly natural, light peals that took a thousand stones off her shoulders.

"No, I did not, Mr Katz. I did not. And as mad as it all may seem, it still worries me. It's all riddles and mysteries and things I'm beginning to quite forget, even though I really shouldn't. None of it makes a lick of sense. Do *you* like riddles, Mr Katz?"

"Do you know anything about our legal system?" he responded wryly. "You *have* to love riddles in my job. Actually, I heard a good one the other day from a dear friend who – like me, like you – loves riddles as well."

"Oh, let's hear it!"

"All right. Who knows – maybe solving it will help you work out your own problems. They work like that, you know. Expand the brain or exercise the mind or something. Make you think differently about things. Here goes:

"I have mine and you have yours
It's needed in a painting
But in the end none agree on
The meaning of the thing."

"Oh, that's a tough one," Alice said, thinking. "It could be anything. Value? Colour? What is it?"

"You must figure it out yourself," Katz said with one of his maddening little smiles.

They had stopped walking and were right in front of Aunt Vivian's house.

Alice had the sudden thought that he was going to tweak her nose, or do *something* – when suddenly one of the senior partners noticed them again.

"I say, is that a camera?" George asked, looking owlishly at her obviously technical satchel. "I've been thinking about getting one for myself or the wife—oh! Be a dear and take one of us three old codgers, would you? And print me up a portrait? I want to see what it will do!"

"Of course, but the light… oh, you're not listening any more," Alice sighed, feeling this was somehow familiar. Somehow Wonderlandy. The two old lawyers were utterly ignoring her, running hands over their hair and straightening their ties. Vivian gave her niece a sympathetic smile and carefully led them as close to a gas lamp as she could so the flames could illuminate their features at least a little.

For a moment Alice wondered what Wonderland creatures they would be. And then she was taken suddenly by the thought that these three were old friends, all still getting along marvellously without all of Mathilda's silly rules about what was proper behaviour for men and women. She took the picture, trying to remember the Hatter.

"Where does the picture come out?" the other lawyer asked interestedly.

"Oh, don't be ridiculous," Vivian said, shaking her head and giving him a hug about the shoulders. "We must go inside and *develop* the plates. Actually, we must go do that after we take another portrait I have promised. Alice?"

"Goodnight, Mr Katz," she said regretfully.

"Until next time," Katz said with a bow. "And Alice – *do* figure it out. I think you will find the solution may help you. And I depend on your answer!"

"Oh, bother," Alice said, for many reasons, not the least of which was the three older people watching them.

Chapter Eighteen

Charlie was the name of the terrified little six-year-old Alice was meant to do a portrait of. She had beautiful, over-coiffed ringlets of black hair and a perfect little white dress with a blue sash such as Alice herself had worn at that age. With soft words encouraging the exploration of Vivian's rather extraordinary bric-a-brac, Alice eventually managed to coax a smile out of the serious girl. She supposed the aunt wanted a proper old-fashioned pose, as was done with the large-format cameras in studios with velvet backdrops, but she also took one of the girl giggling and hanging off the divan upside down, the paintbrush tips of her thick black locks just brushing the floor.

A hundred years from now, Alice thought as she

developed the pictures, *someone will see* this *photograph and* really see *Charlie. He won't just wonder about the frowning little girl with the composed hands and face in the other photograph. He'll have an idea of what she was actually like.*

She was a little surprised when the 'fun' picture, once revealed, remained the same – Charlie upside down – but the *serious* photograph revealed a Wonderland umbrella bird. "I suppose all children make up the little creatures of Wonderland," she said as the plate dried, thinking of Adina and how delightful that was. Although the umbrella bird in question seemed to be hiding behind a tree and peeping out from behind it nervously.

Alice also developed the photo she had taken of Mrs Yao and the deadly stone. But instead of an incriminating newspaper showstopper, the scene was of a person tall and stern, with dark skin and a dark circlet of black baubles upon her hair. She held her arms crossed over her chest and stared directly at the viewer with an appraising look. A strange weapon was gripped in her right hand, one with three bells or spheres at the end of its shaft.

"A club?" Alice wondered aloud.

Mrs Yao was in the suit of clubs in the other world.

But why?

There had been nothing in her adventures so far that involved any suit besides hearts.

She thought back to two girls on a stifling summer day, long heavy curtains drawn in the study but seeming to hold the heat and dust *in* rather than keeping things cool. A pack of cards, divided, lay between them. Alice had a drooping red bow in her hair; Missy Fedgington a pretty little black bonnet that had fallen to the floor. Their fathers were friends, but these two were united only in boredom and age. Each flipped a card, and despite the extreme lassitude of the afternoon Alice couldn't quite let go of the sting of defeat each time she lost a bout… Little red and black queens, trading cards endlessly in a game neither much cared about.

The memory came back to Alice with force, like a suddenly recalled dream.

You just pull out your cards over and over again, and whoever has the most at the end wins.

She looked at the picture. The black baubles almost looked like a crown the way Yao wore them.

That was it!

In Wonderland, her double was the Queen of Clubs!

"*There's another queen,*" she murmured. "There's another queen in Wonderland! As powerful as the Queen of Hearts, and almost certainly her enemy. Maybe she can help us!"

Alice studied the image in the photo. The woman in it seemed a bit severe and stern – but she didn't seem mad.

Or at least not frothing-at-the-mouth mad. Someone who maybe could be reasoned with.

Well, it was the start of a plan, if Alice could ever get back to Wonderland. She cleaned up quickly, leaving the rest of the plates to develop another time, and practically ran out of the house.

"I'm coming," she promised the Hatter as she ran through the streets.

"To sleep!" she declared, bursting into her house and running up the stairs to her room. "On the nonce!"

(Which really wasn't that hard; it had been an extremely tiring day.)

But she woke the next morning with nothing more than a few half-remembered dreams of pink cheeks and wise eyes.

So she tried napping in the large chair her father preferred to snooze in after dinner.

She tried it on the couch, gazing at the image of the Queen of Clubs before closing her eyes.

She tried it in the garden on a blanket in a warm corner.

She even had a bewildered Mrs Anderbee recite long and rambling stories about growing up in Yorkshire until she drifted off. The old woman was flattered, and Alice's daydreams were full of berries and furze, clear cold spring water and turkey for Christmas. But there was no entrance to Wonderland.

She might have been seeing things, but at one point it seemed like the Queen of Clubs in the picture had turned slightly to look at her. As if to say, *Well, are you coming?*

Time was ticking, whether you were friends with him or no.

"All right, let's look at this logically," Alice said, thinking about her friend Charles and his maths.

The first time, she had chased a rabbit into the other world; the second time, she had been pointed there by a duck. Perhaps sleep wasn't the answer at all; perhaps *animals* were the interlocutors of Wonderland: the Nikes, the Charons, the Castors and Polluxes, the psychopomps. All she had to do was find the right one!

This, of course, resulted in situations that went from mildly amusing to downright shocking. Despite never really having cared about what others thought of her, Alice still had to bear with comments from her family about the fox she chased into the garden, the Scottie dog she *swore* was looking at her funny, the rat that nearly made her usually stoic sister scream.

(Rather than carefully avoid the furry monster the two sisters spied in the street, which is what sensible adults did when encountering the fat urban unafraid-of-humans variety of rodent, Alice knelt down and tried to reason with it. And when the right-thinking rat decided that *this* human was mad and therefore potentially dangerous, and tried to escape, she ran after it.)

There was also the bright blue tit in her mother's garden that she had merely wound up taking a picture of.

All right, Alice said to herself. *Perhaps I shouldn't rely on randomly finding some animal citizen of Wonderland. I should take the situation in hand myself. What else has my crossing over involved?*

Her quick and analytical mind – which had resulted in many a triumph over her father at chess – picked through the things she knew about Wonderland and crossing over, and fanned them out for review: sleep, animals, Unbirthdays. She had been called to Wonderland the second time; had the first time just been chance? What else was there?

Aha! Two people had been present when she had dreamed herself to Wonderland. The first was her sister; the second, Katz. And while her sister was downstairs and extremely easy, at least physically, to talk to, Alice didn't imagine the conversation would go very far.

"Excuse me, Mathilda, could you pause your pamphlet-folding for just a moment to cast your mind back to over ten years ago and remember exactly what I was doing before you woke me under the tree that time in the park?"

Even if Mathilda didn't dismiss it immediately as nonsense, the rest would still prove awkward and unhelpful.

Katz… on the other hand…

This was not, she told herself, also an excuse to see him (it was).

He would *not* be compelled to discuss with her such nonsensical-seeming things merely because he felt about her a certain way (he obviously did).

She was only doing any of this because it was vital for her return to Wonderland to save her friends (mostly true).

There were two problems with her plan. One was that she didn't have an answer to his riddle, and the other was that showing up randomly at his office might seem impetuous and a little desperate – especially to outside observers.

So she would start at the Square, where apparently he spent some of his time.

On the way there Alice stopped at the little fern (now a few inches taller and more unfurled) and paused to ask if it could help her.

It remained haughtily silent on the matter.

The Square was also strangely silent. There were fewer children than usual, and those extant were quiet and subdued.

"Hello," Alice said gamely to the closest boy. "Is Mr Katz here, by any chance?"

The boy shrugged. "Katz hasn't been here today. We was hoping he'd come. Josh… they took Joshua away. And a bunch of others. Maybe Mr Katz could have stopped it."

"Took Joshua *away*? Who did? Where?" Alice demanded.

"The police and someone else with them. They said they committed a crime – broke a window or something. Josh owes me a turn with his ball. He owes me a turn with his ball and he was going to let me *this afternoon*."

He said it with the timbre of righteous anger but his eyes were wide and wet.

"Broke a window? But that can't be. It was Danny Flannigan. I don't understand this at all. Tell me everything," Alice said grimly, kneeling down to put her face even with his. That was the thing of dealing with children: you didn't lie to them and you didn't treat them like lesser beings. Alice had managed *excellent* results with her little models by being as respectful and polite as she would to a vicar.

"Two police officers just came and grabbed Josh and three of his other friends. Filthy orphans, they said. Josh is no orphan. He's got a sister and a cat."

"Of course. Don't worry – they are probably just down

at the police station," Alice said. "I'll go find Mr Katz and we will have this sorted immediately."

All right, maybe that part was a lie, she thought as she straightened up and hurried back out of the square. She wasn't sure he shouldn't worry. She wasn't sure they could have it all sorted immediately. She wasn't even sure where Katz's office was. But she would find it.

Alice hurried down the alleys and twisty little streets, picking up her skirts, heels pounding the cobblestones, foot strikes echoing off the walls. She knew a shortcut that would let her out almost directly on the high street where all the important businesses were; she was as at home here as a rabbit in its labyrinthine warren.

She tried to sort through crazy thoughts and priorities as she fought for breath and ran. First she would try to see about Katz and tell him about what was happening with the children. Hopefully he would be able to do something about that. *Then* she would take the photograph of Mrs Yao to the newspaper. Or maybe to the police. She wasn't sure which. Then she could turn her thoughts back to Wonderland.

So much to do – and how was it suddenly all up to her to fix things? She had no experience in social justice, newspapers, the police or politicians. It was all ridiculous. Nonsense, really.

Once again she passed by the little green fern and,

looking at it instead of the cobbles ahead of her, almost tripped over the curb.

A strong arm stopped her fall – and then grabbed her round the neck, a gloved hand over her mouth.

"HAND IT OVER!" rasped a muffled voice.

Alice tried to tear herself away from her assailant – whose face, she saw, was covered in a scarf to conceal his features. His coat was on inside out to hide any details.

He wasn't trying to strangle her, she quickly realised; he was just trying to hold her still with one hand while he fumbled for her bag with the other.

"Get away!" she shouted, her voice muffled. "Villain!"

She writhed and flailed trying to shake him off.

"JUST GIVE ME THE BAG!" he… pleaded? – still in a fake, raspy voice.

She gave the satchel one hard yank.

He let go.

She went flying back, smashing into the stone wall of a house behind her.

As the world went dark, Alice noticed that just beyond the little fern she had so admired was a green and gloriously exuberant garden.

Chapter Nineteen

Gardens weren't at all unusual in Kexford – except in this part of Kexford, and this kind of garden. Anyone would have blinked twice and fallen in love with it; the perfection of detail, the exuberance of the flowers, the colour of the leaves, the precise yet natural placement of the vines, the bright paint on the house, the neat little cabbages in their artfully dishabille cold frames. Alice immediately saw it for what it was: Wonderland.

And familiar Wonderland at that.

"Why, it's the White Rabbit's house!" she declared.

She put her hand thoughtlessly to her neck, and then head – had they hurt a moment ago? Had she suffered a headache? Whatever, it was all gone now.

And then seven-year-old Alice remembered she was now eighteen-year-old Alice, and this was no harmless little white rabbit: he was a Queensman. "But then again," Alice said to herself, "he didn't seem so harmless back then, either. Why, when he ordered me to fetch his gloves, thinking I was Mary Ann, I went and looked for them just like that! *Scared* to disobey."

But there were other differences in the two visits besides Alice's age and attitude: red heart card guards marched around, looking important and deadly in helmets that revealed only glowing red points instead of eyes. Fortifications had been erected around the house that were not there last time; a new wall here and a sandbag there, all befitting someone important and indispensable to a queen at War.

"Why am I *here*?" Alice wondered.

She had thought that if she made it back to Wonderland she would be returned to the place where she had been plucked so suddenly and horribly from her friends – the battle at the Grunderound. She had prepared herself to go back and face whatever had happened, to rescue those who hadn't made it out – and seek vengeance for those who didn't make it out alive.

Here, except for the soldiers and the walls, all was bright sunshine and peace: no real clues or revelation about the War currently being waged.

"Also, the last time I was here, I was the size of a rabbit, or a lizard, and then suddenly the size of a giant, and became stuck in the house. Poor old Bill! I hope he didn't get captured by the cards. He always has the worst luck."

Alice looked down at herself and then back at the house: she seemed to be about the right size to enter it. Old Alice wouldn't have thought twice about this, but now-Alice wondered if this was on purpose – if she was *meant* to go into the house. Or were there soldiers waiting for her inside? Old Alice also would have gone up the front steps immediately and knocked – or even entered directly without knocking, perhaps feeling a little naughty but mostly adventurous.

"I think I'll at least evade the guards," now-Alice decided.

This proved to not be very hard at all.

Much like Tweedles Dum and Dee fighting over a rattle, despite *looking* scary, the guards were very close to being useless. They marched stylishly and loudly around the house clockwise and widdershins and occasionally slammed into each other – perhaps because it was almost impossible to see out of their fearsome helmets.

Alice waited to make her move until a collision occurred on the side of the house away from her (she couldn't see it but heard the clang of the helmets and muttered swears). Tiptoeing quickly she let herself through the kitchen door – which was almost heartbreaking in its fine carpentry and snugness. There was a tiny heart-shaped window set in the middle, glazed in red glass.

Inside there were biscuits freshly iced and sitting on a pan with the words EAT ME piped on them. More out of habit than anything else Alice grabbed a couple and stuffed them into her pockets. The murmurings of a housekeeper or chef rose and fell from the pantry, so Alice quickly moved on.

She still wasn't entirely sure what she was looking for. Gloves? Bill? War plans she could steal and thus figure out some sort of counterattack? Unlikely. Alice had no experience in the military, as said, and she was fairly certain Wonderlandians didn't work in such a logical, tactical fashion anyway.

What she *did* find was the Dodo.

He was chained up in a small study, certainly not the most uncomfortable of prisons. There was a soft rug and a cheery fire. It was as if the White Rabbit had no real idea of the proper way to go about treating treasonous criminals. The poor bird was perched on the floor, legs drawn up under him, looking bedraggled and tired. There was a gash across one of his eyes, and his wings were folded tight against his body in a far more avian fashion than the creature generally held himself. He had lost some tail feathers and his jacket was torn and missing buttons.

"Oh, Dodo!" Alice whispered in dismay, rushing over to him.

"Alice!" The Dodo brightened. "I knew you would come! I said so. And here you are."

"Shh. Let's see if we can get you out of this," she said, pulling at the cruel iron chain. The cuff was solid enough and sized perfectly for the Dodo's leg, not too tight but not able to slip off, either. There was a heart-shaped keyhole on the side that would of course require the usual Wonderland search for an iron key (with a heart on it as well, no doubt). Alice would bet her camera that the key would be hanging around the Rabbit's neck on a tiny and delicate version of the iron chain around the Dodo's leg. Or dangling from a high bookshelf, or…

"We haven't time for that nonsense," Alice murmured, pulling out one of her purloined biscuits and gulping it down. Then she put a hand on either side of the iron cuff and gently pulled her hands apart.

The metal expanded under her touch, and the wondering Dodo easily slipped his foot out of it.

"Astounding!" the Dodo said, shaking his legs out.

"Where's the Hatter?" Alice whispered.

"I don't know. He ran a different direction than I. There was quite a flummoxing when the cards—"

"Is there anyone else locked up *here*?" Alice pressed, not wanting to get into a long Wonderlandy conversation while they were in danger of being discovered.

"No, just me. I was the only one they brought here," the Dodo said, a little mournfully. "I insisted on parole – on meeting with the White Rabbit. Bill was with me at first, but the housekeeper helped him get away."

Well, that made a certain amount of sense; he used to work here, of course. And poor old Bill certainly deserved a break after all he had been through.

Alice looked out the window. The guards were changing. She cursed herself for missing the advantage of the very ritualized moment that was taking up so much time.

"We'll have to sneak out the *front* – immediately, I'm afraid. Come on." Alice took the Dodo's wing and led him as quietly as possible down the hall. The house, she couldn't help noticing, was just the right size for her in her present form, but not proportionately; it was built for a rabbit's movements and habits. Doors were fatter, rounder and shorter. There were lovely paintings of carrots and dill artfully arranged on the lettuce-print wallpaper along with the usual long-eared silhouettes. Lovely little velvet King

Louis chairs were more like tuffets for resting on with all (four) of your legs pulled up under you.

They passed a delicate set of curling wooden steps, and Alice could have sworn she heard a whimpering from upstairs; a sad, mournful sound much like the Mock Turtle had made.

"There's another prisoner," she whispered to the Dodo. "You go on ahead. I'll meet you by the hedgerow just outside the gate."

The Dodo saluted and Alice had the funny thought of replacing his long-lost wig with a captain's hat.

She tiptoed up a flight of stairs that were honey-coloured and thick and didn't creak at all. The part of her that still liked dolls ached for a house like this. Every decoration was well thought out; care had been taken in each last detail. The tiny window on the stairwell hadn't a speck of dust and the paint was recent.

She remembered the bedroom where she had searched for the Rabbit's gloves, and where she had grown too big and become stuck – that seemed to be the place where the sobbing was coming from. She stepped forward as quietly as she could and peeped around the door frame.

It was the White Rabbit who sat there, weeping.

"Mary Ann," he moaned over a pair of white gloves. "You didn't deserve that. Oh, Mary Ann..."

Crying was a tricky business for the White Rabbit: tears rolled out of his eyes and then got caught up on his whiskers, sometimes flowing down them, causing them to droop and then spring up in an undignified fashion when the tears finally splashed to the floor. But sometimes they flowed back towards his face and matted down the fur there.

The gentlemanly little rabbit, still in the fancy waistcoat – now he also had an armband with a heart patch on it, and what looked like a tiny medal of valour – looked a damn mess.

"I should throttle you where you sit," Alice found herself saying aloud, despite her surprise at his reaction to the girl's unhappy fate.

The Rabbit looked up at her with the mindless surprise of a normal lagomorph: red eyes wide and dead, ears up, paws down. Just like one of his wild cousins right before it decides to bolt.

"I should have your skin for a muff," she added, shocking herself but meaning every word as she advanced. Fury freed her from any fear of stupid card soldiers and consequences.

The White Rabbit seemed to regain his sentience; he settled back into a slump of despair.

"I would deserve it," he murmured.

Alice blinked in surprise.

"I was only trying to do what was best. I was only trying

to *end* this nonsense, this madness. The sooner it's all over the better," he said, waving a tired paw. But his voice had regained some of its irritating officiousness. "I didn't think she would get involved. She only need have waited for the End of Time. I was speeding the Queen along. We already had so many toys… The end is so close—"

"So many toys? You mean like dolls?" Alice interrupted. The Cheshire's riddle… and the brush-child-thing at the Grunderound… Dolls and toys and more dolls! "What are you going on about, Rabbit? The Queen is destroying everything in Wonderland and taking all the toys for herself? *Why?*"

"She wants all the toys, the most toys, of course. What else would you expect from the Queen of Hearts?" he said miserably. "I am helping her… acquire them. Sometimes there is resistance."

"What a terrible rabbit you are," Alice said, wondering if these words had ever been said in English (or any language) before.

"Take the Dodo and go," the White Rabbit said tonelessly, not paying much attention to her. He stroked the little white gloves. "I shall have to call the guards soon enough."

Alice backed out of the doorway, a little shaken by his strange words and behaviour. But before she left she saw that she had been right: there was indeed a fine black iron chain around his neck, on which hung a key with a heart-shaped bow on the end of its shank.

The Dodo, bless him, was right where she told him to be. It was strangely surprising.

"All right then," Alice said, hunkering down in the hazel next to him. "Tell me what happened back at the Grunderound when I disappeared! Was anyone else captured? Was anyone hurt?"

"Oh, there were many people hurt," the Dodo said mournfully. "Although perhaps rather fewer than could have been. The soldiers were very surprised by your sudden disappearance. So surprised, in fact, that they sort of marched into each other and fell into a terribly messy pile. Cards, you know. Terrifying in numbers, especially the higher suits, but a bit of a disaster at times."

"Oh, I'm so glad," Alice said with feeling. "I never meant to leave you, you know – I was pulled away. Just like last time, when I thought it was all a dream."

"I know," the Dodo said, a little sadly, looking up into her eyes. "You have a whole other world to worry about, besides our little Wonderland."

"Well, I don't know if..." Alice started to correct him about her importance in that other world, much less this one, and then decided it wasn't worth the conversation right then. What a funny idea the creatures here had of her, though! It seemed like they could only think of Alice as a silly, useless girl who knew none of the rules of living here – or as some sort of replacement saviour. Nothing in between. "What happened to the Hatter? And the Gryphon? And the Dormouse?"

"The Gryphon fought, raking his mighty claws at the enemy," the Dodo said, eyes lighting up at the memory. "Gosh, he was glorious. I think he tore several cards clean in half. The Dormouse was still on the chandelier, I believe, when it fell. The Hatter—"

Alice's heart clenched.

"The Hatter tried to get all the wounded and children to safety," the Dodo said with a sigh. "I don't know what happened finally, but he was leading a group to the exit. Had a dish and spoon riding on his shoulders last I saw.

"But I knew you would need help assembling your army, now that you're our leader."

"Indeed," Alice said, kissing him above the beak. "Good, loyal Dodo. Thank you so much for your perhaps undeserved trust in me – but *how* did you know I would wind up here?"

The Dodo shrugged.

"You… Mary Ann… the White Rabbit. You're all tangled."

Alice sighed. Of course. Wonderland logic.

"I don't think I have any of the skills the poor departed Mary Ann had for organising Wonderland creatures and calling them to arms; it was utter chaos in the Grunderound just taking care of the wounded."

"We are all very independently minded," the Dodo said with a sniff. "When you identify as a Dodo, you are Dodo all the way. Auks just can't understand things from your point of view. I mean, they *can,* better than, say, whales, but they still do not truly know what it is like to be a Dodo. We have our own special needs and issues."

Alice rubbed her head. Perhaps this was what Coney was really afraid of – Kexford being overrun with a thousand different exotic ideas and votes. Caucus races, indeed. Still, it was a democracy; all viewpoints were supposed to be welcome.

"Except for the cards," he added darkly. "They are all too easily organised into nasty packs."

"Yes," Alice said with a sigh. "If only we could harness that for good."

Then she suddenly remembered: the picture of

Mrs Yao! The queen, dark and beautiful, bearing a club. *A queen of clubs.*

"Dodo! Tell me about the other suits – the Queen of Clubs, in particular."

"Oh, she is a fierce and respectable ruler," the Dodo said, preening his chest a little in thought. "She and the Queen of Hearts have come to blows a thousand times – border skirmishes – but they always manage to avoid a serious game of War in the end. It would be bloody indeed if they didn't."

"Do you think she would help us?"

The Dodo looked dubious. "The Queen of Hearts is conducting a campaign against her own people. Why would the Queen of Clubs get involved?"

"Because she's a good card?" Alice suggested hopefully.

"Well, I don't see much other choice," the Dodo conceded. "And we don't have the Hatter and his good sense to guide us. Since he lost his Nonsense, I mean; it really was a bit of a silver lining."

"Hatter…? Good sense…?" Alice said wonderingly. Imagine a world where the Mad Hatter was considered a reasonable and wise fellow! But perhaps in his own way he had a keener idea of what worked and didn't in Wonderland. "Dear old Dodo. Let us go find the Queen of Clubs, then."

"Dance, dance!" the Dodo suddenly cried, leaping up

and cavorting away without even looking back to see if she were coming.

"What! What are you doing? Have the guards found us?" Alice asked in fright, running after him.

But… it wasn't proper running.

It was *like* Alice was running, but at the same time it was all too sleepy and dreamy to be running. She watched the shape of her legs under her voluminous skirt with something like wonder: they pumped and moved the way they should have had she been actually running in fright, but so slowly… like she was moving through treacle.

She looked around and the landscape seemed to lean forward a bit, objects closer to her blurred as if they really wanted her to run, to be caught up in her tailwind, to finish the reality that her feet were suggesting.

And yet she hadn't moved an inch from her place.

"That's no good!" the Dodo scolded as he bowed and did a pirouette. *"DANCE!"*

"But we're not getting anywhere!" Alice complained. She risked a look behind her. A four and seven of hearts had just noticed the attempted escape and were reacting – very, very slowly.

The Dodo began flapping his left wing while clutching his chest with his right one. "Dance! Or we're done for!" he panted.

Well, running wasn't working and this was Wonderland, so why not dance?

Alice spun, feeling a little ridiculous, hand up as if an invisible partner were leading.

The Dodo's footsteps beat in time.

One, two, if I were you
I'd pick up bricks and put 'em in the mix
A chair, a doe, an isinglass bowl,
Dance the Hob to pay for the toll

Three, four, dance till you're sore
Waltz on nubs to the Queen of Clubs
A mile, a road, we won't be slowed
Until we get to the Queen's abode!

The Dodo was also spinning now, opposite her. She grabbed his wing tips and the two pirouetted along, faster and faster until the force of their spinning flung them apart and sent them tumbling down a hill.

Chapter Twenty

Alice was laughing like a little girl, feet flying overhead, rolling harmlessly through warm, soft grass. *This* was Wonderland at its finest. Dancing from danger and potential death and winding up enjoying a perfect summer day from childhood. She sat up and looked around: of course the White Rabbit's house was gone. The Dodo was carefully getting up and dusting himself off very punctiliously, picking prickly seed heads out of his jacket.

"Can't travel like I used to," he was mumbling to himself. "Age requires more first-class treatment. Carriage boys and service gnats."

"Are you all right?" Alice asked solicitously.

"Far better than our old companions, presumably," the

Dodo replied, for just a moment morose. Then he shook himself out, preened a couple of feathers into place on his neck, and straightened his shoulders. "Come, then! To the Queen of Clubs! It's a bit tricky from here on out, so be on your guard and careful we don't get separated."

Alice stepped cautiously into the grass and looked around. They were in a gently rising meadow at the end of a wide valley of some sort. Grey cliffs like bulwarks bounded either side of the view. Far ahead, dark strips of foliage could be seen weaving in and out of the mild hills. The occasional patch of trees might have hid monsters or jubjub birds, but nothing in the landscape seemed immediately threatening or dangerous.

"There's nothing to worry about here. There's no one around – it's safe as houses," she protested.

"But how safe are those?" the Dodo asked. "They burn down and get exploded by young ladies all the time."

Alice decided not to argue with this, especially since she had been a young lady who had in fact exploded one.

They walked up one hill and down the other side. Over here the grass was grainier and dark green. Just ahead was a beautiful prairie blanketed with little white flowers, which Alice bent down to smell.

"*Oy*, get yer nasty knows away from us," one of them shrieked. " 'Oo nose where it's been?"

"It's like they never been smelled themselves," another one said, sniffing. "If they 'ad, they would think twice about doin' it to others, they would."

"For shame!" a third cried, pulling a tiny bud safely away in its protective leaves. "Stinking away at such a wee one. You… *hussy*!"

"Right," Alice said, standing back up again. "I deserve that."

And so they kept walking.

This hill grew steeper and steeper until eventually it became the green skirt of a small, perfectly square tor – which Alice was fairly certain she hadn't seen before, and should have, considering all had been mellow and field-y with near infinite sight lines a few minutes ago. Just when the way became impossible and nearly sheer, a convenient set of steps appeared, carved into the cliff. Rocks jutted out at helpful locations for placing a hand for balance.

"Of course," Alice said. "How perfectly Wonderland. It always provides – just not in the way you expect."

She self-assuredly clambered up, remembering with ease the movements from a childhood of climbing trees.

At the top was a delightful alpine heath with short golden-green grass and scads of beautiful pink and purple flowers that Alice decided not to study more closely. *Even though* at second glance it became obvious that the glorious sunlight wasn't sparkling off their dew but the petals themselves: each blossom was a jewel, or maybe glass, and chimed gently in the wind.

The Dodo came up close behind her, huffing a little.

"Oh, you can practically see the Queen of Clubs' demesne from here," he said, pulling out a tiny telescope and looking through it the wrong way. He winced when the eyepiece touched the gash across his lid. "It's very tiny, but gets large enough once you're close. See it glitter?"

And there in the distance far below them, like a shiny beetle, was a blob of something black and unsuitable for the world they currently seemed to be in. Unnatural and man-made. The Queen of Clubs' castle!

Alice felt like skipping; maybe it was the air or the height (heights had never bothered her, and they still didn't). She was giddily happy as they walked along what turned out to be a plateau and not a single mountain after all. A little stream trickled out of some decoratively set boulders. Beside it was an old worn sign with bright gold letters that said YOU MAY DRINK ME, IF YOU PLEASE.

"Oh, I do wish we had brought a picnic," Alice said, kneeling down to take a sip.

"You didn't—" the Dodo began.

The ground gave way and Alice tumbled, far less pleasantly this time.

She banged back and forth in what seemed to be an open-topped tunnel. It was hard and cold and so slick and slippery that she couldn't slow herself down despite the hexagonal tiles that tessellated its brown-and-yellow surface. The grooves in between them were too slight and shallow to dig her fingernails in.

She kept falling.

She tried making her whole body stiff and using friction to slow her descent; that resulted in a skinned elbow and her dress tearing apart at the knees.

She hit the bottom with a *thump*.

A tiny cluster of white flowers inches from her face glared at her dubiously as she lay still (in much pain) for a moment.

Thump!

The Dodo landed right beside her.

"Alice! We were doing so well!" he scolded. "And then you had to go and bungle it."

"*Bungle* it? Bungle *what*? What did I do?" she cried, attempting to rise. She ached all over.

She tipped her head back to see where they had come from. The thing she had slid down on was… well… a slide. A brown-and-yellow one that snaked back and forth up the side of the hill to the top with the stream.

"You took the spring's water. You just *drank* and didn't

say please, naughty girl. What kind of leader and saviour are you, anyway?"

"I'm not… But I've never had to say please before!" Alice cried. "This is Wonderland – everyone does just precisely as he, she, or it *pleases*. Without even a modicum of polite and civilised behaviour. The sign said Drink Me, so I drank!"

"No, it said You May Drink Me, If You Please. *Very* proper and polite. You are *here* now, in the vicinity of the Clubs," the Dodo said primly, taking out a pince-nez and polishing it with a thumbfeather. "Rules are rules. And the Queen of Clubs has quite a few of them keeping her safe from the rest of the land. All the border areas around her castle are strict about that sort of thing."

"All right, I can sort of understand that," Alice said thoughtfully. The Queen of Clubs was sounding more and more like a reasonable, normal person every moment. Like Mrs Yao.

She peered closely at the slide they had come down. Through some trick of her eyes or the hypnotic pattern of the tiles, instead of looking hollowed out it suddenly became the very opposite: curvy and full.

The end of it, or rather the head, pulled itself up and hissed at Alice, baring two fangs and a large forked tongue.

"Oh!" Alice said, falling back in fear at the green slit

eyes. But the head did no more than weave back and forth as the rest of the creature stayed glued to the side of the hill.

"A giant snake! What in heavens… *OH!* I understand now!"

She stood up and looked around, carefully inspecting the miniature dell they were now in. There were neat squares of darker grass ahead and to either side of them. On their left was a tree with steps hammered in a spiral up around it, leading to somewhere above the treetops.

"It's a giant game of Snakes and Ladders!" she cried.

"Well, of course it is," the Dodo said simply. "Now will you kindly follow my lead, since you apparently do not have a real enough understanding of the game – or good enough breeding – to proceed properly? If you were actually familiar with Snakes and Ladders, you would remember that traits like Frivolity and Greediness slide you back spaces, sometimes quite a bit. Habits like Kindness and Pity advance you. Your Impolite Behaviour before nearly sent us back to the beginning."

Alice was outraged. First of all, she was an absolute master of games of all sorts in her household. She had been playing this one almost since before she could count.

On top of that, she was nothing *but* proper behaviour. She always said please and thank you and curtsied when she was trying to think of what to say. One could complain about her lack of respect for social convention when it came to her camera, friends or her occasionally mannish walking habits, but in conversation at a polite dinner party she had few equals.

"I beg your pardon! Do you remember the caucus races? And… the tea party? I was polite while everyone else was *extraordinarily* rude!"

"There is a Time and Place for everything," the Dodo said. "And Time is winding down. We could wait for him here, to wrap everything up, or we could proceed to the Queen of Clubs and save whoever is left of our friends. Being Quarrelsome, you know, slides you back five spaces. And so does having too much Pride."

Chastened, Alice flushed – and deservedly so.

"You are quite correct. I am most sorry, Dodo. Please lead the way."

"Take whichever way you like," the Dodo said magnanimously. "Take two if you so desire. It's what you do with them where I shall set the example. You see – Generosity. We should be advancing quite soon enough."

Alice curtsied – *very politely*. "After you, Mr Dodo."

"Thank you kindly, Miss Alice," he said, also

curtsying, which was strange. His tail feathers flipped up and his legs sort of squatted to the side.

Alice decided not to say anything about it. She wondered if *Tact* was an approved – and useful – trait in this game.

Chapter Twenty-One

As it is assumed that the reader has more than passing knowledge of Alice's previous adventures, we can cut to the chase a bit – because otherwise you would be doing nothing at all this chapter except for watching a rather slow game being played by a young woman and an old bird.

They avoided a square in whose centre was a bright pile of all sorts of fancy treasure heaped up on a glass table: crowns and coronets and sceptres and rings and other gaudy trash. But Covetousness was not the way to win the game.

Alice asked the Dodo to forgive her for setting them back several spaces and apologised profusely for it, and so they climbed a rapidly appearing, oddly lonely set of steps (for Penitence) that seemed to lead to nowhere but actually put them on the other side of a fast-moving and deep creek impossible to cross any other way.

She vaguely remembered another stream of water like it – or maybe it was a river – that she had rowed down once and nearly fallen into.

Alice bit her lip at the reminder of her other life. Of course she had to save an entire world here, but she had emergencies waiting for her when she returned to Angleland as well. What precisely they were she couldn't quite remember. Something about children and tea and windows and…

"Catch it over here," a voice said behind her.

She spun around: the Cheshire Cat was on his back in the grass, playing with a daisy. Literally, of course: one claw was patty-caking with the leaves of the young bud.

"What am I to catch?" Alice asked politely.

"Your mind. It wandered off the game board entirely. That's dangerous in Wonderland, you know." He flowed up into a sitting position and the stripes on his tail moved a bit, winking on and off. Alice put out a hand to stroke him; his fur was warm from the sun. How long had he been there – or anywhere, really – watching her?

The Dodo was distracted, muttering to himself, investigating what lay beyond the border of their current square on the sides adjacent to the river.

"I was thinking about how it seems like I have *two* worlds to worry about now," Alice said with a sigh. "A real one and this one. I can't help thinking about the mess I left back home – children taken into custody..."

"Are the ones being thrown in the Queen of Hearts' dungeon and plundered of their toys any less real than your little ragamuffins?" the cat asked, as lazily as ever.

"Well, don't you suddenly become clear as crystal when something ticks you off!" Alice snapped, withdrawing her hand from the cat and putting it on her hip. "Perhaps I misspoke, but I have spent all my life in that other world and only been in this one a few times. And this world... it vanishes or fades from my memory over there, like it's a dream and not real at all."

"Only *this* one disappears?" the cat asked, his hind legs walking up a flight of invisible stairs and then falling down over its edge and down his face. "Tell me about your other... your 'real' world. What is the name of your aunt?"

"Hatshepsut," Alice said promptly. "Auntie Hatshepsut."

She frowned.

The cat waited patiently.

"No, that's not right, is it?" she said with a sigh.

"And what is it that so upset you about your sister?"

"Why, it's her magpie, of course. It's always a bother,

always in my personal things, a real nuisance, carrying her voice…"

Alice *kept* talking, hoping some sense would come out eventually. But it grew worse and worse as she spoke.

The Cheshire Cat said nothing, for once behaving like an English cat, staring at her with large, unblinking eyes as she realised the truth for herself.

"It's like the real—I mean, *my* world erases Nonsense from my memories… things that shouldn't just fade away… But Wonderland replaces real—ah—*my* world's things with Nonsense."

"Very deep," the Cheshire Cat said. He curled himself round, forming a perfect circle with his body. Through it was a well, dark and endless. Alice leaned over and peeped in but couldn't see the bottom. The cat stretched and walked down the tiny spiral steps along its walls (on his own body!) until finally his hind feet followed. "Very… deep… indeed…" his voice echoed back.

Suddenly his face popped out of the sky, upside down, inches from her own.

"One wonders *why* you go back and forth. Why you bring what little you carry from one world over to the other. And what that thing is, and how useful it might be."

"I have no idea what you're talking about," Alice said, shaking her head. "Not a single word this time. And it's not even a riddle."

"A riddle, you say?" the cat said, suddenly frozen in delight. "But I simply *love* riddles. I'd run many a mile to tell a puzzling tale to a receptive soul. But *you're* running *away*, from Time, and the White Rabbit is running *to* him. And the Queen of Hearts bakes her tarts out of the tears of children. While you're off looking for unreliable help, he's sent you, oh, some friends to play with…"

"Unreliable help? What do you mean? The Queen of Clubs is our only hope!"

"When has Wonderland ever been about anything besides Alice?" the Cheshire Cat asked, but not accusingly or sadly. It was more like a statement. "For Alice, I mean."

"I beg your pardon – I am not thinking of myself at all here. *Others* have suggested that I must lead armies against the Queen of Hearts – which really is ridiculous. I know my limitations, and I am not a queen myself – *or* a Mary Ann, apparently. But I am doing my best to help out in any way I can – which is not that much, I admit! But what do you mean the White Rabbit is running to Time? And what friends did he send? To play *what* with us? A greater game? A – meta game?"

But the Cheshire Cat had faded from view, and all she was left with were two slitted black pupils that fell with a tinkle to the ground like stones once the rest of the cat was entirely gone.

"You and your stupid riddles!" Alice said, disgusted. Although he hadn't actually told her one this time.

But *wasn't* there another riddle? A real one, that she had to answer? One that someone had told her she must answer? Soon?

"I think we should proceed, with haste, Miss Alice," the Dodo said, hurrying back to her. "The next squares are clear. No sense lollygagging."

"Are there other players?" Alice asked. A question she realised that she should have posed at the beginning of this particular adventure. No games were played alone except for Solitaire.

"Of course!"

"And where are they?"

"I don't know – around, I suppose," the Dodo said vaguely.

"Aren't we playing *against* someone? What do we win? What do they win? What is the point? Who gets to the Queen of Clubs first gains her support, or the like?"

"Perhaps?" the Dodo responded, a little desperately. "This isn't the area of my expertise, dear girl. I know about

Tortoises and Impeachments. Do let us go, perhaps before we find out the hard way – as losers of the game."

A fair point. Alice picked up her skirts and strode quickly alongside him.

Things were quiet for a few more boring squares – no Snakes *or* Ladders to contend with. On the fifth square she finally saw someone else on the board.

Some*thing* else, actually.

Several some*things.*

At first it just looked like a scene directly out of a picture book on nature: a herd of strange deer cavorting in the field ahead of them. They were beautiful when they leapt, glittering like glass or fragments of something shattering in slow motion. But once they were back on the ground, their running seemed awkward and disjointed. Despite the fact that they had a formidable lead on the Dodo and Alice, she found herself wincing whenever one of them tottered and seemed about to fall. Finally one did, and it had a very hard time picking itself back up again. It rolled and stuck out its long legs and rocked and…

"They haven't any knees!" Alice realised. That was why they looked so unreal and graceful in the air and terrible on the ground.

"What don't? Who? *Oh!*" The Dodo put up a pair of opera glasses (again, the wrong way round) and then shrieked, dropping them. "*Bonetalopes! Run!* Have they seen us?"

"They have now," Alice said dryly.

The delicate creatures turned their long ears towards the two. They pawed their tiny, sharp hooves into the ground and lowered their graceful necks so that a dozen pairs of terrifyingly metallic horns were all aimed at Alice and her friend. Then they cantered awkwardly into a menacing arrow formation with a leader in the front. He (or she) emitted a strange noise – like the honk of a horn but also the call of a bull, with a little bit of a mockingbird trill at the end.

The creatures charged.

Alice shrieked.

The bonetalopes suddenly fell back, snorting in frustration. They had hit the border of their square and could go no farther.

"Whew," the Dodo said, pulling a – still clean! – white handkerchief out of his pocket and wiping his forehead. "We're safe!"

"That's what the Cheshire meant! These are emissaries of the White Rabbit sent to stop us. But they are playing by the rules," Alice said slowly. "They can only go forward."

"Well, that's a relief, then," the Dodo said.

"Yes, as long as we stay here. But we have to *win*."

Her mind began to race – just as it did when she was

playing against her sister or a male companion at any sort of strategy game. It was as if dozens of little Alices broke off from the main Alice of her mind and went running around in all directions, looking for an answer or a way out. Twenty heads were better than one.

"Sometimes," she reminded herself, "you have to dance when you need to get somewhere." Or do the thing that didn't seem to make the most sense.

"Look!" she said aloud, pointing. "If we go up a square we can Quarrel, and then slide down that snake over there." She pointed, grabbing the Dodo's arm.

"But that's preposterous. My dear girl, we can't go *back*..."

"No, do you see? Two squares up from there is *Pity*, whose ladder takes us one square ahead of the, ah, bonetalopes."

"Lose on purpose – go *backwards* so we can go forward? I suppose it will work," the Dodo said dubiously, looking the wrong way through his glasses again.

"Come on!" Alice cried. "Let's do try it!"

This felt right and Wonderlandy, and she nearly skipped with eagerness to test her theory.

The Dodo, however, being a bird – even an ancient one – was, like all birds, not overfond of snakes or serpents. The idea of *purposefully* mounting one to slide down its awful, scaly back was almost inconceivable. He pulled an old colander out of one of his pockets and put it over his head to blind himself.

"Coo coo," he said echoingly from inside.

They stepped into the next square, wing in hand.

"Oh, I'm sick of it!" Alice declared, trying to figure out a good Quarrel. "All of your… talking! And Nonsense! And… setting me up with young gentlemen I don't at all desire to have a conversation with, much less marry!"

"Eh, what?" the Dodo asked from inside his colander.

"Stay out of my life, you ridiculous thing! Imperious sister! Keep to your own banal little life, with your ridiculous views on what is and isn't right. Get married to that big wooden block of a sheep and leave the rest of us out of your idea of what a perfect Angleland should be like!"

"I beg your pardon," the Dodo said, echoingly, yet with some dignity. "I don't really care a huffle's ruffles about your Angleland, and I do not take kindly to your tone, Miss Alice…"

"Choose a side, you ridiculous bird! You don't even know my sister or her magpie, but you know *me*! I cannot believe you would defend her! Impudent avian!"

The poor, mostly extinct bird was having a difficult time indeed with his end of the made-up row.

"Er… *you*!" the Dodo tried, thinking hard. "Then!

Go take a… long walk… off a, let me see, very short couch! Yes!"

"*Go stuff it!*" Alice cried, grinning.

And so the snake, with a dull, confused look in its large golden eyes, tossed them into the air and onto its back, and the two went sliding down back a number of squares.

They landed with a double *thump*, right next to each other this time. And, having been prepared for the slide down, Alice wasn't injured at all and managed to leap directly up again.

After rising, the Dodo put his colander away with specific movements and affronted dignity. "Well, I'm not surprised that your sister wants to rein you in a bit. You do seem like a bit of a Monster."

The square they were in was greener and moister and cooler than the ones around it. Little trees and bushes cast some much-needed shade on the otherwise open landscape of the game.

"Oh, a tea rose, most excellent," the Dodo said, delightedly taking in their surroundings. "Just what we need."

Alice was about to admonish him for his nonsense, but of course the tea rose had fat buds that, when closed, made perfect teacups, complete with steaming, delicious-smelling tea within. Actually, a nice cuppa didn't sound too bad right then.

"All right, on to the next square, and Pity," Alice declared.

"Why is it a pity?" the Dodo asked, a little dumbly.

"No, it's the 'Pity' *square*. We have to get ahead now."

"I already have a head," the Dodo squawked, outraged. "You were the one who seemed to let your mind drift back there. And you've lost your mind completely if you think the ground is pitty; seems like it's fairly flat and even to me."

"Never mind," Alice muttered. *"Nonsense."*

They stepped to the next square, where a beautiful, swaying ladder as light as mist rose into the air just out of their reach. Its other end dangled languorously on a moss-covered stone just beyond the bonetalopes.

Alice closed her eyes and summoned the faces of the spectaclesbird and mirrorbird taken away by the policebirds.

"I Pity the poor children, snatched from the Circle, to who knows where."

"I Pity your sister," the Dodo muttered. "Your temper is formidable."

The ladder unrolled slowly and deliciously into Alice's outstretched hands. The frustrated bonetalopes whickered and whinnied in frustration a square behind them. They really were beautiful in their own fragile, clumsy way.

But Alice still had to resist putting a thumb to her nose and waggling her fingers at them.

As she climbed onto the next square, she saw a funny white cloud hovering directly above them. One didn't have to look very closely to see its strong resemblance to a rabbit, and of course it was all fluffy and white. As the winds blew it, a paw seemed to drift to a fob and pull out a watch – and did the cloud wink at her? A younger Alice would have been delighted. An older Alice watched it uneasily and wondered what the Cheshire Cat meant when he said the Rabbit was running towards Time.

Just then a little spiral snout poked its head over a stump, and sparkling black eyes regarded Alice unblinkingly.

"Hello!" she said to it. "I'm very much afraid I don't have time to talk, but…"

A second curlicue snout popped up.

"Toves," the Dodo observed. "Slithy ones, at that."

"Are they dangerous?" Alice asked.

A third snout popped up. The three creatures seemed to confer, somehow rubbing their corkscrew snouts along each other's without getting them tangled.

"Not when taken singly," the Dodo said thoughtfully.

A fourth and a fifth tove crept around the bottom of the stump. Their paws were a little too large and strong for Alice's liking, claws a little too curved. Much like a badger's.

Which, if Alice remembered correctly, was also relatively harmless when encountered singly, and as long as one didn't back it into a corner.

Now there were a dozen.

And they started creeping closer.

"Dodo," Alice said uncertainly.

Pinned to the fur on the breast of these beasts were tiny ruby-red hearts.

She grabbed the old bird's wing and ran, pulling him after her.

The toves brayed and launched themselves forward.

Alice felt a sudden pain in her ankle: she hadn't moved fast enough! One of the creatures had successfully connected with her flesh. She tumbled to the ground and the force of her fall knocked the horrible thing off – but not before she had felt it actually turning and squirming, trying to work its horrid, dangerously sharp snout farther into her skin.

With a moist-sounding snarl another leapt forward. Its claws raked furrows into Alice's side, slicing her clothes into a thousand tiny ribbons.

She scrambled up off the ground as best she could with the searing pain in her ankle. The toves hissed and lunged at her. The poor Dodo whimpered, surrounded by six toves lowering their heads and getting ready to drive their snouts into his belly.

Alice desperately felt around in her pocket for one of the biscuits she had taken from the White Rabbit's house. Swallowing it all at once without chewing was, of course, Mildly Impolite. A small snake slithered up and around her and the Dodo and pulled them down – right to the square with the bonetalopes.

"Out of the frying pan..." she moaned.

"How dare you even speak of such a thing! Some of my grandbirds were murdered in a hot skillet with crusty breading!" the Dodo shouted at her.

But the biscuit's effects were working their way through her system.

Alice looked around for something to do. The Queen of Clubs' castle was in view but far ahead of them: a beetle-shiny square of blackness nestled at the base of the distant mountains, behind a formidable river.

She reached over... *pulled.*

The game board stretched and distended like an India rubber ball. Alice's stomach felt like it was doing the same thing. Nevertheless, she hooked her thumbs into the best hold she could – the far riverbank – and heaved it mightily to herself.

"Come on! Run!" she told the Dodo.

"That's cheating!" the leader of the bonetalopes cried. She sounded and bugled, a fearsome beast with no fewer than six sharp knife-horns sprouting from her skull. The fierce thing lowered her head and galloped madly, nearly breaking her slender kneeless appendages in fury.

The Dodo leapt up onto the tongue of stretched land and ran down to the castle, getting immediately smaller like a trick drawing or an illusion.

A tove rammed itself into the meat of Alice's calf and began twisting around, working its spiral deeply in.

Alice screamed.

She had never experienced pain like this in all her life. She could *feel* the sharp and deadly tip moving through her flesh, cutting sinew and muscle.

The bonetalope leapt.

Alice let go and fell. The land snapped back away from her. She grasped desperately at the riverbank, but instead plummeted into cold, wet blackness.

Chapter Twenty-Two

Alice awoke.

A light breeze brushed her cheeks; it smelled dry and sweet. The bed she lay on was soft and giving in all the right places. A thick, clean linen sheet that had been draped over her body protected her just enough from the air to keep her warm without overheating. The light was unobtrusive. Nothing sounded of clangs, honks, shouts, horseshoes on cobbles, large wheels over ruts, the cries of deliverymen or women, or students getting their exams back. Nothing smelled of coal. Everything was peaceful and serene.

She awoke, but not in Angleland.

Alice's first real emotion that pushed through the blackness of recovering from collapse was *relief*.

The very last thing she had thought before passing out was how she was just going to wake up at home, yet again losing the immediacy of the dangers in Wonderland while being forced to deal with the problems in her own world.

(Only to return at a later time, perhaps, with things having gone from terrible to even worse.)

Alice's second emotion was… nothing.

Not joyous or sad or scared or angry. Just peaceful.

There was no one else in the room and she could, for the first time in a long time, just pause and think and *be.*

She pondered what would have happened if she had died in Wonderland. Would her spirit be trapped – freed – there? *Here?* Would she die in the real world? Was there a God and Heaven for Wonderland? Was He as full of Nonsense as His creations? Would she never have to return home to boring reality and stodgy sisters and flowers that stayed firmly silent…

… and young men with rosy cheeks…?

Could she remain forever in a world where your words were constantly twisted? Where nothing and no one behaved properly? Where it was all Nonsense all the time, whether you liked it or not?

"I should like a world in between, I think," she murmured to herself, finally stirring a little. "Fancies and whimsies who don't quite know their place, but don't try to kill you, either. They remain delightful or annoying but small and easily dealt with. And same with the real world. Small problems and some sort of consistency.

"No, that sounds more like a wish for an end to all problems than a real world for living in. Very lazy of you, Alice. How about… large, eventually solvable problems in a world with rules that may not make sense, but at least stay consistent? And with friends and creatures and places that are occasionally prone to Nonsense?"

She sighed and sat up. Her hair had come completely undone and fell a little lankly around her shoulders. Her dress was gone but her underclothes remained. With only a little bit of aching, she managed to push herself up into a sitting position, resting her back against a positively enormous pile of pillows.

She wasn't in a proper room at all but more of an open space symbolically delineated by airy stone arches that dipped from the ceiling almost to the floor – but then broke off suddenly as if they had grown bored by the whole process. Beyond the arches on one side was an outer wall with giant (strangely indefensible) open windows. On the other side of the bed, wide corridors – or perhaps other connecting rooms – continued onto infinity, with interior walls angling in and out here and there.

Everything was pale grey stone, vaguely pearlescent, like a shell Alice might pick up by the sea and spend several long moments gazing at before deciding to keep or toss. The inside of a purple mussel, perhaps, fascinating in its silveriness that might have been the beginning of a gem – or just a stain from the mud in which it lived.

All of which made her question: had she won the game? Was she in the Queen of Clubs' castle? Because it didn't look very black, as it had from the outside…

Alice's worries were somewhat relieved when a giant stoat, black as night (including her pinafore and apron and little nurse's hat) came quietly padding in on hind legs. Her neck was curled and crooked so she could carefully watch and balance the items on the shiny black tray she carried: a little black cordial bottle that said, of course, DRINK ME in silver curlicue letters, a glittering obsidian cup, and a black digestive biscuit that Alice at once decided she wouldn't put anywhere near her mouth no matter what it said on it. It looked eminently inedible and very disagreeable.

"How's the patient? Took quite a nasty fall there," the thing rasped in a voice far more deep and masculine than Alice would have expected.

"I'm right as rain. I feel marvellous," Alice said, obviously stretching the truth, quick to block any suggestions to the contrary.

But a shooting pain up her leg caused her to wince despite her best efforts.

The nurse carefully set the contents of the tray down on a little bedside table Alice was fairly certain had not been there before. Then she gently pulled the sheet off Alice's lower half. Her left calf, where the tove had pushed its snout fairly far into her muscle, was bandaged tightly and redolent of some sweet-smelling salve. But the flesh pulsed and throbbed with an almost unbearable magnitude when she pointed her toe or moved it at all.

"Toves is difficult critters," the stoat clucked sympathetically. "They pick up all sorts of nasty things from livin' under sundials – poisons and bad humours. Your leg is infected. We cleaned it out best we could, but not sure we got all the charms and nasty beasties out."

Alice was about to open her mouth to correct this outdated notion of science and medicine; thanks to Monsieur Pasteur, everyone knew that infection wasn't caused by magic or spirits or creatures of the usual kind. Merely tiny, microscopic…

And then a small blue thing, less a bug than a sort of star with too many legs, pulled itself up out of her bandage and looked around warily.

The stoat snapped out a paw faster than Alice could react (and anyway her reaction would mainly have been to scream in horror).

Triumphantly the nurse held up the thing and crushed it between her claws.

"Got 'em!"

Alice turned away, worried the nurse would pop it into her mouth.

But the stoat was far too professional for that and daintily put it back on the tray and covered it with a cloth.

"Most likely that'll be one of the last of them, don't you worry," she said soothingly. "Now drink your medicine."

Alice dutifully took the tiny – very heavy! – cordial glass after the nurse filled it to its rim with a thick, viscous black liquid. She was a little vexed at the amount and tossed it back as quickly as she could, uncertain whether to expect the nasty codfish-oil taste that came with real-world medicinal draughts – or the sort of complicated, delicious concoction that was the specialty of Wonderland.

It tasted of nothing.

Literally.

It was like… thick water. Sort of refreshing, but hard to swallow.

Immediately Alice felt a lovely warmth relaxing all the hard bits inside her, unknotting them, loosening the pain, unravelling the things that oughtn't have been tangled, burning out whatever evil creatures remained in her leg.

"Your wee might be a bit lavender for the next week. Pay it no mind," the stoat advised, and then padded away, her long tail bobbing in the air.

Alice, feeling much better, rose out of the bed that was so oddly placed in the middle of nowhere and saw more things that she hadn't noticed before – that probably hadn't even *been* there before. Most apparent was a dress hanging from the air that was obviously meant for her. It wasn't at all like her old dress; it was shorter and had what looked like wide trousers instead of a proper skirt. The sleeves went only three quarters of the way down and were finished in knitted ribbing rather than a proper cuff. The material was a very flattering herringbone grey that looked like it might sparkle a bit in the right light.

Over the right breast was pinned a glittering brooch: three black and sparkling clubs held tightly together. As from a deck of cards.

"So I did indeed make it, and this really *is* the Queen of Clubs' castle," Alice murmured, pleased and perhaps just a trifle bit smug. "I don't fancy wearing her sigil, though. We haven't treated yet – nor even talked. I can't go around wearing a queen's favour without knowing where she stands on certain issues."

She smiled at herself in gentle mockery as she spoke. On the one hand, she sounded like a little girl trying to seem as if she understood the world and politicians and all that occurred between them (as Mathilda's magpie did). On the other hand… she did, a bit. She knew about the nasty Ramses' party line and the coming mayoral elections and the problems with anti-Semitism.

(No, that wasn't quite right. But the feeling and basic thrust of it was.)

So maybe she wasn't an ambassador or spy, but she knew enough to ask: what was the Queen of Clubs' position on the Queen of Hearts' waging war on her own people, and would she help?

"Funny that," she said thoughtfully. "It's like what the Cheshire Cat said: I *do* carry a bit from the real world over here. Just enough sense or something to help me out. What do you call that? That little thing, that angle? That way of seeing something differently from someone else?"

Sighing at her funny memory in this funny world, Alice carefully unpinned the brooch and put it on the pillow on her bed, and only then donned the strange outfit.

She wandered the halls of the castle a little shocked by her own freedom. Certainly there were a number of strange courtiers and servants who gave her stern looks as she passed, but when questioned they directed her reluctantly to the Queen.

(The only ones who didn't respond at all were an ordered column of creatures that might have been nuns or anhingas; it was hard to tell. They walked with padded feet and bowed heads and crossed wing tips, wearing either headdresses or feathers.)

Club guards stood at attention outside certain 'rooms' or paraded in twos down the hallways – but did little more than give her a once-over.

The castle was also a little too free in its own architecture, Alice thought; she passed through rooms where private meetings between council members – and one assignation – were apparently going on.

Decorations looked careless and hastily done, although they all matched. Asymmetrical tapestries on the walls and rugs on the floor were black or grey. Tiny occasional tables up against the walls would have a single piece of grey or black bric-a-brac, sometimes a vase holding a flower that looked just-picked and often droopy.

Some of the windows that looked out onto the world outside shouldn't have, as they were on interior walls. Alice stopped by one and stood on her tiptoes to peep through. Clearly depicted like an early Renaissance painting was the entire board of Snakes and Ladders. The game spread out in the plains beyond the snug little valley where the castle sat, guarded by its silvery moat. Cards and other creatures were fixing the bank of the river that Alice had accidentally ripped out when trying to save herself and the Dodo. She felt bad about that, of course, but wondered at the richness of the loam thus exposed, and the bucolic nature of the scene. It was the thematic opposite of her coming upon the cards painting the roses red or the dying boxwood maze; these creatures were working together quietly to repair nature, and, for all it seemed, happily.

Alice hurried on and eventually found – well, if not the throne room, then at least the Queen's sitting room. For the Queen herself was there and sitting on an elegant, tall chair. The Dodo was also present, relaxing on a tufted couch with a cup of tea and an owl of state perched uneasily nearby, craning his head around on a long accordion neck. He kept the nearly-extinct bird fixed in his sight with large unblinking eyes. A little white dog chased both its own tail and a shiny black ball on a grey shag rug. A low table was set with all manner of nibbles and treats – though none of them was sweet. More of the black biscuits, some bright orange cheese and finger sandwiches that were black with bloody-red filling of some sort. Nothing looked appealing in the slightest, though it made a pretty picture. The Dodo, Alice noticed, wasn't actually sipping his tea.

"Your Majesty," Alice said, dipping into a low curtsy.

The Queen turned an elegant head slowly to look at her.

She was tall, very tall, as tall as the Queen of Hearts had been short. She was serene, reposed and had eyes that were black all the way to the edges – no whites at all. Her cheekbones were high and sharp as a stylised statue's and her hair was black and shiny and intricately swept into rounds and balls around a headpiece of similar construction, so it was hard to say where one began and the other ended. A long, draping golden veil hung from her crown over her shoulders and down her back. The rest of her dress was a familiar mix of checks, six-pointed stars and club insignias in dark blue, black and gold.

"More like the real card," Alice thought.

"Alice! So glad you're well!" the Dodo cried. "Bit of a close call there!"

Alice stuck out her leg – the bandage and wound were utterly revealed by the scandalously short dress thing. The pain wasn't too unbearable. She wondered what would happen when the black drink wore off.

The Dodo went pale upon seeing the scope of the damage.

Even the owl hooted, unable to help himself.

"Congratulations on winning the game," the Queen said formally, bowing her head a little bit. "You'll want a prize, of course. Here."

She nodded, and a thing that looked part hedgehog,

part jay shuffled forward with a small wooden chest, which it opened with great ceremony. Inside was a strangely familiar pile of gaudy junk, though not, obviously, really junk: there were giant sparkling jewels hung on golden cords, bangles covered in silver bells, teeny tiny diamond crowns on hair clips and all sorts of chunky, tacky dinner rings.

Alice selected a pretty little wristwatch whose large dial had pearls marking the numbers. It was the most tasteful thing of the lot, and anyway Alice had always wanted a wristwatch. It would leave her hands free for her camera while she was timing exposures and the like.

"Thank you, Your Majesty."

"I chose a tie pin." The Dodo preened, showing a golden stick that had NUMBER ONE WINNER engraved on it with diamond stars like fireworks all around.

"You risked life and limb to come and see Ourself," the Queen said in a resonant, deep voice. "Almost no one tries the game, much less wins it, these days. Especially after that nasty little rabbit let all those nasty, dangerous creatures into it. Very curious – normally toves don't attack people so immediately and so viciously."

"Yes, but my leg would tend to disagree with that," Alice said with a wan smile.

"Really? What do you have to say for yourself?" the Queen demanded of Alice's leg with interest.

For a moment Alice was terrified her leg was going to answer back. She didn't know what she would do if that happened.

"I think both I and my leg are most grateful for the ministrations of your servants," she answered quickly with another curtsy.

The Queen seemed to like that, sniffing a little.

"We – I mean, my leg, the Dodo and I – have come here to beg Your Majesty to help an ailing people..." Alice began, clearing her throat.

"Oh, we weren't expecting that," the Queen said, a little nonplussed. She patted herself all over and found a single coin – golden, shaped like a club – and tossed it at Alice. "You don't seem like a beggar."

"No, Your Majesty, if you please." Alice curtsied again, but honestly couldn't keep her eye off the curious golden coin. It was very shiny and intriguing. "I've come to ask for your aid against the Queen of Hearts."

The Queen of Clubs' eyes widened at that. Then she laughed. She shook up and down, stiffly, like an old man in a corset pretending to find a joke funny. "Why do you need our aid against her? We have *been* against her, with all our clubs and soul, since the beginning of Time. We have played War against her over and over."

"And who wins?" Alice asked politely.

"Sometimes we do, sometimes she does. More often ourself," the Queen said, perhaps lying. She looked a little sly. "I grew tired of it. It's boring."

"Some say it's not a proper game at all," the Dodo put in, trying to be part of the conversation. "Because the cards are random, but set at the beginning of the game, and there is no actual choice or any additional random elements during play – you just flip cards and the outcome is predetermined..."

"Don't be absurd," the owl cooed.

The Queen held up her hand impatiently. "We have no time for Nonsense right now, Dodo. We sense this girl has urgent matters on her mind. Now, have we answered your question?"

"I beg your pardon?" Alice said, blinking.

"We have told you: we are always *against* the Queen of Hearts. Is that all you wanted to know?"

"Ah—no, Your Majesty," Alice said, dropping into yet another curtsy while she thought, confused. "I was wondering if you would be—ah, *actively* against her. As in, help her subjects overthrow her."

"Help her subjects overthrow their *queen*?" the Queen of Clubs demanded. Her mouth went square, or maybe trapezoidal, her upper lip dipping down and the corners pulled taut and outward in disgust.

Alice could see how that idea might seem a little controversial, at least in another queen's eyes.

"Your Majesty, she is out of control, executing and murdering and locking up and torturing her own people, many of them for seemingly no reason. And taking all their toys," she added. She still felt it sounded foolish, but the Dodo nodded seriously and the owl let out a low whistle of shock.

The Queen's face froze as if it was on its way to another expression but she had forced it, by will, to stop.

"Taking… all… their toys, you say," she said slowly.

"Yes. But also ravaging the countryside and executing people and—"

"They are… *her* subjects. She may rule as she wilt." But even with her formal, toneless voice, Alice could tell she wasn't convinced by her own words.

"Do you know Mary Ann?" Alice tried.

"Of course. Who doesn't?" the Queen said, rolling her eyes. Probably. It was hard to tell without any whites.

"The Queen of Hearts had her killed, after torturing her first. I think—I think she blinded her, or ripped her eyes out, or something of the like." Alice trembled as she spoke, picturing the photograph.

The Queen went pale – perhaps. Her skin didn't change colour but gave the impression of changing somehow.

"Mary Ann?" she whispered. "The White Rabbit's – the *Rabbit's* – girl?"

"Yes, and it's horrible. But I've seen similar things done to people you might not have heard of. Children and lizards and most of the Hatter's tea party. The Hatter lost an eye to one of her jubjub birds. She's killing and maiming everyone who wants to stop her from taking all the, um, toys."

The Queen tapped the armrests of her chair with long and pointed black fingernails.

"And it doesn't even make any sense – or Nonsense, either," Alice said, more to herself or the world than the Queen. "I don't know what she expects to gain from any of it."

"Why, she wants to win, of course," the Queen said in surprise. "The girl who has the most toys when she dies wins. At the end of it all, of course. Everybody knows that."

Alice thought about it.

"So she means to die? To what? Gather all the toys in the world and then…? At the end of all *what*, do you mean?"

"The End of Time, you silly girl. She is going to bring about the End of Time, and the End of Wonderland."

Chapter Twenty-Three

Alice had thought herself a sensible girl – outside Wonderland, of course – but for some reason she just couldn't make her normally logical, aphorism-stuffed mind chew through what the Queen of Clubs had just said.

"But—" Then Alice decided to shelve her follow-up question and move on to the next-most-obvious piece of information that seemed to be missing. "*What* does she win? If Time itself ends, if it's all over, if Wonderland itself is over and everyone – including herself – is gone, what is there left? To win?"

"She just *wins*. Everything. What can't you understand, girl?" the Queen huffed impatiently. "She is the *winner*. If she has the most toys. When we all die."

"Does she—does she then alone get to live through the End of Time?"

"It's the End of Time, you little fool," the Queen said, leaning forward to look her in the eye. "We don't know how Time works in *your* world, or what he works *at*—"

"Perhaps he's a druggist," the owl suggested.

"Perhaps a druggist." The Queen nodded. "Or a cobbler. But *here* the End of Time is what it sounds like. He – and everything – *ends*."

"But then," Alice said, reluctant to anger the Queen but unable to let the confusing issue drop, "if the Queen of Hearts… along with everything else… ends… what is the point of her winning anything?"

"Because she *wins*. Because she—Is there something wrong with this girl?" The Queen turned in desperation to the Dodo, who shrugged and gave a mild smile like the grandfather of a particularly dull but pretty granddaughter.

"All right, all right," Alice said hastily. She would just have to accept it; this was Wonderland, and their worldview was simply not her own. Winning was important even though you weren't around to enjoy any of your toys or acclaim or spoils. The End of Time was indeed the end of everything, but apparently not enough to whip immediate panic and terror into the hearts – or clubs – of the locals. That's just the way it was.

"So she wishes to acquire all the toys, or most of the toys, and then bring about the End of Time quickly so that she may be judged to be the winner," she said as slowly and clearly as she could.

"Finally the girl is making some sense," the Queen didn't really whisper to her owl. "It took an awfully long Time for her to do so, however."

Alice thought hard. She had won Snakes and Ladders; she could figure this out, too. Right?

Her 'plan' up until now had been to throw herself on the mercy of the Queen of Clubs – a feckless and rash thing, considering the general self-interest and irrationality of all the Wonderland natives. She needed something that had much more tooth, much more appeal to a Wonderland type.

"Do you think all the toys of all her subjects would be… enough… for her to feel comfortable about her chances of winning? Or might she decide it's not *quite* enough, and she should seek beyond her borders for other kingdoms' toys as well?"

The Queen of Clubs narrowed her eyes and looked thoughtful.

"Aha," Alice thought. "*That's* got her attention."

"We do not know. This is a thought normally only given to queens to consider because of its political ramifications.

From the likes of *you*, this sounds like a tactical question, child. As if you are looking for ways to draw Our Royal Self into Hearts' ridiculous folderol."

Alice was surprised at how quickly the Queen saw through her cunning and, yes, manipulative plan. The ruler of the Clubs was much cleverer than many a Wonderlandian.

"Well, yes; that's why I came here," Alice admitted, holding her hands out. "To seek help from you in any way I could. The Queen of Hearts is destroying her own kingdom, plundering it and killing and torturing and locking up her subjects without stopping. I *had* hoped you would help stop this travesty out of the goodness of your heart—"

"Our *WHAT*?" The Queen stood up on her little footrest, which made her taller still. She seemed a mile high, and a trick of the light caused her eyes to look depthless and terrifying.

"Your *clubs*, I mean, Your Majesty, forgive me!" Alice immediately jumped off the couch and curtsied as low as she could, bowing her head. Her golden hair fell around her shoulders and sparkled in the sunlight. Perhaps that nudged the Queen's judgment positively. "The goodness of your clubs, I meant to say."

"You are forgiven," the Queen said haughtily, and sat back down.

"... but even if you were unmoved by their terrible plight, perhaps you might choose to get involved to protect your own people and their, ah, toy resources."

Did that sound wise? Academic? Clever? Alice had a vision of herself and the Queen dividing up a globe while intently discussing the Doll Mines of Eastern Europe or the Toy Boat manufacturing centres of the Outer Hebrides.

"But of course," the Queen said, narrowing her eyes so dramatically to look down on Alice that they almost entirely closed. She smiled and said with warmth: "That is what a queen does: protects her subjects. Why do you think we put our castle here, at the end of a terrible game on one side and open to the Unlikely on the other?

"We are very much protected in this narrow valley. If the Queen of Hearts ever chose to turn her armies towards us and invade, she would have a hard time of it indeed.

"Our toys are safe."

The Dodo was blinking long, feathery eyelashes at Alice, obviously still keeping all his faith in her but wondering what to do next, where to go from here. His trust and loyalty were frighteningly endless. Alice steadied herself under his avian eye.

The Queen continued on blithely:

"We will not involve ourself in the domestic affairs or troubles of other queens. We have no proof of what she is doing, or if it is out of the normal way she reigns." She sniffed.

"Oh, you have evidence enough, I'd wager. I wager you have spies – knaves and the like – who keep you informed," the Dodo said unexpectedly. "If the Queen of Hearts keeps her eye on you, you most certainly do the reverse, and contrariwise," he added, sipping his tea a little too smugly through his long beak.

Then he coughed, ruining the effect, obviously having forgotten he hated the black stuff.

The Queen of Clubs darkened – really darkened, her skin going shiny and black like onyx. She glowered.

"*Please*, Your Majesty," Alice begged. "The Queen of Hearts is a monster – maiming, executing and torturing even those once loyal to her! *You* wouldn't do these things, would you?"

"No, but We are a good queen." More than a little self-congratulatory.

"To her own people," Alice thought angrily. Of course… if this were the real world and she were arguing with a real head of state of Europe, she could almost see some logic behind the Queen's thoughts, as backwards and uncaring as it might have seemed. The Queen of Clubs was indeed a 'good queen', but if she interfered in another queen's rule over her own people… what was to stop someone else from doing the same thing to her? What if a king thought that being made to wear little pins of clubs was malicious and cold-hearted, and invaded to 'save' these people? Because *he too* thought himself good?

Alice could argue about the plight of the Heartlanders until she was blue in the face, but Clubs here wouldn't do anything that might eventually jeopardise her own rule.

"Now, if her subjects actually rose up against her, *lots* of them, we mean," the Queen of Clubs said softly, "that would be a different matter altogether."

Alice blinked, slowly processing what she said with a mix of suspicion and intrigue.

"If a majority of people judge they are ruled by an evil queen, a vindictive, Heartless, cruel tyrant, and they have had enough, and they make that known – why, we would be more than happy to step in and lend them a hand. Perhaps even a flush or a straight."

The owl craned his head on his long accordion neck around in surprise at his mistress's words.

"We would do it out of the generosity of our own clubs," she continued serenely. "And only take as our fair reward in the end any toys our soldiers seized from the deposed despot."

Aha. *There* was the Wonderland angle. Alice strongly resisted rubbing her forehead in exhaustion. She wasn't sure it was a faux pas before royalty, but it seemed like the sort of thing that might be. She also tried not to sigh.

"So," she said instead, taking a broad, shallow breath, "if we can adequately demonstrate that the subjects of the Queen of Hearts are all – or mostly – resisting her efforts to mow them down and seize their property and bring about the End of Time and all of Wonderland, that they are ready to overthrow her themselves, then we may count on you for military assistance?"

"You may *count* on anyone you like," the Queen said generously. "Even our dog, if you wish, although there is only one of him, so it would be fairly short counting. We will commit troops. Pairs of troops, even."

Alice had no idea how to do what she had just proposed. From the savage and brutal drumming her friends had taken to their inability to organise for even the smallest, slightest operation, the task of organising a revolution seemed hopeless. But at least there was a chance now. She would take it.

"This is just the sort of thing Mary Ann would have been so good at," the Queen said a little sorrowfully. "She knew just what to say, and she knew everyone, and she knew what to say to everyone when she met him."

"Also, she knew the heart of the Rabbit," the owl agreed, bobbing his head up and down. "And all his plans. And therefore… all the Queen's plans."

"Yes, upon considering it, we are… unsurprised at the removal of Mary Ann by violent means," the Queen agreed. "It was very efficient of the Queen of Hearts, we will give her that. But we can't imagine it endeared her to the White Rabbit."

Why did their talking about Mary Ann *still* irritate Alice, even a little? The poor girl was dead, had died trying to save everyone. She deserved to be thought of as a hero, not an impossible ideal to live up to.

Alice was ashamed of her inner self, and promised Penitence later when she had time.

"I shall depart at once to rally the people," she said aloud, getting up to curtsy again. "How will you know when… enough people have decided to throw in together against the Queen of Hearts? Even with, ah, spies, they can't be everywhere at once."

"Take this."

The Queen nodded to her owl.

He heaved and coughed and coughed and heaved most terrifyingly. Alice looked over at the Dodo for confirmation that this was normal Wonderland business – owls coughing up fewmets or pellets in public at the will of the Queen.

But the Dodo looked horrified and embarrassed and uncomfortable and started nodding his head back and forth as if he too were about to be sick, or were looking for a place to hide or excuse himself to.

Finally the owl reached a crescendo and leaned over. The Queen put out her hand. He promptly coughed into it a small and perfect ivory-coloured egg.

Alice blinked in surprise. Wasn't the owl a boy? But, and also, was that how eggs came in Wonderland? And…

The Queen smiled, satisfied, and turned the egg over with her long black fingernails. On its shell, raised just a bit, was a perfect set of black clubs. The Queen extended it to Alice, who took it with both hands as carefully as she could.

"Take this with you. Keep it safe at all times. Reveal the will of the people to it. If all is as you say, we shall come when it is expedient to do so, with our army."

The Queen stepped down from her chair. Somehow she was now wearing a thick black cape with a long train that extended out of the room. It appeared just in time for her to turn and have it elegantly and dramatically swirl out around her as she left.

"You will exit out the back door, of course," she said, not bothering to turn round. "The bonetalopes were following you to the front – and the snakes didn't get *all* of them."

"Thank you, Your Majesty, Yes, Your Majesty," Alice said, leaping up and curtsying, although she wasn't sure it was necessary since the Queen wasn't even looking. Even so, there was a pair of black cassowaries who now stood guard on either side of the door through which the Queen had exited, with rather mean looks in their eyes. So perhaps it was just as well, for form's sake.

An all-black mome rath with particularly large and heartbreaking eyes and a platter balanced on its head bumped into Alice's leg, obviously encouraging her to put her used tea things on it. She didn't have any, of course, because the tea and its accompaniments looked disgusting.

"Well, this is exciting," the Dodo said (pensively, not excited-sounding at all) as they followed the creature through the halls. "Actually, everything has been rather *too* exciting lately. This is less exciting than some of the previously exciting things. This is *more* than usually exciting but *less* than recently exciting. And less violent too, with any luck."

"What is?" Alice asked, trying to pay attention. But they were passing what looked like a miniature bakery crammed into one of the castle's strange room-alcoves, and tarts and cookies had been set out to cool on an open window that hung from the ceiling. She couldn't help sneaking a couple, just in case. The cookies were pink and sandy and said EAT ME on them in little nuts that might have been pecans, but she wasn't certain; Alice had never seen them before.

"… the Unlikely," the Dodo was saying. "I haven't been there since I was a fledgling."

"And what was it like?"

"It was *Unlike* anything else, you silly goose," the Dodo said, rolling his eyes. "The Queen is right – you *do* take a long time to get things through that head of yours."

This, of course, made Alice feel a bit glum. Especially since she had failed in the one task she had set herself once they had begged her to take over from Mary Ann: to secure help from the Queen of Clubs.

"Dodo, do you have any thoughts about how we are to go about this? I'm afraid we haven't had much luck with gathering the forces of good so far."

"You gathered the tea party," the Dodo said philosophically. "And brought us to the Grunderound. And you came back and rescued me. So there's two of us now."

"Oh, I really had thought to be able to turn the whole thing over to Mary Ann when we found her!" Alice said, trying not to whine. "I'm afraid the Queen of Clubs is quite right. I'm really not a very good saviour, in comparison to her."

Was she hoping for him to disagree? Just a little? She peeped out the corners of her eyes to see his reaction.

"Well, there's no one like Mary Ann," was all he said.

"There's no one *like* anyone else in Wonderland," Alice

muttered. "Not you, not Bill, not the Hatter—oh! That's what we'll do!" She clapped her hands. "We will talk to and rally all the Heartlanders we see along the way, of course, but *first* we shall find the Hatter! Assuming, of course, he made his escape and isn't… well, gone.

"Without his Nonsense he seems to have moments almost of clarity and purpose, and he certainly knows how to talk to all Wonderlandians."

Suddenly Alice was afraid she might have insulted the Dodo. Dear, kind, kind-of-ridiculous Dodo, who was loyal to the point of waiting on the enemy's very stoop for her to return. Who stayed by her side through Snakes and Ladders and the toves and meeting the Queen.

But he didn't appear to notice any undue compliments given to his friend, or rather, did not seem to be bothered by it.

The black mome rath indicated the end of a long corridor with a careless twitch of its leg and then scooted back the way they had come, bouncing off the walls back and forth as it (he?) went.

The ridiculously long hall narrowed down to a ridiculously tiny end, but of course by the time they made their way along it, everything had shifted and they stood at a giant blank wall in the middle of which was a drab, unremarkable little kitchen door. A giant sign above it said

EXIT, with an arrow indicating the door just in case the reader didn't quite get it.

"All right," Alice said, putting her hand on the – slightly greasy? – knob. It swung open, crookedly, like one of the hinges wasn't fastened properly. The light was so bright after the dark, cool halls of the Castle of Clubs that the Dodo blinked and squawked and Alice shaded her eyes.

They stepped outside.

Alice expected many things: a forest made of broccoli, a vast plain that dissolved into a hazy swamp, a brightly coloured and garish market town with blue onion domes and flying desk chairs. But what she saw instead was…

Home.

Her home.

Chapter Twenty-Four

"But… But… I don't understand!" Alice cried.

The house wasn't actually, but *seemed*, much larger than it should have been, taking up most of her frame of reference. There should have been other houses with lawns to either side of it but she couldn't see any, as if they weren't quite important enough to show. Everything was perfect and real down to the last detail, including the cracked keystone over the second window to the left of the library.

Except…

Alice frowned.

In the real world – or back home or whatever – the window with the cracked keystone was on the *right* side of the house if you were standing in front and looking at it. A quick ascertaining of other pertinent details further proved her sneaking suspicion: the house had been reversed. Her mother's little kitchen garden could be seen poking out the *left* side of this one.

"Astounding," Alice murmured. Someone else probably would have said *creepy* or *disquieting*, but this was Alice in Wonderland, and everything was amazing.

"Dodo, this is where I live!" she added with excitement.

"Of course," the Dodo said offhandedly, straightening his cuffs. "Very Unlikely it should be here at all."

"Right," Alice said. "I know we're on a mission to unite the Heartlanders, but I would love just a peek inside. I could show you my room!"

The Dodo shrugged. He seemed neither interested nor anxious to go on. Then again, she remembered from her first visit that in Wonderland all things had a habit of leading to the same place. Avoiding her house or going into her house might not have any effect at all on defeating the Queen of Hearts.

Alice practically skipped up to the front door, which tried to sidle out of her grasp once or twice before reluctantly letting her in. It seemed to be just peevish, though, not really set on keeping her out.

"Oh, look!" she cried. "Everything's the same... but different!"

At first glance it appeared to be exactly like her real home (in reverse). Beyond the symmetry, however, all other details were slightly askew. Portraits on the wall were occasionally empty of people, as if their subjects had grown bored and wandered off. Many of the smaller inanimate objects – like her mother's favourite vase and a blown-glass sweet dish – had little faces and personalities. Alice tried to see what the sweets were in Wonderland; in the real world she had eaten all the good ones, and only the liquorice were left. But the dish scuttled away from her. It made little tsking sounds that were almost too high-pitched to hear, and that was really the most vexing thing.

"I'm not a child any more," Alice protested. "I can have as many sweets as I want!"

"Seems like you don't keep your place in very good order," the Dodo chastised. "You should really reprimand it more. Spare the rod, spoil the house, as they say."

"I should do," Alice agreed.

The pianoforte was asleep and its keys unsettlingly warm. The wax fruit in the basket laughed and dissolved under her touch. The fancy carpet slowly revealed scene after scene of distant meadows, other places.

"If the rug at home were really like that, I should never leave the living room!" Alice declared, fascinated. How much her childhood would have changed with the magic views. She might not have done anything else at all.

The downstairs fireplace was unlit and Alice had the distinct feeling that the hearth was yawning every time she turned away. And the…

She suddenly turned back to the fireplace, realising something else was amiss, even for a Reversed, Wonderland House.

There was the little broom for sweeping the cinders, there the scary black iron poker she had not been allowed to touch when she was little. But in place of the little shovel normally used to lift out the coals was a dark green shovelbird. It stood very still and held its shovel-beak downwards the way the real shovel would have pointed. Its dull orange legs were held tight together to imitate the handle and it seemed to suck in its breath to make itself skinnier and more normal-shovel-like.

There was a scratch across its breast and right eye and a bandage just above its right knee.

Alice felt her heart melt.

"Oh, what is it about the eyes?" she asked the Dodo sadly. "The Hatter, your own injury, and this poor fellow here. What does it mean? The Queen of Hearts always seems to be trying to take out your eyes. Why?"

"Why *could* be next, I suppose," the Dodo said

thoughtfully, scratching the healing wound on his own brow. "That makes sense. Eyes, Wise, and then she'll go back round and do the Ays, Ease, Owes and Yous, too."

Alice shook her head disgustedly and turned her attention to the (other) bird.

"Hello. I won't hurt you," she said gently, not holding her hand out for fear of scaring it further.

The shovelbird opened one eye and regarded her blankly.

"Come on, come on," Alice cooed. She reached – slowly – into the pocket of her new outfit and pulled out one of the biscuits from the Castle of Clubs. "Here you go. This is my house, and I'm not going to hurt you."

Slowly the bird took awkward and bobbling steps around the other fireplace tools, untangling itself efficiently if not gracefully. It came to within about a foot of Alice and regarded her for a moment – then shot out its shovel-beak and scooped the biscuit out of her hand, neatly and expertly prying it out of her fingers with its pointed tip. It threw the treat up in the air and let it fall precisely down its throat and into its stomach. Alice could see the shape of the biscuit as it travelled down the inside of its scrawny neck.

"Very good. Mostly. Come with us! The Queen of Clubs has told us that if we stand up for ourselves, en masse, against the Queen of Hearts, she will come to our aid and help overthrow her!"

This was Alice's first rousing speech to get Wonderlandians on her side.

It was not, she reflected, very good.

The creature looked at her sideways, then began to peck at the ground, looking for missed crumbs.

"All right. I suppose you still have no real reason to trust me," Alice sighed. "Well, when we depart I shall still endeavour to take you with me, rather than leaving you here, hiding amongst the ashes. Although… isn't it funny…" She bit her lip, remembering. "When I was… very little… I used to wonder what it would be like to hide there myself. I imagined Father mistaking me for the poker and picking me up by the head and poking at the logs with my legs… I must have been very small to imagine that, if I could have fit there. Mrs Anderbee and my nurse were always scolding me to get away from the fire.

"I wonder if there are any more refugees hiding here, in places where *I* used to hide! Dodo, I'll look in the kitchen, you in the pantry. No—let's make it the other way round. I used to tuck away in the pantry myself and pretend the pies were boats that would take me away to Puddingland."

"There is already a Puddingland," the Dodo pointed

out. "Or wait – it's Puddinglane. Or maybe Penny Lane. In my eyes and all that…"

"Pudding is in your eyes?" Alice asked.

"Better than pennies," the Dodo answered sagely. "That would mean I was dead."

"Too true." She patted him solicitously. "We wouldn't want that. Come now!"

The copper pots and pans in the kitchen had obviously been gossiping or engaged in some other inappropriate activity, because the moment the two walked in they immediately flew apart from their tight little crowd and tried to rehang themselves on the proper hooks, banging and making a noise so thunderous that Alice had to cover her ears.

Actually, on second glance they seemed to *enjoy* the noise they were making, and didn't look like they were trying to sort themselves out at all.

"Stop that at once!" Alice cried.

This only made them bang and clang even more loudly. Now tinny laughter and minuscule jeers were added to the clamour. One saucier actually paused long enough to stick his thumb to his handle and waggle his fingers provocatively at her.

"Stop it right now!" Alice ordered. She popped a biscuit in her mouth and opened her hands, surrounding the pans

– at least visually – and then brought her hands together until they almost touched.

The pots and pans and lids shrank, of course, their wails getting higher and higher pitched as they almost disappeared. Alice waited a moment, then opened her hands again. They grew and screamed at her.

She clapped her hands all the way closed.

She waited a moment.

Then she opened them, slowly, and this time the cookware was silent and looked thoroughly chastised.

"*Thank* you," Alice said, a little shortly. Somewhat hangdog, they made their way back to the rack and hung themselves up in the proper position. "I have no issue at all with you socialising – it's your behaviour while you did so that was unseemly."

"Quite right, too," the Dodo said. "Keeping an orderly house is the first tenet of civilisation. Oh, I found these, hiding in the stockpot."

Huddling in the palm of his wing was a family of mice with ribbons for tails and buttons for eyes and pocket-handkerchief corners for ears. They were calico and shivering miserably.

"Are you fleeing the Heart soldiers?" Alice asked, trying not to squeal with delight. One of the smaller ones, probably a baby of some sort, held up a wee doll and shook it defiantly. The toy was no bigger than the nail of Alice's smallest finger and had what looked like poppy seeds sewn on for eyes. "Oh dear, she's going after toys as small as that?"

The mice nodded fiercely. One of the other children began to cry – presumably because her toy had already been lost to the Queen of Hearts. Reluctantly, her brother held out the doll for her to touch for comfort.

"This is madness," Alice swore.

"We're all mad here," the Dodo said a little sadly, obviously thinking of the Hatter.

"You know," Alice said gently to the crying mousekin, "I used to hide *my* doll – her name was Sophia – in the stockpot. We played hide-and-seek, and it was terribly hard pretending not to know where she was. I would try to make myself forget – because *Mathilda* wouldn't hide her. Ever. She was never up for any sort of game, except for charades with family and friends. What a wet blanket she is."

"That's unusual!" the Dodo said, intrigued. "I would have thought in a boring world like yours she would have been a girl, like you."

Alice decided to ignore that. It wasn't likely the Dodo would ever meet Mathilda, so she would never really have to explain it all anyway.

"Come with us, little mice," she offered, trying again.

"The Queen of Clubs has promised to help as long as we try to rebel against the Queen of Hearts ourselves. If she sees the entire country is aligned against the bad queen, she will come with troops and save us all."

The parent mice shook their heads and drew their children close.

"Well, please think about it. Here: not a bribe, just a parting gift." She pulled out one of her biscuits and broke it in half, handing over a piece. The adult mice grabbed it with tiny claws like pins.

As they turned away into the pantry, Alice frowned, thinking.

"Dodo, how are all these creatures escaping the Queen of Hearts making their way here? Wouldn't they have to go through Snakes and Ladders first and win it?"

"There are many different ways into the Unlikely." The Dodo shrugged. "But most are tiny."

"Succinct, and yet meaningless," Alice observed. "Oh, look – what a surprise. A mome rath in the pantry."

A bright pink-and-green one, its head tuft a darker pink. It stood out amongst the quietly murmuring pots of jam and old biscuits like a bright chintz-print curtain in the middle of an ancient wood. It did not belong there at all; for even the Wonderland version of her house had colours duller than the rest of the imaginary world.

This creature showed no hesitation at all and immediately threw itself into Alice's arms. It was a little shocking, and very furry, and exceptionally soft. She hugged it back, trying to ignore its rather oversized eyes.

"It's not a monster – it's just a terrified little thing," she told herself.

"There, there," she whispered aloud. Should she offer it a biscuit? Did it even have a mouth? Was it rude to offer a biscuit to something that didn't have a mouth? "I didn't only play pretend things in the pantry. I always ran there when I was—when I was sad, or scared. Or felt bad."

Her head swam for a moment with déjà vu. She suddenly felt that she was comforting a much younger Alice, and not a ridiculous little Wonderland creature. The room didn't spin, exactly, but she felt light-headed, like things were shifting behind her eyes, her brain resettling itself for a different reality.

"Dodo," she said quietly, putting a hand to her head. "We are still in Wonderland, are we not?"

"We are where we've been," the Dodo said kindly. "I've always been here. Still am."

"I'm not really *home*, at a different time, am I?" she asked, looking around. For when she didn't look *too* close, the bizarre differences weren't readily apparent, and the movement of normally inanimate objects out the corner of her eyes seemed more like the beginning of dizziness or a fainting spell. "I'm not in the past when I was a little girl – or in the future, when I'm wandering about the rooms, old and mad?"

"You might be old – I don't know how folks age where you're from – but you're certainly mad," the Dodo said soothingly.

"You don't think it's queer that in each place where I've had a memory of hiding – either an object or myself – we find another refugee of the Queen of Hearts?" She knelt down to look the Dodo dead in the eye. "*Specifically* in each place I remember, and nowhere else? As if… as if they either knew somehow it's where I hid and felt safe, or… they're all in my mind to begin with?"

The Dodo just blinked at her, and for a frosty moment all she saw were blank avian eyes.

"Dodo, please tell me! Are there mome raths in my head?" Alice pleaded. "Do I carry my Nonsense around with me everywhere? Even back in Angleland? Is that what the Cheshire meant? What does it all mean?"

"It means that, with all these good fellows we're finding, we have a great head start on telling everyone about the Great Hearts Uprising!" the Dodo said, patting the little mome rath on its head in a fond but ultimately patronising manner.

"But, but…" Alice fretted. "This is very perplexing. I

feel like I'm on the edge of a great precipice, or a sudden expansion of my range of knowledge. Where do I *go* when I am in Wonderland? Or is it just my mind, while my body stays at home – possibly asleep? Does any of it come back *with* me? Literally? Do the little mome raths and calico mice sneak a ride in my… mind house here? How is it I forget facts and figures and memories from the world I come from while here, and while I'm over there, Wonderland seems to drift away entirely? For when I'm over there, I almost entirely forget the importance of what is going on *here*."

"That," the Dodo said, "is tragic. That's like paying a painter with a squib instead of a penny."

Alice regarded him steadily. Here she was having an attack of existentialism and all she got was Nonsense.

The Dodo shrugged. "I'm a politician. Talk to a philosopher about these issues – you can usually find them scavenging in the rubbish bins. Talk to *me* about caucus races. But I shan't have any constituents at all if the Queen of Hearts takes their toys and murders them."

What world do I really belong to? was a question that flitted through the forefront of Alice's mind for only a tenth of the tick of a second hand on a fancy grandfather clock. It was actually irrelevant. Both worlds needed saving.

"I've forgotten what's really important. It's not what's

going on my head at all – it's real things happening to real people, in Wonderland *and* Angleland," she said, chastising herself. "I've entirely lost my perspective."

Suddenly she blinked.

"*Perspective!*" she cried aloud.

"No one is answering to that name," the Dodo said, looking around.

"No, listen!" she said excitedly.

"I have mine and you have yours
It's needed in a painting
But in the end none agree on
the meaning of the thing.

"The answer is *perspective*! It's a riddle my friend told me. I forget his name."

"And yet you remember the riddle," the Dodo observed.

"Why, that's true, isn't it?" Alice said slowly. "How can I remember that so clearly?"

"You must remember to tell it to the Cheshire when you see him again. He *loves* riddles. More than the Hatter, actually. Now, I think you were going to show me your room?"

"Quite right," Alice said distractedly. She felt the way she did sometimes when a conversation with someone had not gone quite the way it should, and even though she played and replayed the dialogue in her head later she couldn't figure out what had gone wrong, but still felt bad about it. She needed a good sulk or quiet sit by the window, possibly with a kitten.

Who had told her the riddle? He had said it was important. That he depended upon it, or something of the sort.

The weight of this and two worlds fell heavily upon her and her shoulders. So many people depended on her now!

But as she put one hand on the banister, suddenly she felt exactly the opposite.

Not knowing quite how it had begun, Alice found herself slowly floating up the stairs, drifting with purpose, one finger keeping her anchored to the railing.

"Of course," she said in wonder, as if she had only just rediscovered this method of taking the stairs – how could she have ever forgotten? "I must remember to do this when I get home – what a much better way for moving between floors! I'm surprised no one else has started the trend already."

The souvenir etchings of foreign places that hung on the wall animated themselves most pleasingly as she passed them by: a little sailboat in Venice made its way past Saint Mark's; crows circled the onion domes of St. Petersburg while banners snapped in the soundless wind. A salmon leapt and sparkled – in a sepia sort of way – out of a very detailed waterfall.

"I never noticed that before," she observed.

"Lovely, just lovely," the Dodo said, floating behind her. He had on a pair of reading glasses this time, but they balanced on his beak awkwardly, their arms extending the wrong way, out away from his face.

At the top of the stairs was a broom dog who apparently couldn't remain in hiding while there were messes to clean up. His long, whiskery beard and moustache, like those of a very healthy Scottie, made a sort of brush; sweeping his head back and forth allowed him to tidy together a neat little pile of dust (and if he missed something, the other brush, the tiny one at the end of his tail, jotted forward and finished it). Alice had seen one very much like this on her first trip to Wonderland, but that dog had been brown, and this was more ash coloured.

Some of his whiskers were bent and broken, but otherwise he seemed all right.

"Hallo there, good boy," Alice said, putting out her hand. Like most Wonderland creatures he was diffident at best; a shaggy ear rose up, leaving his bristles to sway back and forth below, but then he continued sweeping up. "I wish we had you round back home. Then Mrs Anderbee could have a rest and put her feet up now and then. Perhaps have a cup of tea while you did the parlour. I wonder who you are in Angleland."

As they approached the doorway to her own room, she saw that the shadows inside were slightly off. And though the house was a mishmash of memories and history, Alice immediately grew tense. Something was *wrong* in there. There was something extra. Something alive.

Waiting for her.

Alice took a deep breath and put her hand on what would have been the Dodo's shoulder had he been a human. He bobbed his head but said nothing.

She stepped over the threshold, the heel of her shoe making rather more noise on the wooden floor than she would have liked.

She expected cards to attack, she expected the executioner dog, she expected many things…

… but not the quivering lump just beyond the bed, which looked as though someone were doing a poor job of crouching down and hiding behind it.

"Ahem," Alice said, clearing her throat.

The lump rose and grew hesitantly, taking on the form of a rather… large…

Top hat…

Chapter Twenty-Five

"Hatter!" Alice cried.

The hat rose more, appearing to grow. A face appeared under it: cautious, framed by crazy hair and finished with a gaping wide mouth that revealed two large buckteeth. His one good eye blinked slowly. In place of the tiny top hat over his injured eye was half a pair of cinder goggles. The mica lens was dark, hiding whatever lay beneath.

"Hatter!" Alice cried again and threw herself over the bed in a most unladylike move. She wrapped her arms around him and squeezed.

"Alice…?" the Hatter said slowly and unsurely, a ghost of a smile beginning to form on his wide mouth.

"What what, Hatter old fellow," the Dodo said. "Good to see you're up and about."

The Hatter came out of his crouch – he had been hunkering down to protect a number of small beasts. Amongst them was a cat the size of an egg, several mome raths, a teakettle with legs and what was probably a dragon fly: a tiny lizard with outsized eyes and leathery wings, smoking a bit from its tail and mouth.

"Nearly wasn't. Up and about." The Hatter looked down at himself and patted his own shoulders and chest. "Nearly grabbed by those nasty cards. They knocked what remaining Nonsense I had right out me. I'm afraid they might have got the others… I haven't seen the Gryphon or Bill, though he *is* very small."

"Bill is fine. He escaped with help from the Rabbit's housekeeper," the Dodo told him.

"But… the Dormouse?" Alice asked hesitantly.

In answer to this the Hatter took off his hat. There on his bald pate slept the silly little thing, both his front paws in plaster and paper. The Hatter put his hat back on, as gentle as a mother.

"Oh, Hatter, I'm so relieved. What a terrible time it is," Alice sighed.

"He's a right ready misbegotten toethrower these days, pardon my language," the Hatter muttered. "I shan't be sending him a present at Christmas, I can tell you that."

"But what are you doing here? In my bedroom?"

"Where else would I be?" the Hatter asked curiously. "Safe as houses in your house. Safest in your room."

And if Alice didn't think too much about it, there was a certain sense to it.

"Of course," she said softly, squeezing his shoulder. "Of course you're here, in my – sanctum sanctorum. You always have been. You always will be. You're the Nonsense in my head that mustn't be ignored. You're the piece of me that maddens everyone, my sister the most."

The Hatter gave her a tired smile and said nothing – which might have been the wisest thing he ever said.

"Hatter, I've been to see the Queen of Clubs—"

"Why?" he asked, surprised.

"So we can form an alliance with her and defeat the Queen of Hearts."

"But they are always at War anyway," the Hatter said. "And they're both queens. Why would she help us? And what's to stop her from taking all the toys herself, and taking over Hearts if she invades?"

"Do you have a better idea?" How quickly her feelings had gone from relief at seeing him alive to frustration! "I'm *not* Mary Ann, and *I* don't have any better ideas."

"Does the Queen have all the toys yet? Or is she still gathering them?" the Dodo asked quickly, trying to change the subject.

"Funny you should ask that. We saw *cartloads* of toys being loaded up and hauled off on our way here. Apparently soldiers are going to every house and confiscating toys – and then burning the houses."

"It sounds like maybe she hasn't enough yet. So if she ends Time now, she may not be able to win," Alice said thoughtfully.

"Aha! That is what she is doing? Trying to be the one with the most toys in the end?" the Hatter said, nodding in realisation. "She already has lots. Scads. Mountains. But knowing her, she will probably make twice as certain that she has enough, and *then* send the White Rabbit to stop the Great Clock."

"That's very tactical of her," the Dodo said. "I always do that with my halves. When two and two is four, I always say eight, just to be twice as certain."

Alice ignored him. "Hatter, that was surprisingly logical and concise. Well done."

But he began to shiver. "I *told* you they knocked the Nonsense out of me. I'm not myself—no, don't follow up on that one, Dodo. It doesn't look good for me."

And to be sure, he did look a bit pale and wan around the edges. Hungry. *Tall.* Alice was fairly certain that neither sense nor nonsense was a necessity to living healthily in the real world, not in a meat-and-potatoes sort of way – but who knew here? Maybe it was bad for the soul to be lacking in it, and the flesh soon followed.

"Alice..." he began softly. "Why did you leave us? When we needed you most?"

"I didn't *want* to, Hatter!" Alice cried. "I wanted to stay and help you – I didn't know what to do! I was terrified but prepared to fight until the end. I had no idea at all that I would be whisked away back to my home. If I *made* it happen somehow, I am dreadfully sorry.

"The first time I left Wonderland I was so, so sad and missing home, and then I was attacked by the Queen of Hearts, and I woke up elsewhere, and I was *glad* to be home. For a while, anyway," she admitted. "But *this* time I had no desire to go home at all! Maybe home just yanked me back, somehow, sensing I was in danger."

"Hatter, old fellow," the Dodo said gently, "this stupid girl came into the Rabbit's own house to rescue me. Surrounded by cards and guards. She is not wanting in will or bravery."

"No, of course not," the Hatter said quickly, but his good eye never left her two blue ones, as if making sure she was still there. "Forgive me. I had supposed that with Mary Ann gone, you would naturally disappear as well."

"I am *not* Mary Ann," Alice growled, almost stomping her foot. "And she didn't *disappear* – she was *murdered.*

Please do not confuse the two. What happened to her was the direct result of an order by the Queen. Do not just chalk it up to the random happenings of Wonderland. And I came back and was nearly killed by a herd of rabid toves and almost lost a game of Snakes and Ladders while trying to get to the Queen of Clubs – which is the best way I thought of to save everyone. I realise my methods are more real-worldy than Wonderland's, but that's all I have to work with!"

"And if we win?" the Hatter asked unexpectedly.

"I beg your pardon?" Alice asked, still fuming but trying to calm down. Oh *why* did comparisons to the poor dead girl upset her so?

"If we win… will you stay?" It wasn't quite plaintive; it was genuinely curious. "Forever?"

Alice blinked.

"Why, I… I don't know, Hatter."

Things in Wonderland would be different if they won, and she was the reason. If it was anything like last time, they would probably make her a Queen of Something and maybe listen to her now and then.

But… what about the real world?

What about Mayor Ramses and the mome raths of the Circle?

And Mother and Father would miss her. Maybe her

sister, too, although perhaps she would be too busy trying to avoid the scandal of having a missing sister to really weep for little Alice.

And that boy… there was a *boy*, wasn't there?

And if she won there, in the real world?

If she saved the – whatevers, and defeated Mayor Ramses and… well… *somethinged* with the boy… she wouldn't think about that bit right now… would that be winning? Would it be enough that she would never want to return to Wonderland? What if they made her Queen of the World over there? Or even just the Americas? Would that be enough to occupy her ideas and banish thoughts of borogoves and bread-and-butterflies?

"Let's concentrate on defeating the Queen of Hearts right now," Alice said, a little too swiftly. "My personal future is far less important than stopping her from imprisoning and executing innocents, and then ending the world."

"Too true, too true," the Dodo cooed.

"The Queen of Clubs says she will help if there's a mass uprising against the Queen of Hearts. She must see that this is what the people really want. So we must convince the otherwise timid and skittish inhabitants of the realm to come together, face their fears, and resist rather than just running away and hiding – *as welcome as that idea might be*."

Alice addressed this last bit to an umbrella leaning casually up against the wardrobe, trying to look like an inanimate object rather than the vulture it really was.

The normally spooky, beaked head looked around at her in almost comical chagrin.

"Have you ever had a thought you couldn't catch?" the Hatter asked. "It just… skitters around the edges of your mind while you're having an argument with someone, and only later does it turn up and you say to yourself: *yes*, that is what I should have said? 'Where were you when I needed you most, you silly little thought?'"

He nodded, using his chin to point out the various hidden creatures around the room. It was the same as trying to catch the creatures of Wonderland and reason with them, was what he was trying to say.

"Well, until someone comes up with a better plan, this is all we have. We shall just have to try," Alice said firmly, pursing her lips. "And lead by example. Creatures? Wonderlandians? *Les enfants?*" She clapped her hands together the way she had seen foreign governesses do when taking a number of their charges to the park. "Attend me now. It is time to go."

A dozen different Wonderland natives stuck their large-eyed heads out of various hiding places. While Alice wasn't entirely surprised to see a mirrorbird step down off her dressing table (fancy and new and not from her real house) or a pencilbird sneak up off her tiny child's desk (got rid of years ago), the eighteen-footed raterpillar crawling out from under the bed was a bit of a shock. But the thing that looked a little bit like a garland and a little bit like a string of pom-poms that fluttered through the room on uncertain wings was most surprising of all. Alice was afraid it would tangle up in her hair somehow. It settled itself rather endearingly around the Dodo's shoulders, where he thoughtlessly adjusted it like a muffler and patted one of the yarn baubles on its body.

"Very fetching," Alice said approvingly. "Let us depart; it is time to leave the Unlikely."

And trying to project an aura of unquestionable, calm leadership – again, like a foreign governess – Alice left her room and floated down the stairs, not daring to look back to see if anyone followed.

Chapter Twenty-Six

She did, however, *hear* the Dodo and Hatter pattering down the stairs behind her; apparently they didn't float, or didn't choose to. And she very much hoped the soft susurrus and mushy cloth sounds that were just on the edge of her hearing were the rest of the small and assorted Wonderlandkind following.

"And what if I throw open the front door," she thought as she reached for the doorknob, "and we are immediately surrounded by Heart cards?"

When she did open it – at a speed somewhere between bravery and caution: too slow for real bravado but too fast to do any actual good should there have been a danger – there was nothing.

Well, not quite nothing. For one thing, the Queen of Clubs' castle was no longer in view. Perhaps it was behind the house now, or perhaps it or the house had hidden itself entirely elsewhere. Whatever the case, the grounds that now spread out below the house were soft and infinite. Rolling hills and friendly trees invited the viewer to walk, no, *run* into their embrace, propelled by half-recalled memories of childhood. The air that blew was sweet, somewhere between bedstraw and the sea. A tiny, jolly train rode over the crests of hills and disappeared, only to reappear again with white puffs of smoke that bubbled up to the sky in the shapes of fish, and whales, and miniature suns.

Alice was at first enthralled and then immediately suspicious.

None of her companions gave the view a second thought, but they all piled up around the doorway – behind her, of course – and looked out at it with their owlish eyes.

"Well," Alice said, trying to sound bright. "Here we go!"

The other not-quite-nothing revealed by the open door was a bright piece of fluff lying in the middle of the walkway, too slim to be the tuft of a buried mome rath. Alice went to pick it up, but it was far heavier than it looked and somehow *caught* – on the scene itself, it seemed.

"Excuse *me*!" a voice cried out in purple indignation.

"Oh!" Alice dropped the furry bit, but it stayed angrily where it was in the air.

And then, of course, the rest of the Cheshire Cat appeared, walking back and forth above the ground with the hauteur only a truly affronted cat could pull off.

"What are you doing out here?" Alice asked, scratching him on the back of his neck. He stretched to better enjoy it, the tip of his tail extending far beyond its supposedly natural limits, the space between the purple stripes increasing to a foot or more. Then it snapped back into a tight coil. "Why aren't you hiding inside with the others?"

"I haven't been invited in," the cat said with cool dignity, suddenly flipping on his back and wearing a top hat, spectacles and a gentleman's general appearance.

"Lovely hat, Cheshire," the Hatter said from behind Alice.

The cat rolled his eyes. "Of course *he's* here. Before she took off your head she would have to take off your hat, wouldn't she? And that would be difficult..."

The Hatter doffed his hat to reveal the Dormouse. The cat's eyes widened and he leapt at the poor sleeping thing with the yowl and frenzy of a real cat, glasses and hat forgotten.

The Hatter immediately clamped the hat back down on his head and held it there hard, over his ears. The Cheshire screeched to a halt in mid air, barely stopping in time to keep from colliding.

"Choose a side, cat," the Hatter growled.

"I dare say, Hatter old boy," the Dodo said, alarmed. "It's just a *little* bit of nonsense. How far gone are you? Ease off!"

"I choose *inside*," the cat said, opening his mouth wide and walking his tail and hind end into it until he entirely disappeared, having swallowed himself.

"No, on the contrary, outside is better." His voice came out of the air, sounding far away and hollow. He reappeared in the air before them, lying contentedly on his side.

Alice took a deep breath to steady herself.

"Cheshire Cat, can you help us? We need to drum up—no," she said hastily, "we need to *encourage* everyone to resist the Queen of Hearts on their own, and then the Queen of Clubs will help stop her."

"And the Queen of Diamonds shall dine on fine sums and the Queen of Spades will call for all ransoms," the Cheshire sang.

"I'm *serious*, cat," Alice said, frowning at the fact that she sounded like the Hatter. "People's lives are at stake."

"Mary Ann tried to rally them to a man, and now she is no more," the cat said thoughtfully, looking at his claws. "What makes you think you can do better than she?"

"I *know* I'm not Mary Ann! But I am trying my hardest! And besides, I bring… an outside *perspective* to the whole thing!" she surprised herself by saying.

"Here's a riddle, liddell Alice: then why are you trying to *be* Mary Ann? Why are you pursuing such a complicated plan?"

"Do you have a better idea?" Alice demanded.

"I don't. But I'm a cat, sweetheart." He twirled and flipped around and regarded her with lazy eyes. "Mary Ann and the Rabbit and the Rabbit and Mary Ann. There are always two. Me and…"

… he grinned and disappeared.

"Bother," Alice said, kicking the dirt he had been floating over. "He always makes me feel itchy and stupid. Come on, you lot. Which way do we go?"

Two of the mome raths, a big and a little one, toddled forward and threw themselves onto the ground, making an arrow.

"Fine," Alice hissed and tried to march with some dignity in that direction.

The landscape changed in just the sort of way Alice now expected; that is, she expected it to change unsettlingly but couldn't of course predict what it would change *into.* Somehow the summery hills faded and the little band entered a dark forest of positively enormous trees – far larger around than those in the Tulgey Wood. The ground rose in humps about their roots. It was so dark on the path that Alice couldn't clearly see what kinds of leaves or branches were overhead; pine, she thought, considering the cylindrical shape of some of the silhouettes she managed to make out. But there was no inkling of dark green or light green or any green at all: this was apparently an autumn forest where the tones were all brown and grey and black and shadow.

Sometimes the trees shivered.

And instead of muted bird calls and the riffling through leaves by small animals, there were strange, deep-throated mumblings and murmurings. Like a conversation you couldn't quite catch a word of, the sounds drifting maddeningly just at the edge of comprehension.

"Where are we?" Alice asked the Hatter and the Dodo. The smaller creatures followed them like a multicoloured parade with their own murmurs and snufflings, the broom dog bringing up the rear. It would have been very jolly indeed if the mood in the woods hadn't been so mysterious and grim.

"Still at the edge of the Unlikely, I suppose," the Dodo said, looking around.

"The Droozy Forest, I think," the Hatter said

mournfully. "Shan't make it out of here without a scratch, that's for certain."

At this the Dodo reached over with his big and seemingly buffoonish beak and raked it across the Hatter's left wrist. It left a ragged line of broken white skin and a few pricks of pink blood.

"What was that for?" the Hatter demanded in outrage.

"Now you have a scratch. Now we can leave," the Dodo said simply.

"I really don't know how much more of this I can take," Alice muttered. She was beginning to remember a much younger Alice weeping in the Tulgey Wood, tired of all the nonsense. Could she even *imagine* living here forever? Even if she were queen? Her penchant for nonsense was less than when she was a child, but more than the Hatter could endure right now, and far more than most adult Anglishmen and women would put up with. "I saw a train on the hills – could we take a train to Heartland?"

"Why would we take it there? It belongs here," the Dodo said pointedly.

"Is there a *station* around here?" she asked through gritted teeth.

"I believe so."

"Well, let's get out of these woods as fast as we can and find it," Alice decided. She doubled her speed and walked with her chin in the air, away from the mystery of the whispering trees.

A train; that was something reasonable. And civilised. How badly could Wonderland muck up something so real, so mechanical, so invented by humans?

She thought she saw the path lighten a little before them, as if it were opening up, just past the two argyle oaks. Maybe this was only a small wood, like in a park! Yes, a town park. Then the train station would be nearby, and…

… Argyle oaks?

Alice stopped. She took a look – a really *good* look – at the trees around her. They all stood in pairs, well matched. The swells at the bottom of each that she had thought were boulders or roots were dully shiny, black and brown. *And laced.*

The cones and cylinders that sheathed the fat trunks were wool, of course…

"mumble mumble Alice not a chance…"

"little upstart, mumble? *Cut her down to size…* sssssize… size… card cutter will…"

"Hallo!" Alice shouted, trying not to panic. "I can hear you! It's very rude to talk about someone who's *right below your nose*!"

"thinks she's so important… irrelevant as a hat on a tove…"

There was faraway grown-up laughter. A pair of stockinged feet in ladies' heels tapped a little up and down as if unable to conceal their mirth at whatever scornful thing was being said.

"I can't tell precisely what you're saying, but I know it's about me!" Alice continued. "And I know it's very impolite. What is that? About a cutter?"

The legs and feet, now that she recognised them as such, were very, very conventional. There wasn't a bright sock or Dormouse hidden amongst them. They were *very* real world.

A horrid thought occurred to Alice: did she actually know these people? She couldn't recognise them, of course, but then again she didn't spend much time admiring people's footwear. "Something I shall strive to correct in the future," she admonished herself.

Then conversations started up again, incomprehensible and quiet and casual, as if everyone was trying to talk over an embarrassing moment. As if *she* was an embarrassment to be quietly ignored by everyone. And hopefully removed.

"Hello! I'm real! I'm right here! Hello!" Alice waved, trying to maintain her anger but feeling queer, like she was fading from the inside out.

"Fancy sensible Alice, talking to the trees," the Dodo said, not unkindly. "Dear girl, the train station is up ahead."

"But—they're talking about me," Alice protested. "I heard them. Didn't you hear them? They were making fun. They said… I wasn't important. They were laughing, like I was a joke…"

"Of course they were, dear," the Dodo said soothingly. "Wind in the branches. Let us go, then. Have a butterscotch?"

He held up a tiny boiled sweet wrapped in paper. Unsure what else to do and feeling very blue, Alice took it.

"Is there any such thing as a card cutter here, Dodo? Is it like a dealer, or someone who just cuts a deck of cards, before a game?" she asked glumly.

"A dealer? Oh no, not at all. The Card Cutter is *terrifying*," the Hatter said, looking pale and serious. "Don't even mention his name! He'll smell it!"

And there, before them, was the station.

Chapter Twenty-Seven

The ticket booth was made of paper. Printed-page bricks, grey paste from old wet fish wrappings as mortar in between, the sign DROOZY STATION in rolled newspaper sections. The window had oiled paper to let light in, and the praying mantis who sat there wore a crisp white paper hat.

"Well, step up, step up," she snapped, but not unkindly. "Where's it to be, then?"

"Good afternoon," Alice said, a little distracted. "I'm sorry, I arrived here rather more suddenly than I expected."

"That's the National Railway for you!" the mantis crowed, which was strange, and then blew a little horn in triumph, which was also strange. "Now, will you be going first class or premium?"

"I don't know how much it is," Alice admitted. "How much is a one way, no return, to Heartland?"

The mantis blinked, which was hard, for she had no lashes – or eyelids, for that matter. "The Local-Nine to Heartland is not recommended, for reasons of bloody civil war. Try a different place instead. The park not too far from TulgVapCo station is lovely this time of year, I've heard tell."

"No, I'm afraid it's Heartland," Alice said, putting her hands in her pockets. "One ticket for me and all my..."

She turned, but no one stood there except the Hatter, who was now a slightly stooped, middle-aged, very plain Hatter – with a large hat, to be sure, and a prominent nose, but that was all.

"... and my friend here," she finished lamely.

"Perhaps they've gone ahead," she told herself. "Perhaps they're running to tell all their friends to pass the word along about the Queen of Clubs and how they should rise up against the Queen of Hearts!"

She felt a little sad without the colourful mome raths and the Dodo and the shovelbirds. It was scary to lead them but lonely without them.

"No sale," the mantis said briskly, and reached up to try to slam the oiled paper down.

Without thinking Alice reached up as well. Despite having shorter arms than the giant insect, she managed to grab the ends of the paper window first and rip it away from the ticket seller – to rip it out of the wall entirely, in fact.

"I'll have my ticket to Heartland, thank you very much!" she said, huffing a little. "And so will my friend!"

The mantis made a terrible hissing, clicking noise with her mandibles. Alice stood firm in the face of this terrifying display. She had held one once as a child, and though it was unsettling and surprising how strong the slender and fragile insect's legs were, it had neither bitten nor tried to.

The present mantis finally reached under her desk, ripped two tickets off a roll, and sulkily slammed them down in front of Alice. "No return indeed. I'm on my tea break now. Good day. And good *luck*."

"Charming lady," Alice murmured. She turned and handed her companion his ticket as if he were a child. "Don't lose this, now—or shall I keep it for you? Where did everyone go off to?"

"Away. To… rally everyone." The Hatter shrugged, putting his hands in his pockets and falling into step beside her. It seemed like the most natural thing in the world. Hair grew out of the insides of his ears. His striking half goggle had become a frayed-looking eye patch.

"Well, that's good! Just as I thought."

They wandered over to the single track that came out of

the hideous Droozy Forest. A heavy mist lay over the land now, so it was impossible to see the tops of the 'trees'. Alice hoped it turned to rain and soaked the trousers of whosever legs made the forest.

A train charged in, blasting smoke and screeching to a halt far more unpleasantly than the little choo choo she had seen far away on the hillside. Alice took the Hatter by his arm and made for first class, holding her head high and trying to look like she belonged. She didn't *not* belong, considering that all the other passengers waiting were, in order, a half-empty jam jar, a cow with very long horns, a pair of furred creatures that resembled ducks but for their manes and tails, a small gaggle of eggs with feet and a woman with a giant crab on her head.

Once she and her family had taken a leisurely boat trip to France and her father had sprung for chaises on the fashionable part of the deck. Alice had watched with amusement as her mother, somewhat surreptitiously, tried to adjust and tie her shawl around her hat the way the rather more glamorous (and younger) wealthy ladies just starting out on the Grand Tour did.

(Mathilda had also seen this and proceeded to lecture her own mother on the sin of vanity.)

Now Alice sort of wished she had a crab to put on her head as well.

They had a nice cosy little compartment to themselves. A kindly old walrus took their tickets and clucked when he saw their destination.

"Ahh, I wouldn't go there given the *choith*, mith. It ain't a thafe plathe for vithiting theeth dayth."

Alice supposed the tusks were why he lisped.

"Thank you," she said politely. "But we have unavoidable business there."

"Well, all hail the Queen of Heart-th," he said unemotionally. She noticed, as he waddled to leave, that amongst the black scrimshaw figures that decorated his tusks, a new and blood-red heart stood out. It made her uncomfortable.

Alice shivered and turned back to her companion. "Dear Hatter, are you feeling all right? It seems as though every last bit of nonsense has been just… drained from you."

"That's it, exactly." The Hatter nodded. "I've seen too much and none of it is funny. The Queen of Hearts has ruined the world, or me. You've got to stop her, Alice," he begged. "Please."

"I'm trying, dear Hatter. I'm *trying*." Alice put her hand on his.

Poor man! He was all dried up by the horrors of the reality he experienced. All that was left was sense, and it was aging him terribly.

Was this happening to all of Wonderland?

Was this the future of all its dreams and creatures? Was it too late, even if she prevented the End of Time? Saving the world was one thing. Fixing it was another.

"Here, I'll just go fetch us some tea from the dining car," Alice said, trying to put worry and panic aside. "And maybe a biscuit or two. That should do us worlds of good."

The Hatter nodded morosely and looked out the window.

"Perhaps I can find him a talking tart, or something else," Alice thought as she gracefully wended her way down the swaying aisle into the next car. "The next thing that says Eat Me or Drink Me I'll give *him* instead of taking myself."

She passed all manner of passengers and then the smoking carriage, which was, literally, smoking. Closed, impenetrable and grey windows showed nothing of the world outside; and its occupants were betrayed only by a scaly tail or tentacle snaking out the bottom of the door. After that was a luggage carriage, which narrowed down considerably and which Alice had to turn sidewise to get through. It wasn't so bad in her new Land of Clubs outfit, but it was still a little tight. And then a man stepped out in front of her.

She didn't see him at first because he too was turned sideways; and card thin as he was, practically invisible even in his luxurious velvets and silk.

And ridiculous feather.

"Alice!" he purred, blocking her way forward and angling himself so she was forced into a luggage area.

"Knave! You… disgusting *pig!*" Alice cried, spitting angry. She wished she *could* spit, like she had seen other people do. Of course Mathilda and Alice had not been raised that way at all and Alice was afraid it would come out all wrong if she tried it now.

"Actually, not a pig at all!" she then added, thinking of the toves. "They are at least honest about their alliances and loyalties and affections!"

"Why, Alice," the Knave said, and she honestly couldn't tell if his surprise was genuine or mocking. "Did I break your Heart?"

"You betrayed me and my friends and may have got some of them killed!"

"Oh, is that all," the Knave said, a little disappointed. "It's War, darling."

"It is *not* War!" Alice hissed. "It is an insane tyrant wreaking violence on her own people. And what *you* did was not an act of war – it was an act of cowardice. Going traitor and running to the Queen to reveal the location of the Grunderound condemned dozens of innocent victims without you having to risk yourself at all, or take a single shot yourself! You don't even have the honest awfulness of a regular enlisted man ordered to shoot. You had a choice, and you hid behind the Queen's skirts when the real violence occurred!"

Perhaps the Knave flushed, perhaps he went pale: it was hard to tell behind the shiny finish of the card.

"I'm sure the innocent will be let go," he mumbled.

"Mary Ann was executed, the Hatter was *almost* executed—"

"*They* were enemies of the state! They broke the law. They conspired to overthrow the Queen."

"A mad queen. An *unfit* queen! A queen who was locking everyone up and torturing them and seizing their property and killing everyone! An insane tyrant!"

"The law is the law, Alice," the Knave said with a smile. "The Queen is the queen. Even in your world there is a queen who rules."

"*My* queen would never attack her own people, or try to bring about the end of the world."

"So she fancies herself a *good* queen, eh? To… *everyone*, really?"

Alice regarded him frostily. "Victoria would never take toys from babes. And what about this whole business about the Queen *winning*? I have heard that once she has enough toys, she will bring about the End of Time and therefore the end of the world, and *that* is how she wins. Are you really in favour of that?"

The Knave gave her a brilliant smile. "I'm but a knave, with no power or say in these things: the pursuits and glories of queens and kings. The game of thrones. Whatever happens, I intend to stay on top until the end."

"What a pleasant philosophy. It allows you to feel no guilt and just float along with whatever those in charge decide, leaving you free from thought or duty beyond the next moment."

The Knave sighed. "What are you even *doing* going back into Heartland?" he asked wearily. "It is the exact wrong place for you to be – you made it out of there, you should *stay* out. There is a price on your head: a thousand tarts and a jack-in-the-box confiscated from one of the auntlions."

"How did you find me?" Alice countered. "Have you been following me?"

"Of *course* I've been following you!" he said, exasperated. His entire countenance of bravado and enthusiasm fell. He simply looked tired – like everyone in Wonderland now. "Initially we thought you were dead, or trampled, or otherwise gone forever after the raid on the Grunderound. When it was obvious you had somehow escaped, the Queen had me find and follow you."

"You couldn't have followed where I had escaped to," Alice said. "You cannot go to Angleland."

"*Some* can. And do."

A narrow panel of window that lit the dark luggage area

flashed with the changing scenes outside, at one point showing an orchard whose fruits were all shiny black letters sparkling in the sun. Alice had a single glimpse of a pleased-looking rabbit, a brown one, holding up an *E* and getting ready to take a bite.

"But I cannot. I admit that road is closed to me," the Knave finally said. "Be that as it may, I picked up your trail as soon as you returned to our fair land. There is still a price on my own head, you know? The tarts. The stupid, stupid delicious tarts that I ate in the Forest of Forgetting. I am to repay my misdeed by serving the Queen in whatever way she wants."

"So what now?" Alice asked.

She made herself look in his eyes – his printed, black eyes.

"Now I turn you in," the Knave said – perhaps a little too flatly. Flat as a pressed card. Both were silent for a moment.

"Or maybe I rip you in two," Alice suggested. She had no idea if the new powers she had in Wonderland would work; she had no biscuits or drinks left. But her hands twitched, delicate fingers posed to grab card and *tear*.

"Or maybe you call for the Hatter," the Knave said. "Or maybe the conductor. Or, perhaps, you will simply push me out under the door…"

He wasn't mocking her this time; his eye slid to the thin space under the door from which the roaring sound of the wheels on the track came. He *would* fit.

He was… suggesting it.

"Why?" she asked softly.

He shrugged and smiled sadly.

"The next time I see you, I will have to take you in. Listen to me: do not return to Heartland. It will mean your death. The Queen is so furious about you and Mary Ann she would be likely to set everything aside just to hunt you down and punish you. There are those… unlike me… who do not have a paper heart. They have scissors to rend and cut and destroy."

Alice's eyes widened. Scissors to *cut*?

"You mean the Card Cutter? The Droozy Trees mentioned something about it… the Hatter was terrified!"

The Knave shook his head impatiently.

"Do it," he whispered. "Now or never!"

"Hatter…?" she called. *"Hatter!"*

Then she took the Knave by his side and carried him to the door like a piece of mail delivered to the wrong address, when one slips it back through the slot and out. *"Hatter!"*

The Hatter came rushing in just in time to see the Knave get sucked out the car and fly into the fields beyond, picked up by a fresh breeze, turning over and over into the blue sky until he disappeared.

He did *not* arrive in time to see the Knave give Alice a saucy little wave before he went, or the kiss he blew.

"Oh," the Hatter said, surprised but not crestfallen. He saw that Alice was unharmed and safe, and that was enough for him. He had no obvious machismo, nor any desire to be a hero if it was uncalled for. Only when it was needed. Alice rather appreciated that; it was so contrary to all the men and boys she had known (except for her cousin Cuthbert). "You're all right, then. Was that the Knave?"

"It was indeed," Alice said, breathing heavily from her exertions and – whatever else. The new outfit she wore had a much looser corset, which made the process easier and more pleasant, but she wondered about how good it was for supporting her back. "Either he was just information gathering, or there really is a price on my head. Or Mary Ann's head. I'm not sure the Queen can tell the difference – I'm not sure any of you can."

"Oh, that's not fair," the Hatter said reasonably.

"Let us do go get that tea," Alice decided, patting her trousers clean. "I have a feeling it may be a while before we have another chance."

Chapter Twenty-Eight

The long-faced gentleman behind the counter in the dining carriage regarded them gravely when Alice ordered two cream teas and a packet of sweets. She realised she hadn't even thought about payment – it was always somehow just handled in Wonderland – and the attendant definitely looked distrustful of the situation.

"What is your affiliation?" he asked carefully around his large teeth, avoiding any hint of a horsey accent. "You don't wear any indication."

"I wasn't aware one needed to when travelling by rail. What is *yours*?"

"The great National Rail, of course." He sniffed through wide nostrils. "It is beyond any *local*, geographic loyalty. I am a citizen of the world. Your tea, miss." He turned his back on her. Alice raised an eyebrow at the Hatter.

"Mind he doesn't introduce you to the biscuits," he whispered. "I know this breed."

"I had no idea Appaloosas were so rude," Alice murmured.

But the fellow didn't say another word, keeping whatever prejudice he had against the pair of travellers to himself while sliding over a tray of biscuits and scones along with a waxed bag of candies that seemed to be shuffling themselves in an attempt to get comfortable for the ride. EAT US was scrawled in clotted cream and underlined in jam – raspberry, it seemed – on the tray.

"Very posh," Alice said with admiration. "Eat up, Hatter old chum! With any luck these will have you feeling like your old self again."

They perched on the stools and she nibbled a scone while the Hatter literally threw everything else into his mouth. Alice just barely managed to keep back the bag of sweets but was delighted to see his maw did seem a little larger and out of proportion compared to a normal human man's. Perhaps he was going to be all right.

But then he took a little flask out of his pocket and carefully poured out a single shining silver drop into the steamy depths of his tea.

"Hatter!" Alice cried in dismay. "And before noon!

"I think," she added, unsure.

"It's all right. It's just mercury," he reassured her. "To feel like myself again."

"But that's poison!"

"Yes, so are arsenic and all the other things the ridiculous women of your world use to keep your complexion perfect," he said with a shrug. "I do this to keep my Madness intact."

"How do you know that? About arsenic and the women of my world?" Alice asked suspiciously. Of course she and Mathilda never did such things; between parents who thought they were perfectly beautiful as they were and simple level-headedness, the most they ever sneaked was (newly – for Mathilda, at least) rouged powder and simple cosmetics.

"Cheshire," the Hatter said with a shrug as if it were the most obvious thing in the world. "He has a friend over there."

Alice sipped her own undoctored tea and wondered.

"HEARTLAND," the walrus cried hours or minutes later, walking through and taking the ticket stubs off the back of the seats. "All idiot-th off to their violent fate."

Before Alice had time to look round and collect her things and then remember that she had no things to collect, the train was quite forgotten and she and the Hatter stood on a platform next to a higgledy-piggledy stack of dishware for a ticket house.

A nicely cobbled road led away from the station… bright red and sticky, dripping with blood.

"Alice," the Hatter said, looking faint.

Everything the road led to and past was crimson and wet: trees, walls, small churches, postboxes. Alice stepped forward – hesitantly – and knelt down to take a closer look. The Hatter clung to her side.

(Was he perhaps just a little shorter than before the tea? Ungrowing back to his old size? She couldn't be sure.)

"It's only paint," she said, trying to soothe him – but she leaned over to take a sniff, just to double-check. "She has covered absolutely everything in paint."

There were also signs posted *absolutely everywhere* along the road.

HEARTLAND

THE QUEEN OF HEARTS LAND

KEEP OUT UNLESS FEALTY SWORN

ALL TOYS CONFISCATED AT BORDER

TRAITORS WILL BE EXECUTED

UNDOCUMENTED TRAVELLERS WILL BE EXECUTED

EVERYONE WILL BE EXECUTED JUST TO BE SAFE

THE WINNINGEST QUEEN EVER

THIS WAY TO GREAT HEARTLAND

THAT WAY FOR LOSERS

HEARTS WILL WIN

"Well, one can't accuse her of being unsure of herself," Alice observed.

"We are going to walk down that road to our death, aren't we," the Hatter said morosely.

"Have a sweet," Alice suggested, holding out the bag and shaking it at him as she would at a small child or a dog. He grumpily took one and ate it and then smiled like a tot who had accidentally picked his favourite flavour.

Alice took the egg out of her pocket and, feeling a little ridiculous, held it up and 'showed' it everything, wondered if the Queen of Clubs could see somehow. "This is what is left of the land out here," she narrated as seriously as she could.

"Come on then, Hatter!" she added brightly, stepping carefully onto the road to not get paint on the sides of her shoes. "We're off to change hearts and minds. Remember that: hearts and minds."

"Please don't say that. Don't say *hearts*," the Hatter begged.

The area just beyond the train station was desolate and unpopulated, at least as of recently. Scattered across arid fields were the still-burning ruins of what once might have been farmhouses. The smoke that puffed up from these fires made heart shapes that would have been perfect for Valentine's Day had they not been so dreadfully black and oily, dripping down desultorily to their points.

The sun and moon met briefly in the sky and must have had some sort of argument; the moon retreated back the way it had come, even sulkier than before. The sun glowed stronger and more smugly after, and the day grew hot, and the paint on everything dulled and cracked.

"Brings a whole new meaning to 'watching paint dry', eh?" Alice asked, nudging the Hatter. "Get it? *This* time it is really quite fast."

"Might as well be as fast as a sliggerdoo," the Hatter said sadly. "Might as well be as slow as a Racing Lorikeet."

Alice didn't say anything, afraid of getting her hopes up. But his words were silly and he *had* seemed to shrink a little. And his hat might have been just a touch bigger than before.

The first inhabited hamlet they came to was a tiny farmstead. Only half of the orchards around seemed to have been set on fire, and these smouldered ineffectually anyway. The minuscule houses hunkered down and bowed out like animals against whatever attacked.

"Hello?" Alice called, turning off the main road and onto a dusty path that had been only splattered a bit rather than painted. The dust shrugged off the liquid, as expected; it beaded up and dried in ugly pots and divots.

"Hello?" she cried again. "It's Alice. I'm here to help. The… *recoveringly* Mad Hatter is here. Hello? We're not going to hurt you!"

Eventually these constant and vaguely soothing words produced some result: several very strange furry creatures dressed in farmers' overalls poked their heads out of doorways, holes and wells. They were sparklingly golden and almost perfectly round and didn't seem to have any eyes at all. Their large, adorable noses tested the air rapidly like rabbits'.

"GO AWAY!" one cried out, turning towards Alice, having apparently found her by scent or sound. "Leave us to mourn our family and farm in peace."

"There will be no peace for anyone," Alice called back reasonably. "There will *be* no more anyone. Once the Queen of Hearts has a significant pile of toys, she plans on bringing about the End of Time and ending the world."

One of the golden moles howled at this and clutched its baby – which was the tiniest, roundest, cutest thing Alice had ever laid eyes on, and despite the urgency of her mission, her fingers actually itched to hold it.

"No more no more no more," another one cried. "Bring the bandersnatches and dovercoots, but let it be over finally."

"She's speaking the truth," the Hatter said, raising his voice. "She's been to the Grunderound. She's had messages from Mary Ann. In a sense, she was *sent* by Mary Ann."

"Mary Ann?" one of the creatures said softly.

"I bring this," Alice said, pulling the egg out of her pocket. A dozen noses, some whose owners she couldn't even see the rest of, quested at and queried the air excitedly. She turned the club so it was facing them, though she had no idea if they could see it was there – or if they merely hungered for fresh egg. "We have an ally in the Queen of Clubs. If she sees that everyone is opposed to the Queen of Hearts, she will come with her armies and save us."

"And Mary Ann arranged all this?" a different mole – or perhaps one of the first ones, Alice honestly couldn't tell – asked hopefully.

"No, *I* did," Alice said through gritted teeth. "But… because Mary Ann summoned me."

The Golden Moles whispered to each other and conferred in a snuffling, whustly way.

"Mary Ann will bring the Queen of Clubs."

"Armies of cards will go to War and we shall be saved."

"We shall be saved and all our toys returned."

"And the End of Time shall *not* come earlier than usual!"

"We hear," a female mole spoke up. At least Alice assumed it was female; its voice was slightly higher and it had a bright blue kerchief knotted neatly around where its neck would have been had it not been such a delightfully round creature.

(Of course, this was Wonderland, and one shouldn't make assumptions.)

"And we feel. We will tell."

"We will tell! Mary Ann and the Bringers of Hope!"

And then, without another word, the creatures all went tail up – although they didn't actually have tails – and snuffled down into whatever earth was closest to them. Alice watched with alarm as their shapes pushed up dirt and zoomed just below the surface faster than she felt was strictly acceptable for underground speed without a pre-made tunnel. If they hadn't been so cute and furry in person they would have been terrifying.

"Just imagine if they travelled like that in Mother's garden and lawn back home," she murmured.

"That went well. I think," she added more loudly.

"In fact they *were* faster than sliggerdoos," the Hatter mused. "But don't expect everyone we meet to be so agreeable."

———

And of course no one else at all was like that, because no two people or groups of people in Wonderland were alike. The next thing they came to was a very tiny, very detailed castle, accurate down to all the loops and the garderobes. Alice walked around it grinning in delight, wishing she had something like it as a little girl. She could easily have crouched and hidden in the bailey – with a good book or two, or maybe a snack – and had her dolls man the battlements.

Comfortably tucked inside the walls were several toddlers armed to the teeth, one with a crown on her head that seemed to be made out of hawthorn switches and paste gems.

Alice tried to make her case as well as she could to such an audience but was cut off immediately.

"WE CAN DEFEND OURSELVES! BE OFF WITH YOU!" one baby – whose nappy dipped precipitously – shrieked.

"But you're just wee little bairns," Alice said, alarmed. "And I see there's a dolly over there in the corner, and a stuffed bear. The Hearts army will seize it all immediately."

"WE ARE PROOF AGAINST THE QUEEN OF HEARTS!" the queen baby screamed. "NO ONE SHALL CONQUER US WHILE THE DOOKIE TOWER STANDS!"

"The—oh, I see. But here, look." Alice brought out the egg, wondering if it was perhaps a bad idea: if the Queen of Clubs saw these obstreperous babies, perhaps she would assume that more Heartlanders wanted no rescuing. "The Queen of Clubs shall come and save us and protect us if only you will resist, in word if not deed, the Queen of Hearts' plan. You know she intends to destroy the world?"

"WE DO NOT RELY ON FOREIGN ARMIES," the little queen shrieked. "AND NEITHER SHOULD YOU IF YOU HAD ANY SENSE. SAVE YOURSELF, OR SAVE YOUR WORLD YOURSELF. OTHERS ARE FOR NAUGHT BUT CHANGING NAPPIES AND BUYING MILK."

"Well!" Alice said, putting her hands on her hips. "Aren't you a naughty bunch of babies!"

At this the quartet began to scream and cry and shriek louder and grow red in the face. Hurriedly Alice found a dummy in the eastern ramparts and stuck it into the queen's round, howling mouth. The baby shut up immediately but continued to glare at Alice with large, beautiful eyes.

"Told you," the Hatter said as they wandered away.

"Yes, but they were just babies," Alice said, unsure what she meant. "In any case, in fairy tales these things always go in threes, so at our next place we should get a real idea of how things are going to go."

She was silent for a moment as they walked, still brooding on the interaction.

"But really: 'Other people are for changing nappies.' How rude."

"Well, could you imagine a bunch of babies touting the benefits of self-reliance instead?" the Hatter asked. "At best it would be rather ironic, wouldn't you say?"

Alice honestly couldn't tell if that was Nonsense or sense. She was beginning to lose track.

Somewhat foolishly, Alice didn't question how they were able to move so freely down the main road – which was dotted with signs specifically to intimidate people like them – without their actually being hunted or captured. She was Alice. This was Wonderland. And though every place and every person here was different, they were all gifted with a singular lack of an attention span. Alice had no doubts that the Queen, having had the road painted red, had promptly forgotten it.

Instead her thoughts wandered. She wondered if Mary Ann had ever been on this very road before all the terrible things began. If she had, there was a chance that Alice's shoes actually trod in the other girl's footsteps! That was a strange thought. She shivered, imagining ghosts and ghostly tracks disappearing as she erased them with her own – presumably – same-sized feet.

An unexpected squeak came from inside the Hatter's hat. In response to the Dormouse's warning, the Hatter grabbed Alice and the three of them went tumbling off the side of the road together, rolling and imprinting themselves with the terrible paint as they did.

Alice was about to indignantly protest this rough treatment and the ruining of her Land of Clubs outfit (which she was really growing to like) until she saw the cards marching down the road towards them.

But it wasn't just cards this time; there were all sorts of nasty-looking creatures alongside: angular and spined, tall and scrappy, pustule-covered and bulbous – all wearing shiny ruby-red armour that glittered in the sun. One, in a giant helmet sized for his deformed head, sat on the shoulders of a large sad creature with long hair and short tusks. This ox or yeti pulled a caged cart that was full of toys – and several hapless victims as well, who tried to claw their way out of piles of doll arms and miniature trebuchets and lead soldiers.

The Hatter put a hand over Alice's mouth before she could cry out in shock and anger.

The Dormouse stayed awake long enough to lift up

the edge of Hatter's hat and give a low, sad whistle at the scene.

One of the rear card guards whipped round, having heard the sound.

The three friends froze.

Alice tried very hard not to close her eyes: if death or capture was coming, she would meet it head-on and ready.

It was difficult.

A long, long moment passed as the entourage moved on down the road, disappearing, and this one clever card stayed behind, searching back and forth across the road, using his spear to prod the bushes.

Seconds ticked by.

The card drew close to where they hid.

Finally he spat and spun round, marching after the rest of his comrades.

Alice and the Hatter shuddered in relief – but the Dormouse was already asleep again.

Chapter Twenty-Nine

After recovering for a bit the three continued on – but more carefully now, keeping to the edge of the road and remaining much warier. The way soon split, a smaller road leading off to the right. Of course the fork was marked with signs.

ORNITHSIVILLE THIS WAY – LOYALISTS ONLY!

TOYS THAT WAY

Each sign was stamped with the rabbit symbol, hastily and sloppily, so white ink ran down and mixed with the red paint on the wood. It made a rather pretty shade of pink, if you didn't pay attention to the meaning.

"All the way back round again," the Hatter murmured in wonder.

"Ornithsiville! Like from the Greek *ornitho*, meaning *bird*?" Alice cried. "Is that the village where we first saw everyone so craven and beholden to the White Rabbit?"

"Yes," the Hatter sighed, closing his eyes. "It would be madness to go back there, right into the hea—ah, *belly* of the sycophants and Queen loyalists."

"But that is precisely where we should go, to change people's minds," Alice pointed out. "If the Queen of Clubs saw that we rallied *those* cowardly birds, she would be sure to help us!"

"Of course an Alice would say that sort of thing," the Hatter muttered.

But she felt with all her being that this was the right decision, especially since her companion said it was Madness. And that was also what *he* needed right now, more than anything else. Didn't he seem to shrink just a smidgen further?

Also there was the matter of the egg. Nothing in Wonderland made any sense, so perhaps there was no real connection – but it was extremely curious that the Queen of Clubs had chosen to send Alice with an egg, and here she had wound up back in a village of birds.

"I suppose it could have been alligators," Alice murmured to herself. "Or crocodiles."

There was something different about *those* eggs, of course; and of course right now she couldn't remember what it was. Were they soft, unlike chicken eggs, or was it that they were inside out? Gooshy and yellow on the outside? They were opposite of birds' eggs *some*how…

They took the way to Ornithsiville and followed it assiduously, even when it curled around itself and spat them out only a foot over from where they had entered the roundabout.

(This was doubly odd because she was sure there had been no solid road into Ornithsiville when they had come through last time; it seemed to be just plopped in the middle of the country, like everything else in Wonderland.)

In the market a woman was arguing with a man, quietly and furiously, in cheeps and whistles, as he shook a piece of paper at her and raised a Rabbit-stamp threateningly. She had two mewling chicks at her feet. One was mostly human, the other as fuzzy and large-beaked a fledgling as there ever was.

"Here now, leave her alone," Alice said, moving forward and making shooing motions with her hands. The bureau-grackle hopped back. "Can't you see you are upsetting her children?"

"If the Rabbit knew she was hiding a ball along with some extra fine alfalfa sprouts, he would *come* for her children, and her, too!"

"Never mind that; I have an announcement to make that will change everything. Hatter, a hand?"

She went to climb up on the birdbath, but of course the Hatter paid no attention and just began clapping: enthusiastically at no one and nothing in particular.

"How droll," Alice muttered. She was glad to see his Nonsense coming back so strongly, but did it have to be when she needed him? Setting her boot carefully against the marble, she managed to hoist herself up and then balance on the edge with only minimal swaying.

"Good people of Ornithsiville! May I have your attention, please? Hello? Just a moment of your time, that's all I ask! Hi! Over by the fountain here! I have an announcement to make!"

Immediately the birds turned their bright eyes to the plaza centre and began to flock towards her. Monocles flashed in the light; top hats were removed so others might see.

"Oh, another bloody politician. I thought they had migrated already," a swallow groaned.

"I heard there is to be punch and pie afterwards," a grouse told him knowingly.

Someone set up a stand to distribute flyers and buttons; Alice couldn't make out the insignia or the slogans. Lemonade was served, which caused a bit of a row because there wound up being no pie at all.

A hundred or more birds were now facing Alice, scratching the ground, preening and impatiently waiting for her to begin. Although she was high up and out of their immediate reach, she couldn't help being a little flustered by their sharp eyes and sharper beaks. Not a crowd to stick around in should the mood turn ugly. Some of the cocks had truly formidable spurs.

"Ladybirds and game, and men," she called out, "the time of being afraid is over. The time of hiding your toys and paying ridiculous tribute to those in charge is over. The reign of the Queen of Hearts itself is over! If you want it.

"I come bearing great news: the Queen of Clubs will aid us with her forces and liberate—"

"… liberate us from cards of the Heart, and return all our toys – yes, we've heard all that already," a pinch-beaked goose squonked.

Alice blinked in astonishment.

"And *we* heard it from a Dodo," a short, bushy ground owl said with a great burr of an accent. "Much more reliable source than a human girl, I might add."

"Hatter!" Alice cried out in delight. "They've already been through here, spreading the word! All of our friends!"

"Didn't I say they had gone ahead?" he replied a little peevishly. "Back at the train station when you were bullying that poor mantis?"

"So you're with me? And against the Queen of Hearts?" Alice called out.

"We've been discussing the notion at our committee meetings. There's some question of the seriousness of the claim," a bird yelled back. "Some proof of the Queen of Clubs' intentions would be helpful. Mostly we're with the Dodo. And Mary Ann. Some of us, anyway. She is almost as good as a bird. You should hear her sing."

"But she's..." Alice didn't know what to do. This time it wasn't even irritation at the constant mention of Mary Ann. The poor girl was dead. Did she dare tell this crowd? Didn't they know already? Would this dampen their spirits?

"Mary Ann lives on," she said, neither telling the truth nor acknowledging the comment. "But you must work to bring about your own salvation. I know it's been hard having your, ah, toys confiscated, and watching your friends be imprisoned, sometimes tortured, sometimes killed. But no one – no Mary Ann – is going to leap in and save you if you don't try to save yourselves.

"Make your rebellion known and the Queen of Clubs will see and bring in her armies. She will fight the Queen of Hearts and win, freeing you all. But she needs to see you *want* to be liberated. She will not invade to take another queen's domain without recourse."

"Fie on *all* your queens," a brant spoke up, bobbing his head and trying not to squonk in the middle of his speech. "But if Mary Ann says we can save ourselves, we will do it. I've *seen* Mary Ann. Plain as that girl up there on the fountain. Actually, that girl looks ever so much like her, in fact. Never seen no Queen of Clubs. But if she speaks for Mary Ann, I know we're saved."

There were murmurs in the crowd, birds nodding and looking towards Alice and commenting on the similarities. Alice's head spun. They were agreeing to do what she asked only because they thought a dead girl was still alive and asking? Or because Alice somewhat resembled this girl? None of it made any sense. It was all, of course, Nonsense. What was real were treaties and pacts and armies and weapons.

It took someone from the real world to see that. Someone with real-world perspective.

"This is ridiculous," Alice complained down to the Hatter.

"You still don't get it, do you?" the Hatter said with a

sigh. "This whole plan is ridiculous. It's not about armies – it's about you. It's *always* been about you, Alice."

"Seems like it's more about Mary Ann," Alice muttered. But she carefully took the egg out of her pocket and held it up. *That* caught the crowd's attention.

"What's that she's got?"

"An egg? Is it *her* egg?"

"Can human girls lay eggs, too?"

"No, *but they eat them*!"

"Lord sakes! IS SHE GOING TO EAT THAT EGG?"

"What's that on it?"

"Why, it's an egg in the suit of Clubs!"

"She speaks for the birds!"

"I'll follow that egg anywhere!"

"Down with the Queen of Hearts! Down with the Queen of Hearts!"

"Hooray for the *Quack of Clubs*!"

"FREEDOM!"

As they shouted and Alice held the egg, club side out, a crack appeared in its side.

The crack grew and grew like lightning over a field with a distant horizon, when you can see the whole bolt crackling from end to end. Its points divided and divided and became more cracks until the egg was riddled with them and the shell was more like a jigsaw puzzle than a solid surface.

Suddenly it exploded.

A white owl, adult, fully formed, complete with an accordion neck, took off directly into the sky as if winging its way to the sun. It hovered for a moment high up, sweeping its wings while scoping out the crowd and feeling the wind. Then it swooped away, off in the direction of the Unlikely.

The crowd oohed and aahed and gasped.

"So that's how that works," Alice observed, watching it go.

Chapter Thirty

"It can't be that easy…" she added, tearing her eyes from the sky and resettling them on the crowd. Birds were talking excitedly, arguing viciously, taking great gulps of lemonade, and affixing various pins to their feathers. Some of the brooches were of hearts, some clubs, some rabbits, some funny-looking question marks that looked like they were cut through with an exclamation mark. Some, worn by the most decadent, old or philosophical, showed an image of a clock with the minute hand approaching thirteen.

"Let's go find the Dodo. We must be right behind him," the Hatter said, but whether or not he was responding to her thought she couldn't tell. "I'll bet the Gryphon's with him, too. They both have wings, you know."

"But if the Queen of Clubs is being summoned, or told, by that bird thing, then she will be on her way very soon with her army. Directly to the Queen of Hearts' castle, I presume, to wage war there. We should continue in that direction, spreading word and raising support and then helping the Queen of Clubs any way we can."

"I was afraid you would say something like that," the Hatter moaned.

The two (three with the Dormouse) quietly slipped out the back way of Ornithsiville.

"I very much would like to avoid the Forest of Forgetting," Alice said. "We should go more directly across that checkered plain."

"As you wish," the Hatter sighed.

They drew away from the bird village and closer to the castle, taking Alice's journey backwards, and the landscape and environment began to change. Immediately, of course, not with the slow progression of colours and geography one might be used to in a world more like Angleland. And as she walked through this shifting landscape Alice realised she hadn't asked the Hatter to lead, or even troubled about how to get there. All actions and signs – some quite literally – pointed to the Queen of Hearts. That was where the next, hopefully final, confrontation between everyone was to be. So of course Wonderland would take Alice there.

She wondered what it would have been like to grow up as Mary Ann, used to travelling by inevitability. It had taken three visits for Alice to get the hang of it.

The checkered plain came fast and quick but now it was dead and dusty. The red paint had completely coated and dried on the bushes and grass, killing the plants entirely and rendering them into bony, crimson blots on the landscape. The sky was dark with bloody red smoke and the air had a pungent thickness to it. Ugly embers danced in the upper reaches, round and down and only eventually out, like malevolent demons from books in Alice's world. Like nothing at all from Wonderland.

"I don't like the looks of that," the Hatter said despite being unable to turn away.

Alice found herself filled with a sort dread that she had rarely experienced since she was a child: a fear of even greater terror to come, of the future punishment from the *other* parent after the first one has yelled, promising worse later.

She took the Hatter's hand and he squeezed hers back, a little absently, but hard. They walked silently like a very grim Hansel and Gretel into the desolate landscape.

Far too soon they came upon the cause of such rank pollution.

Blocking out the sunlight and sending the land around

them into shadow were giant piles of things smouldering and burning and releasing great oily red billows.

Covering her mouth with her hand and trying to breathe only through her nose, Alice approached the closest heap. She thought they would be toys – which, admittedly, didn't make sense because the Queen had to actually have functioning ones to win (she assumed). But what sense was there in anything now in Heartland?

In fact the things on fire were everything *but* toys. Chairs, bicycles, teakettles, pencils, baby blankets, eyeglasses, plum puddings, lamp glass, bricks, pantaloons, cupboards, snuff boxes, policemen's hats, loaves of day-old raisin bread, saddles, stoops and stairways, leather bags, bonnets, stamps from printing presses… everything and anything Alice could name was mounded into these giant, endless piles of burning rubbish.

The Hatter looked and poked at the pile interestedly; even the Dormouse stuck his head out and pointed at a silver teaspoon that shone a bit in the flames. The Hatter dutifully picked it out (wrapping his hand in his muff first) and handed it to his companion, who sighed in delight and promptly went back to sleep, cradling it for warmth.

Rushing around the base of these hills were giant ants pushing soiled red carts. Using some reason or logic or pattern known only to herself, each would reach into a cart, pick up an object – feelers moving about in the air as if receiving signals on what to do – and then fling it onto a particular bonfire.

Suddenly one of the smaller ants began gesticulating wildly with her feelers and arms.

I got one! I got one!

Alice put her hands to her temples, not meant to receive that kind of communication. It hurt. The Hatter pulled his hat all the way down over his head.

A dozen other ants rushed over to this crying one, their feelers flurrying.

The ant held up her find: a tiny doll missing its head.

Rubbish is it rubbish

Is it a toy

Is it a doll without a head a doll

Is it something to play with

It is if a brother popped the head off

Is it still a game?

No matter, look! the first ant said, triumphantly digging around her cart some more and holding up a tiny thing covered in hair. *Here is the head! It* is *a doll, by any definition! A* toy*!*

A toy a toy a toy! all the other ones joined in.

Clacking her mandibles with glee, the ant rushed away, holding the toy aloft.

Immediately the other ants clambered up the side of her cart and began methodically going through the rest of her stuff to see if there was more luck, if there were more toys.

"That's very clever, I suppose," Alice said, taking the Hatter and drawing the two of them back away from the uncomfortably large insects. "Using ants to sort through everything. Like the fairy tale about the princess spreading the sacks of grain out over grass and making a poor suitor try to find them all and refill the sacks – and some friendly ants doing the job for him."

"Certainly, except the headless doll was horrible, and the giant ants are horrible, and *all of this is horrible*."

The Hatter pointed. There was a slowly charring skeleton in one of the piles and Alice couldn't say for certain whether it was a corpse or a model from a scholar's laboratory.

The rubble shifted as something finally collapsed, too charred to hold weight any longer, causing the skeleton to turn slightly, as if it was looking at Alice.

"Oh," Alice said, spinning away and swallowing, trying not to throw up. But as shocked as she was, she was more worried about the Hatter, who looked grim and impassive. He was straightening out again, taller, with a smaller hat and head.

"Ever have a Flying Butterscotch?" she asked quickly.

"No, what's a—"

Alice took out a sweet and lobbed it at his head. It hit the rim of his hat and fell down – right into his open mouth, which he readied just in time.

"To the castle!" Alice said brightly, popping another candy into her own mouth. She closed one eye and moved her hand as if to brush the burning pile away… and so it slid into the background improbably and unnoticeably, a trick of the eye made real.

"To the castle!" the Hatter agreed, sucking on the sweet and taking her hand again and skipping. Alice was on the point of telling him not to skip with a sweet in his mouth, for he might choke – but wisely decided not to.

(It was good she had kept that packet of sweets. Just like someone had told her – who was it? Always keep a packet of sweets on you? One's life might depend on it? She couldn't quite remember…)

The ants took no notice of them, just as they wouldn't in the real world unless a mischievous younger Alice had put an obstacle in their line of progress: a rock or a bit of honey, say. When the two companions made any effort at all to look at the carts or bits being sorted they both tried to keep their observations light. "That's an unusually shaped ottoman" or "My aunt used to have an eggbeater like that." Otherwise their progress was mostly silent amongst the rubbish heaps except for the clicking sound of the ants.

Then a strange feeling began to come over Alice. A creepy-crawly scared one – and oddly, it had nothing to do with the ants.

She spun round to regard the desolation behind her. It was like being at a fancy, crowded party and something was stepping on her dress. Or was about to.

"What are you doing?" the Hatter demanded the third time she stopped. "You're as nervous as a tove pup in a blanderpatch."

"I feel like we're being followed," Alice admitted, once again turning round and scanning the horizon. The Hatter looked with her, but all they could see were the mindless ants.

"There's nothing behind us at all," the Hatter said.

"That's because your death is in *front* of you," came a whispery dry voice.

Alice spun back round.

There stood a skeleton, closely resembling the skeleton from the burning pile of rubble before: there were char marks on his bones here and there. Perhaps it *had* been him. On a closer look he was strangely angular, with dead geodesic eyes and an upside-down trapezoid for a skull.

Also he seemed… flat. Thinner than a card even when he curled around to draw his sword, an evil-looking half scissor. The hole where his nose would have been was the only part of him that was curved; it looked like an upside-down heart.

"The Card Cutter," the Hatter whispered, his voice thick with fear.

"Hello," Alice said with a little curtsy. "We're just on our way through, if you don't mind…"

"But I *do* mind," the skeleton said, inching closer. Its flat and bony toes made tiny *clink* sounds against the ground. "I am the evener of odds. I make all games fair. I am the great equaliser. I wipe out cheating advantages. I am here for *you*."

"Whatever for?" Alice demanded, trying to keep her voice from shaking. "I never cheat. Much. Any more. I'm an adult, not a child."

"You are definitely trying to cheat, little Alice. You are bringing a whole new deck into this game. It's not fair for the Hearts."

"I beg your pardon!" Alice said. "Your Queen has all the weapons, all the soldiers, all the armies, all the power, all the toys—"

"Not all the toys, yet," the skeleton interrupted. "Soon."

"—all the roads and towns and prisons and garrotes

against the hapless folk of Heartland, and you accuse *me* of cheating because I want to *even* the odds? By bringing in an equally powerful ally?"

"She was not in the game at the beginning, when the rules were called," the skeleton said, shifting his stance and grip on the scissor half.

"There was never any precise beginning to this madness, and no one ever called out the rules!"

"So you say."

"It sounds to me like you are just rationalising whatever reason you were sent after me," Alice snapped. "Or you can only do as you are meant to, and the Queen of Hearts somehow twisted the words and rules around to make you think this is the right thing. When really—"

But whatever she was going to say next, probably some handy bit of Alice wisdom, was cut off as the Card Cutter suddenly and silently brought his scissor-scythe down at her head.

The Hatter yanked Alice out of the way.

But not *quite* out of the way.

For one seemingly endless, silent moment she saw a neat triangle of cloth break free from her trousers and drift to and fro towards the ground. A short lock of hair, no more than a comma of blonde, followed. Already on the dirt was a scrap of Alice's shoe leather, the precise colour and shape of a trimmed nail that has fallen to the floor – but larger.

"ALICE!" the Hatter roared, pushing her away again.

Time restarted. The Card Cutter swung, the scissor half this time going *snicker-snack* despite the absence of its opposite twin.

Alice twirled out of the way hysterically, unsure what to do. There had only ever been one real fight between her and Mathilda, and that had involved hair pulling.

"Do something!" the Hatter hissed.

"Unfair—" Alice cried as the scissor half *clanged* down again on the road next to her, temporarily sticking itself between two cobbles. Without a grunt or a huff or any sound at all, the too-thin skeleton bent himself upon freeing it. Alice stumbled up and jabbed her hands in her pockets, but panicking fingers couldn't manage to find the packet of sweets now.

So it really seemed like a good time to—

"Run!" she cried, grabbing the Hatter by the hand. No fighters, they. It was survival, not cowardice.

They barrelled down the path around and *past* the skeleton; what little sense Alice kept made her choose to at least run away in the direction of their eventual destination. The Hatter's legs were much shorter than hers now and he had a hard time trying to keep up – especially with one hand on his gigantic hat.

Although her own heartbeats and breath were loud and fear seemed to make a noise of its own, after a little while Alice couldn't hear anything else at all. The only sounds in the world around her were things crackling and shifting in the burning piles of rubble. There was no hint of pursuit, there was no *swish* of the scissor half.

Alice was torn. On the one hand: excitement! Had they really evaded their attacker so easily?

And on the other: unease. Had he let them go because they were heading into the lion's den, as it were? Closer to the castle?

Should they have danced away instead?

But her emotions were quickly settled by a discarded and dirty card blown by the wind; it arced overhead and drifted down in front of her.

The Card Cutter rose up, brandishing his scissor half triumphantly.

Alice and the Hatter stopped their forward momentum just in time.

"You cannot escape equity," the skeleton said with a broad bony grin. "Fairness comes for everyone in the end; everyone becomes food for the worms, equally. This world is almost over. Consider yourselves the lucky forerunners into the next."

Alice turned to run again.

"We cannot escape him," the Hatter hissed madly, teeth chattering with fear. "He can go anywhere – appear anywhere. He cuts down cards wherever they are. He is unstoppable."

"I'm not a card!" Alice cried, both to him and the skeleton.

The skeleton made a mocking little half bow. "Yet you look like you are trying to become a queen; you play in the Queens' Games."

He suddenly lunged forward, twirling his weapon and bringing it horizontal this time, intending to cut the two friends in twain.

The Hatter and Alice ducked.

The top of his giant hat was lopped off.

"My hat!" the Hatter cried, grabbing it on either side of its brim. Alice pushed him out of the path of the skeleton's riposte: having spun all the way round, swooping his weapon out like a scythe, he let it continue its momentum *up* and over his ivory shoulder only to come straight back down on top of the two.

"Alice!" the Dormouse cried, popping out the top of the Hatter's sad hat. "The sweets! *EAT THEM!*"

Alice dug desperately into her pockets again – but was so distracted she wound up tripping over her own feet. She stumbled and fell into the dust and dried paint, hitting her head against the Hatter's shoe.

She did manage to pull out a single sweet, a liquorice, and pop it in her mouth.

Her tongue recoiled from the hated taste. She forced herself to swallow.

Her view of the sky was cut off by a grinning skull: the skeleton took one strangely delicate-seeming foot and kicked the Hatter away from Alice. The poor man went flying.

The Card Cutter raised his scissor half into the air; it sparkled prettily, golden and sharp.

"*You* shut up like a telescope," Alice whispered, holding out her hand and seeming to catch his skull between her thumb and finger. She squeezed them together like she was crushing his head.

There was a terrible sound that must have been bone on bone: grinding and squeaking and sandpaper grit like teeth forced to do something they shouldn't.

Whether the skull became small and fell off its neck, rendering the skeleton deceased; or whether it stayed on but the whole thing was such a drastic and sudden change that the skeleton couldn't cope; or whether whatever it had for a brain or soul shrank into uselessness along with its cranial protection, Alice never found out.

Its arms were still moving, caught in the middle of its last blow, and the scissor half came down squarely into her Heart.

Chapter Thirty-One

"Alice!" the Hatter cried.

"It's funny," she thought, looking at the scissor half that stuck up out of whatever you called the part of your body that was sort of between the ribs. The fleshy, lumpy, beating bit.

"A Diamond, is that it? Or no, the Spade?" she wondered.

The scissor sort of swayed back and forth and for just a moment looked like it was as thin as the skeleton itself, but of course even so it was pure sharp golden metal.

"Brass, maybe," she decided.

"Vile thing!" the Hatter swore, grabbing it with both his hands – and almost cutting his fingers off in the process.

"No!" Alice started to shout, for though she had little knowledge of medicine, she did have a feeling, or maybe remembered a story, or… The point was, one didn't…

Whatever it was, it was too late.

The Hatter pulled the scissor out, and with it came great pumps of blood. Real blood, not red paint. It smelled of meat and copper and as it flecked her lips Alice could taste it. The Hatter's eyes widened in shock, and unable to think of anything else, he grabbed his hat and held it over the flow. It didn't work very well without its top.

"Things aren't… supposed… to hurt… in Wonderland…" Alice murmured.

"Alice, you have to go home now. Go back to wherever Alices come from," the Hatter begged. "You will die here."

"No!" Alice struggled to sit up. "You'll *all die* here! The world will come to an end! Patch this up – bandage it… It's not going to kill me… I cannot die in Wonderland."

But whatever shock had reduced most of her initial pain took this moment to wear off. A strange sloshing went back and forth through Alice's whole body, half nausea, half heat, half something else.

Half scissors, she thought. A bright white light of pain like nothing she had ever experienced before divided her chest from her torso, as if the sharp weapon had relodged itself there.

She cried out, unable to stop herself.

"Alice, go home, that's an order," the Hatter said, saluting her. "Come back as soon as you can. You're no good to us dead."

"Might make a good martyr for the cause..." the Dormouse suggested sleepily from the middle of his balding head.

"We already have Mary Ann for that, you heartless rodent," the Hatter said without feeling. "Alice... we need *you*. Alice. Only Alice. Alive. Come back to us. Soon..."

"I don't know how!" Alice said, feeling blackness come over her. It wasn't pleasant like falling asleep. It was like a thousand delicate crabs had dropped on her slowly from above and were pinching their way into her. Why did her stomach hurt if her arm was nearly cut off? Wait, *was* it her arm?

"Don't..." she said, grabbing the Hatter's hand.

She tried to memorise it: the little hairs, some of which were grey, around his knuckles. The dimples of pores where they entered his skin. A tiny scar. An actual fingerprint. All these things, unique to the Hatter, and as real as, as real as...

Chapter Thirty-Two

She came to in an alleyway.

Alice felt strangely encumbered and kicked her legs, trying to get out from underneath the quilts and nooses that held her down… and then realised that it was all just her own skirts, pinafores and various assorted underthings. She had been thinking of her other outfit, her Wonderland one.

"The Hatter! The Hatter's hand!" she cried, trying to remember. It was an older man's hand, still with a little plumpness around the knuckles but thinning out around the bones. "No, no! *Details!*" But her clever brain substituted descriptive words for specific facts, glossing over *exactly* what he looked like with what he probably *should* have looked like. The way any brain will do upon awaking, filling in the forgotten or unimagined bits of dream.

Large hat, crazy hair, large nose, short stature, like a children's illustration in a book of funny poems…

"The Card Cutter! We were almost at the castle! We showed the egg to the Ornithsivillians and the Queen of Clubs will come! We almost *won*!"

Two of the children from the Square were standing over her, staring at her worriedly. One was Zara. Alice had no idea what the boy's name was.

"Mistress Alice, are you all right?" the boy asked solicitously. "You're very white."

Things were drifting in and out of focus.

"I need to get back," Alice said, trying to hang on to the feelings she had just a few moments before. Unfortunately all it involved was tremendous pain and then a faintness, with all the cares of the world lifting away from her.

The *Card Cutter*. The burning piles of rubbish. The mad queen. The end of the world… the desperation…

Hold on to it, Alice! she told herself.

She screamed in a very un-Alice way: more of a forced groan made loud as her entire body and soul tried to expel the real world and its sensations that infringed on her mind.

She raked her nails along her arms, leaving long white scratches and trailing pinpricks of blood like pearls. Pain would focus her. Pain would help her remember…

"What are you *doing*?" the boy cried. "STOP IT!"

Zara was more practical and simply reached over with her two strong and chubby hands and grabbed her.

"I'm just trying to remember," Alice said calmly.

"You could tie a string around your finger, maybe," Zara suggested with an insouciant irony that seemed far too young for a girl of seven. Then again, that was how old Alice had been when she spoke back to monsters and creatures from that other world.

Just not adults of this one.

Alice gave her a wan smile. It tasted terrible. She smacked her tongue around somewhat impolitely, trying to dispel whatever it was.

"Your camera's gone," the boy said, picking up her bag and shaking its obvious lightness. He peeped in. "Other stuff is still in there, though."

"My camera?!" she cried in dismay.

Then:

"No, wait, that is not important. The *other* things are more important. An entire world…"

"I really think you should go to the doctor," the boy said seriously. "You have had a fit or something."

"No, I'm fine. Perhaps I just fainted and someone came along and saw me and stole my valuables."

But that wasn't precisely true, was it? She had a memory of tripping, and an arm, and not being able to breathe, and an assailant…

"You still have your necklace and ring," the little girl pointed out promptly.

"And your little purse with money in it," the boy said, taking it up and shaking it.

"Someone has mugged me to… just take my camera? Why not everything else as well?"

Her arm itched for a moment as she thought about the implications of this. She scratched it idly and then remembered why the injury was there.

"No, no, this is all irrelevant. There are other things to worry about." She rose to her feet, unsteady but determined. "Little darlings, thank you so much for my rescue. If it wouldn't be too much trouble, could I offer a reward for you to see me safely home?"

"No reward," the boy said simply. The girl spat in disgust.

Aha! Alice thought. That *is how it's done. I should take note!*

"Can I reimburse you for the task of helping me get there, then, and carrying my bag for me?" she asked politely.

"And can you remember all the strange things I may say along the way, if I ask later?"

"Home or *vrach*?" Zara said, rolling her eyes.

"Doctor," the boy translated.

"Home. An extra penny if you don't mention the doctor again," Alice said with a smile.

And actually it was good that they went with her: walking was a little harder than it should have been. Her head was swimming with the remnants of her dream or having fallen; reality moved slowly around her, landscape and objects only slowly catching up to what her body and eyes told her was going on. Sort of the reverse of Wonderland, where the scenery sped up on you. Every time there was a sudden change of altitude, a slope down or a step up, she wobbled and the world spun. The worst was a set of four steps down. At the base of them everything went dizzily blurred and a sharp pain drilled itself into her chest with an intensity so great she began to black out.

"Alice, is that you? *Get away from her at once!*"

Alice jumped at the shouts as an unwanted pair of intruders came over to investigate her decrepitude.

It was, she saw from the light shining painfully off a half dozen buttons like angry little suns, a police officer, and—

"Are you all right? Begone, vermin!"

She closed her eyes. Coney. Of course Coney. *Again*

Coney! Even when she was trying to avoid him, he reappeared in her life. Like… almost like…

She had it on the tip of her tongue but couldn't quite place it.

"I'm fine," Alice moaned in irritation. "I'm all right. I've just been robbed…"

"You little *thieves*! Officer, take these two away at once! This is the body – the girl, I mean – I told you I saw in the alley! These two must have been stealing her blind while she lay prone!"

"No, no, no." Alice was finally able to pry her eyes open enough to glare at the hateful face of Coney, pale and surrounded by a halo of ridiculously glassy pale hair. "They *found* me. They saved me. Someone knocked me down and they came upon me…"

"A likely story. You're too forgiving, Alice. Officer, search these two at once for the missing camera!" Coney ordered.

The policeman gave the kids a distrusting but mild look. "They're filthy, thieving, foreign gutter rats, to be sure," he said almost regretfully, "but I don't think there's any place on their selves they could *hide* a camera. And why would they stick around after the crime?"

Alice raised an eyebrow at Coney.

"To… put you off the scent…?" he asked lamely.

"I am happy you are all right," Zara said with a perfect curtsy, holding her patched but mostly clean pinny in between delicately arranged fingers as she did so. Alice was pretty sure only she – and possibly the police officer – saw the sarcastic sparkle in the girl's eyes as she performed the manoeuvre.

Brother and sister turned to go.

"But wait—" Alice said, fumbling for her purse. The boy gave a quick, nearly undetectable shake of his head. His eyes flicked to the two men. With a hot lick of shame and anger, Alice understood: giving them money would just encourage Coney to claim they were profiting off her neediness. The policeman would question the children further, prolong the encounter – who knew. It would cause problems. The kids wanted to get out of there as quickly as possible without any more fuss or attention. "*Thank you.*"

The siblings ran off, happy to escape.

"I'll see you home," the policeman said, offering her a hand up. "And when you have rested you can make a complete report to us about the theft."

"Take me to my aunt's. It's closer."

"I'll take care of her," Coney told the police officer with a man-to-man smugness. Alice dearly wished she could have done something to him – she couldn't remember quite what, but in Wonderland she could have effected a physically final response.

"Just you take care to come by the station, or I'll have one of my men drop by your house," the officer said – ignoring Coney and his looks. "This is a strange and serious thing. You still have your jewellery, and your purse. The miscreant just wanted the camera. The sooner we can get all the details, the sooner we can apprehend this criminal – and protect other ladies as well."

Alice nodded dully. These were all excellent points and he was only doing his job, but aside from the annoyance of having to acquire a new camera, it was all unimportant. The police officer tipped his cap to her and strode off.

She endured the walk to her aunt's as best she could, putting up with Coney's careful holding of her arm and constant exhortations to lean on him if necessary. It was agony. Fortunately Vivian's house wasn't actually too far, and the relief she felt when she saw its odd, green-painted door was as perfect and complete as lemonade on a hot summer day.

"Thank you," she said politely and succinctly as she opened the door. "I'll be all right now."

"Should I see you in? I really am… I really am worried about your health. I hadn't realised it was *you* when I saw your unconscious form on the ground. I just ran and fetched the policeman…" He did indeed sound worried, all unctuousness aside.

"No, pray do not come in." She stepped over the threshold and turned round, holding the door half closed between them before delivering her final word.

"I never said that it was my *camera* that had been stolen."

She slammed the door in his face.

With her head still aching she stumbled through the blessedly cool, dim and, for once, incense-free interior. Vivian came out, covered in clay and frowning; myopically concerned.

"Alice! You look terrible. Is everything all right?"

"Not at all. I've just been manhandled and mugged by a truly loathsome individual so he could steal my camera… for, I assume, some image he thought was captured on the film. *Evidence* of something. But all that was on that plate was a harmless little blue bird. He left behind all the other plates in the bag, because he's an idiot as well as a thief. I must develop them all immediately to see what he was after."

"Alice, that's dreadful! What hap—"

"*But far more importantly,*" Alice interrupted, holding up her hand, "there is a whole fantastic world under siege that I must return to at once. The villain who stole my camera is simply a distraction. I'm beginning to forget what it was all for."

Her aunt stared at her through gradually narrowing eyes, like a lizard overcome with cold.

"You haven't been in my personal things – taken anything from my rosewood cabinet in the studio, for instance?"

"No, Aunt Vivian."

"All right. Just checking. So… this camera theft. You aren't hurt – physically – and you don't seem to be overly upset by the crime. Although I must point out your dialogue is just the slightest bit off for… normal society. Just a word to the wise. You may indeed want to see a doctor for any lingering effects of your trauma.

"But as for your other concerns – your 'fantastic world', I mean. Am I to understand that you are upset less about the crime and more because the camera thief is a person from Porlock, interrupting your visit to some sort of private Xanadu?"

"Let's say yes, Aunt Vivian. But if Xanadu were real, and in danger of being destroyed."

"But Xanadu *was* destroyed the moment Coleridge awoke. He never went back."

"I can. I have. I must again."

Vivian was silent for a moment.

"All right. What can I do for you now?" she finally inquired, brisk and businesslike.

"I have promised everyone so much, in both worlds," Alice said with an impatient shake of her arms. "There, I must save the world. Here, I need to develop the film I have left. And I still have to go to the newspaper with that photo of Mrs Yao. Also, I could use some tea."

"And sandwiches, no doubt," Vivian said, nodding seriously. "I'm on it. Go put on one of the work pinnies and I'll be right back with a plate. I love my brother very much," she added – seemingly without emotion – "but really I do wish you were my own child sometimes."

Alice had a lopsided smile on her face as Vivian strode away. She loved her aunt, too, of course. But there was something more. What she felt was the sort of affection she could only compare to her feelings for the creatures of Wonderland. Love, but also a delight that such creatures should exist in the first place.

And a certain amount of curiosity, she had to admit. There was always some *holding back* with the Wonderland denizens, some further truth or mystery they took their own time revealing. Alice wondered, for a moment, what her aunt's was.

Chapter Thirty-Three

Of course all the plates she developed wound up displaying only Wonderlandians – at least for Alice. And none of them portended anything good at all.

The first photograph was of Messrs Tweedledee and Tweedledum. They were, just as Alice had expected, Gilbert and Quagley Ramsbottom. They grinned and held hands and wore Heart badges.

"Of course," Alice muttered. "They look positively gleeful."

The second was of the Dodo. With a giant sheep – a ram – who was weeping.

Alice nearly dropped this one when she picked it up. The Dodo was looking directly at the camera and had his wings out in supplication: *come back.*

"I *will*! Oh, Dodo, I am trying!" she cried.

She fished around in her bag until she found the monocle that she had sort of co-opted from her aunt. Who *was* he, anyway? In this world? There wasn't a lot of help from the background, most of which was blocked out by the giant sheep. It seemed like basic Wonderland scenery… a grassy plain, some trees, what looked like a train… *There.* Closer in, almost hidden by the ram's girth, was a side table that seemed put there for the posers' extra things so they wouldn't have to hold them. But instead of the Dodo's wig, or one of his telescopes, or a bell for the sheep, there was a pair of gloves with particularly large, ugly leather bows on the wrists. They didn't look *feminine* and *delicate* so much as that they perhaps more properly belonged on a dog's collar.

Alice would have known those gloves anywhere.

"Mathilda…?" she said in wonder.

She sat back, gobsmacked.

The Dodo. Sweet, loyal Dodo. The least nonsensical of all the tea party. Always proper. Always trying to talk politics and caucus races. He had trusted that Alice would come back… and walked right into the enemy's hands, knowing she would rescue him. He believed in Alice.

Of course Willard wasn't *really* the Mad Hatter and Mrs Pogysdunhow was much, much nicer than the Queen of Hearts (probably; she had always been all right to Alice and Mathilda, at least). Headstrewth wasn't at all sheepish, although in some ways he was large and harmless.

The other-world doubles possessed only the shallowest of similarities.

But…

What if under all her annoying pastimes and lectures and recriminations Mathilda really did think she was doing the right thing? That she was merely reining in the crazy people? What if her trying to manage Alice's life was because she wanted her to be happy – but *exactly like herself*? It wasn't from a lack of kindness or love, but a lack of imagination. She literally didn't know any other way of being.

Thoughts for another time, Alice told herself. It was indeed something to consider, but not when there was a world to save and a mystery to solve.

The last photograph was a nightmare that Alice almost dropped in revulsion.

It was a trio. The Caterpillar, a Scottie dog and *the March Hare.*

Who was a corpse.

The Caterpillar looked terrified, as if something was about to hit him in the face. The Scottie was screaming, looking at a golden watch at the end of a fob made of beetles.

And the March Hare… was stiff, and white, with unseeing dull eyes and his arms crossed over his chest.

Alice let out a wail before she could silence herself.

She *knew* the poor thing was dead. The Hatter had told her that. But that was very different from seeing such ghastly proof.

This was the photograph of Aunt Vivian and the two lawyers. Ivy was the Scottie dog, Alexandros was the March Hare.

Alice wiped the tears that were spilling silently out of her eyes, trying to keep that last thing in mind. The March Hare might have been dead over there, but here he was alive and well. Some part of him remained.

"I must get back," she whispered. "I must avenge him."

Reluctantly she pushed this photo aside.

There was still the mystery of what Coney wanted from her camera. There was nothing incriminating in any of the portraits. She shuffled through all the photographs again and again, trying to see something new.

"How goes it, dear?" Vivian asked, popping her head into the spare room where Alice was investigating her negatives. She had been as good as her word; a three-tiered tea set of sandwiches had already been delivered to and utterly demolished by her niece, not a crumb remaining, as well as two small pots of tea.

"Please tell me what you see here," Alice said tiredly. She held the up the old image of the Queen of Clubs posed with her clubs, now raised high above her head in a warrior's pose.

"Oh my goodness, that's Mrs Yao and her broken window," Vivian said, putting on her pince-nez. "She is holding up the offending brick – is she not? Oh no, it's a stone. And a note? What does it say? It's too small for these old eyes, and too backwards."

"I can't remember precisely. Some rubbish about 'go back home'. I'm taking it to the newspaper. I want everyone to know about it. They've already taken away several children – who I think cannot even write in English – for the crime, falsely and with no evidence. I think if I had the photo enlarged enough, the handwriting might give away the identity of the perpetrator. *Oh…*"

Alice suddenly realised the truth.

"*This* is the image the thief wanted to steal! He thought it might incriminate *him*! And he's so stupid he thought it was still in my camera somehow!"

"Brilliant! You're a regular Dupin!" Aunt Vivian cried. "But… who knew that you had taken that photograph? Besides Mrs Yao and yourself, I mean?"

"Only my sister and Headstrewth and…" And big sheepy Headstrewth had a big sheepy mouth, though he never really meant any harm with it. "Anyone Headstrewth told, which is probably everyone. Honestly, Aunt Vivian, I'm pretty sure the thief was Richard Coney. He appeared shockingly quickly after I came to – with a policeman in tow, no less – and seemed to already know about the theft."

"Ooooh, lovely," Vivian said with a hard, toothy smile. "Put that photo in the paper and *everyone* will figure it out for him or herself. Whether or not Coney is convicted of the crime, I would say his time in Kexford is over. And maybe Ramsbottom's, too!

"Are you going to the paper now? I could do with a walk. And so could you, by the looks of it. You're as pale as a mushroom from being in the darkroom so long. Let me fetch my hat and walking stick."

One couldn't say no to Aunt Viv; she was a force of nature when she cared to be. What Alice really wanted to do was lie down and sleep for a thousand hours – and hopefully reawaken in Wonderland.

But she rose and tidied her work, and finally summoned up the energy to meet her aunt at the front door – when it burst open and Mr Willard exploded inside.

"I have done it!" he announced grandly, his pale blue eyes blazing and a shocking grin revealing a set of very square, very even yellow teeth.

"Done *what*, Mr Willard?" Aunt Vivian asked, coming

in with her hat – one of his creations; there were several birds on it – and a walking stick with a silver wolf's head for the grip.

"Why, what you suggested: I put my name in for mayorship of our fair town!" He gave an extended, exquisite bow.

"Oh! Good show, Mr Willard, good show indeed!" Aunt Vivian said in surprise. She reached out and pumped his hand vigorously. "I am very, very happy about this turn of events."

"To be sure," Mr Willard said with a put-on, aristocratic smile. "We need to plan, to politicise, to figure out what our next steps are. Posters, pamphlets, pro-Willard advertisements!"

"Oh, and pins," Aunt Vivian said sagely. "People love the pins."

"Precisely!" Willard agreed, cackling.

"Well, by lovely coincidence it is definitely teatime, so let us away to Hendrick's for a bit of artemisia and some political planning! Dear, do you mind if we walk you to the café and you go the rest of the way yourself?"

"I'll be fine, Aunt Vivian," Alice said with a smile. "I fear no further camera thieves."

"Let us proceed thence," Willard said with a bow, gesturing to the open door. "After you, my lady. May I count on your support in the election?"

"If I could vote, you would absolutely have my vote," Alice said, a little archly. "But you may have my *support*, only if you would promise to help out the children of the Square – in a thoughtful, reasonable fashion."

"But of course!" Willard said indignantly. "And because you asked, it shall go to the top of my list. Along with democratising the local textile mills and turning over the means of production to the workers."

"Ah, yes, you may need to put a bit of your socialism on the back burner if you want to win," Aunt Vivian said bluntly. "We can discuss this further over drinks."

The three walked out onto the road full of goodwill and some hilarity. Even exhausted and sick about the March Hare, Alice found her mood a trifle lifted.

I shall just go to the newspaper with the photograph, inform Mr Katz of poor incarcerated Joshua and his friends, and then I can finally concentrate on going back to Wonderland, she told herself. *Just like that!*

As they approached what passed for the high street in their small town, the three saw what appeared to be something of a festival going on near the large fountain. A table was set up and clustered around by a crowd of all sorts of people: young, old, children, adults, mill workers, farmers and townspeople. There were brightly coloured toy balloons and ribbons and bunting strung about.

Birds, for some reason Alice suddenly thought they resembled.

Ramsbottom sat behind the table. His beaming, jocular visage seemed to light on each and every person's face, and his right hand moved faster than a magician's to shake a hearty hello. During this he also somehow managed a quick – and hatefully smug – look over at Alice and her party. Coney was right beside him, handing out pins, looking harried – and a little pale when he saw Alice.

"Mr Willard," Ramsbottom called out in cheerful aggression. "I heard that you have declared against me. Best of luck."

Mr Willard started to roll his eyes, but Aunt Vivian hit him on the arm.

"And to you," the hatter added quickly.

"I'm running, too," said a quiet man at a small and lonely table all his own. Alice thought she recognised him from around town – the post office, perhaps.

"I am Mallory Griffle Frundus. My platform is primarily predicated upon a complete and long-overdue overhaul of the metropolitan sewer system and imposing *some* regulation on the out-of-control growth of factories along the river – all while encouraging progress and creating jobs for those now squeezed out of agriculture. Pin?" He held out a blue-and-red rosette with FRUNDUS – FOR US! written on it.

Alice smiled sympathetically. "I'm afraid I am supporting Mr Willard here, but I will wear your pin, too, if you think it will help."

"Oh, anything would at this point," the man said with good humour. "I'm also having a little breakfast gathering Tuesday, a forum where people can come and discuss the issues important to them. Mostly as it pertains to urban improvements, of course. Sewers, schools and the like."

"*We're* having a big rally that day, too!" Ramsbottom announced. "A *Pride for England* parade. All citizens from *good* families are welcome. And by 'good' I don't mean wealthy. Solid men of the earth, as you people like to say, are invited – anyone is, as long as they have hearts shaped by centuries of generational love in the nurturing warmth of English soil."

Alice sighed. Really understanding Ramsbottom was like deciphering a riddle. And what she saw at the end of it was more broken windows, hate and fury in the guise of patriotism. How much did those signing his petitions and taking his balloons understand and wilfully join in on? How much did they not *quite* understand, but went along with anyway?

"Everyone loves a rally," Coney added half-heartedly.

"I don't think I shall be able to make it," Willard said.

"Loving our fellow man can take many different forms, but this is not one of them."

"Alice, will you come?" Coney asked nervously.

She gave him a look, but before a real answer came out of her mouth, Ramsbottom's grin went even wider.

"I'm afraid it's men only to march, anyway. Women may watch and then clean up, with a bit of punch, of course, provided by my campaign. As it should be in politics in England."

Whether he was referring to women in politics or free punch in politics it was hard to say, but the would-be mayor raised his voice for the last bit and looked to the crowd with an *am I right?* wave of his arms. The crowd responded immediately with cheers; who knew which thing they were cheering, but he had them in the palms of his oily hands.

Alice, Vivian and the hatter left the square melancholy and disturbed.

"This is bad," Willard said darkly. "Not just for my campaign – but for Kexford in general. It's like he's whipping the masses into some sort of beast of hate. Mrs Yao will not be the last of the victims of this state-sponsored xenophobia."

"I don't disagree," Aunt Vivian said with worry. "I don't know what to do – even if you don't win as a mayor, there has to be *something*."

"Auntie," Alice said slowly, thinking about what Ramsbottom had said, especially about women. "Do you think the newspaper will *listen* to me at all? Will it print the photo and story if it's given to them by a woman?"

"Alice," Aunt Vivian said sternly, "it is your photo, and it is Mrs Yao's story. You're *her* friend. You must stand up for women everywhere by insisting they listen to you."

"But if the point is to get notice and justice for Mrs Yao, isn't the most important thing that the photograph just gets printed, however it gets there? Isn't *that* what really matters here?"

"Both are good points. In the end, however, you can and must only do what *you* feel is right," Willard said kindly. "Welcome to the world of politics, Alice. In the end, it is all stuff and nonsense."

Chapter Thirty-Four

"Stuff and Nonsense."

What a strange – and particular – choice of words, Alice said to herself.

She considered all the twins of the two worlds: herself and Mary Ann, the Dodo and her sister, the March Hare and Alexandros… Was there more to it than that? Were events, geographies, all of *life* mirrored as well? Did the mayoral race and Ramsbottom's rally somehow have something to do with events or goings-on in Wonderland? Was the Queen of Hearts' insane, murderous game somehow fuelling events in Kexford, investing the upcoming election with otherwise dismissible emotions and meaning? If Ramsbottom won, if the children in the Square continued to be hassled and locked up for crimes they never committed, and Mrs Yao never received justice… was this all because of their doubles?

Or was this just the madness of England?

Or was there an in-between answer: did each world have some sort of effect on the other?

What if the mad goings-on in England somehow polluted Wonderland? Alice suddenly wondered.

What if the Queen of Hearts was bitten by whatever bug that made her decide to win the silliest and last of all games – because of what was happening in Kexford?

Also, the Hatter knew about things from this world because the Cheshire Cat had told him – presumably because the Cheshire had been here himself at some point. And the Knave had said some people could go back and forth! Not just Alice. There was some sort of fluidity between the two places; ideas and personalities and even people could sometimes pass through whatever walls normally kept them separated.

Then… possibly… whatever she did to solve the problems of one world would help the other. Or the reverse: if she failed, it would destroy both.

It seems terribly unfair, she thought. *It seems like I've been given a hopeless task, or pieces for a game with no rules at all and a shifting number of opponents, and told that everything depends on my figuring it out and winning.*

How very Wonderland.

As she walked, the street grew busier and more cluttered with shops and offices in what passed for the town centre of Kexford. Alice watched all the businessmen and servants and people shopping and chatting and waving hello to one another and wished she had someone *she* could talk to. About everything. Someone both logical and a little mad. And perhaps not quite as close and concerned as Aunt Vivian (bless her, though).

Her subconscious already knew what she was thinking and Alice laughed a little at her false naivete. She paused, debating the pros and cons, at a literal crossroads. Then she took a left turn, knowing her mind had been made up a long time ago.

There it was: ALEXANDROS & IVY, BARRISTERS-AT-LAW. Gilt on richly stained wood.

She hesitated just a moment – was anyone looking? Was there going to be a rumour about young, single Alice approaching a law firm by herself? This particular law firm?

She went in.

(And what would Mary Ann have done? Just stood, helplessly, assuming England would take her to wherever she was needed next?)

The interior was cool and dark with heavily stained wood. Everything smelled of ink and paper and musty books and fresh polish. A secretary, seated at a large desk, leapt up upon her entrance. He was ageless, skinny, perhaps needed to wash his hair, and gave her a look of such dismissal that she very much wanted to pull him by the ear and yell into it the way her neighbour sometimes did with her grandchildren.

"May I help you?" he asked, looking like he had no desire to do any such thing.

"I'm looking for Mr Katz," she said politely. "I have some business with him."

"Do you have an appointment?"

"I don't," Alice admitted. "But I'm sure he'll see me."

And she was. There might be a veritable hurricane of nonsense flying around, but he had stayed by her at the park and covered her with his jacket. He had given her a riddle. He would see her, as definitely as she would smile upon seeing his rosy cheeks.

"I will check to see if he wishes to be disturbed," the secretary said in such a tone that Alice immediately knew he would most likely go upstairs, pretend to confer, then come back down and tell her sadly that the barrister was busy.

"I'll go myself. It's no problem," Alice said serenely, heading up the stairs with one delicate, gloved hand on the banister.

"No, I must insist – he mustn't be disturbed…" The clerk went to stop her, putting his hand out.

Alice just widened her eyes and paused: that was all. Her meaning was clear enough. You *dare* lay a hand on a lady? And expect to keep your job?

He would not dare.

The man crumpled as visibly as a bachelor's button when the sun goes in.

Alice gave him a frosty nod and continued upstairs. Any incipient panic she had about looking like an idiot once at the top was quickly dispelled: unlike in Wonderland, the doors here were labelled clearly with neat little plaques. She knocked on the one that said MR A. JOSEPH KATZ, ESQ.

A voice from inside: "*Drat it, Brigsby, I* said *I would go over to Mrs Bickler's later and...*"

The door opened.

"Oh, it's you."

He was startled.

Alice found she had held her breath.

They stood there alone in the upstairs, him on one side of the door, her on the other, this situation arising only because she had decided to come see him. This *moment* only existed because she had sought him out, and that fact hung in the air very palpably. His brown eyes seemed extra wide and deep. She felt her own cheeks start to go as red as his were. The moment dragged on. Neither one of them said anything.

"I have solved your riddle," she finally said. "It's *perspective*."

"Indeed!" His eyes crinkled in relief and merriment. "And have you found that answer helpful? For other things in your life?"

"Yes, but not *entirely* helpful, and not for all things. There are some problems riddles cannot fix, I'm afraid," she said with a sigh. "And I have such a problem. Not a legal matter – a personal quandary, if you will, and I would dearly love an outsider's perspective, if you have a moment."

"For you, I have every single moment, all of them," Katz said frankly. "I'll clear my appointments for the day – for the next week, if you like."

Alice smiled.

"I hope it doesn't take that much time," she said, stepping in.

"I do," Katz said with feeling. Then he grinned. "This is de*light*ful!"

His office was small and well-appointed and full of books. His desk was mostly neat – tidy blotter, expensive but simple pens and inkwells, stacks of papers in neat little piles; the only off thing was the *Kexford Weekly* in an untidy heap in the middle as if it had been thrown there.

"Oh!" Alice said. "That was sort of what I came to see you about."

Katz made a sour face and threw himself into his chair with the strength and lankiness of a young man not quite grown out of childish acrobatics but constrained by the very nice suit he wore. Alice couldn't help noticing how pretty his lips were even when pursed in distaste.

"Is it about 'Ramsbottom's Rally'? They're going to be burning down houses by the end of it, the silly fool," he spat. "Always a good idea to rally up the proletariat with hate and free punch."

"Ah, no, although Aunt Vivian and Mr Willard are equally concerned as you. I am, too," she added hastily. "I just don't see what can be done about it. It's a free country, Mr Katz, and Ramsbottom is allowed to have a rally if he wants and has all the permits."

"It's a free country for you and Mr Coney," Katz agreed. "There are some of us who might find it uncomfortable to continue living in a town where he holds sway."

Alice took this not *quite* as a slap in the face. Here she was showing up wantonly at his door and he was flinging their differences in her face and making her feel bad about it.

"Yes. I suppose I am free. But how did you vote in the last election?" she asked pointedly.

"Why, for Garretty, of course. He… Oh." He looked at her in wry amusement. "I see what you did there. You didn't vote, of course. Because you're a woman. Well played, Alice, well played. I am quite justly put in my place."

She smiled. "I think perhaps you've never had an opponent quite like me. At any rate, I came for advice from a friend, not to spar. *This* is why I'm here." She fished the photo of Yao and the stone out of her purse and handed it to him. He had to squint and hold it under the green-shaded lamp to see it clearly.

"I don't understand," Katz admitted immediately.

"Some ruffian threw a stone through Mrs Yao's window with a nasty note attached – you could read it, if the picture were a bit larger – suggesting she leave town before worse things were done to her shop. She has had to replace the window at her own expense and the police have made no effort to try to catch the true villain. Instead they rounded up a couple of very innocent children from the Square and have them locked up. I thought maybe having this picture in the paper would put a fire under the police, as it were, to find the actual villain, to let the children go… or at least I shall wake local sympathy to her plight."

"Hmm, not a bad plan at all," Katz said. "Plus it's a nice advertisement for the tea shop – it would certainly help her business. Alice: 'English white saviour to the rescue' again, eh?"

"You're very disagreeable sometimes, Mr Katz," Alice said, narrowing her eyes at him. "It's not about me at all. It's about my friend, and the children in the Square. I am perfectly willing to not even have a credit to the photo – I am here considering having *you* bring it to the paper, since they may not even accept one from a woman."

"Well, there I think you're wrong. Not about my being disagreeable – I am entirely. I'm a *barrister.* We're always disagreeable. If we agreed all the time there would be no court cases at all.

"I think everyone in Kexford knows Alice, the town photographer, and it would only help to know that you were involved with this. Say…" He pulled out a magnifying glass and held it over the photo, frowning. "I still can't entirely read what the note says, but that handwriting looks *awfully* neat and flowing for some random thug without schooling, much less an immigrant from Russia… Just look at the flourishes on the end."

"Yes… I'm fairly certain I already know who the miscreant is. The police, with some actual effort, could also figure out who wrote out the note and paid someone else to do the actual dirty work. Probably the same person who stole my camera in an attempt to get the film back."

"Your camera?" Katz asked, blinking. "Someone stole it?"

"Yes, rather mugged me for it. I shall deal with all that shortly."

"Someone *attacked* you?" Katz asked, standing up. "And stole your camera? You seem very calm about the crime that was perpetrated upon your person!"

"There are so many things going on right now, Mr Katz," Alice said wearily. "As strange as it may sound, it is not my greatest concern. My brains are fine. The camera can be replaced. The perpetrator will be caught. I have other things to attend to. I have a world to—ah, a world *of* other concerns to get back to. Other things need saving more than I do, Mr Katz."

"Such as what? What could a young woman like you have to worry yourself with – what *other* things?"

"I wish I could tell you. It would ease my mind considerably to share some of these troubles," Alice said with a wan smile. "And afterwards you would never speak to me again – you would send me to straight to the mad-house."

"Oh, I doubt that," Katz said, raising an eyebrow. "I mean, we don't need a special house for that. We're all mad here."

Alice looked at him sharply. But he was just smiling his usual guileless smile… with perhaps a bit of extra sparkle in it. She had the urge to curtsy, to take time while she thought of something to say. The moment drew out, and it was rich and full like a slant of late-afternoon sunlight through a dusty window.

"Why isn't your name on the sign outside?" she finally found herself saying, rather stupidly.

"Oh." Katz rolled his eyes. "I am not a partner yet – another six months and another connection with the right solicitor, I think. It's coming, don't you or my mother worry about that. Look, though, I have all the proper paraphernalia!"

He went over to a small wardrobe and with more energy than strictly necessary pulled out a robe and wig with a flourish.

"I even have a mirror to make sure not a whisker is out of place."

He opened the wardrobe all the way and revealed a simple but long looking glass that showed a slightly warped version of the handsome young man: his jowl pulled out to ridiculous horizontal lengths and his toes disappeared into pinpoints. He grinned and put the wig loosely and lopsidedly on, and the overall effect made Alice laugh – out loud, for the first time in days, in the real world.

"All right, it's a bit of a carnival deal," he admitted, putting the wig back after making one last face. "But as soon as I'm a full partner I'll get myself a really nice one. And a house," he added quickly.

He looked uncertain – and hopeful – and nervous – and—

And Alice found she was enjoying all of it rather much.

"A *house.* Indeed, Mr Katz. I hadn't realised they were required for barristers, or solicitors, or even clerks. Along with the uniform, I mean."

Katz flushed but also grinned with good humour.

"Let me take care of your photograph – *and* Mrs Yao, and the children," he offered. "What's a little more pro bono between friends? Anything that will ease your mind and lighten your troubles would be pleasure for me. And it would allow you to concentrate on your… other… concerns, whatever they may be. Saving the world."

"Thank you, Mr Katz," Alice said, standing up and preparing to say goodbye. She was relieved – she felt she really could trust him to do the right thing. But she was also sad the interview was coming to a close. She put out her hand. "But I'm not, ah, saving the world. I just need to… need to find a way to…"

"To get back to *that world*?" he asked softly.

"I have no idea what you're talking about, Mr Katz."

But he was pointing at the mirror.

Alice gasped.

Somehow, rather than the dusky and half-lit view of Katz's office that *should* have been reflected, there was instead a scene of a grim but sunlit field: of checkerboard squares, and fires burning, and smoke…

Alice looked back at the barrister and found herself reaching for a camera she no longer had.

Katz shook his head. "You know who I am in that other world, Alice. You don't need a photograph."

"Kat-z," Alice said slowly. "Cheshire Cat!"

He executed a bow, and just as easily she could imagine him disappearing halfway through, or tumbling all the way over in a somersault, or something else ridiculous but graceful.

He didn't, however.

"But how? And how do you… *know* all this?"

Katz shrugged. "How do you travel back and forth so? My other half can, and he comes to visit. He brings me riddles."

"And you give him riddles in return," Alice said slowly, suddenly seeing all her recent interactions with the Cheshire in a whole new light. They had *both* been trying to help her, all along.

In infuriatingly mysterious ways.

"Return to Wonderland," he said, looking her in the eyes. "Save their world. But… come back to mine."

"That's rather forward of you, Mr Cat."

He grinned. But it wasn't *just* like the Cheshire Cat's smile. There was warmth in it, and even love.

"I'm not the single young lady who goes knocking on strange barristers' doors," he pointed out.

"Hmmph," Alice said, sniffing. "Excellent point."

He gave her his hand. She picked up her skirts with her other one and began to step through the mirror – which was all soft and fading, just as she somehow expected.

She stopped before she was all the way through to turn back and look at him.

"Well then, Mr Katz?"

"Well then," Katz said. He leaned forward and brushed a tendril of hair out of her face. "Good luck, Alice. Remember, time is always on *your* side. Or your wrist, in fact, if you're wearing a watch."

And then she fell backwards into Wonderland.

Forever and Ever Alice

Chapter Thirty-Five

She didn't so much *plummet* as sort of drop and float at the same time.

"*Flop,*" Alice decided.

Fast and violent but also peaceful and quiet. End over end, head over heels, slowly turning round as though she were a leaf making its leisurely way from a branch to the ground. Her skirts billowed out around her and she was a little sorry to see they were her clothes from Angleland, not the smart suit the Queen of Clubs had given her. Still, the layers of fabric blossomed and fluttered like a pretty flower as she continued her journey downwards.

She flapped her arms and tried to spin herself the right way up. She kicked her legs to propel herself through the air faster, but to no avail. Gravity took the girl with her own sweet time, like a thistle seed, through low puffy clouds and air pockets of different temperatures, fluttering through flocks of fast-flying birds.

"Geddoutta the right lane, it's for fast fliers and passing only!" an angry goose squonked at her.

Far, far below, like one of those amusing paintings for which you need a magnifying glass to view all the details properly, was a vast board game – *field* – upon which two opponents – *armies* – had drawn up their sides. Literally drawn, though not so much like a picture as from a deck of cards, of course. These soldiers were neatly arrayed into rank and file on either side, but there were dozens upon dozens of other red and black cards patrolling the edges, organising the support, trying to spy and checking weapons.

Alice wondered where the Spades and Diamonds were.

"Ah well, adventure for another time, I suppose."

On the side of the red cards, defended by them, were the giant slowly burning piles of rubbish – and one *really* giant hill of toys.

All the toys in the world, it looked like.

There was every kind of dolly: folksy ones with no faces and angelic French porcelain ones whose eyes closed when they were laid down to nap. There were food carts and model trains and tiny velocipedes for tots and wagons and hoops and those little wooden ducklings on a rope you pull along whose bills snap open and shut and whose heads nod as they go. There were lawn games like croquet and darts, and many beautiful rocking horses, and tops and marbles and music boxes and jack-in-the-boxes. And there were things that Alice couldn't quite categorise, for they were toys unique to Wonderland and unfettered by English imagination.

And on top of this, grinning horribly and kicking her legs and shaking an evil black and twisted sword above her head with glee, was the Queen of Hearts.

Alice was so immediately filled with rage that she wanted nothing more than to reach down and shake the stupid little card queen until her head popped off like a flower.

"You… *stupid*… *murdering*… little… *spoiled brat*!" Alice screamed, thinking of the worst words she could. "I will destroy you!"

She had no plans beyond smashing herself into the nasty little creature from above; even now-Alice had her moments of acting without thinking.

Which is why it was a good thing she had friends.

Sensing something amiss, the Queen of Hearts stopped her laughing. She looked up with big, bulgy eyes that popped even further when she saw what was coming at her from the heavens. Her mouth opened wide, wider, wider still as if she couldn't decide whether to scream or to swallow the approaching danger.

Alice felt her own mouth pull back into a dry grin. All her teeth were exposed.

It wasn't really at the *last* moment; she had quite a good number more feet to go, really, but nearabouts the end something like a violent wind *wooshed* through and seized Alice, knocking her off course and carrying her aside.

(Of course the very angry and frustrated Alice couldn't see the Queen of Hearts' reaction; suffice it to say that the Queen merely looked perplexed for a moment, then took it in stride. "Must have been about to rain cats and dogs, and then the impounder came," she decided – quite reasonably for Wonderland.)

"*No!*" Alice cried. "Let me *go*!"

"Killing yourself and the Queen won't save the world now. Not even killing the Queen and lightly injuring yourself would save the world," came the voice of the thing that had seized her. Alice saw that she was in the grips of four strong claws, two leonine and two eagle-y. But no sooner had she noticed this than they switched directions quickly again and she had to focus on not losing the many sandwiches she had eaten back in Angleland.

Just as her stomach righted itself they were done: the wind stopped and was she released. Alice tumbled unprettily to the ground, and the Gryphon just stood there for a moment preening a stray spot on his neck without saying a word – he was half lion, after all.

She rose unsteadily to her feet. They were in a tiny wood that jutted out into the battlefield, a strange little peninsula of trees and thicket that felt protected and safe. A small assortment of Wonderland creatures were also there (hiding), including the Hatter, the Dormouse, the Dodo and Bill.

"Hatter!" Alice cried and ran over and hugged him. "Dodo!" she added just as happily. "Dormouse, Bill," she said, carefully taking their tiny appendages and shaking them delicately but properly. "And Gryphon. Sorry I struggled, but..."

"No worries. My rescues are always affronting. It's just the family way."

"I'm so glad you're all safe," Alice said.

"We are not *all* of us," the Hatter said. "But we are glad you've not bled to death, or however you do it in that other world of yours."

"I see the plan worked – the Queen of Clubs is here to save the day!" Alice said, admiring the two armies in the distance. Her royal friend rode a giant, fuzzy creature Alice decided to call a *buzzywhump* for future reference. It was mostly calm but pawed the ground occasionally with its furry front hooves. The Queen wore a black helm with a set of shining black clubs on top and a long black horsehair plume behind. The older accordion-necked owl sat on her shoulder, wearing black feathers for the occasion; his child, or tiny twin, was perched right next to him. The Clubs army was dealt out on either side of the Queen as far as the eye could see, some riding black pigs.

Alice thought it most interesting that the Queen was down in the fray, as opposed to remaining above her army like the Queen of Hearts.

On the other side, Tweedledum and Tweedledee raced round and round the base of the toy pile in opposite directions, singing. They crashed into each other, of course, falling down onto their backsides with their legs kicking into the air. Then they leapt up, rather more adroitly than seemed likely, shook hands, bowed, linked arms, and twirled around each other. Their ruby-coloured heart pins glittered in what little light there was.

Alice couldn't decide if their antics were amusing or chilling.

"*Surrender now!*" the Queen of Clubs ordered, raising her club. "You cannot hope to win this game of War."

"What do you mean? *Win?* And win *only* War? I intend to win *all* games! The last one! I shall be the one with the most toys!" the Queen of Hearts shouted back, laughing baldly. She nearly cut herself on her own sinuous black blade with her dramatic antics.

"She *can* win, can't she? The Queen of Clubs, I mean?" Alice asked a trifle nervously. "That's a lot of cards out there. More than enough for a game of War."

"*You* tell *us*," the Dodo said, not unkindly. "You're the one who arranged all this."

"I? Yes I did, but I couldn't be certain exactly how it would turn out… and what else was there to do? No one has told me that yet," Alice said a little peevishly. "It was the only solution I could think of that I could effect."

"It doesn't involve *you* at all," the Hatter said cryptically. Or maybe not so cryptically, considering the eyebrow he raised at her like a duelling pistol.

"Why are you even here?" the Queen of Hearts was shouting to the other Queen. "Is it just to witness my excellent royal winning of the last game?"

"We are here to free your people, and to take over whatever worldly possessions and treasures you have as our reward," the Queen of Clubs shouted back (a little too honestly, in Alice's private opinion). "You have betrayed every noble responsibility of being a queen. You have scared, tortured, killed, seized, imprisoned and stolen from your subjects willy-nilly, without even a warrant or an advertisement in the newspaper about it. You are, in a word, unfit to be queen. Step down willingly and we shan't execute you too much."

At this the Queen of Hearts threw her head back and laughed. "Step down? When I am about to *win*? We'll have one final count, and then it's game over – I win forever!

"Rabbit! Rabbit! Where is the list? How many toys do I have now? Rabbit…?"

The Queen of Hearts looked around, at first in annoyance, and then in complete perplexity. "Knave! Where is that dratted rabbit? He's supposed to be doing the tally for me!"

The Knave, Alice saw, was at the base of the mountain of toys along with several of the Queen's closest advisers (one was the Knave of Accounting – of course he would be in charge of lists of toys). None was the Rabbit, however, and all were shaking their heads and shrugging and denying and looking in general very worried and excitable.

"We shall execute the Rabbit twice as much," the Queen of Clubs announced. "For being a traitor to his own people as well as carrying out your ghastly orders."

But no one was paying attention to her.

The Knave put a reluctant foot on the base of the pile of toys, then gave up any pretence of trying to climb the ramshackle structure at all.

"No one has any idea where he is," he admitted loudly.

"WHAT?" the Queen of Hearts shouted, putting a hand to her ear.

"He's gone AWOL!" the Knave shouted back.

Then a little thing, something like a vole but with a longer snout and red eyes and webbed feet where its ears might normally have been, scrabbled up to the Knave and whispered something in his ear.

"Apparently he's gone to the Great Clock—*What?*" the Knave demanded in surprise, interrupting himself. He asked a question, quickly and quietly. The thing nodded. "All right. Apparently he's already gone to the Plain of Time, to push the clock forward."

"But that's ridiculous!" the Queen said as thoughtfully as was possible for her. "We haven't done a final tallying. I don't know if I have enough toys yet."

"They're all about to be *mine* anyway," the Queen of Clubs said helpfully.

"And what about the Ticket Master?" the Queen of Hearts' owl called out. "Have you checked against him? He has been collecting toys since the beginning of the last age. He definitely had more jacks than anyone else, acres of them."

"Yes, there's no point in ending the world until we know for certain," the Queen of Hearts agreed. "There may be no point in ending it at all. That rabbit is a traitor! He'll ruin everything! Off with his head!"

"*Surprise attack!*" the Queen of Clubs suddenly yelled.

A black card ran forward and threw himself down in the middle of the battlefield, directly between the two armies. He flipped himself over.

He was a nine.

All the spectators – where had they come from? They were suddenly there in the stands, *oohing* in impressed surprise. The crowd was a perfect cross section of Wonderland: creatures from the Unlikely and the land of the Clubs were bright-eyed and eager, well-dressed and passing bags of snacks to one another. Those from Heartland were tired, bloody, sad, wounded, fixed up with bandages and slings and eye patches. But they looked towards the battlefield with hope.

"Odds, odds on the war, on the end of the world, on the number of toys," a genial pig in a cap shouted, walking up and down the aisles waving pound notes in the air.

"I'll take seven to one against the Queen of Clubs," a duck declared, handing over what looked like a small bag of buttons.

"Lemonade, punch, quizzes and liquorice comfits. Biscuits and breaderflies," a woman with a tray of concessions called out.

"We're all going to go with the end of the world in a few moments," the Gryphon reminded her. "No one could possibly finish a bag of comfits in time."

The woman shrugged.

"This is terrible!" Alice cried. "I don't understand! I had solved everything! Oh, *why* is the White Rabbit going ahead to try to end the world if the Queen of Hearts isn't ready?"

"Of all the questions that pertain to this situation, is that really the one that's the most ripe?" the Hatter demanded.

"But the two armies – won't *they* determine the winner? And what about the Rabbit? What do we *do*..."

She looked around at their expectant faces, as if she were about to pull a March Hare out of her hat.

"No, what do *I* do," she said slowly. "I am the only one who can get us out of this. That is what you have been saying all along. I just didn't believe it until now. That I had anything to offer Wonderland at all – compared to you natives."

"I told you she wasn't a stupid girl," the Dodo said mildly, stirring his tea. "She just takes a while to get to the right answer. She's slow, that's all. But I think everyone in Angleland must be. Don't be hard on her."

"Where is the Plain of Time?" Alice asked.

"Oh, it's a terrible adventure off," the Gryphon said,

frowning. "First you have to go through the Labyrinth of Shifting Persimmons. Then you must cross the Sinking Sea. If you survive that, there's the land of—"

As he spoke the Dormouse tumbled down from the Hatter's hat with a large iced biscuit, aiming for the Dodo's tea to dunk it.

"Yes yes, *no*," Alice said, seizing the biscuit out of the poor little mouse's hands. She popped it into her own mouth. "Sorry. Seized for emergency measures."

Then she stuck all her fingers together like she was holding a very tiny, very sticky ball – and drew them apart.

Inside the space she created was a scene of a surprisingly serene, if empty and endless, prairie. Stuck in the middle of it was what looked very much like Big Ben, if Big Ben went to thirteen instead of twelve.

"Wish me luck," Alice said, stepping through.

"We're counting on you," the Dodo said, raising his teacup.

"It's one rabbit," Alice said, knowing exactly how stupid she sounded. "How hard can it be?"

Chapter Thirty-Six

The Plain of Time smelled funny.

"This," Alice said, "is how one can tell it isn't a dream at all but reality: one doesn't remember smells in dreams most of the time."

The air was… burning a little? There was nothing precisely she could see, but something definitely reminded her of the scent of *blue*. Sparks. Clean, like before a thunderstorm or after a particularly close lightning strike. The opposite of the smouldering piles of rubbish in Heartland. She felt the hairs on her arms rise and her heart quicken. Something exciting was about to happen.

And yet it didn't look like a place where anything

exciting happened, ever; it looked like an African veldt or a flat alpine field that extended endlessly. The grass was low and not green and vibrant emerald like a proper field, but shades of straw and sage. The flowers were delicate and tiny. The shadows were strange because the sun and all the moons stood next to each other in the sky in a kind of a standoff. The sun had fire, of course, but there were at least eight moons in their different phases, and some of the horns looked quite sharp indeed.

The clock tower stood in the middle of the field – or really, it could have been at either corner, at the bottom, or near the top, because the field went on forever, so who could say where the middle was, really? If clocks read the same in this world, it looked like it was about an hour and a half until thirteen o'clock. Whereas through the doorway, the Great Clock had seemed austere and severe ruling over the empty space, up close she saw that it had rosy cheeks and a cheeky smile and eyes that looked left and right with the seconds. Surprisingly friendly for something that could bring about the end of the world.

To the right of her was the White Rabbit.

They caught each other's eyes for a long moment. He wore his little waistcoat. He had his pocket watch (with heart-shaped fob) out but the face seemed to be cracked. The *Rabbit's* face was still and strange and his red eyes held hers with no fear – but also not with the blankness one normally associated with lagomorphs.

It was a pause before the storm, the breath before a tirade, a last moment of peace before the crying began.

Then he slipped the watch into his pocket and took off.

On all fours, like a rabbit.

"No!" Alice cried and raced after him.

There were many disadvantages for the girl.

For one thing, she was not made for running in the way a rabbit is. The poor dear had only two legs. Also her dress, corset, crinolines and underskirts were ridiculously confining. (A giant and satisfying *riiiiiip* could be heard as she opened her stride up just a little more, forcing the pace of legs below her a little faster.) Her shoes were stupid. She was not used to exercise.

She *did* have the fate of a world and panic within her, but whatever drove the Rabbit drove him mercilessly and madly.

Alice was larger than the Rabbit, which was a little bit of an advantage; her steps were three or four times his body length. There was a moment when she felt like she could have, if she just knew how, thrown herself over and on top of him.

But rabbits are made to evade meat eaters; the way they

run is tricky and wily. He would suddenly change direction, zigging and zagging with each leap, as confounding and frustrating as any rabbit a child has chased at dusk. It is like they can always predict the straight, boring paths of the house-apes who chase them.

The Rabbit danced around a small boulder; Alice leapt over it.

The Rabbit cleared a trickling not-quite-stream in a single hop, and Alice's leather boot went deep into the mud, becoming stuck there for precious seconds.

The Rabbit suddenly cut right, a perfect ninety degrees right, and Alice tripped over him trying to stop and change her own direction.

She could hear nothing but the Rabbit's hind feet beating the ground like a drum – and her own breathing in her ears, too loud and not enough.

The Rabbit made a mighty jump and landed on the first step of the clock tower. Without so much as a pause he leapt up and up and up, clearing several stairs at a time and never resuming his upright, human stance.

Alice practically fell over the first step, tumbling forward and hitting her hands hard on the fifth and sixth one. She bled but continued her forward and upward motion, all her limbs now out of sync and staggering.

She had to keep going. The world depended on her.

Around and around she followed the Rabbit up the outside of the tower.

She looked for biscuits in her pockets. She tried to make a window or a door while trying not to trip.

All too soon – or too late – she was on the walkway that led to the giant hands of the rosy, smiling clock face.

The Rabbit had the hour hand in his paws.

"NO!" Alice cried.

The Rabbit swung hard, and pushed it to thirteen.

"It had to be," the Rabbit said.

The ground – the whole world – began to shake. Alice flung up her arms to try to balance on the narrow walkway.

"*NO!* There has to be another way. There is always another way in Wonderland!" she cried in despair. She grabbed the hour hand herself to pull it back, but it didn't budge. The Rabbit didn't even try to stop her.

As Alice struggled and groaned, her dress stretched and ripped more, this time at the seams of her arms. The cloth shrank up her biceps as it tore, exposing her wrists and forearms.

And also the watch she had won from the Queen of Clubs.

"My watch…" she murmured.

What was it someone had said?

Time is always on your *side, Alice. Or your wrist, if you're wearing a watch.*

The Rabbit was looking at her curiously but bleakly. The tower began shaking so hard that she stumbled, almost falling off the platform. Strange cracks of purple and black lightning split the sky.

Alice grabbed the knob of the watch with her right hand and pulled.

Everything stopped.

Everything…

… was…

… silent.

Chapter Thirty-Seven

Alice fell forward from momentum, her body already used to the movements of the crumbling world. An ugly black streak of not-lightning froze in the sky; the waxing half-moon was caught in a look of surprise and horror. The Rabbit's eyes were glassy and wide like a taxidermy's.

Alice sobbed, catching her breath. The sound carried strangely across the prairie.

All was still except for her.

She didn't pause to ask *now what*. Perhaps little Alice would have done that.

Ever so carefully she popped open her watch – which also had thirteen numbers on it, each in a different style and font – and tried pushing its hands backwards.

Like the one on the tower itself, the hour hand wouldn't budge.

Neither would the minute hand.

Tentatively, holding her breath, Alice tried the second hand.

Success!

She sobbed again, in relief.

She wound the hand backwards… once… twice…

… and was plucked up through the air, pulled backside-first like the hand of God was playing dolls with her. Her hair waved the wrong way, and despite her body repeating the motions that had led her to where she was now, in reverse her mind wasn't pulled that way. She still *thought* forward and could examine the strange course she and the Rabbit had taken across the field.

Suddenly she stopped with a jerk, half in and out of the window she had created to get to the Plain of Time.

Two minutes and fourteen seconds.

That was as far back as she could go.

Perhaps the window was the end point; perhaps time couldn't travel through it the way it could through local space. She was frozen at the beginning, right before the Rabbit had come up next to her. She could see him hopping towards the tower but just starting to turn towards where she had popped out of nowhere.

"This is an easy fix," she said. But her words sounded strange and dead, as if they too couldn't travel through time-stopped air.

She made for the Rabbit, taking her belt off. All she would have to do was tie him up when he was frozen like this, and the game would be over.

"No," she told herself, despite the horrid sound of her voice. "No more game metaphors. We're done with that."

But as Alice approached the White Rabbit, the air around her seemed to thicken, like she was pushing against a strong wind. She closed her eyes and dug her feet in but the force grew stronger in response. Soon it was as hard as walking through water or mud. A hollow booming sound emanated every time she forced a foot or a hand forward even an inch, trying to split the air with her fingers.

Finally she ground to a complete stop. She could push no farther. And she was still several feet from the Rabbit.

Well, if she couldn't get to the Rabbit, the obvious answer was just to go to the tower, perhaps with a stick or a stone, and wait for him there, and bop him over the head.

Alas, Time had other ideas.

As she walked farther away from her starting point, once again the air built itself up against her. She was little more than halfway to the Tower before she couldn't budge, even by sliding her feet forward in the dirt a smidgen at a time. The booming sound became unbearable.

"All right, then. I can't stray far from my point of origin, in time *or* geographic locality," she concluded. "I'll just set myself right in front of the Rabbit, as close as I can to him, and grab him when he runs by. He'll be so surprised at my sudden appearance that he will be unable to do anything but continue barrelling forward into me. It's a trap that practically sets itself."

She went as close to the Rabbit as she could and walked back and forth in front of him several times, checking the angles, making absolutely sure she was directly in front of his path. No room for error.

Then she hunched down with her hands out like a wicketkeeper in cricket, ready for catching.

She took a deep breath and put a finger on the watch knob.

"Three… two… one… *go*!"

She hit the button.

Chapter Thirty-Eight

Time restarted.

The White Rabbit started moving – but slowly, as if Time was warming up, stretching.

Suddenly he shot forward.

His sometimes-human eyes saw the girl who had somehow appeared between him and the clock tower. They widened in shock. It was obvious from just that little movement that he had no idea Alice was capable of anything like this – anything at all surprising or dangerous. Alice would remember that later.

But right now she was too busy being confronted with a simple fact of nature. White Rabbits in waistcoats with pocket watches aside, rabbits in general were creatures of the wild with very little brain – but very lots of instinct. He might not have understood *how* Alice got there, but this puzzle meant nothing to the rabbitiness inherent in him.

Without thinking he thumped his hind legs to the side and darted around the unexpected obstacle.

Alice cried out in dismay as he whisked by her, his inside leg beating the ground twice in a double thump to make up for the hard right turn. Rabbit fur flew up Alice's nose.

Being human (and a Victorian one at that) the girl had very little instinct and very lots of reason: it took her a precious millisecond or two to process what had happened and then turn and run after him.

Although her plan hadn't worked out the way she had expected, she was at least much, much closer to him than in their previous race. Alice made herself run harder, pumping her arms and legs and running on her toes. It was easy because her dress was already torn.

The Rabbit bounced around the large rock as before; this time she cleared it without pausing.

There was the stream and bog – he leapt straight over it. She wasted a second or two pausing to see what was the best way through so she wouldn't get stuck like last time. There was a tuffet that looked perfect for pushing off from – and it was. Strong and sturdy and springy, it gave her an extra foot or two of lift, which recovered a little of her precious lost yards.

The Rabbit made one human mistake: looking round back at her just as he began to leap up the tower stairs.

Alice threw herself forward to grab him but missed and once again tumbled against the hard stone steps, scraping her palms *and* her shins this time. With a shriek of frustration she pushed herself to her feet and practically crawled up the steps before rightfully regaining her footing.

Despite all her flailing about, she was right behind the Rabbit. By the time the two reached the top, he was once again within grabbing distance.

Without a thought for the danger of the unfenced catwalk and the height they were at, Alice lunged forward and clawed at him.

One finger got a bit of waistcoat; the luckier left hand got what felt like a neck-fold and a little bit of flesh.

But the rabbit thumped and kicked and his hair shed into her fingers; he slipped like a jacket out of her grasp with great clouds of white bunny fur.

He leapt straight up and caught himself on the hour hand of the clock. His weight and momentum were enough to pull it down to thirteen.

The world began to shake.

Alice pulled the knob on her watch…

Chapter Thirty-Nine

It was something to have the entire world stopped and frozen and to be able to scream as much as she wanted. No one heard and everyone waited for her to be done.

Finally Alice wiped her forehead with her wrist – careful not to nudge the watch. She glared at the dumb rabbit dangling from the hour hand and for just a moment had a vision of him strung up with a brace of other conies over the shoulder of a hunter returning home from a good day's work.

Immediately she felt sorry for that; the White Rabbit was an intelligent being who deserved neither being filled with shot nor being eaten.

Although he *had* decided to end the entire world, killing

everyone in it, and of his own volition! Not even on the Queen of Hearts' orders; he was a would-be mass murderer!

She slowly wound the second hand of her watch widdershins, watching everything carefully in reverse as she was pulled back towards the start: the beginning of the race, the boulder, the bog, the stairs, her falling…

Then she took a moment to breathe and think.

She walked out to the boulder – the air only thickened a little at that distance – and, breaking back multiple nails and scraping her fingertips raw, managed to pull it out of place and turn it on its small side, revealing a hole in the ground. This she covered with grass and rushes.

She dusted off her hands, pleased with her work.

"He's so intent on the clock tower he won't have noticed things in the landscape shifting. He'll just be barrelling forward and *pop* – if he doesn't crash head first right into the stone he'll definitely get stuck in the hole, even for a moment."

She smiled, stretched, and got herself ready.

"Three… two… one… *go*!"

She hit the knob.

Chapter Forty

Time restarted.

The stone *did* catch him off guard.

He almost leapt right into it. At the last minute he tried to change direction but fell back into the hole.

"Ha!" Alice cried. "I have you now!"

Like a child's toy – or Bill, pushed out of a chimney – the White Rabbit shot straight back up out of the hole, powered only by the fire of his hind legs. He hung in the air for a moment like a confused balloon and then dropped back down, touching a single left claw onto the top of the upright stone.

He used that to push himself off again, and continued towards the tower.

"Damn!" Alice cried.

She chased.

He ran.

He bounded up the stone steps.

She tripped.

Not quite as badly this time – she didn't even scrape her hands. Merely reddened them.

He leapt for the clock's hands.

"I did it for—" he shouted.

Alice pulled the knob on her watch. Time stopped.

Chapter Forty-One

Time restarted.

Time restarted.

Time restarted.

Alice added a gash to her forehead, a slightly turned ankle, an abrasion all up her left calf, several puncture wounds to her arms, and embedded grit in her cheek. She lost a boot.

She also lost her bodice trying to rig up a net to ensnare him.

She screamed and kicked and threw stones at the Rabbit. They slowed down as they approached his frozen form and dropped equally slowly to the ground, far out of harm's way.

She stood in her undershirt and corset, covered in mud and sweat and blood, her hair down around her, looking like a witch from *Macbeth*.

She lay back on the grass of the Plain of Time for a while, watching the strange moons and sun and chewing on a stalk of timegrass.

"It's just another stupid Wonderland riddle," she mused. "I can't capture the rabbit. I never could. Not before, not now. That's apparently just not allowed. Alice never gets the White Rabbit.

"So what *can* I do? Just let the world end? Someone told me that time was on my side – I have figured out that part at least, with the watch. But if I can't get the Rabbit, who can? How can I stop him? How can I stop him from getting to the clock and ending the world? What do I have that is unique in solving this? How does *perspective* solve this?"

She regarded the tower, the strange thing out of a child's dream or nightmare. It seemed so harmless with its rosy cheeks and rolling eyes. Even the ancient stone steps could be seen as part of the block tower an imaginative child had built while muttering to herself about Time and rabbits and Snakes and Ladders and games of War and piles of toys and suns and moons and stopping the end of the world. Being a hero. So many different games of childhood all mixed together in the mad mind of a lonely child. All of them old and familiar.

Alice blinked.

"*Perspective.* I don't have the right one!

"You're given a rabbit and a tower and a countdown and think you've got to stop the rabbit. But you're playing the wrong game, Alice," she said, beginning to grin. "Forget the rabbit! The *tower* is the object of this game! Just *GET THERE FIRST*!"

She smiled, rose and kicked off her other boot. She stretched, and got herself ready, crouching down the way she had seen serious runners do.

"Last one there's a rotten egg," she told the frozen rabbit over her shoulder.

"Three… two… one… *go*!"

She hit the button.

Chapter Forty-Two

Time restarted.

Alice didn't look left, right or behind her. She didn't even bother to imagine the surprised look on the White Rabbit's bewhiskered face as she suddenly appeared out of nowhere in front of him, running to the same goal. She ignored him.

She pumped her arms and dug her toes into the soft ground. It was really quite delightful, feeling the two connect with a primal joy she hadn't experienced since she was a young girl at the beach. The earth was pushing her off with each stride, *helping* her spring along to the finish. Her long golden hair streamed out behind her, shedding the dried mud and blood.

For a brief moment something white appeared below and to the right of her, perilously near her feet. It was the Rabbit, pushing faster and harder than ever. He was so close she could have wasted a second and kicked him – out of her way, out of the race.

She didn't.

She concentrated on running and pulled ahead.

She worried for one ecstatic moment as she cleared the bog that she was actually losing precious moments in the air as she hung there below the absurd celestial orbs.

But she landed and went on regardless.

The steps.

She was there first. She just had to not—

—fall.

Without thinking she lengthened her legs and leapt. She didn't worry about landing.

And so she touched down seven steps up, and the falling-forward momentum at the end of her jump only propelled her farther along.

Around and around she ran, two, three steps at a time, leaning into the tower and letting her own weight keep her safe.

Alice could hear the tiny stony *thuds* below her of a rabbit's hind feet pounding the grey stone.

She broke out onto the catwalk below the clock's face

with a scream of triumph. She swung round to face the White Rabbit, who tried with one last, valiant bound to leap *over* her and land on the hour hand. Alice punched straight up above her and knocked him into the clock's nose, where the two iron hands were attached.

The Rabbit fell in a crumpled heap at her feet.

"HA!" Alice cried, kneeling down and seizing him. "*I WIN!* The Queen of Hearts loses! The world is safe from your terrible mistress – and your own terrible, terrible acts of villainy!"

The Rabbit was shuddering and shaking. Alice turned him to face her, to make him look her in the eye – and saw that he was sobbing.

"The Queen can't hurt you," she said hesitantly, confused. "Any more than I and my friends will, I mean. She has lost. The world is saved and she will be punished. You will be, too – but in a fair trial."

"Win…?" the White Rabbit moaned. "I never wanted her to *win*. I don't care about winning. I wanted to end it all."

"I beg your pardon?" Alice asked, unsure she heard him properly. Adrenaline and triumph were still raging in her ears and making it hard to understand.

"End it… End her raids, tortures, executions, imprisonments, looting, burning… End it all. End the pain. End her reign. End the world where my Mary Ann was killed."

"*You?*" she eventually asked, trying to understand. "Wanted to destroy the world? You? Not the Queen of Hearts? Coming here to speed up the clock wasn't all a plan of her invention?"

"She wanted to have all the toys when the world ended, whenever it was due," the Rabbit said, pointing miserably at the clock. Tears rolled down the fur on his face, eventually sinking in and matting it down. Without thinking Alice pulled out what remained of her last handkerchief and tried to hand it to him. He didn't even see it. The little, respectable, ridiculous White Rabbit no longer cared about such picayune niceties. For some reason this was more shocking than anything he had said. Alice did her best to wipe away the majority of tears herself as he lay prone in her lap.

"Once she was sure she had the most toys she probably *would* have advanced Time so no one would have a chance to beat her, and win. I don't care. I just want this world to be over, to restart with Mary Ann alive again. Even if I didn't know her, even if we never met again. *She* would be alive. And safe. And no one would be in pain or in prison any more. Everyone would come back. And maybe even the Queen of Hearts would be reborn as someone better. Who knows?"

Alice's head was whirring.

"This clock doesn't end the world? It… restarts it?" she asked.

"It does both, you dim thing. Ends one game and starts the next. Don't you know how games on a timer work? You really are such a dull girl compared to my Mary Ann. Sometimes. But sometimes you outwit the Rabbit…" he mused.

Alice put a hand to her temple, exhausted and confused by this revelation, unmindful of the dried sweat and bits of dirt that flaked off as she did so.

"THREEE CHEERS FOR QUEEN ALICE!"

Alice leaned over – dangerously – and peeped at the plain below.

There was a small but growing crowd of bedraggled and excited Wonderland creatures, clapping and shouting and leaping up and down and capering about.

"She's saved the world!"

"She beat the Queen of Hearts!"

"She wins!"

"I didn't…" Alice began, standing up to address them better. The rabbit was still in her arms, prone, apparently unconcerned with whatever happened next.

Suddenly there was a curious weight on Alice's head.

Cradling the Rabbit with her left hand, she reached up cautiously with her right and found exactly what she expected there: a giant crown, probably golden, heavy and ornate and, from the glints she saw reflected in the clock face, very, very, sparkly. A cape somehow slipped over her shoulders and Alice hoped very sorely that the soft fur at the edges wasn't ermine. She had seen several ermines on this adventure.

The crowd below her was very large now: she could pick out, like shapes in the clouds, the people from the various places she had been: there was a contingent from Ornithsiville, mostly dignified but with one enthusiastic cider seller. The Queen of Clubs stood at the head of a fantastic procession, riding her buzzywhump. She smiled broadly at Alice, apparently not at all displeased at her coronation. There was the horse at the head of a train, toasting her with a cup of foul train tea.

Alice's heart leapt when she saw the Hatter, Gryphon, Dodo and some of the others waving madly at the very base of tower, telling anyone who would listen how *they* knew her *personally*. She waved back, which was now hard with a rabbit in one hand and a sceptre in the other.

"Bother!" she swore.

Carefully, being sure not to trip on her cape, she made a long, slow descent from the catwalk. At the base of the steps was a ceremonial float that had been prepared in her honour, complete with a high chair that looked a bit like the clock tower for her to sit in and wave from. It was so rickety she felt far more dizzy and unsafe atop it than she had at the top of the clock tower itself.

The Queen of Hearts was in a cage on a wagon, pouting furiously. At first Alice found it hard to be angry with such a ridiculous creature… and then she thought of Mary Ann, and the March Hare, and the Hatter's eye, and all the insanely horrible things the Queen had perpetrated against the good people of Wonderland.

"You are a vile creature," Alice told her coldly. "Without a bit of Nonsense in you. You are directed, cruel and hateful. You don't deserve to live – more than that, you don't deserve to live in *Wonderland*."

The Queen of Hearts' eyes bulged wider than seemed possible. Of all the things she had expected from Alice, this was very obviously the furthest from it – and worse than anything she could have imagined.

Suddenly two bright, ball-shaped boys popped up between the cage and Alice's float. From their mouths came a grating, wheedly apology sound. Alice's ears nearly crumpled with horror.

"We are sorry, Alice, Alice."

There was Tweedledee.

"Alice, we are *very* sorry."

That was Tweedledum, and he raised his eyebrows at his brother to show how much more sorry he was.

"She took all our toys—"

"But said we should have new ones—"

"Once the world was over," they finished together.

Alice looked at them levelly.

Was it worth pointing out the ridiculousness of what they said?

"Can we sing a song for you?" Tweedledee asked.

"It's a very good one," Tweedledum added eagerly.

They opened their mouths—

"Nope," Alice said, spotting some people in the crowd below she would much rather spend time with. She slipped down the chair and ran over to them, still cradling the White Rabbit. The Hatter regarded the creature with a raised eyebrow.

"I think he is punishing himself enough," Alice admitted. "He wanted to end the world to stop all the terrible things that were going on – and because he didn't want to live without Mary Ann."

"Hmm," the Hatter said thoughtfully.

"But now we're all safe, and the Queen is behind bars, and we can all live happily ever after," Alice said with a grin. Mice and gnats were replacing her outfit – discreetly – with a golden gown, and she didn't even mind.

"Yup! At least for another hour or so," the Gryphon agreed happily.

"Yes, at least for—*What?* What do you mean?"

"The clock," the Hatter said, pointing at it. "This day's almost over. World's about to end."

"Well, we must stop it!" Alice jumped up, putting the catatonic rabbit back on the wagon. "Let's go and move the hands back…!"

The Hatter looked at her as if she were Mad. "You can't stop the end of the world. Silly girl. Maybe *you* stole my Nonsense," he added suspiciously.

"But! But! That's terrible! All of this was for nothing!" Alice shouted, feeling panic take over her body, arms and legs.

"Not true at all," said the Cheshire Cat, rubbing against her legs. "You beat the Queen of Hearts. You prevented her from winning. You caught the White Rabbit. You won, you became queen, you stopped all the pain and misery in this world."

"But you only have an hour left!" she shrieked.

"All games end, Alice," the cat said softly. "All dreams get woken from, eventually."

"The same game forever would be *boring*," the Dodo put in. "Even for me."

"Yes, definitely time for something new," the Hatter agreed.

"But I don't want you to…" What? Die? Disappear? Restart? "I don't want to say goodbye."

"Then don't," the Gryphon said, shrugging. A forked tongue came out and licked her tears. It was warm and wet like a dog's; not entirely unpleasant.

"But what do we do?" Alice asked plaintively.

"That's up to you now," the Hatter said simply. "You are Queen."

Alice looked around her. All the creatures of Wonderland she had met and saved, she had avoided and fought with, she had sung songs with and run from, all the cards and bandersnatches and mome raths and borogroves and paper people and dragon flies, the animals and birds and insects and people, they all looked at her expectantly.

(The Knave looked at her curiously, toasting her with his cider.)

"I..." She thought hard.

What else *was* there to do?

"I... declare teatime and Nonsense until the End of Time!"

Chapter Forty-Three

An ear-deafening roar the likes of which even Wonderland had never heard before went up from the Plain of Time. Everyone danced and shouted and cavorted and jumped and flew. There was cheering and a ticker-tape parade, the pops of some sort of cannon or gun or perhaps champagne, and a walrus band that marched through blowing their tusks. Tea was served all around, from large and small kettles into endless souvenir coronation cups. Trays and trays of EAT ME cookies were distributed. It would not be too much to say it was the largest, happiest, most raucous party anywhere at any Time.

Alice sat on the wagon, dangling her legs over the side, one hand on the slowly recovering Rabbit, the other on the

Cheshire Cat's back. Her sceptre was being used to stir some lemon into a cup of tea the size of a church. Her crown was cocked on her head.

She felt very, very strange.

She wanted to cry, but it was obvious that no one else was sad – or wanted anyone sad around them at the party.

"Maybe this time I'll come back as a cobbler," the Hatter was telling a pretty young chicken eagerly. "*That* would be a fun change."

"Not me. I shall be a Dodo, I think," the Dodo mused. "Maybe with a different wig."

"Cheshire," Alice said, suddenly remembering, "You told me that *Mary Ann* was the real hero. You said, 'If you want my advice… you'll find her.' "

"And you did," the Cheshire said, bathing his tail. "You found her… or a hero… or something that led to all of this. Inside of you. Oh, but you have needed so much of my help! I even sent Katz to help you find your way back, through the pond and the old tree…"

Alice sighed, for once not distracted by thoughts of the boy (though it was nice to remember his name). "I wish I could have known Mary Ann. I feel like I've been right behind her, just missing her the whole time, unable to catch her – like the White Rabbit. I was foolish to be jealous of her for so long… It's just that she always seemed to know what she was doing, and everyone loved her for that. She knew who she was and what to do and how to bring about change in her world. It made me feel so useless and unsure of myself. I should have just learned from her. And I suppose I did, in a way.

"I would dearly love to meet her. I suppose… with the world beginning again… she will come back. Will I ever be able to return here again, Cheshire?"

"A man cannot walk into the same river twice, for later he is not the same man and it is not the same river," the Cheshire answered.

"I am not a man and this is not a river," she said, rolling her eyes. She gestured at her friends, who were now singing, even the Dormouse. "Will they even remember me?"

"Katz will remember you," the Cheshire said with a grin, his body fading in and out of existence. He walked up and down clawingly in her lap like a real cat, albeit one that went invisible. He sighed in contentment as he settled himself down and curled up. "I can't remember a single thing *now*."

And they all lived very very happily until the clock struck thirteen.

Chapter Forty-Four

Alice woke up slowly.

She was at home in her own bed, and it was morning, late but not too late; there were shafts of pale golden sun on the wall in front of her. She watched it for a while, feeling sad – no, *melancholy*. She did not turn over and try to go back to sleep, however. She just lay awake in silence. Dinah regarded her out of one blearily open eye.

When she finally went downstairs for breakfast no one was there, which was a relief. She sat down and had the first, hot sip of tea all to herself. She closed her eyes and just felt the quiet inside her, the quiet. It wasn't an *empty* feeling. It was a pause, a breath before a birth. It was waiting.

The paper was next to the butter, folded so that the top

of the front page showed: RAMSBOTTOM RALLY TUESDAY NIGHT. Alice shivered. There was something so stark and ominous about the words. They foreshadowed truly dreadful things to come. In this world villains weren't even whimsical – the streets would never run red here with milk paint, but with real blood. Alice was back in the land of no Nonsense *ever*. Possibly *for*ever.

How could she fix *this*? She had saved a whole world – somehow; the details were fading a bit now. But she knew she had managed to do it because she had the advantage of coming from the real world, with a real-world, strategic mind. Here she was just an ordinary citizen of England, no special advantages or perspective whatsoever.

Mathilda came in, and when she saw Alice sitting there, started to open her mouth – and then closed it. She sat down and made her own tea instead, but without the extra clinks and noises that very obviously stated I AM MAKING MY TEA AND NOT TALKING TO YOU – which tactic *both* sisters occasionally employed.

Mathilda shuffled through some letters and then said, very casually, "I don't think Corwin and I will be attending the rally tonight."

Alice blinked, surprised but remaining silent, waiting, gazing at her sister over the rim of her cup.

"It's all a bit…" Mathilda scrunched up her face, looking

for just the right dismissive word. "Ugly. Corwin and I feel very strongly England should take care of its own first, mind you. But those in the Square *are* England's own now. And we should treat them with nothing less than charity."

"Hmm," Alice said, not wanting to say anything to jinx the moment. She nodded, as if this was the logical and proper, the *only*, conclusion to come to.

"And Corwin is especially sorry for ever suggesting we introduce you to Coney," Mathilda added. "He will come round later with his own apology and probably a very large, very ugly gift. Please just nod and take it and do what you will with it later."

Alice smiled. "But why this change of heart for him, all of a sudden?"

"Corwin… looks for the best in everyone, perhaps to the point of certain blindness. But even he has no trouble at recognising criminal behaviour."

She held up a copy of the morning *Kexford Weekly*.

There on the front page was the photo of Mrs Yao. There was even a blowup and a callout of the note she held – the handwriting *very* clear – and a plea for any good citizen who recognised the handwriting to report the miscreant to the police immediately.

The photo was credited to *A*.

Everyone in Kexford would soon figure out who both the perpetrator and the photographer were.

"Actually, I find myself running out of some of that oolong that Mrs Yao carries," Mathilda added contemplatively. "I may drop by her shop later. She could use the business to help pay for this bit of nonsense."

At no point did Mathilda actually apologise.

Aloud.

But it was enough.

Alice opened her mouth to say something nice and meaningful and sisterly, but what came out was…

"Bit of nonsense! *Nonsense*… But of course! That's *it*! I *do* have an advantage and perspective different from everyone here! Take *that,* Mary Ann! Mathilda, you're a genius!" She leapt up, kissed her sister on the cheek, and ran out of the room.

"Well," her sister muttered after she had left, "at least someone in this ridiculous family finally recognises that."

A one-time visit to the esteemed law offices of Alexandros and Ivy was unusual. Twice would have been suspect. So instead Alice went to the Square and grabbed the first child she found – Zara, the one who had found her after her camera was stolen.

"Hello! I need a favour – I need a message sent to a friend. Would you do it for me? I'll pay you for your time," she said, opening her purse.

"It's Katz, isn't it?" the girl said flatly. With neither intrigue nor condemnation.

Alice looked into the eyes of this little girl who was not her, whom she had never been. But there was a spark in her eye, an Alice-spark. Humour and wilfulness and curiosity. It just came out differently. The little girl tried not to grin wickedly and mostly succeeded.

"Yes," Alice admitted.

"Is it a love note?"

"No. Not yet, anyway. Look, do you want to earn a ha'penny or not?"

"Always," the little girl said promptly. "But can I still earn it if I know where he is, and it's not at his work, and it's a public place where you can meet and talk, but it's very loud, so the two of you won't be heard? *Perfect* for a secret meeting?"

Alice pretended to think for a moment. "Oh, all right. You drive a hard bargain."

"He's at the Samovar right now, reading the news and probably being grumpy."

This was a café run by an Englishman, but with sort of a Russian theme because he loved Russian novels. All the students who could afford it went there to discuss literature, play chess and toss around revolutionary ideas that they would then forget later, in their cups.

"Thank you kindly! A pleasure doing business with you, Miss Sarah. Here's your reward."

The little girl looked at the big copper coin she was handed in wonder.

"I don't have change for a full penny," she said regretfully.

"Oh no, it's all yours. A ha'penny for the information. Another for your silence."

Zara grinned and curtsied and then ran off, overcome with eagerness to share her fortune with her friends – or at least the news of it.

Katz *was* at the Samovar, but he wasn't reading the news; he was considering a chess problem laid out on the table before him. The pieces were exquisitely carved red and white bone but the board was chalked in on the table by what seemed like a fairly tipsy hand. Katz was frowning at it so intently he didn't see her walk up.

Alice reached out and tipped over the red queen.

"Alice!" Katz cried. His face broke out into a smile that encompassed all of him and made it seem like all days would be sunny forever. Alice wanted to live in that smile.

"What a surprise! Twice in one week, and both times unexpected."

She sat down across from him. A quick look round revealed students in robes, students in plain clothes, a few old professors, and even a couple of Aunt Vivian's librarian friends (who looked a little disgusted with the ruckus around them).

"Can I get you some tea?" he offered. "It's terrible."

"Lovely offer, but no thank you."

They were both silent for a moment, but it wasn't as awkward as it was supposed to be.

"Are you really the Cheshire Cat?" she finally asked, softly.

Katz smiled broadly and shrugged maddeningly. "I don't think I *am* him. I know him. He knows me. We are one of a kind in our separate worlds."

"That's a Cheshire answer if I ever heard one," Alice said with a sigh. "Will he remember me if I ever go back? Will any of them?"

"No one could ever forget Alice," Katz said, taking her hands in his.

"Will I—will I see them again?"

"I think it's a fairly good possibility. But who can say? Did you come just to talk to me about that other place, and that other me?" he asked, a little accusingly.

Alice smiled. "No, of course not.

"I came to talk to you about what we could do about Ramsbottom's ridiculous rally."

His hands froze on her own, skeleton-stiff. His jaw didn't *quite* drop, but did fall a little, along with the rest of his face.

He recovered himself quickly and pulled back from her, releasing her hands and sort of shaking out his shoulders, moving his jaw this way and that to dispel any lingering emotion.

"Oh, of course, of course. Most excellent. I'm interested in hearing any of your ideas. It's going to be a terrible thing, no matter what happens, really… you know… bad for the community… and bad… just… in general…"

Alice couldn't keep a straight face. She burst out into peals of naughty, hysterical giggles, covering her mouth with one gloved hand as prettily as any coquette – but really afraid of spraying her companion.

"Of course I want to talk to you about *other* things, too, you silly goose! You're as serious and sensitive as—as, well, *I* was when I first went to Wonderland."

He looked confused, his handsome face a funny blank until it relaxed into a rueful smile.

"You… I… certainly…" The barrister was at a loss for words. Then he grinned and indicated her hands. "May I?"

"Of course," Alice said, presenting them. He took them properly this time, clasped them together and kissed them.

"This is going to be difficult," he said, soft and serious. "Your family, my family…"

"All amazing and new things *are* difficult," Alice said, squeezing his hands back. "But most turn out to be worth it. And everything else is Nonsense.

"Which, ironically, is actually the other thing I came to talk to you about…"

The day of the rally was grey, chilly and a little damp, which might have already tempered spirits some. Mathilda had announced primly that she and Corwin were "going to take a ride in the country with Mother and Father"; they were going to avoid the whole situation entirely. And while it seemed a little cowardly, Alice couldn't entirely blame them.

"I'm afraid we shall miss all the fun," Alice's mother said wistfully.

"Yes, I think I would prefer *anything* to sitting in a bumpy carriage on a cold and wet day with that giant sheep of a man looking at what – fields? Forests? From a distance? I don't think there's even going to be a picnic," Alice's father added mournfully. "And whatever am I going to do with *this* now?"

He pulled out a ridiculous multicoloured scarf fringed in gold coins and draped it around his head. "I had such plans!"

Alice was overcome and hugged both her parents at once.

"Corwin is here," Mathilda said, coming into the room and pulling on her hideously ugly brown gloves, the ones with the big bows. Her big man came through the door after only a single knock – rude! – carrying a large box.

"Hello, everyone!" he called genially.

Really, Alice thought, wincing, *he would be ever so much more tolerable if he just lowered his voice!*

"This is for you, Alice!" he bawled, shoving the box towards her. Then his face went a little red and his voice *did* lower, uncharacteristically. He even looked at his feet. "I… ah… we… You know, he seemed so… but then, of course… Butting in where we're not wanted, obviously! Turned out… even if they don't prosecute," he finished.

Alice nodded, trying to look serious.

"Thank you. I very much appreciate the apology. More than *any* gift," she said, and opened the box.

Then: *"Oh!"*

"My goodness," her father said, looking over her shoulder.

It was a camera. A top-of-the-line, latest-model version of the one that had been stolen.

"*Thank* you," Alice said again, really this time.

Even Mathilda looked surprised. "Hm," she said, apparently having still expected something ugly and unuseful. Alice wondered at that: it seemed as though her sister hadn't told him what to get. Whatever faults and prejudices and incorrect views Corwin had, at least he paid attention. He knew what was important to Alice, which meant he knew what was important to Mathilda. Alice might not agree with him on anything, but it was obvious he loved her sister and his heart was in the right place. Even if his mind and his mouth weren't.

Still, conversations at Christmas would be a struggle from now on.

Especially when… eventually… Alice introduced them all to Katz. Then things would get *really* interesting.

At the market Ramsbottom grinned and kept his spirits up like a carnival ringmaster; he even wore a spotless grey tailcoat and top hat with a bright red rose in it, like some sort of showman. His brother was more discreetly dressed, in browns, quietly helping set up the stage and directing crowd management. Coney bipped and bopped around him like the White Rabbit Alice knew him to be.

(Also soon to be as irrelevant as a prone lagomorph.)

Almost everyone from every part of Kexford was

assembling for the thing, eyeing the now-empty tables soon to be set with punch and treats – but only *after* everyone paid attention nicely to the things that were to be said. And cheered appropriately.

Alice watched this all from behind a tree.

She wore a little-girl Alice outfit; short dress and ridiculous oversized blue sash, gigantic blue bow in her hair (there were wide, French-style knickers under the dress, so it was all proper). The bright-coloured scarf her father had was tied around her wrist. He was there in spirit.

"All ready, darling?" Katz asked, slipping in next to her behind the tree.

She reached out and squeezed his hand excitedly. "This is going to be *brilliant*!"

"I can't imagine this is going to do wonders for my career," Katz said with a sigh, indicating the bright purple-and-white striped union suit he wore under his more proper jacket and boots. An extra bit of the material hung off his back like a tail.

"That's what these are for," Alice pointed out, slipping on her Venetian mask and indicating that he do the same. "Oh look, they're starting. Remember: wait for the signal!"

The crowd had filled out as much as it was going to. Gilbert looked out over them, preening like an Ornithsiville native, sticking his chest out and grinning. Red, white and blue flags had been handed out to the audience and were being waved most patriotically. Everything looked perfect.

"My friends and fellow countrymen," he bellowed with a grin. "Thank you for joining me! We are gathered here to celebrate government and our glorious England! But not all is perfect in this great nation of ours. Recently there has been a trend of…"

"There they go!" Alice whispered. "Perfect!"

From the far side of the market came two dancing clowns. They wore matching caps and had their clothing pulled up over upside-down skirt hoops, the resulting effect making them look like giant, perfectly round balls. On their chests each wore a giant pin, one of which said GILBERT and the other of which said QUAGLEY. They held hands high in the air and pirouetted around one another, trying to look serious while balancing on their toes.

The crowd roared in laughter and approval.

The look on Gilbert's face was *not* approval. It was very, very dark.

But he knew his audience.

He put on a game grin and shouted: "All right, yes, very amusing. The hats are a nice touch."

"I WANT TO BE MAYOR," the Gilbert clown shouted.

"I WANT TO KICK LITTLE CHILDREN," the Quagley clown cried.

"THEY'RE SO DANGEROUS!" the Gilbert clown agreed. They nodded, shook hands and bowed.

"Who are those two?" Katz whispered.

"Friends of Aunt Viv's. Poster painters and onetime performance artists," Alice whispered back. *"NOW!"* she added, shaking the multicoloured scarf up and down as a signal.

Suddenly, from all around the crowd, children came running: the children from the Square, wearing bright capes and flower crowns and holding bouquets. They threaded in and around everyone in the audience, giving people flowers and tossing handfuls of sweets in the air.

"FOREIGNERS! GET THEM!" the Gilbert clown screamed.

"LOCK UP THE CHILDREN! LOCK THEM UP!" the Quagley clown cried. The two ran into each other, fell down, and then ran after the children. Poorly.

The audience ate it up. Everyone was laughing.

The real Gilbert was fuming.

He cleared his throat.

"A joke's a joke, but these are serious times, my people—"

"NOOOOOOO! MY ENGLAND! MY PRECIOUS ENGLAND!"

This was Aunt Vivian herself, powdered white like

a ghost, with ugly red rouge and a black beauty mark (and mask). She was wrapped in layers and layers of old-fashioned dresses, three corsets at least, all black, and trailed a black lace train. She walked on shoes with almost stilt-tall heels and towered above the crowd like a theatre monster.

"BETTER TO DIE A WIDOW THAN LIVE A WOMAN!" she cried, then swooned into the arms of a sturdy-looking young fellow at the edge of the crowd. His friends whistled and jeered. At first he looked uncertain, but then he got into the spirit of it – and gave her a kiss.

"OOOH, YOU CHEEKY YOUNG MAN," Aunt Viv said, hitting him lightly with her fan.

"KICK THEM OUT! KICK THEM ALL OUT!"

This was a clown policeman with a club made from a giant piece of bread. He pretended to check everyone's identifications. "PAPERS! BIRTH CERTIFICATES! CHRISTENING RECORDS! NEWSPAPER ARTICLES!"

Gilbert and Quagley – the real ones – were now shouting at each other, arguing with very heated-looking faces. They couldn't be heard at all above the din. Coney looked sort of wilted beside them.

"Ready for our grand entrance?" Katz asked.

"Of course!" Alice answered.

And because they were wearing masks and no one could see or know, they kissed.

For the *second* scandalous time.

Then they joined the throngs of other clowns coming out of hiding, dancing with the audience, playing horns, throwing flower confetti into the air, and generally sowing Nonsense.

"Because, of course, the real world needs some Nonsense, sometimes," Alice had said to Katz at the Samovar, when originally revealing her plan. "Not *all the time* and not *never*. Just enough to remind us when real things get too ridiculous to be borne. And sometimes we have to create that Nonsense ourselves."

"What the real world *needs* is an Alice," Katz had said back to her. "And Wonderland, too."

That was the first time he had kissed her.

Willard came in at the very end of the performance, riding on the shoulders of one of the stronger clowns. He wore nothing too silly beyond a giant red, white and blue hat he had designed himself. He waved and threw sweets and shook hands and kissed babies – both real and clown doll.

And afterwards there was punch for all.

Epilogue

Dear reader, I suppose you have questions. You, unlike the Dodo and the Hatter and the Dormouse, are not content with things just being as they are – you must know the *future*, the *outcomes*, the *reasons*. So I shall give you three answers, and three only, for that is the magic number in fairy stories.

Question Number Three:

Was Willard elected mayor, thereby saving the town of Kexford and all its inhabitants forever – or, perhaps, condemning them to life in a humourless town where each worked according to his ability and was given according to his need, forever?

Answer:

No, he was not.

However, his bid for the position (and takeover of Ramsbottom's rally) brought to light some of the less palatable beliefs of the other party.

So it was Mallory Griffle Frundus (*Frundus – For Us!*) who was elected. And he did a very good job of renovating the town sewer system.

(Even Willard grudgingly approved of his negotiations with the factory owners to get fair wages for their employees in return for some zoning by the city.)

Once elected, Frundus was asked what he thought about the unruly immigrant children in the Square, and was taken there by certain prejudiced members of the community to observe their foul and disgraceful behaviour. He watched the children for a moment, frowned, and then declared:

"You're playing marbles all wrong! Let me show you how we did it when *I* was a lad."

Question Number Two:

Did Alice and Katz marry and live happily ever after?

Answer:

Yes.

It was difficult – very difficult – at first; neither set of parents approved of the arrangement. But love and gritted teeth won out.

(Also grandchildren. Grandchildren have a way of smoothing out the worst, most cranky old people.)

Katz became a full partner in the law firm; Alice became even more Alice, exhibiting her photographs and touring Europe with him and occasionally Aunt Vivian, who introduced her to such strangely familiar venues as the Cabaret Voltaire. You will not have heard of Alice when reading about the early Dadaist movement, but you can rest assured she was there and played an integral part in their formative years.

Question Number One:

Did Alice ever make it back to Wonderland?

Answer:

Why, dear reader, I think you already know the answer to that.

One thing was certain, that the white *kitten had had nothing to do with it; it was the black kitten's fault entirely. For the white kitten had been having its face washed by the old cat for the last quarter of an hour (and bearing it pretty well, considering); so you see that it* couldn't *have had any hand in the mischief.*

Alice was sitting curled up in a corner of the great arm-chair, her large, round belly finally comfortable now that its tiny occupant had settled for a bit. The kitten had been having a grand game of romps with the ball of worsted Alice had been knitting into a tiny sweater, rolling the ball up and down till it had all come undone again; and there it was, spread over the hearth-rug, all knots and tangles, with the kitten running after its own tail in the middle.

'Oh, you wicked little thing!' cried Alice, catching the kitten, and giving it a little kiss to make it understand that it was in disgrace. 'Really, Dinah ought to have taught you better manners! Now, if you'll only attend, Kitty, and leave my knitting alone, I'll tell you all about Looking-glass House. Everything there is reversed, and the sweets run away from your hand. It's positively delightful.

'Oh, how nice it would be if we could only get through into Looking-glass House again! Let's pretend there's a way of getting through into it, somehow. Let's pretend the glass has got all soft like gauze, so that we can get through. Why, it's turning into a sort of mist now, I declare! It'll be easy enough to get through—' She was standing up, leaning on the chimney-piece while she said this, though she hardly knew how she had got

there. And certainly the glass was *beginning to melt away, just like a bright silvery mist…*

Unravel new twists in the tales that you
know and love in this series of thrilling

Mirror, Mirro

What if the Evil Queen poisoned the p

Can Snow defeat an enemy who will st
at nothing to retain her power… includ
going after the ones Snow loves?

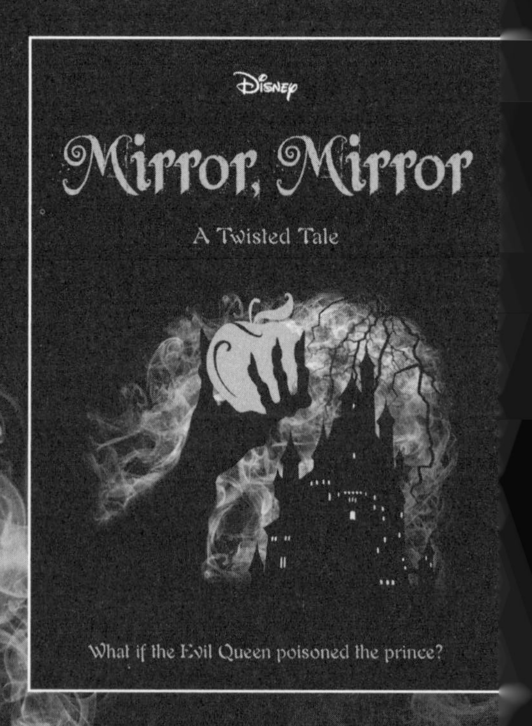

Straight on Till Morning

ndy went to Never Land with Ca

When Captain Hook reveals his sinis
for Never Land, can Wendy and Tin
ve Peter Pan and the place he calls ho

Disney

Straight on Till Morning

A Twisted Tale

What if Wendy went to Never Land with Captain Hook?

What if Anna and Elsa never knew eac

When Elsa, Queen of Arendelle, remembers a
her past and mysterious powers reveal thems
embarks on a journey to find the missing p

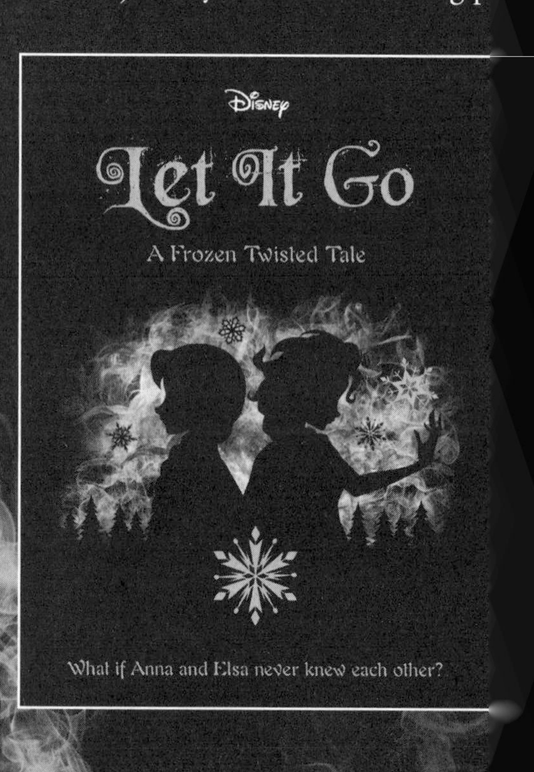